Chadwick Wall

RISINGHAWK
PRESS
Austin

Publisher's Note

This is a work of fiction. None of the characters, business establishments, or events is based on actual people, living or dead, or their lives or circumstances. All material is a product of the author's imagination. Any resemblance to actual people, businesses, or places is a coincidence and purely unintentional.

Printed and Published in the United States of America

Risinghawk Press
in association with
Violet Crown Publishers
ISBN-13: 978-1-938749-21-6
ISBN-10: 193874219

ISBN-13: 978-1-938749-20-9
ISBN-10: 1938749200

Dedication

To the late Theodore Temple Wall, Jr.,
a greater father and best friend than I could have asked for.
Soulful man, brave and full of hope,
I will always remember and honor you...
after all, as you often said, I was your "Lieu."

Acknowledgments

To those who most nurtured me in the writing craft:
my parents, Sandy and Ted
Dr. Walker Percy
Brother William Parsons, F.S.C.
Dr. Thomas McNabb Carlson
and my Novel in Progress writers' group

And to those who helped this novel come to be:
my brother Ryan, Cynthia J. Stone, Lara Reznik,
Lt. Col. Tosh McIntosh, USAF (Ret.),
Will McGaughey,
and on their great sailing trips,
Demian and David Perry, Amy Miller,
and, of course,
Captain George Sargent Grove, USN (Ret.)

Author's Note

My father first drew this emblem in his college years to represent the Wall family monogram, fashioning the letters proudly, in his own way. He used it on official documents, maps, business records, correspondence, luggage, and on all of his artwork. He continued this practice until the last year of his life.

This emblem will always represent my family, especially my father. And more than this, it symbolizes the extraordinary flair and zest with which he approached life. It enhances my memory of him as a man who was naturally creative and always wanted to create, but in his own manner. And so, following in his tradition, I have forged this novel in my own style.

dead reckoning n In navigation, the judgment or estimation of the place of a ship, without any observation of the heavenly bodies; or an account of the distance she has run by the log, and of the course steered by the compass, and this rectified by due allowances for drift, leeway, etc.

–Noah Webster's 1828 English Dictionary

Chapter One

The city knew full well the hurricane somewhere out there in the Gulf neared minute by minute but still New Orleans kept to her usual ways, echoing with jazz and sirens and the laughter and shouts of debauched revelry.

Jim Scoresby quickened his pace eastward down Decatur, sweating through his rumpled blue suit in the fierce August heat, passing tourists stumbling in their drunkenness and street urchins sitting on the pavement against the wall. Jim crossed Esplanade with its stately live oaks and eighteenth-century Creole houses and continued down Frenchman Street.

As on most nights, Frenchman hosted a frenzy of live music and revelers. Every other open door revealed a musical act within. Jim nodded at the doorman and ducked into Snug Harbor. He walked up the dimly lit stairs to the music room with its faint blue light, took a seat, and ordered an Old Fashioned. Jim leaned back and gave a contented smile at the stage.

Freddy Beasley, nearing seventy, stood before the crowd like a beleaguered but steady tower, his quartet behind him. His black, wrinkled hands gripped the trumpet as he pushed his soul through it into every smoky recess and nook of the club. A gray porkpie hat crowned his head, and he was dressed in pressed dark green slacks and a short-sleeve button down white guayabera. His face sharpened with intensity as he blew his note harder into his trumpet. His eyes found Jim's as his lips, behind the brass mouthpiece, drew into a faint smile.

Jim felt his phone buzz in his breast pocket. It was his father.

After draping his suit coat over his chair, Jim walked down the stairs and out the front door to a few feet away. His father was not yelling, but he was close to it.

"Son, I got your text. Why did you quit your job?"

"A million reasons. It was taking up all my time from finishing the house renovation. People are unreliable. Prospects stood me up all the time, even earlier today. Remember, it was commission only."

"I told you not to take this one to begin with, didn't I? Now you've got little chance of income for a while. I can't keep footin' money for your Paw Paw's house."

"Dad, I'm getting there. Just—"

"The hardest thing for you is to *finish anything*. No finishing your novel. No completing the renovation. You're probably all liquored up now, but you come home first thing tomorrow, help me load up. I told you this is a major storm. I'm evacuating to Granny's tomorrow. I need your help gettin' loaded up. Then you better leave with us for Meridian."

After a long pause, Jim mumbled that he would comply, and replaced the phone in his breast pocket.

Back inside the club, the band had finished its song and its members stepped down from the stage to accept a tray of drinks from a waitress. Freddy walked over and sat at Jim's table, and Jim reclaimed his seat.

"Nice song, Freddy."

"What's ailin' you? Sum'n's gettin' to you."

"I just spoke with my Dad, and told him the news. Today I quit my job at the agency."

"Ah, well, that was a long time coming. You got to have a day job, but at least you closer to where you want to be. Cheer up."

Freddy patted his shoulder and leaned back in his chair. Jim envied his confidence and perennial sense of peace.

"I take it yo' daddy didn't handle the news so well?"

"As you'd expect, he being always after me. He's hit his limit with me. All that money he lent for the renovations. My grandfather's house needed to be finished months ago."

"Oh, you best believe, it might be finished in the next few days."

Jim set his glass back on the table and shot Freddy a searching look. "But not in the way I'd want it finished. I catch your drift, Freddy."

"That's all in God's hands now. I keep telling ya to pray. Whole city needs to right now. I stopped years ago, but started back last night. Ha." Freddy excused himself and walked back with his water bottle to the stage, where the quartet members were resuming their previous spots.

Jim sat, half watching and half meditating while Freddy went through another of his famous numbers, this time on the guitar.

Maybe this would really be the Big One. But the mayor had issued an evacuation order last year for Hurricane Ivan, and despite all the mass evacuations it hadn't even grazed New Orleans.

And perhaps Jim couldn't work anything to completion. He felt like driving to Mid-City and throwing himself back into renovating. Perhaps he just needed to forget today and just sink into the oblivious depths of sleep. And then, of course, there would be tomorrow.

Freddy's bloodshot eyes met his as Jim rose and tossed cash onto the table and snatched his suitcoat. Within the old man's gaze, Jim recognized a tinge of assurance and warmth.

Chapter Two

"One more load," his father said, wincing and winded, sweat coursing down his brow as he carried a box to the trunk of his Land Rover. Jim lifted his box from the floor of the den and trailed his father. They had been at this for what seemed like hours.

Time to get back to Mid-City.

Jim lowered the box into the vehicle and began to walk back to the house.

"Now, son, when your Mama and your brother return from gettin' gas, we're leavin'."

"Dad, I told you. I'm staying behind, going to guard Paw Paw's house. I'm a grown man, you know. And I've got to check on my friend. Remember ol' Freddy?"

"Damn it, his family can take care of him. Things 'bout to heat up really fast down there, boy."

"Ha. You might be right about the latter, but you're wildly incorrect about his family."

"You know, Jim, the time you've spent with him," his father said, "you could've spent a lot of that with your own father. Your own blood, who loves you. Who invested in you your whole life."

They were now inside. Jim walked to the counter and yanked his father's work truck keys from the hook on the wall, just under the cupboard.

"Oh, no you don't," his father boomed. He lunged and seized Jim by the shoulders. They grappled, his father straining to tug him back, while Jim struggled to break free. Back and forth they shoved, for half a minute. Suddenly his father swung Jim sideways. Jim banged hard against the lamp table. It tipped over and the lamp and the antique decanter shattered into a hundred shards on the wooden floor. Jim immediately leapt up from the ground and tore past him.

"I'm leaving Granddaddy's Chevy," Jim said, already winded, "and just using the work truck. It's banged up, on its last leg anyway. You're too damned worried 'bout your possessions."

Jim shot through the door, sprinting to the dented and rusting 1976 Ford truck. He unlocked the door, gunned up the engine, and, as his father jogged closer, Jim lurched down the long drive, accelerating as he spotted in the rearview mirror the silhouette raising its hands over its head and throwing them down in frustration.

Jim felt his heart sink with sadness as he turned from his father's property onto the narrow road and pressed steadily onto the accelerator, hearing the engine seem to growl, then roar, as he shot under the vast branches of the oaks and past the towering pines.

Nearly an hour later, he slapped the three dollars into the open palm of the tollbooth attendant and drove onto the Causeway Bridge. Jim contemplated the twenty-four miles left to travel over the brackish lagoon of Lake Pontchartrain, the memory of the shattered lamp and antique decanter, his father's shocked face, frightened that his son could be hurt.

He saw his father's silhouette shrinking in the dirty rearview mirror, and recalled his father's strength, despite his fifty-seven years. He now saw the tall wall of pines bordering the lake, it too shrinking in that same mirror.

Jim muttered an expletive at the sight of the two continuous, bumper-to-bumper lines of cars and trucks coursing northward on the other side of the twin-span bridge, and the nearly complete absence of vehicles, both before him and behind him, on his own southbound span. Soon the lights of New Orleans materialized on the horizon.

Chapter Three

After a minute of Jim's pounding on the door, the porch light turned on and Freddy appeared. He looked like he had been sleeping.

"Well, my, Jim. You came back. For me?"

"Mostly. No wonder you didn't answer your phone. Sleeping?"

Freddy didn't answer but motioned for Jim to follow him inside. The house carried its usual smell of cigars.

"Want a drink? We still got power. A cold beer?"

Freddy brought back a tray with a frosted glass and a Dixie beer can for each of them. He set it down on the coffee table and sat down in the corduroy recliner, at a perpendicular angle to Jim.

"I could turn on the TV but it's just gonna worry us," Freddy said. "I was watchin' it earlier. You know I ain't got no cable but WWL showed that the storm was pretty much headed this way. Grazes us to the east, much better than if it hits just to the west of us."

"No use worryin' about what we can't change," Jim said. "I say we listen to some music, tell some stories."

"And don't forget, drinks and cigars!" Freddy said, throwing his hands above his head like a victorious Olympian.

"How could we forget?"

Freddy pulled two cigars from his humidor on the table beside his recliner, clipped the ends, and gave Jim his.

They sat, speaking of music and their families and the city they loved.

Soon Freddy reached over and lifted his wooden guitar from the couch and began to strum it and hum.

"Hey, Freddy," Jim said. "Let's hear some of those recordings again of your music."

The old man rose slowly out of his recliner and put a record on his stereo and in a matter of two minutes it could have been Mardi Gras in 1975. "Rampart Rag" filled every inch of the room. It was a song Freddy originally played in a jazz format. Now they were hearing Freddy's funk version.

And Freddy didn't immediately sit back down in his recliner. Instead he disappeared into his bedroom. When he returned and yelled "Hurricane party!" he sported his green and yellow and purple Mardi Gras Indian headdress and his long gnarled scepter that resembled a club or walking stick.

Jim exploded with laughter as the old man strutted around the room, peacock-like, with long, pausing strides. Jim continued to laugh and clap with rhythm as Freddy pumped his spear above his head in his war dance.

Freddy strode into his kitchen and appeared minutes later with two more cold Dixie beers. He turned down the volume a couple notches and Jim related the events of the past day, about the quarrel with his father and what he had seen on the Causeway.

"Soon, Jim, soon you be onto some great things," Freddy said. "You still very young. We always are learning, but now you really in a learning stage. You gonna get into somethin' soon to prove yo'self and it ain't just in rehabbin' your grandpa's house."

Jim felt that warm solace come over him that Freddy's words often gave.

Then the electricity went out, and with that, the lights and music. Through the thin walls came the sounds of the wind lashing outside, the creaking trees, and the waves of rain punishing the roofs and adhesive-taped windows.

"Party time over," Freddy said.

Jim felt for the lighter on the lamp table and flicked it on. The dull flame lit up the room with the faintest glow, casting eerie shadows on the wall behind Freddy, who sat staring over at him from his recliner with a sort of sadness.

"Let's find your flashlight," Jim said. "Then we can pack you a bag and get over to my house. There's lots of food and a gas lamp. And I can start up the fireplace if we need more light."

They ground out the cigars and Jim followed Freddy with the lighter until they located the flashlight, which Jim shone on him until the large canvas bag was filled.

They plunged into the storm, with Jim steadying Freddy on their march through the pelting rain and winds until they reached the work truck. Jim drove it the few hundred feet up the street and parked in front of his grandfather's house. Minutes later, they were warm and safe inside, reclining on the living room couches beside the small gas lamp.

Freddy had lost his joyous spirit. He reminded Jim about his late wife, now dead several decades, and his ex-girlfriend now living in New York. Freddy had moved back down to his hometown a few years ago and she and all his children from his first marriage were living in the New York area.

"This hurricane here could be 'the Big One' the state always feared, Jimbo. And very timely. My nurse didn't show up yesterday with a new delivery of insulin. My grandson living here, my only kin here, decides not to answer his cell phone. Well, he finally did, admits he already in Shreveport."

Jim wondered if his parents and brother were now safe in Meridian. Immediately after he felt a glow of pride within him that he hadn't followed, and left Freddy.

"Least your family dudn't desert you," Freddy said. "Don't know what's with families these days. Now I'm more in trouble than I been in almost forty years."

Jim said nothing, remembering the drama in his own family. Freddy administered his own insulin injection into his stomach.

Soon they finally slept, Jim on the couch, the old man in the guest bedroom.

When Freddy stepped toward one of the windows the next morning, he swore loudly. Jim sprang from the couch and rushed to the window. A good ten inches of water stood in the street. An Orleans Parish school bus full of people plowed down the road, dividing the swelling water, while the men, women, and children stared with fright out of the windows.

Jim turned his cordless radio to 870 AM. Garland Robinette, who had retired as anchor of the local news in the early '90s, was filling in a radio spot on WWL. A woman in the Ninth Ward called in. Jim barely understood her words for her weeping. She had fled with her children to their attic as the water first started to invade her house. She screamed that she had no ax or hatchet to chop a hole in the roof. And the water was slowly rising around them.

The line abruptly went dead. Jim slowly raised his head. The old man stared back with an unsettling expression, somewhere between horror and resolve, as his chest heaved with a faster breath.

Chapter Four

That Monday, they waited as long as they could, atop the foldout stairs. Until they knew it was inevitable. Then, with the water mere inches below them on Tuesday morning, Jim Scoresby took up the ax that for forty years lay among the cobwebs and dust of the crawl space in his late grandfather's shotgun house, and he hacked his way out of the decking of the roof.

Jim and Freddy crouched on the searing shingles, watching the dark waters rise a few inches every hour. And there it was, lapping inside the crawl space, around the foldout stairs. With terror and despair, Jim realized, though much of New Orleans had braved the winds, the levees had failed. Entire neighborhoods would drown.

"Dang, this roof hotter than *hell*! We gonna fry like bacon up here," the old funk guitarist said, and then smirked. "Now, what you think of your view of the Second Great Flood?"

Jim stared down at the water welling up around the foldout stairwell. "God help us," he mumbled.

What had come was surely the end of many lives and many homes. And his great times at parades, smoky jazz clubs, storied piano bars and grand old restaurants would now be mere memories.

When he looked aside a minute later from the cavity in the roof, Jim spotted Freddy twenty feet away, standing against the chimney, near the roof's terracotta ridge. The branch of the pecan tree stretched over the roof, granting some shade to the old man. Freddy squinted into the horizon, a look of resignation spread across his face.

Jim trudged up the roof and grabbed onto the chimney for balance. "You seem so alert, Freddy. So, what're *you* thinkin'?"

Freddy had looked sickly when Jim found him, bedridden, two days before.

"This wasn't even the Big One, Jimmy boy. I think Betsy and Camille were stronger. But I see them weak levees done broke. This whole city gonna flood out, man. This time the *whole* bowl gonna fill up. Reminds me of that ol' blues song by Memphis Minnie and Kansas City Joe."

The old man started to sing softly as he looked out over the rooftops. Jim knew the lyrics, but it was still spine tingling. The verse about the unending rain causing the levees to break, that tears and prayers would be futile, caused his heart to quicken in his chest.

Jim couldn't bring himself to comment. He remembered with a pang of guilt that at that moment, with better planning, he and Freddy could have already reached Memphis. The old man drew in a slow breath and launched back into song, singing the old verse of the cruel levee causing him to weep and moan and leave his happy home and loved ones.

Jim scanned the horizon. The dark water had closed over the roofs of the cars. It stood throughout the streets and welled up just below the gutter line of the neighboring shotgun houses. His father's 1976 Ford pickup was completely submerged.

"Damn it to hell," Jim said, bringing his hands to his temples, wincing. "How high's that water gonna come up?"

"High as it wants to. Tellin' you now, it may be comin' higher. But not quite up to where we standin'."

"It can't, right? We're probably above sea-level, at the chimney right here."

"Mmm hmm," Freddy said.

"Well! We *might* be sleepin' up here."

"S'all good," Freddy said. "You fetched me outta my bed, after all. I woulda been back in my house, not knowin' what to do. Too old to open up my roof."

Jim took cautious steps down the roof to retrieve the plastic water boxes and white canvas sack of food and valuables. He placed the sack against the ridge nearby. Then he held the water box above Freddy, who sat atop a wadded-up blanket, and poured water into his mouth. Jim placed the water box on top of the chimney and sat in the shade of the limb, just next to the old man, who began to puff a cigar. Jim closed his eyes and tried to sleep.

Jim jolted upright on the spread of blankets. The boom of a shotgun sounded, followed by an assault rifle's staccato, then deep reports of what had to be a .357 or .44. Several house alarms pierced the air, perhaps triggered by the floodwater. Jim reached into the white canvas sack between him and Freddy and fished out the single-action .357. He removed the zip-lock bag of shells and loaded the chambers. Jim ensured the safety was on and shoved the revolver into the pocket of his cargo shorts.

Freddy smiled. "Them gunshots shakin' you up!" he said, trying to add a little levity.

"I usually only hear 'em at the shooting range or the hunting camp."

"You *are* a Northshore boy. Well, at least you come prepared."

The temperature climbed. Sweat trickled down Jim's brow, down the length of his nose, and dripped between his knees onto the charcoal-colored asphalt shingles. He fretted about the old man, about the rising waters and rising temperatures.

Freddy mentioned there was a day's worth of insulin. When would help come? Should Jim swim for it? He couldn't decide. He saw to it that Freddy ate some of the bread and canned tuna, and that he downed it with plenty of water. Freddy's dessert was a shot of insulin. This time the old man put the needle higher up into his belly.

"Damn," Freddy groaned with discomfort. "Insulin done heated up. When it's too cold or too hot, it stings!"

"Sorry," Jim said. "The NOPD or National Guard boats will be comin' through here soon enough. Then we'll get you to the hospital."

All around them expletives and pleas for help erupted: black voices, white voices, more shouting of frustration and fear down the street. Some were drowning, all were terrified. All were waiting, bearing the worst of the flood save what must have befallen the lower areas of the Ninth Ward, Lakeview, and New Orleans East.

He pulled the radio from the sack. Garland was interviewing the New Orleans Police Chief, Eddie Compass. Strong Category Three winds ripped open the roof of the Superdome, with over twenty three thousand people inside. Rampant looting and police retaliation were underway.

Though the Quarter and most of Uptown remained dry, water had submerged a projected eighty percent of the city.

Fires were reported in every neighborhood. The Southern Yacht club on Lake Pontchartrain burned to the ground. Thousands sought refuge at the Morial Convention Center and had attempted to flee by foot or boat. The Ninth Ward suffered the worst. It was virtually annihilated. Its most famous resident, Fats Domino, was nowhere to be found.

At this last bit of news, Jim shivered. Freddy jerked onto his side and crawled a few feet to the roof's edge.

"Freddy?" Jim lunged toward the old man, in case he slipped over the roof's eave into the water.

Freddy vomited as if his insides would come up, too. Then he eased himself away from the edge. Jim held the water box over Freddy's open mouth and squeezed. "That Fats is my ol' buddy," Freddy said after he finished drinking. "Used to play with him in the Famous Door on Bourbon and in Tipitina's. One time, I'd been robbed, and he sent me money for food and a train ticket to get me back from Chicago."

"He probably got out in time, Freddy," Jim said, knowing it was bold and blind conjecture. "He'll turn up in the next few days. He's probably safe and dry up in some Memphis hotel, watching this nightmare unfold on TV."

Freddy lay back on the roof and closed his eyes. Jim switched off the radio, sensing the strain on his friend's nerves. The old man said nothing for an hour. The breath came first out of the mouth alone, then finally out of the nose again.

Jim allowed his thoughts to wander. The storm's casualties surely numbered in the thousands. The beating by Nature and human error was merciless. The homes of his grandfather and Freddy were ruined. The storm flooded, violated the graves of Jim's ancestors, going back into the early eighteenth century.

Lake Lawn Cemetery, where his Maw Maw and Paw Paw Laforet and his Mamere DuBuc were interred, would be smothered in several feet of putrid water, gasoline, and raw sewage. Saint Louis Cemetery Number One with its whitewashed crypts and angels would be hidden under many feet of the same fetid mire.

And what was worse, many of the crypts surely had opened, releasing coffins and remains alike into the dark unforgiving flood. Jim's stomach squeezed at the thought.

The rapid tempo of helicopter blades echoed all about them. The chopper approached from the north.

"Here we go," Freddy said. "National Guard, come and get us. Please treat an ol' fool to some insulin."

People on other roofs waved as the chopper neared. Several jumped up and down in desperation. Jim pulled off his white t-shirt and shot out from under the pecan tree's limb. He waved the shirt and shouted as the chopper started its ascent, and to his horror, sped on toward the east, downriver.

Jim cursed, slamming his wet shirt onto the scalding roof. He stomped over to the canvas bag and pulled out his last remaining clean shirt.

Freddy was now sitting up.

"Others will be comin', Jim," he said in a consoling, grandfatherly tone. "That's just one of many. Look at it that way."

"You're probably right," Jim said. "But how much insulin's left?"

Freddy paused.

"Less than a day's worth."

"Then I don't want to chance it," Jim said. "I'm gonna swim for it. Find some police, doctors. Bring help, medicine, something."

Freddy nodded slowly, his eyes enlarging, as if he was swallowing a large gulp.

"Thanks for that, Jimbo. Really. But that water's filled with all kinds of evil stuff. Every hour it prob'ly gets worse, too. Best to wait. Take our chance with the police and the troops and whoever comes by in a boat. Besides, I lived a longer life—sixty-five. Why you gonna risk yours for me? You twenty-seven, right?"

"Funny you mention that," Jim said in a soft voice. "Twenty-*eight* as of yesterday. Twenty-ninth of August. Saint John the Baptist's feast day, as my mama often reminds me."

"I'll be," Freddy pulled his head back an inch and smiled. He gave a faint chortle. "You didn't tell me. Guess we were all a li'l busy! Just don't lose your head like John the Baptist, jump in no water. Anyway, glad you came back, ol' friend. Don't know what I would've done."

"Know one of my favorite stories about you?" Jim said, attempting some humor. "The origin of your nickname. I guess that's why I never hear you sing!"

Freddy snickered. A few months before Freddy was deployed to Vietnam, Louis Armstrong had visited his hometown and saw Freddy perform at the Famous Door with his first band. Afterward, Satchmo joked with Freddy that he could play the guitar like the devil, but he needed to abandon singing, that Freddy sounded as "loud and awful as a foghorn on a Miss'ippi River tugboat."

Jim pulled out his phone and dialed 911 again and again, but no call would go through. He sat back down in the shade of the limb, a couple feet from the old man. He tugged a flask from the back of his shorts.

"Jimbo, haha! You got whiskey in one pocket, pistol in the other!" Freddy said. "A walkin' country song."

Jim smiled and took a pull of the bourbon. He did not offer any to Freddy, knowing full well the old man had sworn off all spirits years ago.

Freddy reached into the canvas bag. He brought out a wooden box, then produced a cigarette lighter and two Dominican cheroots, the mouth ends already clipped. They sat puffing away in silence as a breeze reached them, gently waving the limb with its green canopy. Jim was thankful for the strong, rich tobacco smell, as the wind had started to waft toward them the stench of burning tires.

"Know what I always thought was crazy, Freddy?" Jim said. "How when these hurricanes are a day away, the breezes are pickin' up. And we can catch the scent of all the cypress and the pine and what's bloomin' that time of summer or fall: azaleas, camellias, magnolias. Li'l closer to the Gulf, there's that smell of the salt air. And all those trees and branches are just bendin', swayin'. Up in Folsom we'd see those tall pines swayin' overhead. That's 'bout the stage in the storm we'd evacuate, my family."

Jim puffed on the cigar, which he knew would last for a good half hour. He thought of his father, and if he would be impressed in the end with his struggle to survive.

"This city been dyin' a long time," Freddy said. "Now it's gonna be on its knees many years. Eventually it'll come back. Not what it was. But it'll always be the only thang like it on the earth."

Jim spotted one of his neighbors several houses away.

Becky Fourchon was petite, auburn-haired, almond-eyed, and with the energy of a teenager. A young forty years old, Becky owned a deli a few streets away. She was untying a canoe from her chimney. While her husband Beau held the rope, Becky lowered herself into the boat. She started to paddle her way down the street.

"Hey, Becky!" Jim called, and then stepped out from under the branch toward the gutter.

"Hey, boy! Jimmy, whatcha say, dawlin'?" Becky said as she paddled toward him.

"Glad you're okay, Becky. Mister Foghorn Beasley and I are up here sweatin' like stuck pigs."

"Freddy up there on that roof?"

"In the shade, under that branch."

"My husband went by Freddy's house when the water was comin' up. Called 'round for him, didn't hear a peep. Glad he's here! Y'all got food, water?"

"Yes, but he needs insulin. We'll run out tonight or tomorrow morning."

"We gotta brainstorm 'bout that one. Ya hear Oschner and Charity Hospitals have gangs tryin' to get into its drugs? Neither of 'em even got power. Just heard it on Garland's show."

Becky was now no more than thirty feet away.

"Y'all know what my Daddy back there just saw?" Becky said, an eyebrow raised. "A ten-foot gator just next to our house. With Bayou St. John backin' right up to us here, ol' bastuhd must've just floated right into the street. Folks been callin' into Garland's show, claimin' they seen gators and snakes in the water all over town."

"Great," Jim said. "I was a hair away from swimmin' for

help a while ago but—"

"No, boy, don't," Becky said. "You got all these reptiles in the water. Then you got human waste from all the sewers, you got cars' leaky-ass gas tanks, benzene and oil from the petrochemical spills. E-coli and maybe cholera just breedin' away in there. You swim and nick ya skin, you prob'ly wind up dead. Graveyard dead. We got some black and white cans of spray paint in all that stuff back on my roof. I'll go fetch it and I'll be back. Y'all need to spray 'NEED INSULIN ASAP' in white on that roof there. In big bold letters. Coast Guard and National Guard will see it when they come back through here."

"Great idea," Freddy said, now at Jim's side. Freddy stood with a slouching stance. His arms dangled limply. His face drooped in turn, the eyelids heavier.

"There you are, my boo! What's happenin'?" Becky said. "You lookin' worn out. Hey, I'll be back with the paint."

The old man nodded and managed a slight smile.

"Freddy, how ya feelin'?" Becky said.

"Thanks, baby," Freddy said. "Gotta lay down. Ol' bones gettin' weary." He returned to his shaded spot as Becky paddled away. This time he lay down on the blankets.

Jim poured some water into Freddy's mouth. Then Freddy thanked him and again took up his cigar. Jim sat next to where the old man lay and started in again on his own cigar. Jim made another try for 911. Again, nothing but a busy signal.

Minutes later, water splashed behind them. Jim asked the old man to remain seated and stepped over to the rake of the roof.

Becky sat in her canoe, holding fast to the gutter. The hint of a smile, not without a tinge of melancholy, played around her mouth as she pointed to a spot in the water maybe twenty feet away.

Coursing directly down the center of the street, where Jim hoped to find a Coast Guard or National Guard motorboat, was a water moccasin. The arrow-shaped head poked like a ship's prow through the water as the torso undulated side to side behind it. The cottonmouth was even bigger than the ones he had seen in St. Tammany Parish to the north. It seemed as plump and long as the Eastern Diamondback rattlers he had encountered once while hunting in North Carolina.

Jim stared at the haughty head and neck of the reptile, older than man himself, and imagined it knew of the great thrashing civilization had just endured at the hands of Nature.

"My," Jim said. "I see Bayou St. John's unleashed all its inhabitants on us."

Becky handed him the spray paint. Jim thanked her, and took his time to spray, "NEED INSULIN ASAP PLEASE," in bold white letters onto both slopes of the gabled roof. He handed the can back to Becky, who patted his shoe twice with affection.

"How's the Foghorn takin' this, Jim?" she said.

"I don't think he's processed this yet," Jim whispered. "He's lookin' really worn down. The insulin's exhausted soon. If something happens to him, it'll rip me apart. He's close to me. I could've lent him my truck; he could've driven north two days ago. I could've met up with him later. I could've used one of my parents' cars. Instead I was too busy peddling insurance. Waitin' too long to plan. Now I just wish I could use your canoe, go for some insulin."

"We need this, though, Jim," Becky said. "We may need to

get my family outta here soon, one by one."

Jim sighed and nodded, then glanced at the spot at the roof's ridge, just under the branch. The old man lay on the blankets. The cigar was gone. He had probably cast it over the edge into the murk. Freddy gazed through the pecan tree's leafy limbs into the azure sky.

"Any boat or chopper comes our way," Becky said, nodding toward her house, "we'll direct it here."

"Thanks, Beck. I'm prayin' for y'all. Tell Beau and the kids and your parents I said hey."

"Will do," Becky said. "I'll check on y'all soon."

Jim walked up to the old man. Freddy's eyes were shut, his hands peacefully at his sides. Jim sat beside him and said nothing.

The old man spoke without opening his eyes. "Know what I cain't get over, Jim? Flood must've taken thousands to their graves. So many with so little. There's gonna be an exodus outta here. N'awlins won't be what it was. But one day many will be back. It's 'specially y'all's duty, the kids with the ideas and the energy, to resurrect her."

At that last line, Jim felt overwhelmed. He could only imagine how thoroughly destroyed the city was. He probably could never feel at home here again.

"But let's not dwell on what's happened. We need to plan our escape here."

"*You* might escape," Freddy said, his head turning, the eyes fixed fast onto his young friend. "I ain't. What been done here... my *body* may escape. But my *soul* will stay. This is too crushin', man, too powerful. What's been done to this place, my memories, what I knew, those I knew, it's gonna crush this ol' heart."

Jim knew he could do little to avoid this last reaction in his friend. He had always said Freddy was synonymous with New Orleans.

"Let's take a nap. Then we can eat later and get you an insulin dose."

"A burnin' *hot* dose," Freddy chuckled. "I ain't told you 'nough. Thanks for all you done for me here. Wouldn't have made it without you. But if I do go, I'm gonna watch over you from the other side."

"Don't think like that, Freddy!" Jim said. "Let's nap. Then we can eat, and you can tell me again about Satchmo and your funk band. And all your times as a Mardi Gras Indian in the parades."

"That costume and my Zulu one." Freddy closed his eyes again. "They in my poor flooded house. Gone."

Jim said nothing. They both drifted off to sleep.

Hours later they woke to the sun setting just below the level of the rooftops. They snacked on tuna and bread, and then Jim administered the injection into Freddy's stomach. The old man winced in pain, releasing an agonizing whimper through clenched, chipped teeth. The insulin was uncommonly hot, but there was no way around it.

Jim had wanted to hear the old tales but he was surprised at how drained they both were. And so again they slept, and despite the sirens and the occasional shout or gunshot, they woke for only brief moments.

Wednesday dawned. They devoured more of the tuna and bread. Jim held the water box over the old man's mouth, slowly pouring out a long, steady stream, and then did the same for himself. They took turns urinating off the roof, under the branch.

Once again a helicopter approached. Jim ran out onto the center of the left slope. He pulled off his white t-shirt and jerked it overhead as he waved with the other arm. The military chopper slowly descended beside the house.

Jim shouted, though he knew his voice was lost in the din of the vast spinning blades. The chopper leveled out one hundred feet above the water. Jim pointed repeatedly to the word "INSULIN" and then at the spot just beneath the limb where Freddy lay.

The rescue officer was a young white man, helmeted, and with his upper chest clad in a harness. The man gave Jim a thumbs-up and yelled something to the pilot. They seemed to argue for a few moments. Then the rescue officer pointed to his watch and made a motion with his thumb and index finger signifying "small." The man withdrew inside the cabin and the chopper ascended, then departed toward the north.

Jim cursed wildly, stomping his feet onto the roof. He walked up toward the limb, the drooping, hangdog look of defeat all about his face and shoulders.

He knew he had to swim for it. LSU Medical Hospital and Charity Hospital were twenty and twenty-five or so blocks away. He had to cover all bases. If the helicopter did not return in time, he didn't want Freddy to be helpless.

"I'm swimming for it, Freddy. If the chopper returns, because of what I sprayed there on the roof, they know where to find you. But I can't have you helpless if it doesn't. I'll rest every few minutes. It's twenty blocks or so, but I'll get there. Probably find someone in a boat on the way. And I'm coming back with insulin."

Freddy just shook his head. A weak voice, weaker than minutes before, escaped.

"Ahh, Jim. Nuttin' good can come o' that. Just you rest here. Chopper will be back in no time."

Jim held the water jug above his mouth and drank deep. Then he set it down, knelt and embraced the old man and kissed him once on the forehead.

"You'll never see me sittin' idly by while your life's on the line," Jim said. He rose and saw the old man's face full of worry.

"No, Jim! Jim!" the old man gasped, but it was too late. Jim ran and leapt off the roof and hurtled into the dark waters just feet below.

Chapter Five

He swam for over an hour, holding fast to trees and walls every few minutes to rest. Soon he saw something familiar moving just a hundred feet away: a tall, slender man in a canoe.

"Beau! Beau!" Jim yelled.

Becky's husband paddled away from him. Jim tried to swim faster, but couldn't. He yelled once more, as loudly as he could, and the canoe turned around and moved toward him. Jim held fast to the trunk of an oak. Seconds later, he saw the relieved face of his neighbor. But within this expression was something indescribable. Beau was holding something back.

"I'm pulling you into here, Jim. Come on. Grab my hand. Push yourself in when I pull."

Beau gripped Jim's hand, steadied the boat, then leaned quickly back, pulling with all of his might as Jim pushed himself up into the canoe, which wobbled wildly in the murky water.

After a moment to catch his breath, Jim said, "Now we can go for Freddy's insulin. He's runnin' out of time." Beau allowed his broad shoulders to droop and wiped his cheeks with the palms of his hands and exhaled loudly. He looked at the floor of the canoe.

"Jim, I checked on y'all a few minutes after we heard the splash. Thought one o' y'all fell off the roof. Freddy was gaspin'. I saw him pass, man."

"No, Beau. Don't just tell me that to get me back to the roof. Tell me the truth."

"It is the truth, Jim. I'm as serious as this storm. He's gone. I came to find you."

It felt like an entire day passed before they reached the roof. Beau paddled away as Jim ran up to the peak.

Freddy's eyes were shut. His chin was pulled up, his mouth gaped wide, his hands contorted in some horrible agony. Jim remembered photos of Pompeii's dead, mummified by ash and lack of air, and those photos of the dead after the liberation of Auschwitz. He imagined the death rattle sounding, then a second later the final, surrendering breath rushing out of the lungs, past the voice box, like the one he heard many years ago at his Maw Maw Laforet's deathbed.

Jim knelt and hugged his friend's shoulders, realizing the old legend's great heart had suffered such a shock Jim's had never felt. That heart had given way, probably hours before his body depleted its last stores of insulin.

The chopper returned an hour later, hovering two hundred feet over the house. A cord lowered the rescue officer to the roof. Jim would not move or speak. The officer, not much younger than Jim, walked toward the spot under the limb.

"Sorry, sir, we were ordered back to base," the soldier shouted with a thick twang. "We took on gunfire just south of here. Gangs, addicts maybe. Drugs ran out." The officer stopped cold just under the branch. The man's eyes widened, if only for a second. "Is this man dead?" the officer yelled over the din of the blades, pointing at Freddy. The officer knelt, and felt for a pulse in Freddy's neck. He turned to Jim with a look of deep solemnity.

"He must have been dyin' when you were signalin' to me earlier," Jim shouted above the roar of the rotor. Jim nearly vomited, but felt compelled to mention one more thing to the stranger. "Know who this was?"

The man watched with sudden interest, an eyebrow rising slightly into the helmet.

"That was Freddy 'Foghorn' Beasley, man. Ever hear Rampart Rag? The band *Gris Gris*? He was King of Zulu, 1974. He was in the '84 World's Fair here and—"

"Sorry, sir, I ain't heard of him," the man shouted. "I'm Oklahoma National Guard. But we gotta go. Someone'll retrieve him. But you've gotta come now. It ain't safe for us just hoverin' up there! There's lotsa others to save."

Jim nodded at the broken shell at their feet, the remnant of his neighbor who that year had become such a close friend. Jim pulled off his own shirt, reached down, and lifted the old man's head, wrapping it with tenderness. He stood up just before the rotor's winds blew the shirt off the roof.

Jim cursed and grabbed the bulky white canvas bag, checking the contents. Among the cans of tuna and framed photos of his grandparents was the plastic case holding Freddy's white Fender guitar. Jim squeezed the canvas hard in his hands and nodded at the officer, who slipped the other harness around him.

The officer led Jim to the center of the roof, locked his own harness, and gave the chopper a thumbs up. He assumed a firm grip on Jim as the cord yanked taut. "We're goin' up!" the officer yelled.

As the cord lifted Jim, he cried out like a newborn infant. Below lay the expired, ruined body of his friend, the Fourchon family sitting on their roof, the gasoline-splotched canals where there had been streets. The school a few streets away burned. A corpse floated down his street, bloated in its clothes like a discarded sausage. The Central Business District loomed ahead, with its multitude of blown-out windows. The Superdome appeared in the distance, its roof membrane peeled back like the hide of a skinned doe.

"I'm comin' back for you, Freddy! We're comin' back to get you!" Jim shouted into the wind as he glanced down again at the corpse.

Jim lifted his watery gaze toward the helicopter, just as the cord pulled Jim and his rescuer inside the open door.

As the officer unharnessed him and fastened him into his seatbelt, Jim glanced around the cabin. An elderly white couple sat just feet away, their eyes locked onto his with an expression of terror. Nearby sat a sixty-something Vietnamese woman and what appeared to be her daughter, perhaps in her mid-thirties. The younger woman was slender; her face had delicate features but was scratched and bruised. Dried blood caked the collar and lap of her blue blouse. She wept without sound, staring at Jim with seething outrage. Her mother's dry-eyed gaze, angled toward the floor, held a combination of the deepest sadness, weariness, even recognition and knowing—she was half-present in the moment, half-immersed in something, somewhere beyond.

Chapter Six

In the near darkness, Jim moved in silence between the several thousand sleeping or nearly sleeping forms, wrapped in blankets on cots. Though it was just past two in the morning, Jim, gripping the stack of thin wool blankets, was surprised at the silence in the auditorium. It reminded him of funerals he had attended, before the music or service started: all silence and whispering within a cavernous edifice. The Maravich Center had not been so silent in his memories of graduate school.

To some of the evacuated, should they still be awake, he would hand out blankets. To those sleeping, he would lay a blanket on top of each person.

Jim was shocked at how many were women, children, and elderly. Earlier that night, medical teams whisked certain elderly away. Jim had learned the shock of the storm and the evacuation had actually killed some of them.

He had long before noted that the crowds were overwhelmingly black. Only rarely did he see a white, Hispanic, or Asian person. He had spotted the older Asian woman he sat across from yesterday in the medevac chopper. He had asked about her daughter, but she just shook her head and turned away. Hours later he learned from a volunteer from Oregon that the young woman had been taken to a hospital there in

Baton Rouge for treatment. As he had guessed, she had been raped before her evacuation. Jim remembered her tears and bloody dress and mouth.

Jim came to a young African-American boy of perhaps fifteen, slight and short and curled up asleep. Once the boy felt the blanket touch his skin, he half sat up, grinned, and nodded as if impressed. "I'm gonna dance at yo' weddin'," he said.

Jim smiled and walked toward the next row. What a beautiful expression. He had never heard it before.

Some of the sleeping woke as well when Jim lowered the blankets onto them. Some noticed his eyes, brimming with tears, and uttered words of blessing. Jim could not control it. Never had he seen such a degree of desperation, and in one confined place.

Between trips to distribute blankets, Jim passed out plastic water bottles to those still awake. Children, pregnant women, elderly men, all sorts of people thanked him profusely as he handed them the water. Eventually, Jim broke for a snack and a moment to rest.

Some of the volunteers were huddled in the corner at an office table. They invited Jim to share some water and sandwiches with them and listen to the radio. Jim heard how Army and National Guard convoys were hours away from reaching the thousands of refugees in the Morial Convention Center, where corpses both lay in open view and stacked in the basement.

The desperation and mayhem had grown so great in the city that two NOPD police officers perished by their own hands. One was Sgt. Paul Accardo, the spokesman for the entire force. Three people in the Superdome leapt to their death from its top tier.

The Maravich Center volunteers met all of this news with curses and gasps. More of an apocalyptic film than reality, but that it was real made it all the more horrifying.

Through conversation, Jim learned these twelve volunteers originated from all over North America, from California, to Oregon, to Illinois, to South Carolina, even Canada. One young man hailed from Salem, New Hampshire. Jim remembered his good college friend Liam.

"What do you think of Exeter? Exeter, New Hampshire?" he said.

"Exeter? Oh, yes," said the young man, somewhere in his early twenties. "Beautiful town. My family would go apple picking there every year when I was growing up. It's not too far from the ocean, either, a few miles. Sometimes you can smell the salt air in the breezes."

"I've always wanted to visit," Jim mumbled, half lost in thought.

Minutes later, one of the volunteers allowed Jim to check his email on her laptop. Among the many emails asking about Jim's condition—from everyone from his parents to his cousins to ex-girlfriends—was a note from Liam himself. He invited any of his friends living in the New Orleans area or affected Gulf Coast to stay with him in his house in Exeter while New Orleans was "cleaned up, and order is established."

Jim put his fist to his mouth in surprise. Starting in the helicopter ride from his grandfather's house over the city to the previous evacuation center, Jim had hoped his friends in New England or Chicago or Memphis would call and extend an invite. Freddy was gone. His grandfather's house was destroyed.

He did not want to concede defeat and move in with his father and his mother. He must stay for a bit to bury Freddy. But now he sensed an opening.

Jim shot off a few reassuring lines to his parents, telling them of his location. He thanked the laptop's owner, a young girl from Colorado, and grabbed a case of water bottles and walked back into the rows of the refugees, many of them no doubt dreaming pure nightmares.

CHAPTER SEVEN

Jim Scoresby's gaze drifted earthward to the once-bustling waters of Boston harbor, its wavelets leaping in the spring wind. His vision seized upon something he had seen only in old black and white photos. Just out past the harbor sailed a lone yacht, a schooner of perhaps one hundred feet. By the shape of it, it *has* to be a Herreshoff, he thought. Other than an oil tanker farther out in the waves, just south toward Dorchester Bay, it was the only craft in sight.

Jim could make out its features from his seat on his apartment balcony on Atlantic Avenue. The nine sails, three quite large, billowed in the wind, full and proud. He admired the hull, wooden and walnut-hued, the coded, multicolored flags in the rigging, the crow's nest.

He leaned forward and brought his face closer to the balcony's old black cast iron rails. His eyes widened, his mouth opened slightly. His lips poised to form a sentence but at that moment his twenty-three year old girlfriend Maureen Henretty paused from her reading, placed the laptop on the stool between them, and exhaled deeply in frustration. Jim Scoresby stared into the cloudless azure expanse of the Atlantic sky. She again took up the laptop and reread the passage aloud.

I, James Ewell Scoresby, am writing this to fulfill a promise: many times in my life, my long-ill father has made me swear that he would see my first novel in print before he passed on. Here I am nearly thirty years old. A half-finished manuscript lingers in my desk drawer (a different tale than this). And I would still go another few years concentrating on living, voyaging to this and then that far-off land, sailing across that ocean, walking in those mountains.

But word of my father's declining health compels me to consider my duties. The next weeks no doubt will find me squeezing this story from my very soul, brewing pot after pot of French Market until the tale is all told. I had intended my debut work to be the manuscript I mentioned before. But the unforeseen events of my last two years merit preservation, even if less than a hundred people will read these words. At last my father will glimpse what he has desired for most of my twenty-eight years. The boy he raised to write must live out his dream.

I myself will not be the only beneficiary of this tale. The strange and unexpected events forced upon me these last two years—I just feel it would be a tragedy not to share them. It began on the 29th of August, 2005.

After many years of living in a variety of states and countries, I had recently moved back to New Orleans, the city of my birth and my first eighteen years. My nine months there selling life insurance and investments, my new apartment in Mid-City, the visits across the lake on evenings and weekends to visit my parents, the nights in the smoky jazz and blues clubs and restaurants of that grand old town—they vanished in an instant. The worst hurricane to punish the area in decades struck on my twenty-eighth birthday, and it robbed me indeed. My home, my new life—all vanished in a vile, dark flood.

"Too nineteenth century," Maureen said. Slightly raising her chin, she studied his profile. "You're reading too much

Melville and Thoreau. I'd say the diction's at least a bit dated. I could see some Uptown New Orleans blueblood speaking this way, maybe decades ago—not some young guy just after Katrina. You could do better."

Jim smiled. He leaned over and caressed the back of her neck, kissing the side of her head. "Ah, my sweet Maureen. You never do mince words."

She rose, clutching her glass of red. "We really should be heading over to Heidi's. The party starts in an hour." She walked into his apartment and shut the door behind her.

Jim groaned and picked up the glass from the balcony's cement floor and sipped the dark ale. Jim again fixed his eyes on the Herreshoff.

The vessel had made good headway in the late April gusts. Now a speck on the horizon, its features were no longer evident. Yet the great ship loomed in his mind's eye as if it were near the shore. He pictured its vast wooden hull, rare, as most in the modern age were of aluminum or fiberglass. He recalled its network of rigging—hemp rope in place of today's machined nylon and stainless steel cords, its wood-reinforced basket of a crow's nest, its figurehead affixed to the bow—all were vestiges of some long-vanished age.

Jim's stare seared into the panorama of dancing waves, soaring gulls, and the two disappearing vessels. He breathed the smells of the Atlantic seaweed and shoreline breeze, brinier and stronger than that of the Pacific.

Though his ears were vexed every few moments by a taxicab's horn, a tire's screech, or a passerby's chatter, his thoughts drifted inward. His mind returned to that day the August before, a day bright and resplendent. Yet the Seventeenth Street Canal levee had ruptured, yielding to the hideous and ravishing invasion of the coffee-brown waters kept at bay by man's weak hand for decades.

Jim shuddered, envisioning the brackish waves of Lake Pontchartrain, waters that had been a friend to him in his boyhood, as they gushed into his New Orleans neighborhood with the fierce dark finality of death itself.

Jim slid open the door. The hiss and spattering of the shower reminded him that his girlfriend was bent on attending the party. Steam wafted into the room, as the bathroom door had swung ajar. Jim walked to his bed and allowed himself to fall backwards onto it. This time no majestic ship appeared in his sights. The fan churned above, and he recalled the National Guard medevac chopper that lifted him off his roof three days after the levees broke. Once more, he saw Freddy Beasley lifeless on the roof below him.

How far he had come in the last few months toward achieving his new dream to rebuild his life in New England. Working odd jobs in New Hampshire for his move down to Boston, where he landed a nice place. Excelling at his new job as a broker. Meeting Maureen.

He wondered if he could ever feel completely at home in New England. Would he ever return to Louisiana? Maureen had said on their first date she would consider moving one day to New Orleans. She had attended Tulane after all, though he had never known her in those years.

Jim descended into a deep sleep. Soon he was sailing somewhere out on the Atlantic on a bright day. Then there was a bright flash of light and he sank down, down, down into the depths of the ocean toward the sea floor like a stone. Death was near as he spied the sailboat far above him in the rays of light piercing the waves.

Chapter Eight

"Jim sells investments at Dad's firm in the Hancock Tower. He's been over there since November. Daddy invited Jim to the Cape one weekend to get him into sails. That's how we met, you might remember." Maureen exalted his latest social rank to a young couple he did not recognize, but whom she knew from her lab job at Massachusetts General Hospital. Jim was resigned to let her do most of the talking. In the distance, joggers on the grassy Esplanade headed across the Charles to Cambridge beyond.

"I've heard of you from Maureen," said the young redheaded woman with a pinched expression, the same look of pity he had often received in his past seven months in New England. Such looks once touched him, but they could often precede some rather bruising Bostonian sarcasm.

"The Louisiana guy! I'm Heidi," she reached out and shook his hand. Jim's father had taught him as a boy to wait until a woman offered her hand. But in Boston a man tried to shake hands as readily with women as with men. "And this is Chris, my boyfriend."

Chris was tall and lanky with a droopy-eyed, bloodhound expression. His skin was strikingly pale and his jet-black hair was slicked back neatly. Jim shook his hand. "I like your place, the view!"

"You were down there for Katrina, weren't you?" Heidi

said, her blue eyes narrowing, her chin slightly lifting and then tilting to the side.

"I was," Jim mumbled.

Heidi shifted her weight on her feet and took a step forward. "That must have been insane. You rode out the storm there?"

"Or did you evacuate?" her boyfriend said.

After a brief pause, Jim stepped into that brutal chill for the thousandth time. Discussing the storm pained him and he abhorred how his eyes would often mist over. Many inquirers had been caring, but some sought merely to quench their curiosity.

"I was living in New Orleans at the time. I rode it out in the city for various reasons. Actually, I grew up about forty miles north of the city. Li'l town called Folsom. Two weeks after the storm, I bought a one-way ticket from Baton Rouge to New Hampshire. Liam, an old college buddy of mine, lives there."

"Wow," Chris said. His bloodhound eyes widened down at him.

"That was surreal, I bet, totally surreal," Heidi said, "even to watch on TV."

"You could only imagine. One day, I know I'll write it for posterity."

"Yes, Maureen tells us you are a writer," Heidi said. "You should definitely write—"

"What I've *always* wanted to ask, though, for the longest time," Chris said, "honestly, why did you guys live at the bottom of a bowl? Below sea level? I mean, my *God*!"

"Yes! *That*... and what's with... I mean, those scenes at that Convention Center and the Superdome and all," Heidi shook her hands for emphasis, "and people lifted off of roofs. All those African-Americans... how do you phrase it? They aren't even *educated* down there... or given jobs, which just compounds their desperation."

Chris said, "I mean, you *have* to admit, it's like a third world country down there. It's like Haiti or El Salvador... crossed with Savannah. Maybe with some inner city Baltimore thrown in."

Jim had heard each of these observations before, although Heidi's was slightly more original.

He looked down at his feet. A hundred scenes from the storm and its wicked aftermath coursed through his mind. For some reason, in the untamable expanse of his imagination, Jim saw his father's face staring at him, with its deep grey-eyed pathos, the brooding brow, and the ruddy liquor-ravaged cheeks, the impression throughout being one of wounded but deeply striving obstinacy. Jim's stomach sank as he then recalled the age-creased face of Freddy Beasley, the bloodshot whites of his eyes bulging with fear as Jim leapt off the roof.

Jim's knees weakened and his eyes watered. The empty glass of Chardonnay slipped from his clammy grasp and shattered on the balcony floor. He felt the eyes of those behind the open sliding door fix onto him.

Maureen, silent for the last minute, shot to his side. She put one hand on his chest, one on his back, her usually expressionless eyes full of deep concern.

"Jimmy, are you okay? Don't listen to them."

Jim lunged forward through Maureen's embrace and grabbed the lapels of Chris' sport coat.

"Hey! Cool off!" Chris said as Heidi tried to wedge herself between the two men. Maureen tried to tug Jim back toward the sliding door.

"Arrogant pissant!" Jim yelled up at the man's face. A woman screamed inside the apartment, and startled voices got louder behind him.

Chris shoved back at Jim's shoulders, his once-pale face now flushed, his sad eyes now offended and outraged. Jim stumbled backward, but his western boots regained their footing.

"Get a hold of yourself, man!" Chris yelled. "Damn! What did I say to you?"

Maureen shouted for them to stop. She swiveled around and wedged herself along with the shrieking Heidi in front of the two men. Chris had frozen, a puzzled look dominating his features. Jim turned and walked slowly through the crowd.

"What's your deal, man?" Heidi said. "Psychotic... hick from Louisiana!"

Jim headed through the door and headed down the stairwell. He thought Maureen uttered an apology or an accusation to the couple, he knew not which. Another female voice, not Maureen's, exclaimed, "post-traumatic stress disorder" as he reached the top of the wooden stairwell. Soon Maureen was behind him as he descended the wooden stairs with long, deep thuds.

Jim panted as he marched down Marlborough Street between the two rows of brownstones. Maureen caught up to him, her face angled up into his, the eyes of cerulean blue suddenly bloodshot, showing hurt.

Jim halted and glanced back down the street. Nobody had chosen to pursue them. "I wish you could see your expression, Maureen. Like it's *my* fault."

"Those two were being crass, but you didn't have to get

physical."

"Maureen, what do you know? You brought me into that lair, probably knowing they're like that. How hospitable! Your friends from work ended up insulting me right to my face, and in front of you! Not to mention they meet someone who, they learned from you, almost *died* down there in that damned hurricane and—and they look me in the face and unload their racially patronizing, skewed views about my city. I'm goddamned sick of hearing people say these things."

"Oh, Jim. Come—"

"No mention of the city's world-renowned cuisine, its jazz, the traditions. No, it's only a third-world backwater at the bottom of a bowl. 'At least we educate *our* African-Americans,' your lovely girlfriend tells me! As if she'd say that on national television."

"I'm sorry, Jim. Look, you're right. Those two can be pretty bad."

Jim had slowed to a normal pace, cooled by Maureen's conciliation. Her hand grasped his. He closed his eyes and released a deep breath. They had argued and disagreed often as of late but in his heart he knew he still wanted to be with her. It wasn't just the porcelain face with its long lashes and brilliant smile and her five feet nine inches of lean yet womanly curve. It wasn't just that unique mix he loved—the face of some Victorian doll seasoned with a dash of the Native American, especially around the eyes. It wasn't just that visage which reminded him of a masklike yet intriguing face rendered in some Modigliani painting. There was her strong education, her ready wit.

Maureen Henretty held many of the trappings and qualities

of a keeper. She came from an even worldlier background and upbringing than his own. She reminded him he had arrived. And she was open to moving down south.

"You know, I know most of y'all aren't like that couple up there. There've been many caring New Englanders who never have seen the Gulf Coast and have given so much. I've known several. And I always wanted to live at least for a time in the Northeast, even since I was a boy. It's just I suspect it may be all too *different* for me up here, as nice as it is. Take that couple—a bit too direct for my taste."

"I just don't think I could leave my parents and my grandparents, I've been thinking more and more," Maureen said.

Jim pretended he did not hear. Her comment jarred greatly with what she had repeated in their two months together. He wiped his cheeks with the palms of his hands.

"You know, Maureen," Jim said, "this is the prettiest street in all of Back Bay. This and a couple of the older ones on Beacon Hill, like Acorn Street, are just amazing. These lanterns and cobblestones remind me of the old French Quarter. The brownstones on this street were built by the Irish twenty years after the Civil War. This used to be all marsh, until they drained it. Gravel was brought in every hour by train to help with the foundation."

"*I* know," Maureen gave her frequent reply.

He hated how self-important she could sound, but to his embarrassment, he often repeated the same stories.

"You know, James, two of those men were my *great-great grandfathers.*"

He wanted to let a little pomp and seriousness out of her.

"Maureen... Irish? But I thought you were a Boston Brahmin through and through."

She shot him an icy glance.

"Just joshin' ya, sweet thing." He grabbed her around the shoulders, pulled her to him, and slapped a wet kiss on her baby-skinned cheek.

"Now I'm *hungry*," she said. Maureen sounded like a ruined child.

Jim laughed.

"Let's walk up to Legal Sea Foods and have some oysters. I'll have some wine, and you can have some of your beloved Harpoon or Sam Adams or whatever, and we can actually enjoy our Sunday again."

Jim sighed. "I couldn't argue with that. But I just... I just don't see how you could be friends with a couple like that back there. Maybe we're two very different people."

Jim and Maureen remained silent as they walked to the restaurant. He wondered if he had made the wrong decision, pursuing her.

Chapter Nine

Mondays were always particularly trying at the Henretty & Henretty brokerage. From the outset at seven-thirty, Jim slogged through the morning, counting the hours until lunchtime. Then he could enjoy twenty or thirty pleasant minutes, but a building dread of the second half of the workday often filled the remainder of the lunch hour.

Jim could not let slip this secret, either in his face or by confiding to a fellow broker.

Maureen's father, Walter, was the chief executive and owner, as Walter's late father had been.

To reveal his true ennui and disappointment would endanger his employment and his courtship of Walter's daughter. Jim even balked at the thought of showing the slightest ingratitude to the venerable old man.

Jim had first met Walter on Boylston at Abe and Louie's Steakhouse one Tuesday afternoon after the markets had closed. At the dark-oak-and-mirror-backed bar, Walter introduced himself. The old man posed a thousand questions as to Jim's experiences during and after the great storm. He also learned much about Jim's struggle as a fledgling writer.

Jim wowed his new friend with the breadth of his knowledge of Scotch whisky and military trivia, unleashing the latter once he learned Walter was a retired Navy Commodore who had served in Korea and Vietnam. After hearing of Jim's certifications and his year at the New Orleans branch of New York Life, Walter offered Jim the new opening at his firm. To his amusement, Jim often wondered which he feared more: disappointing the old man or his daughter.

Those first few minutes after the market opened were like any of the eighteen or so Mondays Jim had endured since his first day at the brokerage in early November. He had seen all the other twenty brokers and the president/floor manager and the IT tech and the HR lady but still there was no sign of Walter Henretty.

The old man lived in Osterville on the southern shore of Cape Cod and owned a townhouse in Louisburg Square in Beacon Hill a few doors down from Senator Kerry. But most of Walter's days were spent on the Cape, and he had a driver take him up to check on his brokerage perhaps twice a week. Regardless, Walter always made a point of popping in each Monday.

The old seafarer rose each Monday long before dawn to inspire his officers and deckhands as they set off into battle. The Commodore would saunter in with some inspiring or even hilarious exclamation, platitude, or dance, and the floor would unleash a cheer every time. But this ritual always occurred before the markets opened. Still there was no sign of Walter and it was nearing eleven o'clock.

Jim dialed away, trying his utmost to reach a client, all the while staring out the window. Jim had earned one of the cubicles against the glass, the Henretty & Henretty version of a window office. He could take in the broad view of the Boston

Common with its famed Frog Pond, the lush Public Gardens, the Financial District and Beacon Hill, some of Boston Harbor, the northern periphery of South Boston and the Four Points Channel.

Even better was the view belonging to the president and floor boss, Walter's younger brother Dewey. Foremost was the magnificent view in Walter's own office. From inside, one could see the Charles, Cambridge, MIT, the Victorian brownstones, and strolling shoppers of Back Bay, the well-landscaped Esplanade, the Commonwealth Avenue Bridge, and the oldest neighborhood in the city, Beacon Hill.

As he held the phone's receiver to his ear, Jim stood and pushed his face against the window. His client did not answer. Jim left a message, pondering as to whether he would remain in his recently attained position at the brokerage. While he was not the broker with the greatest book of business or revenue over the last five months, he showed the greatest increase in monthly sales. At this rate, he may very well make partner in the firm, or at least manager, if he didn't burn out soon in sales.

Jim was searching for another number in the database when his desk phone rang. The caller ID displayed Maureen's number.

"Hey, sweet girl," Jim said.

"All right, James Scoresby. Where do I begin?"

"Should I be sittin' down for this one?"

"Don't make plans for this weekend. There's a surprise."

"Ah, surprises, my favorite! Sounds good, baby. I'll count on—"

"Jim, I told you to stop calling me baby."

Jim sighed.

"Anyway, you'll see what I'm talking about. I think this week will end as a good one. Now, gotta run. I've been corralled into grabbing lunch with Yoshi and the girls from the lab."

At that moment a great laughter-tinged cheer erupted inside the entire fifty-eighth floor of the Hancock Tower. Jim said a quick goodbye to Maureen. He stood and faced with growing expectation the main entrance to the trading floor. Every broker stood. A few clapped as Walter Henretty, two inches over six feet, lithe, and decked in his usual power suit, crossed the threshold with a flourish.

Walter pumped his arms above him as Jim had seen Mardi Gras kings do on their parade floats. He laughed and extended an index finger on each fist. "Top o' the mornin' to you all, good ladies and gents!" he bellowed in his thick Massachusetts accent.

The old man carried much charisma. It just flowed out of him, and Walter would be loved and admired by most even if he was not a man of power or position.

"Okay, you guys!" the old man said. "I just wanted to congratulate everyone on a great March. Now we're well into April and a few of you in particular are still up to a terrific performance. I'd like to give my special congratulations to Jimmy Scoresby for the most accounts opened in the month. Jimmy came all the way from the lazy bayous of Louisiana to remind us Bostonian workaholics how to work our tails off. Keep it up, my boy!" The old man led a round of applause all across the floor.

Jim looked down at his wingtips. He didn't even notice the next two names mentioned. He had once again begun a round of daydreaming, this time a blissful reverie on his last few months of rebounding and his golden future in New England.

The old man tied up his rally with a quick history Jim had heard months ago. Walter recounted his retirement from the Navy near the end of the Vietnam War. He had assumed control of the brokerage house from his retiring father and loosely managed it ever since, coaching certain brokers to great wealth.

The brokers who became the best, Walter declared, "sometimes were the last ones we thought were cut out for the job. Look at Sarah Dougherty... you could see her definitely practicing medicine or the law. Joel Kauffman, you know, we could all see him teaching nuclear physics over at MIT."

The old man pointed suddenly at Jim. "I mean, consider young Jimmy. One would guess he'd teach history or write novels full-time. Look at the guy, will ya? You better watch out, brother!" Walter pointed over to his younger brother Dewey, the floor boss, who observed all these proceedings with a face of glum boredom.

"I know he doesn't say much." Walter shook his head and chortled, his hands on his hips. "But I assure you, Dewey is watching your every move, especially those who could replace him one day."

Walter guffawed and Dewey's thin lips morphed into a Mona Lisa smile.

"Now ladies and gents, Grandpa Walt wishes you a good day and happy selling! Press on! Keep up the good work! This April, beat the hell out last year's and let's give 'em hell in May." As he gave this last rallying cry, Walter raised a fist above his head in a boxer's celebration.

The floor erupted in a cheer and then everyone sat and

plunged fervently to work on the phones and computers. Walter draped his arm around his brother's shoulder and they walked to Dewey's corner office.

Jim dialed another prospect, an attorney he and Maureen had met at the renowned Raw Bar on the Cape in Falmouth. While the three had snacked on the bar's legendary lobster rolls, the attorney inquired as to Jim's occupation, and then complained about the Dow's recent performance. That gave Jim his opening. He made sure to get the man's card before moving on.

The attorney answered. Jim made his normal polite pleasantries and then set in on his pitch. The attorney bit, but said he had a meeting in a few minutes, and that he wanted a call back later to discuss the number of shares. Jim and the man agreed to chat again after lunch, around one o'clock.

Jim moved to another call. He snickered, thinking of the languid, booze-drenched lunches New Orleans professionals, namely the oilmen, enjoyed back in the good years. Such lunches would last up to two hours, his father would tell him. That was as long as breakfast at Brennan's in the Quarter! Though lunchtime in the Big Easy would always run longer than in most cities, now a good many of those oilmen, unlike his father, had settled in Houston or overseas. The best years of New Orleans were long gone.

Jim paused and called his most reliable client, this one in the marketing department of *The Washington Post*. The number had been forged into his memory long ago. Damon Lockland had attended Sewanee with him and been one of his closest friends ever since. Damon was gifted with many attributes: prodigious wit, vast personability, much culture, and a perpetual emotional buoyancy that rendered every crisis just another minor obstruction.

All of which made Damon Lockland a prime contact for any broker to call on an uneventful Monday morning. Damon was incredibly enterprising, ever vigilant for the newest stock or side enterprise to further his small fortune. He had also inherited the keen business acumen of his father and the creative mindset of his mother. Many times in the last few months, Jim had dialed his friend, and Damon had purchased stocks and bonds, and often in great quantities.

Damon answered with his customary good cheer. “How goes it, James Ewell Scoresby? How are sales? Still liking Beantown?”

“Sales are up more by the month. Boston isn’t so bad. I just landed a new pad in the North End with a great balcony view of the Harbor. You and Kathy come on up for a long weekend. We can also drive up to see your dad in Bradford.”

“We were just skiing with him up there at Christmas. While you were back visiting Louisiana. But for you? We’ll be up soon. Just have to set some plans in stone.”

“Y’all talk, then name some dates when you might want to stay.”

“Jimmy boy, ha ha! Sounds like you’re still rocking the old accent and the ‘y’all’! They’ll rib you raw in no time up there! Now, so... you got any inside info for me today? Anything *promising*?”

“Hargrove is, I think, a promising ticket. It’s down a bit. But I do believe with all my faculties it’s gonna go up the next few months just exponentially. It went the same way two years ago. I’d go with them.”

"I've been watching them a bit. They're down to like one-fifty a share now?"

"One twenty-five now, podnuh."

"Podnuh! Ha! The Cajun Yankee! I love it. I'll take a thousand."

"Very well. Thank you much, Damon. Let's talk this weekend about the trip when you get some time."

They bid their goodbyes and hung up. He missed his old friend, an only child who was like a brother to him. Not merely in college, but when Jim lived and worked there in the Capital four years ago, they found many great adventures together on the town. Now Jim hardly got to see Damon anymore. Damon had remained in D.C. and married a brainy, attractive lobbyist from Maryland. Jim's days of gallivanting with Damon in search of beautiful women were dead and gone. But Jim took heart. Kathy was a great pick.

Jim called up the order for Damon's thousand shares and dived back into the chase. He remembered Ken Whitmore, the software executive he met days ago on the commuter rail to Newburyport. Or perhaps he could phone the old doctor from Brookline he had met at the Museum of Fine Arts members' gala.

He dialed both. Neither answered.

Jim sighed and leaned forward, relishing the gorgeous vista before him. A lone window cleaner dangled in front of one of the turn-of-the-century granite buildings in the Ladder District, on the other side of the Common. Somehow, the reckless figure reminded him of himself.

While gloating at his desk, he was not completely content, despite his survival of Katrina and his newfound success. He deep down did not think he was built for sales, nor did he much enjoy it. Perhaps his success as a stockbroker emerged from sheer will—with perhaps a dash of good luck.

Surely there would come a time when the thrill of the hunt would no longer charm him. Jim would find the market unbearable, no achievement or success reinforcing his self-worth. And he would do as he had done before many times in his youth and venture forth into the horizon and find a different quest, a different arena.

Still, he must remain steadfast on his lifelong course of writing and of bettering his craft. He had published some of his short stories in magazines and journals a few years back, and had privately published a short story anthology in New Orleans to local fanfare.

In the last three years he had written little while he travelled the world: Europe, Latin America, the Caribbean, Canada, and throughout the United States. Then he had settled in New Orleans for nine months. He experienced great moments on the town and with Freddy. Then Madame Katrina paid her visit.

In his months in New England, he had often neglected to write, and instead spent all of his time exploring a region far different from the one in which he had been reared.

He must write more, he resolved, as he stared at the lone, bold window cleaner.

A firm hand on his shoulder startled him.

"Hiya, bud. How's it goin' this morning?" The old man smiled, his narrowed eyes gleaming down at him, both wolf-like and benevolent. The silver hair, clipped short on the sides and back, was youthfully preened about two inches upward.

Jim envisioned some bird of prey, its head feathers jutting upwards from the rain.

"Sluggin' away like always."

"I liked your results, my man! Come with me. I want to chat with you."

Jim rose and followed Walter's brisk optimistic march into the corner office.

"Take a seat, Jimmy boy."

Jim sank into one of the two leather seats facing the large mahogany desk. The old man gently shut the door. Jim's gaze swiveled about the room, taking in the framed black-and-white photos of naval and yachting crews, and then the excellent vista through the windows.

"I tell ya this desk was from an old custom house in Havana? From the days of the Spanish-American War."

"It's a beauty, Walter, definitely."

"I'd like a ship captain's desk, ideally a whaler's, something early nineteenth century. And you keep selling your tail off and I'll getcha something. A fella like you might prefer one of those old tall plantation desks with a copper spittoon, Luzianna boah! I know how you guys are! Now don't try to fool me!" The old man cackled mischievously, pointing at Jim with mock accusation.

"That's not me, sir." Jim shook his head. A frequent thought crossed his mind again: Walter was not very serious for a senior military officer, especially one who retired just shy of attaining an admiralty. But he liked that about the old man. Walter revealed irreverence and jest where Jim imagined many of his former rank— despite their virtues—might harbor stodginess, even moroseness.

The old man's eyes locked onto him, cobalt as the plane-dotted skies and the seas they had gazed upon for decades—seas the old commodore once thought to master, Walter once told him, but soon learned he never fully could. Eyes that had seen, he told Jim and Maureen, men braver and younger and brighter and stronger than he was, blown apart by torpedoes and fifty caliber shells, eyes that had seen both enemy pilots and his own flotilla's sailors alike perish in battle from his very own commands.

Jim realized those eyes across the desk had seen a depth of experience his own would never see, eyes that revealed both triumph and defeat that perhaps he would never know. Those eyes could probably see straight through him.

"Well, I know you heard me go on this morning about you. It appears sales is something at which you are quite adept, son." Walter motioned around the room with his hand. "We both know Kauffman and Dougherty lead in terms of monthly revenue. But they're dinosaurs. They're near-lifers who know thousands of people in the region and they've each accumulated a massive clientele."

Walter leaned forward. "But this is *all*, and I repeat *all*, those guys will ever do. Buy and sell money, a lucrative but dull, and possibly meaningless, pursuit. One day they'll leave me and probably get an office and sell as independent brokers."

Leaning slightly backwards at Walter's sudden gruff negativity, Jim said, "Well, they could run Henretty & Henretty here for you."

"Ah, yes," Walter sighed. He stood and spun to face the table behind him. Walter grabbed the decanter of amber liquid, along with two glasses. "Scotch, my boy? Macallan 18?" Walter had already poured himself a single.

"I can't now, Walter," Jim laughed. "I've got to call this client in a bit and—"

"Nonsense, it's the lunch hour. And you're from the town that invented the cocktail, for Pete's sake. Eat after this, then just down a coffee."

Jim took the glass and reclined in his seat.

"So, Jim... I'm saying that those who excel now in this venture here... that is all they will ever do. I'm a Bostonian through and through, so I'll ask you directly: how long do you see yourself in this business, son? Do you see yourself managing this thing? What do you see yourself doing down the line, for the majority of your life? Settling down and writing, perhaps? Becoming the next Updike?" Walter reclined in turn, sipping once from the glass and resting it on a crossed knee.

Jim felt his brow sweating over the directness and seriousness of Walter's inquiries. He could detect a glimmer of humor and affability both in the eyes and mouth. But overall with the stare crowned by raised, slightly beetling salt-and-pepper brows, Jim sensed the old man was quite serious and wanted an answer, and a pithy one at that.

"To be completely honest with you, sir, as you've always been nothing but honest with me, I have skill and a work ethic. And I've had a run of good luck. I hope I don't get myself in trouble now, but..."

The old man's gaze remained fastened onto him, but an eyebrow had playfully arched in what was clearly amused anticipation.

Jim proceeded with caution. "But oftentimes... I don't see myself... as a broker for good. I can do this for a while, maybe running a ship like this, but I want to settle into something with a slower pace. Maybe teaching a bit, travelling, but most definitely I'd return to my writing. That, I believe, is my true purpose."

"From you I'm hearing, '*not a broker for good*' and '*running a ship*' and '*slower pace*' and '*travel*'. And then you mention destiny, by the way, which is quite impressive, I must say, in this day and age. Good to hear that again."

"Thank you, sir."

"Jimmy boy, I believe you have paraphrased the job description for this new opening in another one of my ventures."

Jim's anxiety lifted. His friend was perpetually intriguing.

Walter took a large sip. "*Wicked pissah!* To use the old Bostonian expression. So young Scoresby. Where do I begin?" Walter slapped his hands on the desk. "I've come to trust your word in the last few months, so to put it in a military light," —Walter motioned with an open palm toward him—"or in a Southern manner: you, I believe, are '*a man of honor.*' So I entrust you to tell *nobody* that I've decided to sell my share of this firm to my brother Dewey. It *must* stay in the Henretty line. My father would've wanted it that way. With this enterprise, sonny, it's hard managing my other pursuits."

Jim remained silent, for fear of interrupting the old man's train of thought. The news was unnerving, but fascinating nonetheless. Jim clung to every word, studying the scrimshaw in the hutch behind Walter. He sipped from the glass, savoring the Scotch.

"What really got those mental gears turning was my little discovery last week of Billy McTierney's embezzlement and theft. He managed my boat brokerage, ran a lot of the errands and deliveries and accounts payable and sales himself."

Jim remembered meeting McTierney at the Cape house. He could sense where the Commodore was going. With anticipation, he kept his mouth shut and his ears open, like one of the old seafarer's lieutenants of decades past.

"He was not just fibbing, son. Flat out doctoring up the books, pocketing several hundred, several thousand in cash here and there, borrowing my boats behind my back. I terminated him last week. Truly a sad case. Given your passion for boats and all, I thought I'd broach the idea, the invitation, that I personally train you to run the business. You do know less than the men in my shop. But I'd put my money on it, son, that I can at least *trust* you. You're a quick learner and I can teach you the rest. I'd give you thirty-five percent commission on all the crafts you sell. I'll even pay you a base, full benefits, to boot. I need someone to start—and very soon."

Jim made a move to speak, but found he couldn't.

"Now, son, you'd make out well here in spring and summer and the first part of fall. And you'd winter boats down in the Carolinas, Georgia, Florida. I'd pay for your 100-ton, then your 500-ton license. As a perk, you could join me on *Avalon* in the Figawi race in May. You know, every Memorial Day weekend from Hyannis to Nantucket. We'd compete with old Teddy Kennedy's schooner, *Mya*. A top-of-the-line sixty-footer. Whaddaya say, son? Drink some more of the Macallan if you can't decide and the immortal fairies will whisper to you their counsel." The old man cackled again.

Jim felt the heat creep up from his neck. The old man really did hold him in such high esteem. Jim knew what he wanted, and there was no need to deliberate.

"I'm in, Walter. This all sounds amazing, a great opportunity."

"You can finish the week here. Dewey will announce you are moving on. You can manage your extant accounts, or Dewey will personally manage them. Either way, you should let your people know their money's in excellent hands."

"Where would I live?"

"You could *conceivably* stay in your apartment and commute to the brokerage in Osterville. But seriously. It's an hour and a half drive. I could buy you immediately out of your lease in the North End. You could move into that condo attached to my warehouse in Osterville. Or I could put you up elsewhere on the Cape. I suggest one of the latter options. I know what you're thinking... about Maureen... but she comes so often to visit, you'd be together all the time. She's the very person who lobbied for you to get the job offer. Regardless, I thought of you before I ever told her about my little idea."

"She knows me! But I'm surprised she'd want me to leave stocks as I've excelled here. And to move away from Boston?"

"She thinks this job would be just your cup o' tea."

Jim wondered if this opportunity was her new surprise.

"Well, my boy, you say you're in. Excellent. You're set to move on this soon?"

"Yes, sir, Walter."

"Great. Now if you'll excuse me, I have business to tend to with my brother. You should break for some lunch, Jim. Be responsible: put a little food in that belly along with all that Macallan. And Jim, consider what you want to do with your open accounts. Dewey can work them. Or we can give the money back, or one of your colleagues can work them. You can mull over the living situation at lunch."

"Yessir, I will! Thank you for the opportunity," Jim said, shaking Walter's hand, noting its steely grip.

The old man guffawed, slapping his young friend's back.

Jim turned toward the door, and before opening it, angled his head toward the window. He narrowed his eyes and smiled with contentment. The Charles idled past with its daysailers and occasional sailboats, their sails puffing in the wind like the breasts of eagles on the verge of taking flight.

Jim hoped he could meet the challenge. It had been years since he had worked on a boat.

Chapter Ten

The belfry of Saint Cecilia's rang in noontime a block away as Jim strolled down Boylston toward Whiskey's Smokehouse and Saloon. Inside, he held up his identification to the doorman.

"*Louisiana*? You're a long way from home! There for Katrina?" The brawny man in the muscle shirt squinted down at Jim.

"Unfortunately, yes," Jim said, immediately regretting his glib response.

The roar of the lunchtime crowd was befitting Fenway Park. Music videos played on all screens, and the place was almost as glutted as it would be in five hours with young professionals and students from Boston University and Berklee College. Jim glanced across the room, then meandered through the teeming crowd and took his seat with his three friends.

Most of his closest friends in New England were there except his good friend in New Hampshire: Liam, the actual reason for his move to the region. Jim spotted Bryce Donahue, who hailed from Simsbury, Connecticut. Bryce lived in an apartment a few blocks away on Newbury and Hereford.

"Greetings, Jimmy!" Bryce said. A CPA at Ernst and Young, Bryce often met Jim for lunch at Whiskey's for the famous ten-cent wings, lobster specials, and beer. Bryce shared Jim's near-fanatical love for seafood and they knew all the good spots in town.

"Good to see y'all. Glad we could meet up at 'the club' ! "

"You've got some important news for us, Jimmy," said his friend Duff, an inside salesman and native Bostonian who lived on Bowdoin Street in Beacon Hill. Duff was blind from birth, yet his wizard-like skill at maneuvering through the meandering streets of Boston without a fall or any impact with man or car ranked second only to his zest for meeting and conversing with young women.

"I've got some news, yes indeedy!" Jim said.

"Well, Mr. Scoresby," his friend Patrick Brauner said. Patrick was in his residency at Harvard Medical School. Maureen seemed to be one of a handful of young females not impressed with him. Maureen was even repulsed, detecting a womanizer.

"Cough it up, man," Patrick said. "Alas, you have decided on moving west and pursuing a career as an '*actor*' of ill repute."

"It's a good thing I didn't invite our friend Father Esteban from Saint Cecilia's across the street." Duff was the only friend who did not care for Patrick.

"Yes, this time the priesthood might actually recruit him," Patrick sneered.

"Alright, man, enough of the suspense!" his friend Case said, beating a drum roll with his hands on the table. Though well liked by the entire group, Case cut a unique figure there at the table. He was longhaired, six-three, gangly and his face was weathered a bit past his years from mountain climbing and hiking out west.

"I've told y'all that I've opened most of my firm's new accounts in the last four months," Jim began.

"You yuppie!" Case said.

"Of course, Case," Bryce nodded over his chicken wings. "And well done, Jim."

"Thanks. Walter Henretty has commended me many times. But he's moving me out of the firm. He's transferring me to a totally unrelated side-venture of his, putting me in charge of the Melville Yacht Brokerage down on the Cape, in Osterville. Selling, buying boats, delivering them up and down the East Coast. Wintering them down south! I'll be making out well in terms of pay and benefits, too."

"That's good stuff, Jimmy," Bryce said. "That's right up your alley."

"Hell yeah! Whoo hooo!" Case screamed, raising his hands in the air. This day there seemed to be jubilation but no wisdom from Case. He had apparently taken a break from urging his friends to "carpe diem" or offering them gems of Native American and Eastern religion and philosophy.

"Congrats, my man," Duff said, smiling approvingly. "But who's gonna accompany me to Sunday Mass? And we're losing our trivia partner at the Twenty-first Amendment on Tuesday nights."

"Hat's off to you, Scoresby," Patrick chimed in. "But... *first* you settle down with a girl who hates me, thereby destroying our partnership as wingmen. And in the city with perhaps the most single professional women with a combination of beauty and brains. Then you announce you're taking a job with a ninety-minute drive from here. Jim, this is a farewell party. This is a funeral!" He slammed down his glass of water and huffed with mock anger. "I'm gonna take the day off now and get wasted in sorrow."

"A true New Orleanian!" Jim said. "Now y'all... this is a godsend. I knew all about the old man's operation. But I never dreamed Walter would offer me a spot in it. And to head the thing!"

"Move down there, but you better come and visit often," Duff said. "And I'll text you during trivia. Some of the history, politics, literature questions."

"So are they covering your move down there, Jim?" Bryce said.

"Yeah, when are ya leavin' us?" Case half-yelled.

A man sitting in the booth behind Case turned around for a moment.

"My lease ends in three months. Ol' Man Walt is bustin' me out of it, offered to pay the deposit on a place on the Cape. Or I could set up in the condo that's over the boat warehouse, down in Osterville. I'm opting for the latter. That's where McTierney—the pompous ass running the shop—was living before the old man fired him. The stuffed shirt ingrate didn't realize how good he had it. Lived rent-free. Had a great job with tons of perks and did many things that would have made any boss can him."

"Now you won't have Beantown rents to weigh you down," Duff said. "You can spend that precious money on other things. Like gas to come up to Tuesday night trivia."

"It'll take a chunk out of your monthly barhopping expenses," Case said.

"Well, it wasn't the *worst* announcement," Patrick said. "You could have told us you were engaged to Maureen, had finally developed cirrhosis, or had entered the priesthood."

"Brauner! Shut it!" Duff said.

"Or that you had decided to return to the bayou, which I suspect you one day will do." Bryce winked.

"Now let's stop the shenanigans and order lobsters!" Jim said. "They have two for thirteen, or one for seven. I love their lobster special. Even though the meat's often crumbly, being previously frozen. Lacks the full briny taste. But they're decent, and cheap nonetheless."

Patrick flagged down the waitress. All chose lobsters except Duff, who ordered his usual fish and chips.

"Y'all know nearly every day here in New England," Jim said, "I've enjoyed lobsters, chowder, steamer clams, quahog clams, littleneck clams, cherrystone clams, mahogany clams, or a combination of these."

Even from his first days at Liam's home in Exeter, the novelty and excellence of New England seafood had never waned for Jim, and his friends all ribbed him for his undying obsession.

"How can we forget the record you set? Captured on video, too," Patrick said. "You men recall the ten pound lobster Jim devoured in my apartment?"

"Ah, y'all, I'll tell you what I shall miss," Jim said. "Grabbing Whiskey's five-thirty weekday pints and wings with Bryce. Meeting up with Case in the ratty East Boston dives."

Jim turned to Duff. "I'll miss Tuesday trivia nights near the capitol at the Twenty-First Amendment with Duff and his buddies. Eating at Durgin Park." Strangely, Jim loved its tradition: the bartenders and waitstaff openly insulting their patrons, and keeping the performance going, never admitting it was all in jest.

"And what else?" Patrick said.

"First Fridays at the Museum of Fine Arts." Jim would join Patrick in doing what all young attendees at that event did: pretend to view the art, but size up prospective dates. At these events, Jim was obligated to "open," as Patrick and his friends joked. Jim would open up conversation with women and then introduce his young friends.

"I'll miss strolling with Maureen to Mass, then afterward buying fresh fish and vegetables at Haymarket's outdoor stalls near the North End. And grilling monkfish or halibut or striped bass on the kettle grill on my building's roof."

Jim was grateful his old Italian landlord permitted this. He learned Jim's great uncle was a famous drummer for Louis Prima.

Jim knew he would miss his friends most of all. But next in line would be these very traditions of the last four months. And Jim would miss the butter and batter aroma of fried seafood that he could discern in streets throughout Boston's downtown, a scent his friends couldn't detect for all the years they had lived there.

When it was time to go, the friends all bade their farewell to Jim outside on Boylston. He would probably see them in a matter of days or weeks. But he had resolved to move in the next few weekdays to Osterville and to occupy the condo. He could take Maureen on her word it was a nice apartment. Jim stepped briskly down Boylston with the crowds scampering back to work after lunch.

Back at his desk, Jim phoned the attorney to take the order for shares as he had promised. Jim then arranged a deal with Dewey to turn his accounts over to the house. Later that afternoon, Jim called his clients to offer the option of either working with another Henretty rep or claiming the balance of the money in their accounts, as he would be "moving on to another position in the coming days."

When six o'clock struck, Jim joined the workers heading to the nearest T subway station or commuter rail. Soon most would arrive, he thought, in some lounge or restaurant or bar or bedroom, some as far away as Plymouth, Hopkinton, or even New Hampshire or Rhode Island.

Jim descended the stairwell of Arlington station into the oldest subway route in America, going from Arlington Street under the Public Gardens and the Boston Common to the Park Street stop. A subway car approached, screeching. It drew to a stop, hissing loudly. The doors opened with the usual rolling sound. Jim stepped inside. Though a seat was available, Jim grabbed the overhead bar and gestured to an approaching middle-aged woman that the seat was hers. The woman made eye contact with him, but neither smiled nor spoke.

The surging crowd of uproarious students and reserved professionals pressed Jim backward. His spine rested against the window. He turned and looked out of it, keeping his hand on the bar. The reflection of his face exhibited the defined yet somewhat delicate jaw. It revealed the approaching premature grayness about the temples, a product of the events of the last year. Two inches of thick sandy blonde waves preened, like Walter's, upward from his brow. The tight face didn't yet sag with age and world-weariness, despite his recent struggles. But the eyes he could barely discern in the reflection revealed a wounded grimness, a determination—and a certain melancholy.

Jim turned and scanned the car into which he and the nameless others had crammed themselves. A young man in a navy blue suit sitting across the aisle stared at him.

Jim returned the stare for several seconds, and then looked at the unsmiling woman and the students and the office workers and once again he recalled the shelter in the Louisiana State University Maravich Assembly Center. He remembered the vast crowds, thousands and thousands of children and elderly, many of whom had smiled at him, commended him, looked deeply into his eyes.

Freddy would have been proud of him in those days in Baton Rouge, and that realization always consoled Jim—though he still felt guilty surviving the storm. In those days, his life had more meaning than ever before. His adrenalin had pumped too much to grasp the overwhelming tragedy. Would it ever hold such meaning again? Would his life just become desultory, full of dead reckoning, to use the Commodore's old term?

Another thought chased that one upon its heels.

Though Boston was intriguing, it would be good to be sprung from the man-forged and often cold and rough urban life, and once more closer to nature, closer to the sea.

Then he shuddered, realizing he would be farther away from Maureen, instead set out frequently upon open water, that most treacherous substance that fascinated him, yet which he so feared. Water might as well have murdered his good friend. The mere sight of it ushered back that hellish day in late August. Would it always be so?

Chapter Eleven

The movers appeared at his apartment that Friday just before dawn. After two hours, they had swallowed all of his furniture into their massive moving van. They had two more loads to pick up that day, but Jim and Maureen would intercept them in Osterville at the tail end of the weekend.

Jim and Maureen stood idly in the apartment, now empty save for a few balls of lint and pieces of wrapping paper. She winked at him and gave a sigh of satisfaction, yet he stood in silence, surveying the room.

He had expected Maureen to be on edge—or snappy as she had been as of late. Strangely, she had been even supportive of his move throughout, at times even enthusiastic and high-spirited. Though her passion was understated compared to his, this was an accomplishment. Perhaps it was because, in a way, he would be more under her observation in Osterville than he would be miles away from her in Boston. He would be more of a part of her family now that he would be living amongst them. The Cape was not a world away, and when she had her fill of the variety and excitement of Boston, she could relocate to Osterville.

They walked down the creaking stairwell of the row house and headed southbound on Atlantic. Jim pointed out the gulls squawking and circling wildly in the morning mist. A foghorn sounded deep and long out on the harbor.

Jim caught that favorite scent of his, one he had encountered all along the New England coast: seaweed mixed with the ocean's brine, a smell so much stronger on the Atlantic. Maureen reverted to her silent melancholia, but as they turned right onto Hanover for coffee, he hoped he could snap her into conversation. They strolled, as neither was bound for work that day.

Jim motioned to the Charles Bulfinch creation, Saint Stephen's Church, where Jim noted Rose Kennedy had been baptized. They passed the Paul Revere Mall with its magnificent equine statue of the famous patriot, and the wall plaques listing the North End's generations of war dead. He did not comment on it. She was surely familiar with the Revere memorial.

They rambled by the Italian restaurant Strega, where they had their first dinner date that winter night some months ago.

"I need to feed my addiction," Jim said.

They turned into Café Vittoria and ordered two coffees to go: a tall dark one for him, and a smaller vanilla latte for her. At a marble-top table, they waited for the coffee. This café was one of Jim's favorites for its history. Built in 1929, it was the first Italian café in the city, opened when the originally English neighborhood had transitioned from mostly Irish and Jewish to its current Italian phase. Jim admired the mirrored walls, the antique espresso machines, the brass bars framing the marble countertops as an aria coursed from hidden speakers.

"Aren't you glad I took a day off to help you move?" Maureen said.

"I sure am, sweetie." He gritted his teeth but said nothing more.

They walked into a nearby parking garage. Jim kept his truck there—he had named it Betty Sue. His family had balked when they learned he was hemorrhaging three hundred and fifty dollars a month on a parking space several blocks from his apartment. He now half-regretted bringing the truck up a few weeks ago. He refused to drive it through any salty snow during the winter months.

Jim started the old rebuilt hunter-green '58 Chevy. His granddaddy Scoresby had driven it very sparingly during his years as a TVA officer in Mississippi, Alabama, Georgia, and South Carolina. Jim let it warm up for a few minutes.

"Is the engine supposed to be this loud?" Maureen said as she turned and spotted the thick tongue of black smoke swirling from the pipe.

As they drove onto Hanover and southward onto Atlantic toward I-93, Jim let rip a roguish cackle. "This baby is perhaps the only specimen of its breed for a few hundred miles, I bet," Jim said. "The rest rusted out long ago."

As Jim progressed down the interstate toward Cape Cod, he cranked his window down. At ten miles per hour above the speed limit in the rightmost lane, vehicle after vehicle rode his rear bumper one after the next, then whipped around him. Some honked their horns. Every few minutes, a driver would extend a middle finger skyward in a profane salute.

"Not to fret, James. They really love you," Maureen said with a wry smile. "Maybe they're furious because this antique here is such a gas guzzler."

"This is ridiculous, Maureen, no matter which way you slice it. You know, this rudeness is a symptom of something larger. I can't understand—"

"*I* know, James Ewell! This argument will pertain to the erosion of manners and the family structure in Boston, and will be peppered with various references to the Civil War. And how the city of Boston lost 'the moral high ground' it once enjoyed one hundred and forty years ago, and about how your region was actually not the only racist and racially segregated one in the last century. And let me guess, it may end by touching on the years it took to allow Jackie Robinson to play baseball in Boston. By the way, I don't know if New Orleans has always been renowned for its 'moral high ground'."

"Well, sure. And especially not the part of New Orleans the tourists frequent, I agree," Jim said.

"Oh, Jim," she winked at him, her arms folded across her chest. "Why don't you switch to your auxiliary road trip discussion on these Cape drives? You know, your back-up discussion of Squanto and King Phillip's War and the struggles between the Native Americans and the colonists in southern Massachusetts and Rhode Island, maybe touching on Robert Williams and Anne Hutchinson and some other figures."

"You're a psychic!" Jim said. "You know me too well. What y'all have put me through! But then again what *I've* put *you* through!"

He was pleased to see her nod and smile. My, she was so sarcastic. He hoped he could endure it. Was there disdain mixed in? Did Maureen truly value him? Jim threw his arm around her neck, pulled her to him, and kissed the side of her head.

"This move, Jim, I just know will be so much better for you. I'm happy for you."

And this move, Jim thought, was a *strange* one indeed. He was leaving the side of his girlfriend to work and live with her father. Jim was shocked she was so fine with the situation—and even first suggested it.

Chapter Twelve

Having both agreed to reach Osterville as soon as possible that morning, Jim and Maureen took the direct route. Yet normally, Jim elected the scenic route on his drive to Cape Cod. How he loved that drive.

Last fall, Bryce had taken them in his Jeep on that route to the Wellfleet Oyster Festival. That scenic way would take him from Boston, through the footsteps of John Adams in Quincy, through Scituate and Duxbury, and then through picturesque Plymouth.

There he could once again marvel at its famous rock and how small and insignificant it looked compared to how it had loomed in his mind as a schoolboy. He could pass the stately early eighteenth century homes, along tranquil Manomet Beach with its gently rolling dunes and gnarled crabapple trees, over the Sagamore Bridge, then through charming Sandwich.

The route cut south, away from the Cape's northern coast, through still-thick forests and through Mashpee toward the southern shore, curved east through Santuit and ended in the seaside town of Osterville. Jim anticipated regularly taking the next leg of the route, which wound from Osterville through world-renowned Hyannis, through the beautiful towns of West Yarmouth, Harwich Port, Chatham (with its infamous shoals and the magnificent seaside resort hotel with its porch's rocking chairs). It wound northward through Orleans, Eastham,

Wellfleet, and Truro with their horse trails among dunes, crabapple trees, and cranberry bogs.

The road finally ended in Provincetown. There Norman Mailer lived and wrote and, though Jim always told himself he would visit the old man, he knew that he probably never would.

These seaside towns, which combined to form a separate region all of their own, were on Jim's mind as he drove in silence the rest of the way to sleepy Osterville. No doubt he would love life on the Cape. More and more, his days of being broke and feeling desperate after the storm were fading behind into the distance.

When he punched in the keycode at the black wrought-iron gate, Jim's heart leapt into a faster tempo. Jim thought this strange, as he and Walter were already quite friendly and he knew he would undoubtedly thrive at his new position. Besides, Jim had visited the Henretty estate twice since Walter had introduced him to Maureen months ago. He sensed some bold surprise at the end of the winding drive, beyond the great swinging gate and the hovering fog. He pressed the accelerator and eased Betty Sue forward.

Jim steered around the sharp swerves and near-straight lines of the cobblestone drive. He could see maybe fifteen feet ahead of him. All along the lane grew gnarled stubby crabapples and cherries and maples and birches, still bereft of most leaves in the cool April air. Every twenty or so feet stood a large white oak almost as wide as his truck, and a few granite boulders nearly as large. No more than thirty feet to the right of the drive, Jim observed the cairn, perhaps twenty or so stones piled upon themselves.

And just a few feet to the right of the drive stood Commodore Walter Aloysius Henretty, Jr. The old man was clad in faded, slightly wrinkled khakis and a thick gray cable sweater worthy of Papa Hemingway. He drew from his dark brown pipe, grinning as if contemplating a good wisecrack.

Maureen rolled down her window.

"Hey, there, Commodore!" Jim said.

"Good mornin', my boy! Takin' care of my little girl, I trust?"

"You bet."

"I tell ya, son, this ol' beaut' brings back many memories. Ever tell ya that me and an old friend once drove through southern California and Arizona in one of these when we were stationed in Long Beach? He was from New Mexico and this truck was what he and his dad used to—"

"Daddy, he's heard this before!" Maureen sighed, scooting over.

The old man opened the passenger door and settled into the seat beside her. "Ya don't mind my pipe in here, son? We puffed cigars when we rode in here last time."

"Go ahead, Walter," Jim said. "You know I love that smell."

"This blasted fog rolled in here thicker than expected. Proceed with caution," Walter said.

In a few moments the old Volvo station wagon was before them.

"You call yours Betty Sue. Well, remember Miss Maud Adams, the Cape Cod Puritan old maid? I just didn't want you to bump her. Old girl finally died on me this morning when I was about to set out for coffee and doughnuts at Christy's. Need to get her towed."

"You two are the only guys I know who name your cars, and both of them old junkers!" Maureen said.

"Great musicians like B.B. King name their instruments. And people name their boats and ships," Jim said in a plaintive tone.

"Just ease around to the left of her. We can park this baby in front of the garage a ways down."

The truck crept around the station wagon, which showed signs of rust near the left rear wheelwell. Jim turned right and parked before one of the three white garage doors. He yanked the luggage from the truck bed and Walter led them through a door into the garage.

Inside sat the 1982 Ford truck, a black diesel Mercedes from the same era, and an old Triumph motorcycle. Walter had stopped riding the bike years back, though he regularly cleaned it.

Jim remembered the rear wall of the garage, Walter's woodworking area. A faded Moxie Cola and a Narragansett Beer sign both featured a smiling Ted Williams. Pinned to a corkboard were three moth-eaten pennants that looked to be at least half a century old. One read "*Boston College War Eagles,*" next to the one that read "*Boston Latin.*" Another read, "*Phillips Andover.*" Jim spotted the blue and gold flag that read, "*GO NAVY!!*" On the wall below these items hung perhaps thirty tools.

Walter led them through an unlighted hallway into the main house.

"Agh! It's dusty! Mom and Sharon need to do a little cleaning," Maureen said.

At the end of the hall was a vast living room. All around

its dark cedar walls hung life preservers (one from the USS Missouri) and vintage nautical tools, such as harpoons and yacht blocks, and paintings and prints of old yachts, sea captains, scenes of Cape Cod and the Elizabeth Islands, Martha's Vineyard and Nantucket. Mixed in with these items were framed photographs of the old man's years at the Academy in Annapolis, in Long Beach and Guam, and in Korea and Vietnam.

A framed oil painting of General MacArthur in his bomber jacket, officer's cap and with his corncob pipe hung near the photo from Walter's early business days, showing him on the shores of Marin County, with the Golden Gate bridge in the background. Two framed pennants of the Red Sox and the Boston Braves completed his collection.

At one end of the living room, past the nineteenth century furniture and the tables topped with framed photographs and piles of coffee table books, stretched the bay window, perhaps twenty feet wide, with the four chairs and the sofa arranged for a panoramic view.

Jim glanced toward the window with anticipation. On a clear day, one could see miles across the ocean: east to Hyannisport, south to Martha's Vineyard and Nantucket, and all the yachts and boats in between. He was disappointed that not too far beyond the glass hovered that wall of gray fog, defiant in its density.

"You kiddoes come take your seats by the window. I've a fresh pot of coffee. Peet's, your guys' favorite! And Mom is making some excellent seafood chowder for lunch."

"We'll take two coffees when you get a chance," Maureen said. "Daddy, so where *is* Mom?" She and Jim had taken their seats by the glass, despite the obstructed view.

"Kathleen went down to the market. You know, Maureen, your mother still bars getting me tobacco. I have to stock up, stow it in some nook or cranny here. She even tries to steal it from time to time."

"Oh, *I* know," Maureen said.

Jim suddenly stood up. "Let me help you with that, Commodore!"

"You sit yer ass down, boah!" the Commodore thundered in his best Southern drill sergeant's voice.

Jim relented and took his seat.

"How about cream and sugar, kiddoes?" Walter asked. Jim and Maureen agreed.

Soon the old man returned, bearing a tray with an old pewter pot of coffee and three pewter mugs arranged next to a plate of scones, three tiny plates and a little cup of lemon custard. He set the tray down on a small table between them and poured out their coffee.

"Thanks for the hospitality, sir," Jim said.

"Well, you're welcome, friend. Such good manners!" Walter said with an upbeat tone. "Dig into those scones and the custard."

He turned toward his daugher. "Yeah, Maureen, you young upstarts, you and Davie and Abbey, so many of you guys around here! Frankly, I just don't know where all the manners went."

"Oh, come on, Daddy!" Maureen threw her hands up. "We had to endure my own mother who grew sour and rude. 'Cause she had to put up with me. And I admit, okay, I was ruined: I had to deal with the fact that women my age and many not much older, I mean, once my dad entered any social event or setting, they'd swarm my old father. They'd just fawn on him like he was some Hollywood matinee idol."

Jim had never heard it put in just those terms. He had accompanied Walter to a few after-work cocktail parties. Even when Walter dressed more informally than the men around him, even when there were some just as old or much younger—it made no difference. At happy hours in the lounges and bars of the Financial District, like The Vault and The Good Life, the old man would enter. In less than fifteen minutes, he would have one or two, even three women flirting with him. Some were in their early forties. Some were thirty-somethings. Even a few were twenty-somethings as young as Maureen. Perhaps they smelled money, power, or a certain class in him.

Jim believed they mainly sensed what he remembered from his days in Spain: Walter possessed *la chispa*, or "the spark." The life force. The Commodore could be nearer to death than any man in the room, but he lived like he was the most energetic, life-loving, vibrant soul on earth, more than many people half his age. Walter lived each day as if, he once told Jim, he was trying to show heaven how very grateful he was for giving him such a long life.

Women implored Walter to dance, and the old man took them up on their offer, but nothing more. Walter always left with Jim or his other brokers, with no phone numbers and no new companion. Walter was a virtuous man, faithful to his second wife, Kathleen, the mother of his children. Maureen had long since prepped Jim to avoid the subject of Walter's first wife, Dianne, who had succumbed to leukemia decades ago.

"How was the drive, son?"

"Not too bad."

"Be honest!" Maureen said. "We almost got run off, or bumped off, the road by a hundred irate drivers. I don't know if it was such a good idea to bring his old jalopy from the swamp onto these eastern Mass interstates."

"So did they show you... the finger, my boy?"

"You've got that right, sir."

Jim loved the old man. Those who served on the minesweepers with him in the Pacific, he thought yet again, must have had loved him even more. No one could ever replace Freddy. But at that moment Walter was close to assuming Freddy's old role: fatherly direction, with great levity, but without the stern demands and expectations from Jim's own father. The old mariner was shepherding him toward what Jim had longed for: proving himself by establishing himself in a happy new life. And at long last, completing the mission, as his father called it.

"So what's the meaning of the pyramid of stones, the cairn, beside the drive out front?" Jim said.

"It commemorates Chief Wanomet of the Massachusetts Indian tribe, a great warrior who fell in that very spot in the 1640s, in pitched battle with Governor Bradford's English colonists."

Maureen sighed and folded her arms across her chest.

The old man lifted his solemn face and exploded into a laughing fit. "Nah, son, I buried my collie Lucy there. I fashioned that cairn to memorialize her in the most Scots manner possible, she being of such a Scottish breed. So you still feelin' good about the move, son?"

"No regrets at all."

"You'll take to it just fine. I bet you rather fancy the name of the operation: the Melville Boat Brokerage."

"I do, indeed. Herman Melville's one of my favorites."

"You could have called it 'Queqeeg's Boat Sellers' or 'Cap'n Ahab's Boat Brokers,'" Maureen said. "But that would've been way too corny."

"You might be right," Walter said.

"'Blackbeard's Boats' could have been a possibility,"

Jim said, knowing he was getting ridiculous. "The slogan could be 'Just Don't Ask Where We Got 'Em.'"

The old man snickered. "The movers did tell me your stuff will be delivered to the condo tomorrow or Sunday. They're professionals who'll take great care of everything. I tip 'em well, and I've used 'em before."

"You used them to haul Billy McTierney's trash to the condo, didn't you?" Maureen raised an eyebrow.

The old man's eyes flashed with irritation. Maureen shuddered with unease, possibly fear. There was a few seconds' pause.

"When I first met Mac, he was a fisherman on Cape Ann, in Gloucester, a hard-working, decent, working-class man, the kind that forms the very backbone of society, that fills our navy and army and our police and fire stations, that keeps us safe. The man just had two problems, which worsened, festered until they destroyed him. Or at least cost him his job and sadly my trust and our friendship."

His daughter sat in silence, blushing away, but watching her father.

"He liked his drink. Right after I hired him, he wasn't all that bad. And he knew more about boats than anyone I've met in a while. He crewed in the good months on yachts in

Newburyport, Marblehead, and Boston. But his problem worsened, and I confronted him about it. But ultimately, the drink fueled his other problem."

The couple was silent.

"Mac also, God help the man, was quite a gambler, addicted to the roulette table. I had no idea he was sneaking off some nights and weekends to Foxwoods and Mohegan Sun to try his luck. His boozing led to riskier bets. That's when I caught him fudging the books. He blew his cover returning late with a thirty-five foot sloop, a boat he was scheduled to deliver in a few weeks on Cape May, a boat I'd actually already *sold*. I found some pink panties in the cabin section. Not to mention the brig reeked like a frat house. Beer cans, wine bottles all around. I spent the morning really studying his books."

The old man shook his head with weariness. "He had me fooled. He was once a good guy with a few weaknesses that really spun out of control. I chose you, Jim, because I know I can train you, but what is more, because I can *trust* you. Ah, Jim. Beauty, vigor, the mind: they all decline. And sometimes disappear outright, before the last breath. All that remains in the end is honor."

Jim gave a faint whistle. So Walter did have a soft spot for the old hell-raiser. Jim wondered if this lecher had hoodwinked Walter from the outset. Or if McTierney had really been a decent man at the beginning, who simply allowed his addictions to corrupt him. Jim wagered it was the latter: Walter had been around too long, led and read men for far too many decades to have not seen McTierney's faults at the outset. Walter wanted to give Mac a chance.

"Commandeering the boat while I was away was bad.

But the worst thing, Jim, was that he stole money from me. Messing up the numbers in the books. Spending money meant for my daughter, maybe for you guys' kids one day." He shot a comical glance at Jim.

Maureen sucked in her breath in surprise.

"I just had to get him out of that condo, couldn't see his face anymore. That sick man lived on the same property with my loving wife and my youngest daughter and son. I gave him some cash and told him to get out of my sight."

"What became of him?" Maureen said.

"He went back to live with his mother in Maine, at least for a bit. The day after he left, I sent his belongings to his brother, who owns four lobster boats up there. I called him—the man told me he'd give his little brother a job. He inquired as to how much Mac had stolen. And I told him. There was a long silence, and he apologized. I thanked him for giving Mac a job, told him his little brother was still a great fisherman and was excellent with boats, that Mac should be a good employee. I mean, he wouldn't thieve from his own brother, right? A few days ago, I received a little package via FedEx. Guess what was inside?"

Walter must have been much like the New England whaling captains of old with his great yarns, with their superb delivery. Jim clung to every word.

"Two things. A thick stack of hundred dollar bills, totaling a smidgen over... five thousand dollars."

"Wow. I wonder if his brother paid this, or if Mac did," Maureen said.

"Good point. I called the brother and all he would say was, 'Thank you for taking care of my brother. Thank you, Mr.

Henretty, for always taking care of Billy.' When I asked who paid it out, all he'd say was it was a small gesture and he and Mac wanted to make amends."

"But Walter, what was the second item in the package?"

"I knew you'd like this part," Walter said, taking a white paper off the coffee table. He handed it to Jim.

The paper read, in a handsome cursive:

O Captain! My Captain!

I Won't Forget The Generosity and Great Tales. Sorry for everything.

Your Friend,

Mac

"See, the man was a bit literary himself," Walter said.

"I guess he knew the great Whitman elegy. I know you know it, son. *O Captain! My Captain*! I tell you, that poem will send a shiver down a man's spine."

"About Lincoln, yes," Jim said. "That was a great tribute, gesture to the Commodore."

"Aye," the old man nodded, a little watering visible in the fierce blue gaze.

Walter tilted his head back and slammed the remnants of his coffee. He then stood and offered them more. They declined.

"So I figured I'd take you out on the boat today, Jim. Help you get those sea-legs back on you."

Jim smiled uneasily, looking down at the rug. Though lost in thought, he mumbled his assent. In his time onboard sailboats, both on the Cape and in New Hampshire, Jim had learned something about himself. He loved boats, but was terrified of the waters they moved in. He often shuddered upon seeing any dark water, even a large puddle in Back Bay. The irony nagged at him, that water was the symbol of life, health, and vitality in most ancient cultures. What if that fear paralyzed him one day out on the water with Walter and Maureen?

Jim lifted his head. Much of the fog had receded. He had been oblivious to all but the old man. The gulls soared and swerved and swooped in what was left of the rising gray vapors. The sun had broken through the hazy remnants. A few ketches, daysailers, and sloops threaded through waves out on the sound. The Vineyard was invisible from the bay window, but the scene grew more magnificent by the second.

"I figured we could go down to the boatyard and the condo, Jim. I'll show you around. You've been down there briefly, boarded *Avalon* from there. But now I want to get you acquainted with the shop. Kathleen will be back in a jiffy with the groceries. She'll whip up quite a brunch for us all, with the help of our beloved Maureen."

Jim swiveled his face to meet his girlfriend's. Her lips were slightly parted; her eyes glared.

"We've just got some business talk, hon," Walter said. "Tedious for most people, anyway. Plus, Mom needs your help and what she's making... you are basically up there with Emeril himself at making chowder."

"*I* know," she said.

"I got you also a little gift, Jimmy boy, which I'll give to you later. Maureen, if you could remind me of that."

Then Walter slapped his hands on his kneecaps, inhaling deeply and perking up his chin. "So are we ready to tackle it, my boy? Whaddaya say, sailor?" he boomed, smiling.

"Aye, aye, cap'n!"

"You're gonna take this operation to the moon, I know it, son! I'm so pleased you took me up on the offer." The old man was on his feet.

Before Jim had risen fully to his feet, the gnarled but still powerful hand was outstretched for a handshake. "Let's do it! 'For God and the Navy!'"

Jim gave the hand a firm shake. "'For The Union, Indissolvable and Eternal!'"

Walter chortled. Jim kissed his girlfriend on the forehead and followed the old man's fervent pace out into the hall. His own gait was giddy with anticipation. He couldn't wait to see the old man's shop and his boats.

With a pang of guilt Jim wondered how Walter would react if Jim flourished in the shop but became paralyzed with terror while out on the open water. Would Walter then retain him in the job? Jim recalled his own father's words over the phone, that August night outside Snug Harbor, and quickened his pace down the hall behind the old man.

Chapter Thirteen

As Betty Sue rolled down the cobblestone driveway and the oyster shell road with her windows down, the Commodore sat within, puffing thick curls of smoke from his pipe. When the road forked, he directed Jim to turn left. The shell lane curved up over a few hills and around a great sugar maple.

Soon the massive warehouse came into view. Strikingly tall, it was set maybe a hundred feet from the dock, boat launch, and the lapping waters of the Nantucket Sound. Beside the warehouse stood a few piles of tires. The large diesel truck used to tow smaller craft sat parked near the warehouse at the edge of the tall seagrass.

Rusting stilts supported an old lobster boat McTierney had worked on from time to time. Mac had convinced the old man to buy it the year before at a Providence auction, but he had failed to restore the vessel in time for the onslaught of winter. Mac had ripped off all of the shrinkwrap several days ago just before he had been canned. A bird had built a nest in a little nook on the side of the cockpit.

Jim parked before one of the four great doors of the warehouse. The old man leapt out, stepped to the building, and punched a keycode on the pad adjacent to a door. After a beep, Walter started to open the door, but then paused. Jim walked toward him.

"Six four and then nineteen forty two," the old man whispered, mischievously grinning. "Now, whassat, son? What's that code for?"

"Hmm, six four nineteen forty two?"

"If you get this, I have a bottle of vintage 1962 Macallan for you in my study. Never opened. Brought back from a trip years ago to Edinburgh."

"June fourth, nineteen forty-two. It probably wouldn't be a land battle... it's the Battle of Midway! The turning point of the Pacific Theater in World War II."

"Keep it down, son!" the old man whispered as he slapped Jim's shoulder. His eyes flashed, like a wolf near the point of attack. "A man after my own heart," the old Commodore added.

He looked Jim hard in the eyes, raising a hand in emphasis, as if about to launch into some fascinating old sea yarn. "I wasn't there. But my oldest brother Mickey was. He was decorated for service in that battle, you know. Distinguished Flying Cross." He then looked down at his boat shoes. "Old Mick didn't survive that war. I was still at the Academy. He was shot down, lost at sea at Tarawa. Now *that* was truly a *horrendous* battle. Namely the way we kicked it off." The old man yanked the door open. He gestured for Jim to enter first.

"I'm sorry, Walter," Jim said.

Inside the door, Jim stepped aside and panned the spacious interior. He gave a shrill whistle and raised his eyebrows at what was before him: a single craft, and a large one at that. Never had he glimpsed something so arresting at such a close distance.

"Her name's the *John Paul Jones*, son. Now I *know* you

know who that was."

"Patriot, founder of the U.S. Navy."

"Yes, lad," Walter stomped his foot with pride. "Now tell us what you think of that beaut! Your first project."

Jim couldn't form the words. Spanning much of the length of the warehouse was what had to be the very same Hereschoff schooner he and Maureen had seen a week before in Boston Harbor.

"Not many people know about this one, Jim. The Hereschoffs didn't build many schooners. This might be their only one. This is actually their *second* largest craft, second only to the *Belisarius*. That vessel resides in their museum over in Bristol, Rhode Island. Captain Nat himself built this one in 1912. Superstructure originally done with mahogany and spruce pine, with a teak deck. Mac spotted this baby for me at a show in Portland. It was affordable, relatively speaking, because it was not in the best of shape. It needed some repairs along the deck and on the aft mast. She took on water once with the previous owner, a judge up in Casco Bay, Maine. Fella just wanted to jettison the old girl, get some decent money for her. Kathleen blew a gasket when she found out what I'd done. After the sale I was still on top of the world, but about a day later, mainly due to Kathleen's powers of rhetoric, what I'd done set in. I've really gotta tweak a few more things on this boat to turn a profit."

"I could *swear* I saw this *right* off the North End, in Boston Harbor. Maureen and I were hanging out on my balcony just this last Sunday. I knew it was a schooner. The three masts, the fore and aft sails with the foresail being the smaller, the design of the hull... I was almost convinced it was a Hereschoff."

"Jimmy boy, that was this one, all right. I had her drydocked in Maine for the winter until I sold a few boats here to make room. As scandalous as McTierney turned out to be, he did help me flip several good deals in the last few months. Anyway, the original owner had her taken from dry-dock, readied, and delivered this very week. Part of the deal went that he'd pay for the wintering and he would have her in his possession, but he'd ensure she would make the voyage down, that she'd be seaworthy. Or he'd be bound to return my money. A few of our guys joined me in working on her the last two days. And I've been spending more and more time working here, as Kathleen has really lit into my own hull for my little transgression. She cut out this ol' tar's grog ration, hid my Scotch for two weeks!"

Walter motioned for him to follow. "We'll check on ol' *John Paul Jones* later. First I'll show you your office." Walter gestured to the small sliding window near the top of the opposite wall.

They walked around the dry-dock in which the schooner was set, hugging the perimeter of the warehouse, past plastic cans of chemicals, mounds of dirty rags, a few random chairs, an old portable stereo, a few boom lights, and a rolling metal cabinet of tools. Walter plodded up the stairs, his six-feet two-inch frame shaking the wooden planks.

Jim followed behind. He spotted yet another keycode pad. What could the password be? The Battle of Agincourt?

"I did this one for you, mate," the Commodore said in a poor British accent. "One eight one eight fifteen. Okay, what is it?"

Jim pondered the question. The Napoleonic War had stopped in 1814, and had restarted in March 1815. Was it an election or an assassination? No, it must be something military, knowing Walter. A battle fought in the dead of winter?

"You almost got me, Commodore. The Battle of New Orleans. Old Hickory Andrew Jackson and the pirate Jean Lafitte teamed up. Jackson's horses and oxen brought cannon down from Tennessee, right past my hometown.... they went right through Covington and Mandeville. The ox lots are still there."

"My boy. You make me proud," Walter said. "But I can't afford any more trivia prizes." He punched the code and opened the door. Inside lurked the smell of old papers with a faint smell of spilt beer. "This here's the office. Mac spilled a Guinness on that table last week. No one can fault him for a lack of good taste."

The Commodore flipped on the light. "Your new office is where we keep the articles, records of ownership, and the receipts of sale in that file cabinet. It holds records for taxes paid on various vessels. And that one contains all our subchapter-S records and documents of incorporation. In that drawer there you'll find the documents on all the races we'll compete in."

Jim felt his heart rise slightly and fall back in place within his chest. He couldn't recall hearing anything about races. How often would he have to practice on the open water for these?

"And this here's your computer. An Apple, no less! Anyway, on the desktop you'll find a digital rolodex of prospective and past buyers, and in the documents section there's a file on each regional show: the Providence Boat Show in winter, the Newport International, of course, and a few ones in Boston. More on all that later."

Walter clapped his hands once. "I'll give you an introduction on Monday, when everyone's here. I'm ultimately running this venture, but you'll oversee most of it. And of course there are the other men living on the Cape who work here full-time. They help mainly with the labor. You can learn a lot from 'em, but they answer to *you*," Walter said with gravity, pointing at Jim's chest.

"Now get a load of this, sonny boy," Walter motioned to another keypad on the wall.

"Walter, you've got this place rigged tighter than Fort Knox."

"With good reason. Years ago some local cretins burglarized it. They made out with a load of tools, and vandalized the hell out the place. I ratcheted up security after that one, when I built this addition here. Your new digs." The Commodore's hand hovered over the keypad.

"Whatcha got, Commodore?"

"Ten twenty one eight zero five," Walter eyes flashed. "I know you'll get this."

"The Battle of Trafalgar, and the death of England's greatest naval hero, Lord Nelson. His victory reaffirmed Britain as the ruler of the high seas for over a century afterwards."

"*Great* show, my boy!" the Commodore thundered in a much more convincing British accent. "Now, tell me, for a hundred points, and the hand of my daughter in marriage, and for full ownership of the *John Paul Jones* down there... just kidding... in what two liquids was the great Admiral Nelson's body preserved for the trip home to England?"

"Brandy... and wine. Not such a bad way to be honored."

"Excellent! Your most challenging question yet," Walter said as he punched in the code and yanked open the door. "After you, Lieutenant."

Walter flipped the light. The apartment, swept and mopped, was devoid of furniture. Jim smiled at the black marble countertop, refrigerator and well-furnished kitchen. The walls had been painted a neutral white, and were without blemishes. A bay window stretched nearly the entire height of the wall. Two French doors, revealing an exemplary view, opened out onto a balcony. The parking lot and boatyard lay below, and the entire Nantucket sound lay beyond.

"I really like the place! Excellent view," Jim said.

"You'll get used to this just fine," Walter said. "Welcome home. Ya dawn good, sonny bo-ah. Ya dawn good. Now let's get back to the house to see what my sweet girls have in store."

For a second, Jim stood musing on the empty apartment around him. He wondered what the flooded, ruined house of his grandfather looked like. Jim had refused for months to see any photos of the mold, mildew, and gutted ceilings, floors, and walls, the obliterated heirlooms and thus the annihilated family past. His father had sent a team to strip the house, but Jim had several times made it clear he didn't want to hear any details. Freddy had passed on its roof, and the entire edifice might as well be cursed.

Jim followed the old man toward the door and felt the guilt return once more. Jim had survived and flourished. His friend had vanished from the earth, murdered by the storm days after it had passed, and the old Jim had died there on the roof with Freddy.

The new Jim was born—and in turn borne up through the air from the city that raised him into the helicopter— and that new Jim had died to the past with its restless travels and struggles for money and been born into a bright new life of many triumphs. But had he betrayed his roots by leaving the city of his birth and heritage at its darkest hour, and abandoned his old life and passions, and forged their replacements in a new land?

As Jim walked out into the sunlight he recalled his father's words from the phone call days before. "One day, sugar, you will wake up and years will have flown by. I'll be gone. Mother will be gone. And it'll be too late to enjoy the rest of your youth and all you could have enjoyed down here."

Chapter Fourteen

The mahogany table was laid out with the old pewter flatware of a semi-formal Henretty lunch. Jim sat to the right of the Commodore, who filled his chair at the head of the table. Across from the old man sat Kathleen Henretty. At Kathleen's right hand, and directly across from Jim, sat Maureen.

The two women debated shoe styles. The old Commodore had completely disengaged. He stared past his wife toward the Atlantic, watching the two racing motorboats and farther beyond, the lone sloop.

Jim sipped Sauvignon Blanc and leisurely spooned the heavenly chowder into his mouth. Kathleen prepared the seafood chowder before their arrival, but had gone to the market only for more dill. Jim suspected the old man had been keen to leave Maureen behind at the house by any means so that he and Jim could talk business and Walter would be free to relate a bawdy or gore-filled joke, tale, or pun.

Listening with half an ear, Jim stared at his bowl. The women switched their discussion to jewelry. The contrast in voices caught his attention. Kathleen's Rhode Island accent carried inflections borne of Italian and Portuguese immigration and a location between Massachusetts and New York City. Her voice was more mellow and lower than her daughter's. Maureen's voice was younger and more lilting, but just as authoritative.

Jim shot two successive glances at the duo, taking in their faces, hair, clothes, and positions at the table. He chuckled inwardly as he contemplated that he did indeed harbor some guilty but nevertheless understandable attraction to the mother, a dead ringer for a middle-aged Raquel Welch, with the same nostrils that often flared sensually, the same lynx-like eyes harboring an inner fire. That last feature she had passed on to Maureen.

Kathleen Silva Burgoyne must have wielded that allure when, as a girl of twenty-seven, she snagged Walter, fifty-two, lightly graying, tall and strapping, and newly retired. Half French and the remainder mostly Portuguese with a dash of Wampanoag Indian, Kathleen first met Walter at a coffee breakfast at the Our Lady of the Assumption Catholic Church in Osterville. Jim had forgotten how the rest of it went.

"So Walter, Kathleen," Jim said. "Can someone tell me the story of how you met at church?"

"Well, Walter had just been discharged," Kathleen began, "and had returned to his father's estate here on Cape Cod."

Jim noticed she omitted mentioning Walter's first wife had passed a few years before the move.

"Walter rarely missed Mass, rarely missed an opportunity for a doughnut, so he inevitably found himself in the parish hall, where—"

"I was chatting with my new friend, Father Higgins, who suddenly mentions he needs 'to give in to the sin of gluttony and find those doughnuts.' He whispers for me to follow him, that he wants me to meet this young parishioner here for the summer. I see this twenty-something, beautiful, somewhat exotic woman, arranging the doughnut tray on the table.

Kathleen starts blushing at me, and—"

"But what did you say to me to make me blush?" Kathleen said.

"Can you help a poor sailor?!" Walter yelled and pounded the table with his fists.

Jim and Walter and Kathleen laughed in unison. Maureen looked at them, from one to another, with an expression of bewilderment.

"Then," Kathleen said, raising her beautifully arched eyebrows, "Father goes, 'This captain returned from a long voyage and needs some breakfast!' I offered Walter a doughnut, and then another one. We spoke of my summer job at this Hyannis boutique and of my Osterville friends I was staying with for the summer. I'd come to the Cape a month before to learn sailing. My father had taught me to motorboat on the Sakonnet and the Narragansett in Rhode Island but I knew little about sailing. I had said the right thing—but as Walter often jokes—I could have said anything."

Jim took another spoonful of the chowder.

"To your liking, eh, Jim?" Kathleen said. "If only you could see your face!"

"I've seen him eat it at two different restaurants in a single day," Maureen said. "But I know Jim and all his funny mannerisms. He's *really* enjoying that right now."

"It's amazing, Mrs. Henretty, really."

"Please call me Kathleen! I'm not that old yet! But Walter?" Kathleen said. "Address him as Mr. Henretty. He's crossed the line into old."

The old man rolled his eyes.

"Now, Jim, which version do you like better?" Kathleen

directed her large, dark eyes with their long curled lashes at him. "The white-broth Maine style or the red broth, tomahto-based Rhode Island and Manhattan chowder? And do you prefer seafood, clam, or fish chowder? "

Either Kathleen Henretty's Maine-style dish or her home state would be snubbed. Jim aimed to navigate this discussion with stealth. "I love them all. If I was on a desert island with only one of those to eat, it would be a seafood chowder, Maine style. But my tastes change. Maybe in a few weeks it'll be the red chowder."

"Good answer," Kathleen said.

"Are you smooth! Ever consider law, diplomacy, politics?" Maureen said.

"Couldn't have stated it better," the old man winked. "And don't let her make ya sweat, son. I was watchin' you!"

"Walter, *behave*!" Kathleen said. "Aren't you going to disclose the little surprise you have in store?"

"Well, after lunch, we could sit around. Let this delicious food settle and snooze here at the house. Then we could take a trip out on the water. We'll cap it all off with a little cocktail party. Sharon can hit the grocery for hors d'oeuvres. I can round up some guests."

"That sounds *wonderful*, Walt!" Kathleen said. "As long as I don't cook, that is."

"Or *I*, for that matter," Maureen said.

"Don't worry about cooking." Walter nodded at them. "This meal was *excelente*."

"So, Jim," Kathleen said, "tell me your thoughts on the new job. Excited?" She raised her eyebrows in expectation.

"It was one big, unexpected leap," Jim said. "But I'm

definitely hyped. I'm giving it all I've got."

"I bet you liked the shop, Jim," Kathleen said, her elbows on the table, resting her chin on her hands, widening her eyes at him.

Jim shot a glance at the old man, who suddenly seemed ill at ease, almost nervous. "I've got a great setup out there, I really do."

"Don't worry, Walt," Kathleen said, her eyes twinkling. "You can relax. I won't mention that very object of careless expenditure that rests inside that warehouse."

Everyone laughed, including the Commodore.

"So are you liking New England, Jim? Starting to get scared off?" Kathleen said. "Between its fast pace and the winters?"

"I am takin' to it just fine so far, ma'am."

Jim felt himself wince. He didn't know anymore whether or not he was a liar. In a way he had uttered the truth. And in a way, he knew he had said something quite different.

"Please omit the 'ma'am'. I feel like I'm aging two years every time I hear it!"

"Sorry, Kathleen. It's a hard trait of mine to unlearn."

"You call your mother 'ma'am', and even forty-year-old waitresses, am I right?"

"From time to time."

"How are your parents, by the way?"

Jim paused and inhaled slowly, as if stopping before a broad river within his own soul he must traverse. He sensed a fog of sadness descend upon him as the faces of the couple who created him appeared in his mind. Part of him still felt like he had abandoned them, betrayed them.

"They're better, and the same. Saw 'em a few months ago in

Folsom, when I went for my truck." Jim loved how, unlike her daughter, Kathleen often asked about his family. "Dad's business was hurting. Hurricane knocked out a good portion of those offshore wells. Mom's still deep into her church functions. She tells me every day how New Orleans—where she's originally from, not Folsom—isn't what it used to be. How depressing things have become, and how depressed many are in that whole area. As for Mississippi, where my father's from—wind damage crushed that whole lower part of the state..."

"You have a brother, right? How's he taking it all?" Kathleen said after a pause. The soft motherly humanity, the genuine concern radiated from her hazel eyes.

Jim remembered working with his brother years ago, and how his brother had hoped they would work together again after the storm, selling home renovations and repairs and working storm insurance claims. The money would have come much easier, but Jim knew he must leave New Orleans...

"Paul and I have at times been at odds, but we were always close. He and my parents, especially my father, haven't gotten along for many years. Now I don't get to speak with him as much. But lots of my New Orleans news I get from Paul. He runs a big roofing operation off St. Charles Avenue. Slate roofs, asbestos, terra cotta roofs, all sorts. He's quite the businessman. Hit the point where he turns business away."

"That's great, Jim. I'm glad they're all right," Kathleen said.

A flurry of images cascaded through his mind—images of the flooded graves of his ancestors in cemeteries and mausoleums across the city and in the surge-leveled graveyards of Waveland on the Mississippi coast, images of bloated bodies drifting in the dark toxic filth of Mid-City streets, of the teenage boy waking there in the Baton Rouge shelter as Jim laid the wool blanket on him. The submerged horror and pain rose from deep within him like bile.

His family emerged unharmed, but the pain and damage wreaked by the storm on that area was incalculable. Was there any evacuee who had prospered more after the storm than he had? Jim knew that he would have to earn his many recent months of good fortune. Surely no one suspected the bitter guilt he felt.

Kathleen must have read his face, and sensed his unease. "I'll say it again." She clapped her hands. "I just can't believe you and Maureen lived just a few miles from each other, for almost a whole year, and went out in the city all the time and never met!"

Jim glanced at Maureen. The features he so loved impressed him as always, but he could detect no hint of mood or emotion. She just stared back at him, expressionless, as she often did. Then she smiled wryly, ever so slightly.

"They were meant to meet here. Right, Walt?" Kathleen reached over and laid her hand on her husband's.

"Jimmy *was* fated to meet my little girl up *here*," Walter said. "So he'd join our tribe, become a seafaring New Englander like us. And run the shop with me! Now let's bring out that lobster salad!"

Walter slid back his chair and prepared to rise but Kathleen beat him to it, making a start toward the refrigerator. Maureen did not budge, and glanced at Jim with the strongest look of ennui. Jim gritted his teeth, and for a second caught himself wishing Maureen carried the same spirit of Kathleen Henretty that Sunday morning decades before.

Chapter Fifteen

The *Avalon* plowed forth through the choppy blue, its forty-two foot fiberglass hull slicing the Nantucket Sound like a saber. At the sloop's helm, the old man smiled, one hand clasping the wooden wheel, the other cradling his pipe to his mouth.

Jim stood beside him, absorbing his every word. He tried not to look out at the water too much, for fear the other three would notice his shuddering. At least he didn't feel another panic attack approaching. The one months ago on the Sound had embarrassed him deeply. No one ever spoke of it.

Halfway toward the bow, Kathleen retied a line to the mast. Maureen lay on a beach towel on the foredeck in search of her perennially elusive tan. Every few minutes, she would launch into a complaint regarding the vessel's ceaseless jerking and bumping and the poorly chosen day for an expedition. Jim could only discern some of Maureen's words, as the crash and hiss of the waves and the blast of the wind mostly devoured her rants.

Kathleen tied down another line and joined the two men under the canopy. She wedged her smiling face between them and squeezed each man's shoulder. "How are my two boys?"

Jim turned toward the swim-suited Kathleen, ensuring his eyes did not drift down to her prodigious bosom or her flat midriff.

"*This* is the life," he said.

She nodded. For the past few hours, she and Walter had smothered him with nautical instruction. Jim smiled and closed his eyes for a moment. He was learning at the hands of the Commodore with his career at the helm. And he was learning from Kathleen with her two decades of sailing and crewing, often in the Figawi regattas.

Walter turned over the wheel to Jim and commenced a tutorial on steering, then on ancient methods of navigation based on sextants and stars. He spoke of the use of logs, and finally on the advent of global positioning systems and how they had extinguished much of the thrill and excitement of sailing.

"In the old days, sonny boy," the Commodore took a pull off of his pipe and exhaled, then looked Jim hard in the eyes, "when the night skies were clouded over or when the logs were ruined or lost, one had to reach his destination by the use of *dead reckoning*."

"I've heard you use the term… doesn't that mean blind conjecture?"

"It's more along the lines of guessing at your current position based on a previous fix, or location, then factoring in your speed, your elapsed time, your course, without regard to the stars or the damned GPS. Logs and maps can be used, but pure dead reckoning, I like to think, would be done without any of that."

"Sounds like no easy feat," Jim said.

"When done well," Walter said, "it's the mark of a good navigator. Imagine our own Navy men in World War II, drifting in lifeboats, under a cloudy nighttime sky, no rescue in sight. If a sailor could make his way to land based on a kind of dead reckoning, which animals strangely have in great measure, he was a captain indeed. Remember Jack Kennedy in the Solomons? When a Japanese destroyer rammed his PT-109 one night in half? And no lifeboat, no radar or logs, but he got his men at last to dry land. He didn't just get to shore by luck! These days, his little brother doesn't have to use such desperate methods when he races *Mya*—his schooner—against me in the Figawi every year!"

A few feet away, Kathleen snickered from her spot on one of cockpit's two padded couches. After the Commodore quizzed Jim on the appropriate use of the wheel and on general tacking and piloting, he took a seat, draping his arm casually about Kathleen's neck. Jim kept both hands on the wheel and whistled a giddy tune.

Walter sat up straight. "Hey, let's check on our girl. How are the sun's rays this fine day, Maureen?" he yelled. Jim glanced past the mast at the bikini-clad brightness of his girlfriend sprawled on the towel. She yelled something unintelligible. Jim screamed the Commodore's inquiry verbatim.

"Too cold! And the sea's *way* too choppy!" Maureen shot back. "But the sun's just fine. The sun isn't the problem!"

"Oh, Maureen," Jim shook his head and sighed. "Sweet Maureen."

"You've got your hands full with that one, Jim," Kathleen said. "You're on your own. Think of it as a sort of... dead reckoning."

"It'll build character, my man," Walter said. "She'll put hair on your chest! Now tack a bit starboard."

Jim turned the wheel. The boat swung slowly to the right.

"Is that the Vineyard over there?" Jim pointed at the dark mass barely visible on the horizon.

"Many miles away, but yes, boy," the old man said. "And over there in that direction, you have the Elizabeth Islands."

For a few minutes only the rush of the wind and water disturbed the silence. The seated couple was set on allowing their young apprentice to enjoy his time at the helm. But Jim's thoughts had returned to those dark sluggish waters in the New Orleans streets. Just for an instant, Jim shuddered at the sight of the dancing waves. He hoped no one noticed his mounting anxiety.

The Commodore rose to his feet, his joints creaking. "I'm so old! Say, let me take the helm just a second, lad. We need that halyard retied. Not the one Kathleen was on, but that other one there. Knot it again for me." Walter pointed at the mast. "Then you can take the helm back and I'll pour out some of our daily grog!"

Jim scampered up onto the deck and ambled over to the mast. He unfastened the line and reknotted it with care, then yanked it hard.

"Make sure it's taut!" the Commodore yelled. "Now come back, get your wheel, mate!"

Jim rushed toward the cockpit, his topsiders holding firm on the deck. He smiled as he stepped sideways toward the halyard. This was a day to remember. He was learning from two masters, and he would have the helm the entire leg home.

He looked up just as Kathleen and Walter shouted something in unison. The heavy metal bar swung mercilessly like some medieval mace. Jim soundlessly gasped in horror and raised his arm seconds before it would have bashed his face. The velocity of the boom, like a sack from a linebacker, knocked Jim several feet across the deck.

Somewhere near him sounded two pleading female voices and the commanding but frantic bellowing of a male as Jim flipped over the lifelines. The broad dome of blue sky and white clouds and taut white sails spun in a great swirling mix above. Then came the cold shock of the water.

The dark vacuum of the deep crushed all about. A bloated body drifted past. Then he recognized the sounds: the indiscernible prayers and pleas from Freddy's parched lips as he spoke in his sleep. The still-hot shingles seared Jim's back as the gunshots and sirens and shouts sliced through the unforgiving dusk. Overhead, the spinning blades of the medevac chopper. Moments later, his vision locked with a volunteer's bloodshot, watery gaze in the Baton Rouge shelter.

Jim felt a strong tug on his arm. Grandma Laforet's panicked face hovered above his own. When she increased pressure on his right arm, Jim's body became smaller, like a child's. A violent force yanked Jim forth to the surface of the cold Nantucket Sound. A heartbeat later he caught sight of bright sunshine and cresting waves. From the distance came the sounds of clapping and cheers.

Hands gripped him under his armpits. Someone was in the water with him. Jim rapidly blinked the salty brine from his eyes. A foot from his face waited the beautiful visage of Kathleen Henretty, straining with exertion, the eyes flashing with fear, then crinkling with humor.

Chapter Sixteen

The Henretty beach house resounded that Friday night with chatter and laughter. No doubt, Jim was the talk of the party. Though none of the guests had ever met him, Jim seemed the harbinger of Walter's resurgence as naval hero and lord of the high seas.

"So I hear, Walter," said Nate Barnes, a retired doctor, "that against the pleas of your wife and daughter, you relinquished the helm, dived in, and saved young Jim? Kathleen deftly secures the boom, reties the knot, then brings the vessel around by motor to retrieve you two guys while you tread water. Is that right?"

"I heard one laughable version tonight that had Jim as unconscious," Maureen said, "with Walter reviving him back on deck."

Kathleen shook her head and said, "Someone tonight actually heard at the party that the men had climbed back aboard just as I spied a great white shark cutting the water toward them."

"I've got one better," Maureen said. "One guest even heard that the 'drowning' and 'helpless' Jim and I had been saved by Dad, who in a flash swam a full two hundred feet out across the Sound."

At all of these tales, the old man had clapped his hands and laughed and howled with delight, while Maureen and her mother shook their heads with disbelief.

Jim looked down at his feet, a gesture which he realized might have brought him into contact with the swiveling boom in the first place. Soon he felt awkward at all of the attention, as the heat built within his cheeks and on his brow.

The old man pointed out Jim's ruddy face with great glee. However, as the accounts grew bolder, more distorted, even scurrilous, Jim could not help indulging in fits of belly laughs until his eyes watered. Even Maureen occasionally snickered, there at his side.

"By the end of the night," Jim said to the jeering crowd while raising his glass of bourbon, "I will learn that the muscle-bound Walter executed a double backflip into the water, punched a great white in the nose and then saved me, Maureen, and Kathleen from a circling school of sharks!"

Walter roared with laughter.

Jim raised his other hand to gather the room's attention. "Let's give credit where credit is due. I had foolishly removed my vest. It was Kathleen who jumped in after me, while Commodore brought around the boat. Here's to her heroic act!" Jim raised his glass and the guests cheered.

"No worries," Kathleen said. In a red form-fitting dress, she looked like a starlet at the Oscars. "But I don't want it happening again! Like your mom says," and she put an imaginary phone to her mouth, "'*Jimmy, watch out for that swinging boom*!'"

Further laughter ensued.

"Now, everyone, do enjoy yourselves," Walter said. "No more worrying about Jim!"

"I'm worried about how *red* the poor boy is getting!" Kathleen smiled across the room at Jim. After a final round of laughter, Walter and Kathleen resumed their mixing, each working a different side of the room.

"I'm glad to know you're cool with all the teasing and attention," Maureen said. "Now come with me. Meet some more of our guests."

Maureen grabbed Jim's shoulder and steered him through the crowd. A few partygoers greeted him. One intoxicated man slapped him on the back and slurred something indiscernible. Soon Jim recognized Maureen's sister and brother.

"Davie, how are you? It's been about a month!" Jim stretched out a hand to Davie, a tall, athletic boy of eighteen with melancholy eyes.

Davie, his face drooping with gloom, was a bit slow to shake hands. "'Sup, Jimmy."

Davie was clad in his light blue basketball jersey, a silver herringbone chain around his neck.

Jim caught a subtle trace of Davie's usual "cologne" or "eau de Vermont" as Jim had once dubbed the cannabis scent while on a homeward drive with Maureen. He turned to the sister. "And how are you, Abbey? How's the writing coming?"

"A little slow with school and all that. How's yours?" Abbey said, her eyes on the floor. She was always less reticent than her brother. A gifted girl, the sixteen-year old Abbey had been writing since age five, like Jim himself. Abbey's warm eyes were either scanning her surroundings or leveled at her feet.

"I'm busy, too. Lots of work, lots of living," Jim said. "The writing's coming slower than I'd like it to. I'll have a whole lot more to write about soon, if I may prophesy."

"Your muse here will give you lots of inspiration," Abbey said. "And gray hair."

"Shush, Abbey!" Maureen hissed.

Maureen put a hand on his shoulder, and they melted back into the crowd. An unfamiliar couple entered Jim's line of sight. Tall and in their mid-thirties, the man sported longish blonde wavy hair. She wore the very same style, but down to her shoulders. Neither smiled, but their expressionless gaze rested on Jim. All about them hung a thick air of imperiousness.

Before Maureen could commence introductions, the man held out his hand. "Jack Spaulding. And you are Cajunman? "

Jim couldn't repress a smile. He shook hands with the man, whose pompous air seemed to have melted away. "Jim Scoresby."

"I've heard good things."

Maureen waded in. "This is Mom's and Dad's friend, he and his entire family, going years back. They live on the Cape, in Chatham."

"Spaulding. I've heard that surname around these parts," Jim said. "In high places. Y'all *do* go way back."

Jack Spaulding grinned and motioned to the woman at his side. "Jim, meet my girlfriend, Natasha Boyle."

"Howdy," she nodded, blinking frequently and smiling ever so slowly.

Jim detected a hint of curiosity in her look. "Friends of the Henrettys? Then y'all are friends of mine."

"I hear you're getting into sails?" Jack spoke with a bit of the lilt Jim had heard throughout eastern Massachusetts.

"I'm learning from the best." Jim raised and stomped one foot. "The Commodore's reputation precedes him. And I'm in the best portion of the country to learn the craft."

"You're dead on, man," Jack said. "Florida may be the ideal

in many ways, but if you love history and you're more of a sailing *purist*, then you want to learn it here. Despite that we may get only five navigable months."

"I'm glad the first of the five is now underway," Jim said. "It makes us all appreciate the spring and summer more."

Natasha's eyes raked Jim up and down.

"Don't you just love this amazing house?" Jim said. "The old beams on the ceilings, the fireplace over there that a man could nearly stand in. And the oak framing and the pine floors and walls. These old colonial homes were built to last."

"Yes," Natasha said. "I don't believe *slaves* were used to build this one."

"Tasha!" Jack glared at his girlfriend.

"Absolutely the worst thing you could say to Jim," Maureen said. "Trust me."

"Ouch. I wasn't ready for that one, my dear," Jim said, jerked from the cozy nonchalance of his bourbon buzz and narrowing his eyes at Natasha. He raised his arms halfway over his head as if in surrender. "I fear you might've been waiting a long time to hit a Southern boy with that barbed little zinger."

"But she means it out of *love*, Jim," Jack put his hand on his girlfriend's shoulder, laughing.

Jim was almost as shaken as he had been at the Back Bay party. That same tingling heat crept about his head and ran down his spine. Though frustrated at this unexpected rudeness, he couldn't stifle a nervous laugh.

"Easy, Tasha," Jack said. "He's had one rough last year, from what I've heard."

Jim raised his finger for emphasis. "I *know* from our honored friend Walter that this house was built in 1810. Not as old as many in New England. Massachusetts was the first state to outlaw the sale or importation of slaves, in 1796. But slaves were still used here far past that date. So, one or a few slaves *could* have helped to build this home. And one must also recognize this state's indulgence in bonded servants and child labor—and the de facto *human trafficking* in all the plentiful Irish immigrants, Miss *Boyle*." Jim uttered the last word with a nod of the head, all the while holding her gaze.

"He is right, my dear," Jack said.

With amusement, Natasha scrutinized Jim's light brown linen jacket, white cotton dress-shirt, and cream-colored khakis, worn in traditional Scoresby fashion with alligator skin cowboy boots.

"I definitely dig the boots," Natasha said with a taint of condescension.

"It's his personal style," Maureen said. "But I did see that combination around the Garden District in New Orleans. Jim didn't invent it."

"I like this guy. You're quite the cowboy gentleman!" Jack backed up a step and studied Jim with an air of playfulness. "You are the Cajun Colonel Sanders, no doubt!"

"That's a first," Jim said. "Well, to utter the hackneyed phrase, 'So, what do you do?'"

"I own Datagenesis. An identity management software startup in Quincy."

"And he lives in Chatham!" Maureen said. "At the elbow of the Cape. Now *that* is a commute."

"Indeed, Jack. You make that haul every day?" Jim said.

"Like our friend, the Commodore. I work from home, but every two or three days I'll pop up to Quincy just to make sure things are running fine."

"You should see his office at home," Maureen said. "There's a bay window maybe twelve feet tall by thirty feet wide, and Jack's desk is up against it. He can watch the Chatham shoals while he makes his calls."

"The infamous Chatham shoals," Jim said. "Site of the most daring rescue in Coast Guard history. Those shoals are probably as treacherous as Cape Hatteras in Carolina. Yeah, I've seen that old hotel y'all have out there with those white rocking chairs on the porch, overlooking the rocks."

At Jack's side, Natasha was as cold and immobile as stone. There was a moment of silence.

Jim sipped from his glass of bourbon, cleared his throat and said, "I must say I'm definitely, definitely glad to be here on the Cape."

"You and I and my dad and Walt should go out on the water soon," Jack said. "We fish a lot, mainly in my motorboat. In a few weeks the bluefish will be out. You can catch stripers, over two feet long. Toward late June, we go farther out and you can get some good tuna and bonito. Walt can give you my number."

"I'd like that." Jim reached out his hand and shook Jack's. He then thought to offer it to Natasha, and playfully looked at her askance with distrust.

She shook his hand without enthusiasm and withdrew hers quickly.

"Ha, ha!" Jack laughed. "Now you have gotten a little intro to Tasha, eh? She'll grow on you though. And she's a mean cook, you should see! And she can crew like the best of 'em."

"It was nice meeting you all," Jim said and waved farewell.

Maureen followed suit, and they proceeded into the crowd.

"Let's locate the hors d'oeuvres. I'm *hung-gree*," Maureen moaned.

Jim always smiled when she said that, and she at times inquired as to the reason for his amusement. Jim never admitted it, but Maureen's teenage-athlete appetite had expanded her hips and buttocks, and he liked it just fine, though Jim knew she was perhaps three of her vanilla lattes shy of being joke fodder for Patrick.

A throng of guests mobbed the table across the room, and Jim and Maureen were swallowed up in it. Maureen prepared a plate of crab claws and cocktail sauce, scallop cakes, jumbo shrimp, and stuffed mushrooms. They emerged from the crowd and walked a few paces before Jim noticed someone studying him with a curious gaze.

"All this seafood remind ya of home, young man?" an elderly man said.

"You read my mind, sir. It's completely different here, but I love it all the same. I could eat chowder every day. I actually did my first two months in New England."

"Chowda, young man," the old man said. "Ya gotta say chow-da. I tell ya, I watched that hurricane coverage and ya know, your state looked worse than a third-world country: the corrupt politicians and police, so many of the people destitute! I was deployed with the army in Hiroshima after we dropped the A-bomb on it. It looked bettah over there than New Orleans did."

"Well, kind sir, I'm Jim Scoresby." He offered the old man his hand.

The old man took it firmly. "Dick Winslow, son." "Mr.

Winslow, I don't think anyone can fault you for a lack of honesty."

The old man gave a sort of pirate's laugh. Jim turned toward Maureen. His badly bruised forearm ached, and now he felt a great knot in his back, between his shoulders.

"Son, really... how's ya family, I wanted ta ask?"

Jim shot him a piercing glance. Something inside Jim sizzled and popped, like a bubble had burst and then settled down to cool. Jim discerned the man's genuine concern, and remembered that first wave of Katrina volunteers in the Maravich Center. "They're doing better, much better."

"*That* is good," Dick Winslow nodded. The old man then vanished into the teeming crowd.

Jim jolted when Maureen touched his shoulder. "Had about all you can take, eh?" she said. "Sweetness, this boy could really use a li'l R and R on the porch out back. How 'bout it?"

They skirted the crowd's fringe, entered the hallway, and crossed the parlor where they had taken coffee with Walter earlier that morning. A few stragglers lounged about the couches and recliners, sipping their drinks and chatting.

Outside on the unlit deck, despite the temperate air and a sky replete with constellations, there was not a soul in sight. Maureen set the plate down on a small table.

Jim placed a hand on the wooden rail of the deck, gripped his whiskey glass in the other, and leaned over slightly. Maureen did the same, just to his side. Neither spoke.

The unobstructed gibbous moon illuminated the sprawling backyard, interrupted here and there by naturally occurring granite rocks of varying size. Off to the side a few gnarled trees grew in a copse, their growth stunted from a continuous bombardment by thousands of gales and the salty breath of the sea. Farther beyond rose the billowing dunes, their domes sprinkled with waving sea grass. Finally in the near distance sprawled the sublime Atlantic herself, seemingly waiting for Jim to notice her skin shimmering with lightly dancing wavelets, her fresh crisp scent wafting all about him in its striking glory.

Even at two hours before midnight, long after the descent of darkness, a few boats lingered on the water. A powerboat moved along, perhaps a quarter of a mile away. A minute passed of sheer silence.

"I know, Jim. You don't even have to tell me," Maureen said.

Jim had said it all before, and it was all futile. He stared out onto the Nantucket Sound. Yet Jim did not contemplate the ocean now, or anything to do with it.

He lifted the bourbon to his lips. The smoky sweet scent first brought to mind his father, the weary man he had left in the aftermath of that great storm of 2005, a period his father saw as the veritable afterglow of God's wrath. No doubt his father was at that moment sitting alone in his dark living room, while Jim's mother was in bed, set to rise before dawn to lead the Rosary before six-thirty Mass. His father would be sipping this very bourbon at this very minute, staring at the vacuum of the television screen. His mind would rest halfway on other matters, much as his son's eyes searched deeply inward, all the while scanning the moonlit waters.

Jim envisioned the ruddy cheeks and the gray hair of his father, the bangs hanging low onto the great brow. The head rested on the antique fabric of the Victorian chair, the swollen feet drawn up onto an ottoman.

This completed the image of a man worn down by decades spent poring over maps and logs. A man weary from endless hours on rig platforms in disappearing marshes, exhausted by the age-old struggle to find and seize treasure. A man further spent by the refuge sought in fine foods and drink and his few leisure hours before the mind-numbing glass screen.

Jim took another sip of the bourbon. The taste conjured up the old cedar-and-oak-walled corridors of Sewanee in those enchanted mountains of middle Tennessee, truly one of his favorite spots on earth, amidst a land thick with hardwoods and the occasional pine, with verdant valleys and waterfalls and massive rock outcrops and English Gothic buildings. He envisioned the nearby Monteagle Assembly, where the Tennessee cavalry and wily Rosecrans once chased each other through thicket and lane. One could still find log cabins from before that war—they smelled like the charred bellies of white oak distillery barrels.

Next in this display within Jim's mind came that day before the great storm. He saw himself parking Betty Sue back at his father's house in Folsom. Despite his father's angry shouting, Jim had insisted on leaving for New Orleans. And his father had wrestled him, their arms grappling, their hips plowing into sofas and chairs.

Jim saw himself speeding south across the twenty-four mile Causeway bridge through the night that harbored the fierce tempest, the conspirator holding the foul invader at her breast. But Jim was mainly concerned with finding Freddy, and his parents would not approve. All over the radio was talk of the threat of looters, and of the storm being the "Big One."

And then there on the Henrettys' back deck, he

remembered looking down at Freddy's body sprawled on the roof one hundred feet below. He imagined all the places Freddy had seen, his performing for President Kennedy at the White House, his years playing the Las Vegas Stardust, his late nights performing with Louis Armstrong and Fats Domino. If those three men could have seen him dead on that roof, deserted by mankind, even by his closest family, they would have thought it an obscenity, a perverse travesty.

And just when Jim's city and his people could have used him most, he realized, Jim had fled. He had deserted them, like Freddy's own family and friends had deserted him in his time of need.

Still Jim did not weep, nor did his eyes even tear up as they had before—and it was always harder to avoid it all with the alcohol he consumed—and Maureen's hand did not stroke him on the back as it had on Marlborough Street the Sunday before. Instead, a familiar scent snapped Jim from his torturous thoughts.

Jim turned where he stood. Maureen pivoted with him. Their backs to the rail, they peered sideways along the full length of the unlit deck. All about them was that familiar, rich scent of Walter's pipe.

"Dad?" Maureen called.

A lone figure moved with slow, firm steps in the shadows, and then stopped. Walter puffed hard on his pipe, heating the bowl which cast the slightest glow onto his face and tweed coat. A thick puff of smoke rose from the bowl as Walter strolled toward them.

With his free hand, the old man slapped Jim on the shoulder. "Don't take it all so hard, bud. I know it ain't so easy speaking with the likes of my neighbor Winslow and that bitch Jack's about to marry, all in the course of a few minutes."

"Daaad!" Maureen said.

The old man gave a crooked grin, a wisp of smoke snaking devilishly from between his teeth. "It's hard, I know, son, getting adjusted to it all. We're crusty and reserved, often standoffish, and we can cut deep. But you make a friend in New England, and it's usually a friendship that lasts. Jack Spaulding is such a man. You guys will get along just fine. And always know there's always a place at my table and on my boats—and in the shop—for Jimmy Scoresby."

"Thanks, Walt. That really means a lot," Jim said, both astonished and amused the old man could read his very soul.

"You love writing. You're a lover of sails, literature, history." Walter punctuated his words with jabs in the air with his pipe. "You love seafood. You were meant to make your way up the coast to be with us! That's one reason you didn't drown today. Besides that, my Kathleen's a real lioness. Now you two enjoy your night."

The old man turned and walked back down the length of the deck until he disappeared around the corner. The steps faded away on the stairwell leading down toward the lawn. The scent of the pipe ebbed away with the breeze, but still Jim and Maureen stood, meditating in the dark and silence.

Jim felt solace that at that moment Maureen stood by his side. As the turbulent thoughts churned and billowed and burned through his imagination, he counted himself lucky she made him feel less alone. However cold and cutting and condescending she could be, he did have her support.

But was he erring in building a new life here? Or was Walter right, that he was meant to build a new life in New England?

Suddenly the face of Jim's own father reappeared in his mind. Jim imagined him at that very hour, standing on his back patio in Folsom, cradling a glass of bourbon. His father stared wistfully at the stars and silhouette of the tree line, then turned and stared at Jim with expectation.

Chapter Seventeen

The station wagon halted on the cobblestone street before the Henretty family's Beacon Hill brownstone, causing the three seat-belted occupants to lurch forward. Jim and Maureen woke to booming peals of mischievous laughter. Weary of her father's pranks, Maureen sighed and mumbled some indecipherable complaint.

"How'd ya like *that* rude awakening?!" Walter thundered. "That's what ya get, Jimmy boy, for sleepin' on duty. Ten lashes!"

"Oh, Dad," Maureen sighed.

The old man turned on his hazard lights. He and Jim both stepped around to the rear of the station wagon and opened the door.

Maureen slid out of her seat and joined them. She threw her arms around her father's shoulders. "Thanks for driving me up." She kissed him on the cheek. "And good luck keeping this boy in line."

"Good luck with work and all," Walter said. "I'll be calling to check in on you."

Jim grabbed the two suitcases and he and Maureen walked up the steps. Walter lowered the rear door shut and got in the car. The couple stopped on the top step.

"That's fine, James Scoresby. I can take it from here." She grabbed the suitcases.

"Sure?" Jim said.

"It wasn't such a bad weekend, eh, Jim? My boyfriend almost drowns and then is forced to run the gauntlet of a few rude guests."

"It was eventful, I'll say that."

Maureen stood on tiptoe and pulled him to her. She smacked a kiss onto his lips and then unlocked the door, smiling back at him as she stepped into the foyer. "Keep Dad in line, too. Get him to cut down on that pipe."

"I don't think that's possible."

"You'll like the surprise Dad's got in store for you. It'll be good for you, remember. Call tonight to tuck me in and tell me how it went." She winked, then shut the door and locked it.

"I've got a surprise for you, sonny," the Commodore said back in the car.

"So I hear! You've piqued my interest."

They wound around the black cast iron fence and massive oaks of Louisburg Square. On Charles Street, they cruised past the quaint coffeehouses, the shops and pubs, the corner bistros. They turned left on Beacon, passed the Boston Common on the right and the golden domed State House on the left. Jim nodded at the 54th Massachusetts Regiment memorial. Soon they were heading south on the interstate.

His thoughts returned to Maureen. It was she who had made the first intimate move those months ago. It was she, that night weeks before her twenty-third birthday, who had first laid hands on him. It had all begun as a small, ardent flame. Over the weeks it became a fierce conflagration, burning on out of control.

But after their first weeks together, she grew mostly avoidant of intimacy and warmth. Maureen seemed constantly ginned up by her own irritability and the stress of her daily life. She had seemed to seek refuge, release from it all in the privacy of their bedrooms back in Boston.

Now, it seemed, he had become addicted to the contact, but he remained frustrated, as she withheld herself from him more and more. Yet Jim was begrudging in secret, as he harbored some guilt over their lovemaking.

That morning in the Communion line in Osterville, Jim had realized he was tempted to daydream about sex more during Mass than at any other time. Jim wondered if it was the same for other people, or at least for young men. And he wondered as to the reason for this oddity.

Perhaps it was because deep inside he felt fear, during the liturgy, he would opt ultimately to forsake many of the physical riches of life, and Mass-time fantasizing was just the natural rebellion of his psyche against moral or behavioral constraint. His mother and father would have maintained it was the Devil, the Evil One, toying individually with him, aiming to draw him away from the Son.

Jim snickered. He still could not accept that idea. Minutes later, Jim again sneaked a glance at the silent Walter, as the station wagon rolled into one neighborhood after the other, each borough poorer, slightly more unsettling in its gloom, than the one before. The old seafarer sported an inscrutable Mona Lisa-like smile as he gripped the steering wheel. Jim wondered where the old man was taking him.

The row houses and buildings increasingly reminded him of his home city. Two emotions collided within him: guilt over leaving behind a city with such poverty, and determination never to be immersed in such poverty again.

Then he inwardly chided himself. Was he being shallow, selfish? Surely he was lucky to have flourished after the storm, when so many suffered hardship, destruction. He must keep these thoughts secret.

Chapter Eighteen

Walter Henretty parked in the lot bordering the Mount Zion African Baptist Church. As the station wagon eased into its spot, Jim shuddered at all of the parked cars. He could only hope Walter was not putting him up to public speaking this Sunday.

Yet, Walter was not the Dorchester type. Jim had only been in Dorchester twice, or "Dotchesta" as many locals called it. Once was with friends on the way to the Saint Patrick's Day Parade. The other time, Jim had taken the wrong turn and he and Liam lost their way for about fifteen minutes. Jim only heard Dorchester mentioned when it coincided with the butt of a joke told by some Boston professional or in some story on NECN's nightly crime report.

"Dorchester Heights, site of one of Washington's biggest victories," Jim said as they exited the station wagon. "No public speaking involved in this surprise, Walter?"

"Public speaking? Nah. I wouldn't do that to ya, son."

As Walter led him up the steps to the entrance, Jim recognized the church. He had read about its storied history as the oldest surviving African-American house of worship in the Boston area. Its walls boasted a regimental flag, torn by minie balls and shrapnel, of the 54th Massachusetts Infantry regiment, a photograph of the Reverend Dr. King's days in Boston as a theology student in the early fifties, as well as letters and photographs of jazz greats Bessie Smith, Ella Fitzgerald, and Duke Ellington.

Within, the choir sang a hymn with soaring exultation. Walter reached for the handle of the massive wooden door and pulled, ushering Jim before him.

Hundreds of standing and singing worshippers packed the old oak pews to capacity. The choir swayed and clapped to the organist beside the podium as their old spiritual coursed through the rafters and pews and reverberated throughout every possible cavity and cranny of the edifice.

Many of the congregants' faces were angled back toward him. They were not alarmed or irritated, but instead radiated amusement, curiosity, and warmth, as if they had expected him.

Jim's heart galloped. The old man grasped his shoulder. He motioned for Jim to look to his side.

A bespectacled young black man in a gray double-breasted suit smiled and motioned for them to follow. The usher led them around the right side aisle of the church to the second row, where he gestured for them to take their places. Just as they entered the pew, nearly the entire section turned and looked at them.

So many smiles and nods caused Jim's shoulders to relax slightly, for his breath to come easier. An old couple turned and waved. Jim recognized the blond wavy hair of a young man and woman. At the end of the pew sat Jack Spaulding and Natasha Boyle. Jim assumed his standing place beside Jack, who playfully punched his arm.

Again Jim considered what Walter had in wait for him. Jim looked sideways in his pew. The Commodore's eyes were riveted on the singer leading the choir.

This lone figure in the black pinstripe suit appeared to be no more than thirty. His face contorted with emotion as he belted out verse after verse. The man's right hand was held aloft as if reaching to the heavens for aid. His left was clenched into a fist, which he pumped vigorously, rhythmically to the beat of the drummer, who was positioned next to a bassist and guitarist at the opposite end of the stage. The singer's face was youthful and kind yet leonine, and like those in the choir, appeared weighed down with an agonizing yearning.

The choir swayed in unison back and forth like a sapling in the wind. All about soared the mighty notes of a church organ, an instrument which Jim could not see until he turned and spotted the army of pipes rising from the wooden loft above the front door.

Set in the walls were vast stained-glass windows, stretching perhaps twelve feet wide by twenty feet tall, depicting Old and New Testament scenes. Most of the figures portrayed were black. One scene featured a black Jesus, one a black Moses. Jim barely stifled a smile when he noticed that the Roman guards and centurions fell mostly within the Caucasian category.

The singer's final, ten-second note tore Jim's attention from the windows. The man held both hands aloft as if pouring all remaining strength into a final musical plea to heaven. The organ followed suit, sending a powerful blast through the rafters, while the sweaty drummer pounded out a crescendo and the lead guitarist worked his strings with building fervor. The singer brought both of his arms abruptly down to his sides.

The church was silent as a cavern. All eyes were locked onto the young man leading the service, who motioned for all to be seated.

The congregation sank to its seats, and Jim and Walter along with it. The singer approached and ascended the podium. His eyebrows raised, he looked out at the crowd, scanning it back and forth. After a brief pause, he spoke. From the authority of his voice to his diction to his ease before the congregation, Jim realized this young man was not merely the choir leader, but the pastor.

"Friends of Mount Zion African Baptist Church, how are y'all today?"

Hundreds of varied shouts and exclamations burst from all sides of the seated congregation.

"You should be, for today the Lord is risen over the earth. He is beaming down at us with all His love... a Lord who even allowed the great storm that afflicted New Orleans months ago, who allows earthquakes and other disasters, who allows some to go hungry and some of the wicked to go unpunished on this plain, but who has a mighty plan in store for us all indeed! For our guests here, who do not know me, I am Reverend Cordell Ward. I'd like to extend a hand of friendship to you all. And now, let's read from the Gospels. Please open the Bibles in your pews to Luke, chapter sixteen, verse nineteen."

All throughout the church sounded the fumbling and turning of pages. The Reverend began to read aloud.

There was a certain rich man who was clothed in purple and fine linen and fared sumptuously every day. But there was a certain beggar named Lazarus, full of sores, who was laid at his gate, desiring to be fed with the crumbs which fell from the rich man's table. Moreover the dogs came and licked his sores.

So it was that the beggar died, and was carried by the angels to

Abraham's bosom. The rich man also died and was buried.

And being in torments in Hades, he lifted up his eyes and saw Abraham afar off, and Lazarus in his bosom. Then he cried and said, 'Father Abraham, have mercy on me, and send Lazarus that he may dip the tip of his finger in water and cool my tongue; for I am tormented in this flame.'

But Abraham said, 'Son, remember that in your lifetime you received your good things, and likewise Lazarus evil things; but now he is comforted and you are tormented.' And besides all this, between us and you there is a great gulf fixed, so that those who want to pass from here to you cannot, nor can those from there pass to us.'

Then he said, 'I beg you therefore, father, that you would send him to my father's house, for I have five brothers, that he may testify to them, lest they also come to this place of torment.'

Abraham said to him, 'They have Moses and the prophets; let them hear them.'

And he said, 'No, father Abraham; but if one goes to them from the dead, they will repent.'

"But he said to him, 'If they do not hear Moses and the prophets, neither will they be persuaded though one rise from the dead.'

The Reverend paused. "Beloved friends, Our Lord allowed for many interpretations here. But I will deal with one of them. Many of you are familiar with this powerful parable, whether having read it or heard it countless times, or," he extended his index finger, "you know this tale from having actually lived it, as a person of wealth, privilege or even financial stability who had needy souls turn to you in desperation. Or perhaps you were one who had to beg and plead for your supper at one point in your life like Lazarus. Most of us have been there, in one of the roles. A few have lived *both* roles."

A flurry of responses shot from the congregation, all in affirmation.

"Some of you have had the gate slammed in your face, like Lazarus experienced many times. And sadly, some of you who enjoyed wealth or financial comfort, despite the anguished pleas of the needy at your door, have done the slamming." With that, Reverend Ward shut his podium Bible with a loud bang.

A shiver shot up Jim's backbone and dispersed across his shoulders. Never before had Jim heard a speaker wield such dramatic effect.

"Now, friends, if you carefully read the parable our Lord relates," the Reverend approached the center of the stage, "you will find that the rich man, called Dives according to tradition, 'fared sumptuously every day' and was dressed 'in fine linen.' So he wore some of the most expensive clothing of the day and enjoyed very fine cuisine. And he's got a dying, desperate, starving, diseased man named Lazarus just laying out there at that gate, just begging, pleading for some crumbs from the rich man's table. But eventually that beggar dies. And so does the rich man. *And those tables are reversed*," the Reverend whispered.

Despite their soft tone, these words echoed throughout the church's interior.

"Now, in this life," the Reverend said, "many who are in the position of Lazarus do *not* get their just reward... in *this* life, that is. And many like the rich man don't get their comeuppance... in *this* life. And sadly, many Lazaruses in this world, they know full well they're Lazarus. But many on this earth, many in our very blessed and wealthy nation, they *forget* they are dining sumptuously behind that gate while Lazarus is dying and calling out their name out in that street. And actually, many hear Lazarus' cries and *know* they're eating that feast of Lobster Newburg and filet mignon at that table, and they hear that Lazarus crying for even a piece of moldy bread, but on they go feasting! Woe to us all, is what I'm saying!"

A roar exploded from the congregation. Once again the power of the man's oratory rippled down Jim's spine. "Now, some o' y'all got family down on that Gulf Coast and took that storm months ago pretty hard. But all the rest o' y'all didn't *need* family down there. I'm one of 'em. We watched from the safety and comfort of our living rooms as almost two thousand lives were *extinguished*. And some of y'all saw plain as day: there were quite a few Lazaruses dead and floating in those streets of New Orleans."

Emotion rose like steam in Jim's throat. He suddenly felt lightheaded, heat building in his cheeks and on his forehead.

"And some of y'all could see ol' Lazarus hunkered down scared on his roof, or on the streets of the Convention Center, or up in that Superdome. And you could see Lazarus sleeping on his front lawn in Mississippi while his little shack behind looked like a bomb had hit it."

Another roar, this time almost deafening, arose from the congregation.

"You could see Lazarus was often black. Imagine that? But hey, you could also see Lazarus was an old white man, a young Vietnamese woman, a Latino child. Some Lazaruses were dead and gone. Some had been flown up here to our state. Some had been evacuated to the desert towns of Utah and the logging towns of Maine and Minnesota. Many Lazaruses are still around, as they always will be. Ladies and gentlemen, Lazarus is here to stay."

Reverend Ward started to walk back to the podium, but stopped just alongside it. Several cries of affirmation shot from the congregation.

"Yes, brothers and sisters, indeed, Lazarus is here to stay and is right there in front of you. Y'all can hear his feeble knocks at the gate, at your door." The Reverend gave three hard taps with his fist on the side of the wooden podium.

Jim found himself holding his breath at the three eerie beats.

"That's Lazarus knocking at our door. He's still alive out there, maybe for a day or two longer. Are you gonna give him some morsels? Or are you gonna give him a whole dish? Or are you gonna shun him, and turn up the music? What are you gonna do? *You* decide!" Reverend Ward pointed toward the crowd.

A middle-aged man of athletic build shot up in the pew just in front of Jim. He had been sitting next to the old couple just adjacent to the aisle. "Feed him! Love him!" the man shouted.

A wave of people shot to their feet, shouting various words of confirmation. In a second everyone had risen to stand, with Jim, Walter, Jack, and Natasha along with them.

"Yes!" Reverend Ward shouted, pumping his fists with jubilation and marching back toward the center of the stage. "You chose wisely. Our Lord didn't just *tell* this tale. He is the Lazarus at your gate! Conversely, when you help Lazarus, you are honoring the Creator!"

Someone began to clap. Soon a fire of applause consumed the congregation.

The young Reverend motioned for all to be seated. "Now,

many of you know the few souls sent to our church by some of our mission workers down in New Orleans. There is little Dwayne, his sister Teesha, and Ms. Arnette, their mama. But there is a new guest here. I have told you about him, and so have our good friends Mr. Henretty and Mr. Spaulding."

The Reverend nodded toward their aisle. Jim's head started pounding. As long as the pastor didn't ask him to speak or to come up in front of the congregation, all would be fine.

"When the storm hit, this young man lived in the center of New Orleans in a neighborhood called Mid-City. The storm hit on his birthday, no less. And rather than evacuate and seek his own safety, this young man ran looking for someone he knew on his block—a very diverse block of people, I might add, and the waters started to pour into the street. He risked his life to save Lazarus, who happened to be an old musician friend of his. I should mention—let's just say Lazarus was one of our tribe. But that ain't the point. Our young guest pulled Lazarus to the highest ground he could—cut a hole in his own roof. They were up there a few days. Well, in the end Lazarus didn't make it, rest his soul—"

"Bless him!" someone called out.

"That's right, brother," the Reverend said. "And *bless* the young man who helped his Lazarus. *Bless* Jim Scoresby, the young man I'm speaking of, right in the pew there. Everyone welcome him, thank him later for standing up for his Lazarus when he heard the knocking at the gate. He's come with our buddy, Mr. Henretty, today to worship. Mr. Henretty tells us Jim is scared stiff of public speaking. So I'll just do a little of that speaking for him, if he doesn't mind. Don't want our guest to get sick!"

The grinning Reverend snapped his fingers and pointed at Jim, who wiped the imaginary sweat off his brow. The congregation released a wave of resounding laughter.

"No man, no woman should run from Lazarus. Our man Jim actually ran *to* his Lazarus. He went to find him and care for him. That's where one truly gives back to the Creator, through one of his children in need. Now, the Lord God doesn't call us all to be the *sole* providers and to feed every Lazarus in this world every day 'til he's fat with sloth. But our God above does call us to have that special love to aid Lazarus when you learn he's lying out there at the gate. And a select few of you will be that sort who walks *out* of the mansion, if only for a while, to go *past* the gate to find a Lazarus in the streets. If that is you, truly *you* are the apple of God's eye, the very paragon of His creation."

The Reverend paused, and scanned the crowd with a searching expression. "But the ultimate tragedy is to become like the rich man in this parable. Yes, I tell you, this rich man Dives, he shut his eyes to everyone and was bent on only fulfilling his own pleasure. In the end, he destroyed himself, didn't he? In the afterlife, he paid the price for this selfishness. So I tell you all, many of the people of southern Louisiana and Mississippi are lying at the gate. Some will make it on their own. Some won't. You gonna go out that gate and feed 'em? And the people who suffered in that catastrophe, are they the *only* ones at the gate? So I ask you, friends, let us not always stay in the mansion. Let us not stroll to the gate and dole out a few pieces of bread. No, I give you all the challenge. I'm asking you, and God is asking you: go out from the gate and actively seek out Lazarus and give Lazarus the love God gives to you."

With that final plea, delivered in a rising shout, Reverend Ward was met with a volley of exclamations of joy and confirmation, from “Amen!” to “Hallelujah!” to “Praise God!”

Jim was struck mute, moved to the very core of his being. He looked to his left at Jack, and then to his right at Walter. Both men beamed at the stage, and swept up in the subsequent wave of applause, began to clap. Jim looked in front of him, and a little to the left.

The dapper old man and his stately wife smiled approvingly at Jim. The man nodded and laughed.

“His parents,” Jack shouted in his ear above the din.

The fierce applause suddenly morphed into a nearly deafening hymn. Jim looked ahead. The Reverend clapped his hands and led the hymn’s first line, after which the choir erupted in zealous singing, swaying and clapping.

At that moment, Jim ceased to ponder why Walter had brought him to the church. He sensed an unforeseen change within himself, a confluence of peace, love, and hope. Though he usually preferred to worship in a less emotional way, Jim now felt borne aloft by the sudden gust of song permeating every inch of the Mount Zion African Baptist Church.

The congregation stood and joined the choir in singing.

Jim’s eyes roamed the joyous countenances of the choir, the ecstatic mien of the singing Reverend and felt admiration, love—and perhaps a tinge of jealousy—at this mysterious spiritual giddiness. The hymn ascended to its climax. The Reverend marched briskly down the center aisle toward the front doors of the church, singing as he went.

Jim realized he had not been in the company of more than two black people since his days in New Orleans. He felt that rush of heart, the ability to reveal intense emotion and longing so easily—that he missed, that he remembered in Freddy and in so many New Orleanians. Walter must be calling him to get involved in this church.

He had been running from poverty and desperation for seven months. Had he not escaped to only fulfill his own ambitions and comfort? Jim knew he must resolve to no longer run, but the question was: could he?

Chapter Nineteen

As Jim and his three fellow Cape-dwellers stepped through the door, they found the renowned Bob's Southern Bistro on Columbus Avenue aswim with Dixieland jazz. Jim threw his head back and laughed with glee.

At the very rear the jazz quartet was arranged upon a platform. A drummer, a trumpeter, a banjo-picker, and a cellist performed before a rather large Sunday brunch crowd. A puffy-cheeked Louis "Satchmo" Armstrong, a sallow, serious Jelly Roll Morton, a piano-pounding, laughing Jerry Lee Lewis, a guitar-strumming, inward-leaning Leadbelly looked down from prints that festooned the exposed brick walls. There were prints of the New Orleans Jazz and Heritage Festival and the Newport Jazz Festival, some going back to the early eighties.

Under an acrylic painting of the streetcars and live oaks of St. Charles Avenue, one diner looked faintly familiar. Reverend Cordell Ward sat alone in the middle of a long table covered in fine linen. He rose to his feet. "Here are our friends!"

"There you are, Reverend!" Walter said. "Great to see you."

The two men shook hands energetically. The Reverend turned to Jack and Natasha.

"And here are the Spauldings!" said Walter. Reverend Ward first took the hand of Natasha, and then shook hands with Jack.

"Not *Mrs.* Spaulding just yet!" Jack said, then released a

hearty laugh.

Jim detected an awkward nervousness in the laughter. "Reverend Ward, how are you?" Jim said. "I loved the service today. And all the great music! But I won't introduce myself. You seem to know all about me already."

"Well, Jim," Reverend began as he shook his hand, "we have a mutual friend here, Walter, who's told me all about you. And he let you date his daughter!"

"I'm glad he's told you... the *good* things," Jim said with a nod of gravity.

The Reverend motioned toward the seats. Walter walked around and sat next to the minister. Walter asked Jim, Jack, and Natasha to take their seats across from him. Jim was lost in reverie as he stared at the framed poster behind his host.

"That brings back lots of memories, Jim?" Reverend Ward said.

"So many, so many."

"Same here, Jim. I've served mission trips in Louisiana many summers, especially growing up. I love New Orleans. Know it like the back of this hand. So I heard you're a jazz and blues aficionado. I bet you're just loving Bob's! Place has been around nearly fifty years, first over on Mass Ave."

"I've heard of this place," Jim said. "But never been. I honestly feel as if I'm right back home." Jim turned and looked at the trumpeter wailing away on stage.

"Good, good," the Reverend said, his eyes radiating a rare kindness.

The thought began to gnaw at Jim once more: what surprise did Walter have in store for him? Was it merely attending the service? What was the old man putting him up to? Speaking in church next weekend?

Into the foyer of the restaurant, a black woman and a white man, both somewhere in their mid-thirties, led a steady stream of boys around the age of twelve or thirteen. Half of the children were white, and half of them black.

Walter grinned proudly and clapped once. Jack slapped Jim on the back and said, "You will like this new project... much more than trading stocks, I'll wager. I'm shanghaiing you into it!"

"My interest has been piqued all morning," Jim said.

The Reverend and Jim rose. All of the others lagged but a second behind.

"Hello, Reverend," said the white man, short and stocky and with a touch of sagging weariness about the shoulders. His dark blue polo shirt read "South Boston Fire Department Ladder 16." He stopped right before the Reverend and shook his hand. "I brought the whole crew here," he said with a thick Boston accent.

"Great to see you, Tim." The Reverend turned to Jim. "These are the boys from St. Brendan the Navigator Parish in Southie. And this is Tim Murphy, Knight of Columbus and Southie firefighter. He's also one of the youth group leaders at St. Brendan's."

Jim studied the boys. There were three of them, all sporting crew cuts, one red, one sandy-blonde, and one brown.

"And you're Jim Scoresby," Tim Murphy said, shaking Jim's hand. "Nice to meet ya. Nice of ya to help out the kids. But we gotta keep 'em in line. Or they'll try to keep *us* in line."

Everyone laughed.

"This is Scott with the red hair. This li'l blondie here is

Seamus. And this guy with the Bruins jersey, this is Lance. They haven't always been *good* boys, let's just say, and *that's* why they're here."

Jim stepped forward and shook each boy's hand, grinning as he called each boy by name. "Up to no good, Tim's saying?"

The boys grinned in turn.

Reverend Ward then motioned toward the black woman. "Jim, this is Miss Shawna Arnette and her son Dwayne. Her little girl Teesha is back sleeping at my parents' house. The Arnettes hail from the Ninth Ward, and I don't think I need to name the city. They've been guests of my family since not long after the storm hit. Shawna lost her family, so now we at Mount Zion's are her new family. She may go back to New Orleans one day, but she's thinking of staying here. Little Dwayne here will be part of our new project, which we'll discuss today."

Jim gave both a hearty hug, his face smiling but his mind lost in a deluge of memories. "Remember how we say hi in Nawlins."

"I love it!" the Reverend said.

Walter, Jack, and even Natasha beamed.

"I hear you been doin' good in ya new city," Shawna Arnette said. She did look perhaps thirty-five but her eyes alone seemed to belong to an older woman, weary but wise.

"It's my new home, I guess," Jim said. "A new start."

"Shawna Arnette is the youth leader for Mount Zion," Reverend Ward began. "She's brought along not just her son, but a few kids from our congregation. Kids that have been a little naughty, so to speak, but kids who have shown they want to improve. Would you do the honors, Shawna?"

"This here's li'l Jeffrey. And this is LaRon. They look

harmless but they a handful, sho' are. Handful for the law, too."

Jim shook their hands and greeted each boy by name. The Reverend waved everyone to a seat while a waiter took drink orders.

"I am glad everyone could make it," Reverend Ward said. "And meeting at such a local institution, a place with such character. I know, Jim, this may be the first time you have heard of this little plan. It was actually the brainchild of your friend here, Mr. Henretty. He committed you to our brand new project. And Walter, if you could give the finer details."

"One day while sailing," Walter said, "I conceived this idea: that I give my love and knowledge of sailing to young people with the *desire* but not the *means* to pursue this matchless sport. As a youth, I'd dream of sailing a real *Herreshoff* sailboat. I now own one, and my workshop's putting some last-minute restoration into it, to be completed shortly. I'm planning a trip from Osterville all the way around the Cape to Boston Harbor or Dorchester Harbor, haven't decided which. Jim and I will lead the expedition, with help from Jack and the other adults. Reverend Ward will be aboard to represent Mount Zion's three boys. Tim Murphy will lead St. Brendan's three boys. That's fourteen hands on deck, including two hands from my shop. Just enough for a schooner like the *John Paul Jones*. And Jack and Natasha, my two men from the shop, Tim, Reverend Ward, and I—we are all licensed mariners."

"It'd be an honor," Jim said, "to help lead this."

Natasha said, "Good, good." She was warming up to him already.

"I knew you would, sonny boy!" Walter said. Reverend Ward smiled and nodded.

"Jack's right." Natasha leaned back in her chair to see past her boyfriend. "We *know* you'll like this more than trading stocks."

"Now, before we talk further," Walter said, "shall we look at the menus? Whaddaya say we order? It's all on me. My idea, my treat. Though Reverend picked the place."

Everyone studied the menu and a few moments passed. Once again the waiter appeared, as if on cue. Most elected the brunch buffet. Reverend Ward said grace and everyone delved into their plates.

Jim assumed he hovered in some stratum of the celestial regions. He did not know if he had let slip some odd noise or made some face while eating, or if it was the sheer size of his portions, but he soon had drawn the attention of much of the table.

"Sweet heavens, look at that!" Shawna said. "That boy *definitely* growed up down south!"

"My, to eat *that* many candied yams, fried drumsticks," Jack said.

"They call it *glorifried* chicken here," Tim said. "It's pretty famous stuff."

"And eating not just the collard greens, but using his spoon to drink its juice!" Natasha said.

"It's called pot *likkor*," Dwayne said. "That's the best part! Mmmm. My Grammaw used to make greens like this."

"And it *is* spelled p-o-t-l-i-k-k-o-r, traditionally," Reverend Ward said.

"We never had that stuff in Annapolis at the Academy," Walter said. "One must drive quite a ways south to get it."

"*Yuck*!" Scott made a sour face. It's *gross*."

"That and the grits, dude!" Lance chimed in. "Nasty." "Hey, pipe down," Tim said, shaking a finger at them.

"Be respectful, ya hear?" He looked at the adults, his face blushing. He nodded at Jim. "Back in Marines training at Parris Island, we must have eaten tubs of that stuff. Tasty little item there. And that was the *cafeteria* version."

"I can't say I disagree with those two boys," Natasha said. "And grits or hominy is particularly dreadful. Fried chicken can taste okay, and much of the other stuff served here. But it's just so ridiculously *unhealthy*, what people *eat* down there."

"*'Scuse me, ma'am*?" said Jeffrey, one of the two Mount Zion children, with the face of one unable to believe his ears.

Jack and Walter shot Natasha an irritated look. She then sat scowling into her lap in silence. Normally, Jim would have grown flustered, but he knew Natasha had already hung herself. Both faces of the Reverend and Shawna Arnette revealed irritation and hurt.

"Well!" Walter said. "I think it's just fine. And even *delicious*, if I might opine. Collards, turnips, mustard greens. Especially when they're made with lots of ham and bacon." He leaned over and glanced down the table at Tim Murphy. "In our training we seldom had such good food. But they served up some *wicked* Chesapeake crab chowder."

After ten seconds of silence, the visage of the Reverend regained its jovial expression, having spied Jim shoveling in heaping forkful after heaping forkful of Cajun squash and collard greens. "Our man is at it again," Reverend Ward said. "My! A man after our own heart."

A few cackles and snickers sounded around the table.

Jim finished chewing and shook his head. "You can't get

much of this around here. Gotta load up, store what you can. Like a squirrel. I feel no shame!"

Some laughed, but Jim, growing serious, nodded at the stage at the back of the restaurant.

"Now, that's quite a group we've got here. They were playing Dixieland jazz, old 'Nawlins jazz. But I can tell this new song is "Do You Know What It Means—"

"To Miss New Orleans!" Shawna screamed.

"That's it," Jim said. "You got it."

"Famously sung by Billie Holliday, played by Louis Armstrong," Reverend Ward said.

All the adults, and all of the boys, fixed their eyes and ears on the young Asian woman on stage, her hair done in flapper fashion. She stood at the large antique microphone, crooning away, her eyes closed. Her singing was so heartfelt that the cellist, the drummer, the trumpeter, and the banjo-picker faded into the background. The old familiar lump returned to Jim's throat.

He stared into his plate. His mind turned to Freddy, his parents and his brother, his grandmother, his aunts and uncles and cousins still living in New Orleans and the South, all of the friends he had left behind, and the flooded graves of his grandparents.

He again glanced at the stage. The singer brought to mind the young Vietnamese woman in the National Guard chopper. Jim wondered what became of that young woman, built like a delicate bird and so soft about the eyes. Had she started a new life somewhere else like him, but in Houston, Atlanta, perhaps? He had resigned himself to the odds that he would never know.

Feeling the burden of someone's stare, Jim pulled his gaze

with reluctance back toward the table. It was Walter, the cobalt eyes larger than normal, filled with sympathy and a certain sorrow.

Jim turned again toward the stage and imagined Freddy stood swaying next to the singer, his trumpet raised toward the ceiling. For the rest of Jim's days, he knew such music would bring back the spirit and the presence of his friend. But with time, would the great memories fade?

Chapter Twenty

Jim felt nauseous as he and Davie lugged the sofa toward the opposite wall of the condo. Within his belly sat ten-odd pounds of ham, collards, catfish, fried and boiled okra, candied yams, and cornbread. Further contributing to Jim's queasiness was the frequent sight of Davie Henretty rolling his eyes at his father's express orders to move yet another piece of Jim's furniture.

Ten minutes into the moving job, just after the movers had delivered the last of the furniture that Sunday evening, Davie sighed. The Commodore immediately chided his son. When the last heavy item was in place, Walter told the boy he could go. Davie vanished with another defiant sigh—herringbone chain, tank top jersey, signature scent and all—to shoot hoops down the road.

"We had a great day," Walter said. "Glad you met the Reverend and all the gang. Tim Murphy, Shawna Arnette. Salt of the earth, in many ways. And all those kids. In trouble with the law but this idea may help them get out of it. They're under different influences now. And just think—we'll have a hell of a time. You, me, the others... we'll be sailing that Herreschoff all the way to Beantown! It'll be grand."

"I *am* psyched," Jim said. "Your great idea will be even better in practice. I'm very glad you picked me to help lead. Just gotta get my sea legs back. Bury that fear of water I've got, after the storm."

"You will, son," Walter tousled Jim's hair. "Set the alarm for eight. I'll be in Boston for at least the first half of the day. The others will be down there in the shop, though. There's no Mac, of course. But look for a salty old fogey named Bill. He'll show ya the ropes. Bill and I go way back. Tough old bird, but you can trust him more than the others. This man will run the shop for ya. And you'll oversee him and handle the purchase and sale of boats, as well as the research and shopping for buyers and sellers and new vessels."

They shook hands and Walter left. Too weary to set up his mattress and box spring, Jim rolled out a sleeping bag, grabbed a pillow, and climbed in. The week had caught up with him: the few days available for transition from Henretty & Henretty, the late nights, the early mornings, the many surprises.

Jim remembered to phone Maureen. The call went straight to voicemail. She must have gone to bed early. Perhaps she was watching the Red Sox recap on NECN. Maybe she was mad at him for some random reason. Again.

Jim set his phone alarm and rolled onto his back. He stopped fighting to keep his eyes open and surrendered to the advancing wave of slumber.

It seemed as if only a minute had passed before his Blackberry's alarm signaled 7:30 AM. He stirred about in the sleeping bag, then shuffled over to the refrigerator. There was no time to brew coffee. He downed most of a can of Dr. Pepper and then disappeared into the bathroom for fifteen minutes. Soon he sprang, newly scrubbed and clean-shaven, through the door and into the warehouse office.

At the old wooden table sat a fifty-something man who

smelled of cigarettes. He sported a long ponytail of straight, graying blond hair and a grizzled dark blond beard. The sleeves of his blue denim shirt were rolled up. His light blue jeans were slightly stained and frayed at the kneecaps, leading to a pair of worn tan moccasins. He pored over a long map, fragile-looking and yellowed with age, which he had rolled out onto the table.

Jim's eyes focused as he approached the table. The bearded man swiveled in his chair until he faced Jim. "You Jim Scoresby, Walter's new guy?"

Decades of sunlight and hard living had turned his face ruddy and wrinkled, while too much drink had rendered his eyes bloodshot. The head drooped to the side with a sort of nonchalance, an adolescent apathy. The eyes narrowed and angled upward, almost searing into Jim. Despite the advanced age of this old wolf, it would be a decent skirmish.

"And you're... Bill?" Jim reached out a hand and made sure he squeezed hard.

During an awkward silence, the man peered into Jim's eyes for several seconds. He finally broke off his stare and ran his gaze up and down, inspecting Jim from head to foot.

"Well," Bill rose to his feet, his wornout knees creaking. "I hear old man Henretty showed you around." Bill sighed as his hands rested on his hips, an ever-so-subtle smirk-smile playing about his mouth. "Bayou boy, how much you really know about boats, kid? And I mean sailboats." The tone was pure sarcasm.

Jim gritted his teeth. He was not even thirty minutes out of bed. "How's this, Bill: enough to be successful as your new boss, if that's what you're fishing for with that rude tone and that damned smirk." His eyes flashed at the older man. His hands, too, were on his hips.

The older man let out a laugh, neither forced nor nervous. Bill shut his eyes for a moment. "Aw, ya got me, kid," Bill held out his hand. "Just bustin' ya chops a bit. It's a rite of passage in this shop. Ya steered straight into it and didn't look back!"

"I see," Jim relaxed into a half-smile, as he shook the man's hand. "I was about to say, we're all on the same team, and Walter did name me the new manager. He prepared me for your crustiness! But he said you'd show me the ropes. And you're trustworthy."

Bill turned and sat once more at the desk and grabbed for his coffee. Jim peered down over his shoulder.

"Now how's that, hah?" Bill said, looking up over his shoulder. "This is the original blueprint for the *John Paul Jones*, from 1912, the year of its construction. That year the *Titanic* sank, but this baby here was born. Built at the Herreshoff Manufacturing Company, right down in Bristol, where they got their famous museum today. Captain Nat, Nathanael Greene Herreshoff—the old genius drew this himself. This paper came with the purchase of the boat. I could sell this old dog-eared print and buy a damned boat myself. 'Course, that's something Mac woulda done. And we all had to say bye to him. Guess you heard about Crazy McTierney?"

"A few good things. And many not so-good things."

"Yyyyeah. You could say that. I'm sure you and I'll get along a lot better than Mac and I did. I just have a unique sense of... humor, for lack of a better word. I'm a little crabby, but my word *means* somethin'."

"Bill, I like you already." Jim slapped him on the shoulder. "I don't know about when I initially started chatting with you, but you're all right now."

Bill gave a long belly laugh, sounding like a shopping mall Santa Claus. "By the way, Jim," he pointed across the room, "that's your desk there, overlooking the shop, through that window."

"Nice. Yes, the Commodore showed me."

"Walter told me you call him that. We used to call him 'the Cap'n'. But 'Commodore'... that's funny." He rose again to his feet, wincing slightly. "Old knees 'bout to go out. Now, let me introduce you to the guys. Or rather, the local ruffians and scoundrels."

Bill led the way downstairs into the shop. Before them stood the *John Paul Jones*, drydocked in its channel. Jim allowed his eyes to comb over the vessel. The three proud masts—the taller mainmast in the rear and the consecutively shorter mizzenmast and foremast with their crosstrees, sails, blocks, and halyards—had been temporarily removed.

Just below the bowsprit or "widowmaker" that jutted out of the bow was a figurehead. Instead of a mermaid, as Jim half-expected, hung a painted carving representing a ship captain of the Revolutionary War era. John Paul Jones himself.

Jim wondered if this piece was original to the vessel. A few feet away, two men in masks cut a section from the planking of the hull, near the bottom. Each held handsaws against the hull, perhaps fifteen feet apart. The two men stopped after a few seconds and stared at Jim and Bill, who stood mere feet behind them.

"Billy, morning to ya. Is that our new McTierney?" one of the men joked. The men set down their saws. One approached them with a sort of bowlegged gait.

"Just playin', friend. Hey, you're Jim?" the man said. He was portly, nearly bald, with sunburned skin and bloodshot, pale blue eyes. The eyes squinted and searched the new boss as if for some clue to his character.

"That's me," Jim said. "And from what I hear about this Mac character, I'll prove to be a little different."

"I sure as hell hope so, Mistah Scoresby! Mac was a hoot," the man said, shaking Jim's hand. "I'm Donovan Butler."

Donovan slapped the back of the handsome young man next to him. "And this is Joey DaSilva, our *Portugee* boy genius of sailing. Kid comes from a line of seagoing *Portugee-zees* windin' all the way back in this state to the 1600s."

Heavy steps plodded on the schooner's deck. Donovan and Joey turned toward the boat and looked upward. A lone figure stood at the railing.

"Chief, whaddaya say?" Bill thundered.

"If he ain't Mac, man, he can't be half bad," deadpanned the man, almost in a kind of exhalation. Each of the workers laughed.

Jim studied the man. He was tall, with russet skin and long dark hair parted in the middle. He was dressed in torn, paint-stained jeans and a Red Sox t-shirt. Though not unsightly, the face was quite rugged, weathered, and with an aquiline nose broken just below the bridge.

"Why don'tcha introduce yaselves?" Joey said.

"Well, excuuuse my manners, gents," the man on the deck said. "I'm Ted. All the guys call me Chief."

"Ted ain't really a Chief, Jim," Donovan said. "But he's a real Wampanoag. Sometimes we call him King Phillip, after their famous leader."

"You don't mind?" Jim said.

"Not at all," Chief said. "Is it true you're from the bayou?"

Donovan turned toward Jim. "I can hear some accent comin' from ya."

"I grew up mostly in Folsom, Louisiana. Little town maybe fifty miles north of Nawlins."

"Well, Jim," Chief said. "This boat here may be a little different from those little canoes you paddle through the marshes!"

"Don't worry, I do know the difference. I grew up sailing ketches, sloops, spinnakers, daysailers on Lake Pontchartrain and in the Gulf." Jim declined to mention all the elapsed years since he had sailed, that his sailing abilities had since atrophied. He would have to study sailing after work, lest he embarrass himself when the men finally saw him in action.

"Well, Jim," Bill said. "Let's show you around your old Commodore's latest acquisition—all one hundred and six feet of her." Motioning for Jim to follow, Bill climbed up the rolling stairwell, and everyone joined them.

"Here she is." Bill stomped a foot on the deck. "What a beaut, eh? Only seagoing vessel more majestic would be one o' them nineteenth-century barques or clipper ships or brigantines."

"I second that motion." Jim's eyes scoured the boat.

"We got a decent amount o' work ahead of us on this old gal," Bill said. "But at least we ain't gotta redo any of the framing or tinker with the ship's head. She was fairly maintained."

"What work is Walter lookin' to do?" Jim said. "If I remember, he mentioned the aft-mast, a little on the hull, and a little deck repair."

"Yep, some fine tuning. Walter purchased her in decent shape. We *are* replacing that aft-mast and a section of planking on the port side, which you just saw. It'd been a little leaky on the trip down. We're replacing some of the deck and fasteners. We gotta sand and paint the whole deck and hull. It really ain't as much work as it could be."

Jim and the men toured nearly every square foot of the vessel, from the wheel in the pilothouse to the bowsprit, down the hatch and into the galley, the fo'c'sle, the berth area, the head and the sink, the cabins, and the captain's quarters. Jim noted the boat's sheer size and its authentic appearance and condition. Framed prints and photographs from the first years of the twentieth century accented the dark wooden walls of its corridor and rooms.

All furniture and accessories, save in the commode, looked "like they were installed by Captain Nat Herreshoff himself," Jim said upon leading the four men back onto the deck and down the rolling stairwell.

While Bill poured coffee into the five mugs, Jim noticed a paint-flecked, battered portable stereo resting next to a box of fresh doughnuts on the table. Donovan flipped one of its switches.

For Jim, there was no mistaking the unique voice and the melodic soaring of guitars. He raised his coffee to toast his new crew.

"I like it! That band, Boston. It was kind of local, too," Jim said. "This song 'Rock 'N' Roll Band'... that's not one of their best ones though."

Chief uttered with palpable assuredness, "I can tell ya gonna like it here in the shop, boss, with all us workin' boys.

Welcome to our morning ritual."

Jim surveyed the warehouse, his hands on his hips. He knew with certainty he would enjoy working at this brokerage so very much more than the one in Boston. But he could sense the challenges that lay in wait. These men must respect him.

He could not show them weakness, and he could not show he was too much of a novice on the water. Ah, but the water...

Chapter Twenty-One

The sixty foot ketch *Undaunted* rose and fell on the foamy blue like the head of a great galloping steed, as westerly winds bore her that Saturday afternoon away from the Harbor Islands. The Commodore had chartered the craft specifically for that weekend's training. He motioned to LaRon beside him to turn the wheel to the left.

Walter grinned and said, "The day is turning out splendidly."

Jim knew why. The Mount Zion and St. Brendan's boys were responding well to the training and the drills. Jack had led the adults and boys on an abandon-ship drill, a man-overboard drill (with Jack being the rescued). Afterwards, Walter had led a brief tutorial on the bowline knot, the square knot, and the anchor bend knot, through various nautical terms such as "aft" and "jettison" and "starboard," and through a crash course on sailing etiquette and safety.

It was quite crowded under the biminy on the cockpit's couches, where the children sat in their lifejackets. They watched Walter teach steering as he let each boy take the wheel for several minutes.

After many hours, Jim's queasy stomach had returned to normal. He joined Jack, who stood amidships, grasping the mainmast. They practiced with the two chaperones on working the halyards, sheets, and sails, their chief task on the boat.

The Reverend and Tim had impressed Jim with their familiarity with many sailing terms and nautical concepts, such as water displacement, tacking, and capstans.

The two men had, after all, received their Coast Guard licenses some months ago. And since the kickoff in Bob's Southern Bistro, both chaperones had pored over sailing volumes and websites, refreshing their knowledge. They seemed well versed in safety and protocol, as well as in the logic behind certain sails and sailing techniques.

Notably absent that day was Natasha. Early that morning Jim had asked Jack about her. Jim immediately detected a sore subject, from the shock and disappointment in his friend's face.

Though polite, Jack had not been his usual jocular, high-spirited self the past three hours. He seemed only half-present as he had hooked himself around the mast with his right arm and stared blankly out into the waves, shifting his gaze through his wavy blond bangs to acknowledge Jim or one of the other two men, commenting on a question posed or an opinion given.

After Jim enlisted the help of the other three men to lower, and then raise, the sail on the mizzenmast, he asked Jack to instruct the boys on winds and wind speed. Jim wanted to trade places with the Commodore.

He half-squatted while scampering aft of Jack and the chaperones toward the cockpit. Jim grabbed one of the biminy's metal poles and hauled himself inside. He hoped he had successfully masked his fear and lack of balance, his handicaps borne of the great hurricane. Jim knew full well he had not yet regained his sea legs of days past.

"Ahoy, maties!" Jim said.

"There ya are, my man," the Commodore said. "I was just instructing the boys on steering, tacking, and navigation. Each had a few minutes at the wheel. Teach here for about twenty or thirty. My trick is done. Jack and I can freshen everybody up on sails and lines."

"Yes, sir," Jim said, clutching the wheel in his hand. "Keep heading directly east?"

"Do so 'til I get back. And we've got to work on that balance of yours, Jimmy."

Jim's stomach sank. Walter had noticed. The old man climbed the three stairs and marched across the deck with a sprightliness befitting a man forty years his junior. Walter greeted Jack and the chaperones with a wave, then hooked his arm around the mast and commenced conversation.

Jim looked at the boys seated on either side of him. "I guess you now know all about steering this thing, right? Turn it to the right and it tacks left, turn it to the left and it tacks right?"

"Yeah!" said Dwayne, his little friend from New Orleans. "I just learned to steer it!"

"Excellent!" Jim said. "It's fun and scary at the same time, your first time!"

"We just saw a humpback whale, Jim!" said Seamus.

"You did? I was too busy up there at the mast. In a little while we can go up there. Or the Commodore will bring some of y'all up there and he'll show you."

"You talk funny!" Scott collapsed into a laughing fit. The other two St. Brendan's boys followed suit.

"I know, I know," Jim groaned. "I'm from a land—a galaxy—far, far away."

LaRon screamed and pointed past Jim at the starboard

side, out into the waves.

Under a circling gang of seagulls, perhaps two hundred feet out in the water, a humpback whale had appeared. It skimmed the surface, going the same direction as the ship.

A resounding cry arose from the cockpit. Jim and the boys cheered in unison. Even the Commodore, Jack, and the two chaperones ahead of them at the mainmast joined in.

And then in a heartbeat, the whale disappeared, as if disintegrating into the ocean. A collective "ooh" welled up from under the biminy.

"Now that was a sight," Jim said. "I haven't seen the likes of any whale in my whole life. Last year I did see a little pilot whale, dead on Crane Beach, in Ipswich, but today was different." Jim felt his pulse quicken. He sucked in his lips, remembering the bloated bodies he saw last August.

"Maybe the whale's a good-luck sign," Lance said. The yellow-and-black of his Boston Bruins jersey stuck out in disheveled fashion from under his life preserver.

Jim launched into a brief tutorial, touching on the whaling industry, the connection of the wheel to the rudder, the importance of watching for the captain's cues, the characteristics of various sailing vessels, from the ketch to the sloop, the yawl, and the spinnaker. He related the most notable features of the *John Paul Jones*, the year of her construction, and the differences between that schooner and the *Undaunted*. Jim was perhaps thirty minutes into the lesson when the Commodore appeared at the biminy's stairwell.

"Hey, my boys!" Walter said with gusto. "How's the lesson coming along, gents?"

"Lots of stuff to remember, but it's interesting," Seamus

said.

"Good, son. Now Jim, I'm bringing up the chaperones. If you guys could catch up a bit, I'll take these kids to the mizzenmast and teach 'em lines and sails. Fair winds and following seas!"

"Aye aye, Commodore," Jim said.

After bottlenecking at the bow-side of the cockpit, the boys filed up the little stairwell and followed the old man to the mizzenmast. Jim remained at the wheel. Soon the chaperones appeared.

"Lookin' for us, Jimmy boy?" Tim Murphy said.

"Actually, I was! Please take a seat, kind sirs."

Reverend Ward and Tim each sat on a couch. "Hope you weren't asleep at the wheel!" Tim said.

"Nah," Jim said, "there's no rest around those little ones. They'll keep you on your toes."

"That they will," Reverend said in his baritone. "How are you today, Jim? These kids too much for you?"

"Ready to throw in the towel?" Tim said in a jeering tone.

"Not for the world. They've been great so far. No complaining, no fights. I bet they love it up there with the Commodore. I know they're itching to learn, from all their questions."

"Just hope one don't go overboard!" Tim laughed. "Glad we got those vests on 'em!"

Jim bit his lip.

The Reverend said, "I wouldn't let the boys set foot on deck without them."

"See that humpback whale?" Tim hooked a thumb over his shoulder.

"Amazing," Jim said.

"We won't be seeing a sperm whale or a blue whale. They're dadgum near driven to extinction," the Reverend said.

"'Dadgum? Bob's Bistro?" Jim said. "You and I are cut from the same cloth, Reverend. Never thought I'd hear 'dadgum' again! I've come home."

Jim waded into a lengthy discussion of steering, seamanship, and the history and practice of navigation. During their talk, much time was spent alternating at the wheel.

Walter appeared. "Shall we have a little peek at the old GPS?" He glanced at the screen attached to the dashboard.

Jim looked past the old man and glimpsed Jack with the boys, holding up a hand to illustrate some point.

"Yes, sir!" the Reverend said. "After all, we don't know where Jim's really taking us."

"To the end of the world, off the edge, and into the abyss," Jim said. "Or all the way to Bermuda."

Walter placed his hand on the wheel. "Lemme take her a while. You've done what I've asked. But now I've gotta turn this baby around. We've headed just far enough out into the North Atlantic. Now for the final treat of the day."

Jim knew he should feel excitement but instead the worry built within his breast. The vessel was so very far out from shore into the sea. But even greater—Jim feared that the others would see this trepidation.

"Looking forward to it," Jim said, forcing a broad smile. If he could only maintain his grit of the last few months...

Chapter Twenty-Two

With the *Undaunted* moored at the visitors' dock and her life vests stowed away and hatches locked, the brave new world of Lovells Island was now—for the boys of Mount Zion and St. Brendan's—ripe for exploring. Jim and Walter led the train of boys off the deck and down the dock, shoreward. Jack and the chaperones brought up the rear.

They approached the visitors' center. Walter turned and asked Jim to watch over the group while he went inside the wooden-shingled shack to claim his reservation for the campsite.

"Friends," Jim said, raising his arm. "For those who might feel a little seasick, I *am* the bearer of good news: *at least* we're on dry land until tomorrow morning. We'll pitch tents after Walter locks down the campsite. Then maybe we can go exploring!"

A great cheer burst from the crowd, a fusion of the boys' glee and the adults' mock-elation.

The visitors' center door burst open. The Commodore waved a map in the air, an energetic grin spread across his face. "All right, friends," he boomed. "Follow me! I won't getcha lost."

Jim and the party pivoted and pursued the lively old man. Walter led them down a shell path through the two-feet-tall seagrass on the long drumlin bluff above the seashore. To their right was a wall of dunes partially obscured by a forest of seagrass. Just beyond lay a stretch of sand, seagrass, and granite boulders. Next was a narrow strand of shells and sand. Finally there was the ocean beyond, with its symphony of choppy blue-green waves kissing a cloudless royal blue sky. Gulls circled in various congregations within this vast expanse. Crowning this scene lay an island far off on the horizon.

To the left of the path, a wooded copse thick with black cherry, gray birch, and apple trees surrounded a small cranberry bog, dark and still as obsidian. On its surface floated patches of green water lilies with their white flowers. Insects faintly buzzed in the thicket to Walter's left. To his right were the sounds of the squawking gulls and the crash of waves.

"Where are we *going*?" Lance said. Surely the boy was sweating profusely under that Bruins jersey and hoping for a break, a dip in the ocean.

"We're going to an unknown underground bunker controlled by the Irish mob," Jim said.

Tim exploded in a chuckling fit.

"Coool!" Scott said.

"Man, I don't know if that's mah cup o' tea," Dwayne's voice wavered, sounding uneasy.

"They won't take too kindly to you guys!" Scott said.

"Cut that out, this minute!" Tim thundered, his Boston accent flying thick and fast, his finger wagging at his charge.

"Hmph! Shuddup, fool," LaRon stopped and turned toward Scott.

The line halted. LaRon's face grew fierce as he puffed out his chest. "They wouldn't know *what* they comin' up against. We'd put a hurt on dem chumps *reeaal* fast."

Reverend Ward and Walter lurched toward LaRon. Each clamped a cautionary hand on his shoulder and ordered him to relax. Tim Murphy did the same with Scott, and Jack and Jim stepped in front of Lance and Seamus.

"Hey!" the old man roared, raising a clenched fist with an extended index finger. Walter's eyes bulged, his face flushed crimson with fury. To add to his unnerving look, the Commodore had now drawn his lips back like a growling dog.

"I said, *hey*!" the old man boomed. "I better not hear any more of that garbage. We set off on this undertaking for *one* reason, and that kind of mean talk to each other isn't it!"

Several seconds of the starkest silence passed. The old man switched his glaring stare from LaRon to Scott as if attempting to brand his order and threatening expression into their memory. Jim turned to Reverend Ward, who smiled at the old man.

"That's it, boys," Reverend Ward said. "Y'all better do what Mr. Henretty says. Knock it off with those comments. We're better than that."

"We *can* be," Dwayne said in a feeble voice.

"Exactly. We *can*." The Reverend pointed his index finger in the air. "We *do* have the power not to stoop to those levels. Exercise that power and lay off that stuff. Let's have some fun."

"Couldn't have said it better." Walter winked at the Reverend. "Now, let's be on our way, shall we?" The old man marched down the path, his military past still evident in his gait.

The line wended around some crumbling concrete ruins and granite boulders. Alongside the trail lay more bogs and copses of pines, oaks, and cherries as before, with thick masses of brambles. Then the path forked.

"We'll take the route to the left. The road less travelled!" Walter marched up the left course and its slight incline into the woods. The path leveled out. The ground, coated with pine straw, was completely clear of bushes and brambles. Ahead, someone had recently burned a small campfire.

"Ah hah! Gents, we have arrived at our proper destination!" Walter said. "Now if all we grown-ups can get these healthy young upstarts to help us set up camp, we'll be doing just fine."

For the next twenty minutes they assembled the six tents. Jim asked Jack to help him find kindling and any larger pieces of wood. Bit by bit, they stacked the wood in a large pile just outside the circle of tents. Jim and Jack then joined the others in assembling the final tent, finishing just as the sun started to vanish. Tim and the St. Brendan's boys occupied two tents. Beside those tents stood the tent for Jim and the Commodore. Adjacent to this tent stood the two tents for the Reverend and the Mount Zion group. Next was Jack's tent.

After Jim and Walter prepared the fire, the boys roasted franks on long sticks they had fashioned. Jim took this opportunity to take Walter aside.

"Commodore, a favor," Jim half-whispered. "Can I make a quick phone call while y'all do the hot dogs? Got to call your daughter, after all. My nightly call, you know?"

"Oh, boy!" Walter laughed. "You mean you haven't called Miss Maureen today? You better be dialing your phone in the next few *seconds* or you'll be in deep, deep trouble, son!"

Jim walked back down the path toward the ocean. When he was out of earshot, he dug into his shorts' pocket for his phone.

A half-irritated, half-exhausted voice answered. "Jim, what's new?" More of a monotone, declarative line than a question.

"Maureen, hey, how are you, sweetie?"

"Jim, don't call me *baby* or *sweetie*. I've told you before."

"Sorry, I forget. Sorry, I—"

"I'm not doing so great, actually." A pause.

"Maureen, what's the matter? Can I help?"

Another pause.

Jim felt a tingling heat on his forehead and the nape of his neck.

"Maybe, I guess. Ah... I don't know how to begin..."

"Is it something I did?"

"It's not really your fault. I just... it's just been so *difficult* lately. You moved away. I encouraged you to go into the boat business with Dad. Now I don't have you as close and it's just hit me lately. But don't worry, I'll deal with it. Are we still on for tomorrow?"

"Of course we are."

"Good. So I take it you're out now on one of the Harbor Islands for the night?"

"Lovells Island. Charming place."

"Dad used to take Mom and me there sometimes, years ago. We'd sail up from the Cape for a few days, or we'd charter a boat from Boston like you guys just did. You should see George's Island. You'd like it."

"I really want to make it better. Sorry you're going through all this. I know you care about me. You just wanted me to find my niche by helping me get into this boat business and all. I'm taking you out tomorrow. We'll talk about it, all right?"

"Don't worry about me."

"You're strong. I have to return to the campsite now. It's getting dark and I don't have a flashlight with me. Well, least there aren't copperheads and water moccasins this far north."

"Call me when you guys dock tomorrow."

"Will do. I love you, Maureen."

"Love you, too," she mumbled. The three words came strangely, so very fast that they blended into one word.

Then the line clicked. Their talk had not even lasted two minutes.

He trudged back up the trail, his back to the ocean. Once again, there came the old familiar sound of the crashing waves and that sharp yet welcome seaweed-and-brine scent of the north Atlantic coast.

Jim softly exhaled his despair as he entered the woods. Through the near-complete darkness and the web of tree trunks and brush, the fire roared, perhaps three feet high. The crew encircled it, sitting in their camping chairs and on a few scattered logs, roasting their franks.

They greeted Jim as he appeared at the clearing's edge. He took his seat in a chair between Jack and Walter. When their glances met, the old man studied his face closely, a hint of solemnity and concern about the eyes.

Jim looked at his feet, then at the glowing fire. The boys were laughing at something puerile and lighthearted but he was outside of their joy, something that seemed now foreign to him.

He wondered why he now felt downcast. What was it within him? It was mostly Maureen's love, or the lack of love, rather, that he felt from her—despite how much he loved her.

But there was something else. He had achieved so much

since that day in mid-September, when he arrived in the Manchester, New Hampshire airport. He had found more success than ever before in his youth.

But he had become, in a sense, a different person in a far-flung land. And that new person was not loved, at least not romantically. He was truly alone.

Chapter Twenty-Three

The *Undaunted* glided forward on her course, her sleek prow surging its way through the strengthening morning light. The gulls soared and circled, diving about her masts and taut sails. His hands grasping the wheel, Jim inhaled the salt air deeply into his lungs and closed his eyes, as if to draw the moment into his memory forever.

"Attaboy, son," the old yet robust voice cheered at his side.

Jim opened his eyes.

The Commodore grinned. "Relish it. This moment's one of those times that keeps a sailor coming back for more—for all those who love sails and the sea and that 'open road' feeling. Not the open road, rather, but the 'whale-road,' as the ancient Vikings called it. And out here, a guy's more connected with nature than on *any* road trip."

Jim grunted. He was at such peace that he found himself reluctant to speak.

"I wanted to show ya something," the old man said. "See that island back there? The one just near Lovells, where we camped? Know what that is? Or was?"

Jim looked past Walter, who pointed toward the greenish, wall-encircled mass fading into the horizon. "I've heard bits and pieces. George's Island, isn't it?"

"What's its claim to fame, my boy? You should know this one. Right up your alley."

"It's the one with a fort, right? And a prison? Fort Warren."

"Indeed." Walter lifted his eyebrows to emphasize the gravity of the subject, or to further build suspense.

"That island was first used by the English colonists as farmland. Around 1850, the navy built a fort there, which would have been one of the best in our land. It just ended up being technologically obsolete upon completion. See, all the new ironclads and high-powered artillery rendered it ineffective as a major fort. So it became a military training ground. Federal soldiers at the start of the Civil War trained and drilled there. The Second Infantry, while revamping the parade ground there, wrote the lyrics to 'John Brown's Body.' You remember, boy, the great marching hymn of the North? Well, at one point in the war, the fort became a prison. It was noted for the humane treatment of its prisoners: three thousand of 'em if you added 'em up over the years. Among them were some notables. You know of Alexander Hamilton Stephens?"

"The Vice President of the Confederacy," Jim said. "The acne-scarred, ninety-six pound 'little big man' from Georgia. Complex guy."

"How so?" Walter said.

"He paid for men and women, white and black people to be educated," Jim said. "Yet he still wrote and campaigned for slavery."

"Correct. And who was Richard S. Ewell, otherwise known as 'Old Bald Head'?"

"A general blamed by a few of his men for losing Gettysburg."

"I guess you could say that, son," Walter laughed.

"Ewell is my middle name, but there's no relation."

"Hmm. Okay, now who was John Slidell?"

"He was a senator from my state who later became a Confederate diplomat to France. He almost pulled Britain into the war on the Southern side. I grew up near a town named after him."

"Correct. Yep, they were prisoners there. You know, those men were treated so well in there that they wrote letters for some of the Union guards who later went into battle, that should they be captured, they were to be treated by the rebels with the utmost care."

"I like that."

"Sounds like you know a lot of this already. Yeah, yeah, Mr. History," the old man leered askance at him with a look of mischief, "but do ya know about the Lady in Black? Otherwise known as the Black Widow?"

"No, sir. Sounds very nineteenth-century, Victorian."

"You'll like this one. Maybe weave this little yarn into what you're writing." Walter shook his finger, pointing upward. "During what you guys down below the Mason-Dixon used to call 'the War Between The States,' back when Fort Warren was a high-security military prison, there was a Confederate lieutenant there named Lanier. He mailed details on where he was imprisoned to his wife. So the guy's wife came up all the way to Hull and stayed with a Southern sympathizer. In her luggage, she'd brought two items: a pickax and a pistol.

"One night she took a rowboat to George's Island, bypassed all the sentries, and ran to a specific section of the dungeon wall. Behind this, her husband and some of his fellow officers were waiting. They hoisted her up with a rope made of bedsheets, right through a cannon's embrasure.

"The husband hid her for months in the dungeon.

Prisoners built a tunnel with the pickax. One night, many men attempted to escape, right through the tunnel across the parade grounds. They sprang from the hole in the ground. With them came Lanier and his wife, who ran into a corridor. A guard confronted the wife. She aimed her pistol and fired. It was an old black powder box type, exploded upon firing. Instantly killed her husband just next to her.

"The Colonel on duty—guy named Dimick—had no recourse but to hang the wife as a spy. Her only request? That they bury her in a dress, since she'd dressed in a fake Union uniform. Some of the guards found some black robes worn in a recent play put on by some of the rebel prisoners. She was hanged in those robes. To this day, the ghost of Mrs. Lanier is said to haunt Fort Warren. Her spirit's even mentioned several times in prison records.

"You know, Fort Warren was finally decommissioned when I was in Korea. From that woman's death to the time the fort was decommissioned, that prison had *many* documented cases of soldiers seeing the Lady in Black. A few soldiers were court-martialed for discharging their rifles and running. One fella tried to desert after seeing her, literally fled his post."

"Guess he didn't get far," Jim said with a wry smile. "There just doesn't seem to be much room to run back there."

"Ha, I guess you're right. A soldier was court-martialed after blasting his rifle off while on sentry duty. He said he'd seen the ghost and was just scared to death. The best account is of the time three soldiers were walking under the big arched sallyport, or entrance. Suddenly, they saw these footprints starting from nowhere and going for maybe twenty feet and then disappearing. And they were tracks made by a woman's shoes! Where she walked to her execution."

"*That* is quite a tale, Commodore."

"I always did know how to 'swing the lamp.' So you know, that Lady in Black, or the Black Widow, it's almost as if her spirit, or part of it, rather, is imprisoned still on that island. I got a friend who lives on the Cape, in Barnstable. He was garrisoned on that island in the late forties. Swears he saw her ghost. And George wasn't drunk on any Narragansett when he saw the apparition, okay?"

A twinkle of humor peeked out of the old man's eyes.

"I do love those stories," Jim said. "Some are fantasy and some are hallucination. But you know, sir, down in the South we still believe in ghosts." Jim thought of Freddy, and shuddered. "There are spirits, and there are souls, and they are two different things altogether. If you or some writer isn't pulling my leg on that one, that was a *spirit*."

"Speaking of such beliefs, my boy, you and I are the same. I'm of an older generation here that still holds those beliefs. The generation of my children—really mine are young enough to be my own *grandchildren*—well, they've rejected much of the old foolishness. But in many ways, they also rejected a lot of our wisdom and the sweet things. Many admire decadent celebrities and, of course, their own whimsy. But what can I do? I wanted to put Davie in a military academy to straighten him out. What I want to change is that he has little respect for anyone, even his elders. And he's just plain *lazy*. And he runs with a rough crowd. So I considered an academy for him."

"Decided against it?"

"Kathleen cried and begged me not to."

Jim fidgeted with the wheel, turning it to the right.

Seconds later, he corrected it toward the left. He remembered how he and his father that night had grappled, swinging each other in one direction, and then another.

Jim winced at the memory. He had not been grateful enough for the man. But Jim felt like he could never impress him, and Jim mused once again that he perhaps instead sought his father's replacement in other elders.

Jim looked out past the biminy onto the deck. Jack held up a line to the chaperones and the boys, who sat on the deck. They had taken a break from raising and lowering sails. Jim hoped Jack would touch on controlling the boom and not wait until moments before the boat docked in Boston Harbor.

"I know it's gettin' a little rough out there with my little girl. She wearin' ya down?" The old man probably had heard some of it from her and could intuit the rest.

"The new distance between us is taking a little toll on her. She admitted it last night."

"I know my little girl. She keeps so much inside. But she divulged a bit to Kathleen yesterday. You guys just need to visit each other more. Knock off work a bit early, if you have to. The work on the schooner's going swimmingly. Shave a little more time off to see my girl. It's fine."

"Thanks, Walter. I've wanted to visit her more. I suspected the distance would be a little hard on us, but I didn't want to neglect the project."

"Maybe a week or two more, with your men going full blast. Once you finish the deck, we're in the clear. We'll be primed for the big trip up the coast."

"I can't wait. And it's a real treat for the kids."

"I am quite pleased with everything," Walter said.

They looked past the biminy at the group. The boys took turns tying a cleat hitch as Jack and the chaperones looked on.

Behind them in the distance loomed Deer Island and Logan Airport off to the right and the buildings of the Financial District straight ahead. Barely visible on the horizon were the obelisk-like Customs House and the gold-capped State Street building. To the right of these buildings, between downtown and the airport, the beautiful arches of the Zakim suspension bridge spanned the Charles. Across the river, just to the right, rose Bunker Hill and the rowhouses of Charlestown. He had grown nearly as accustomed to these landmarks as those of New Orleans.

Soon they would dock. He would finally be on solid ground, and with Maureen at last. A week had passed since he had seen her. He would be with Maureen, but with Maureen he would have to contend. Jim did, after all, have some vital questions for her.

Chapter Twenty-Four

After the *Undaunted* found its moorings at Rowe's Wharf downtown, and after Tim Murphy and Reverend Ward had spirited their energetic charges away to Sunday services, after Jack's Saab rolled reluctantly away to its strife-filled abode in Chatham, and Walter had set off homeward in his old station wagon, Jim climbed into his truck in the parking garage and leaned his head back against the headrest, his eyes closed.

The truth was he had slept little on Lovells Island, and it had nothing to do with ghosts, loud children, or the snapping campfire. The latest conversation with Maureen, however brief, had shaken him to his core. This had all been her father's idea: Jim's move to the Cape and his leaving the stock and bond brokerage for the boat brokerage. And Maureen had more than approved; she had strongly championed the entire idea. Jim made the leap, and he was happier. But instead she was in the doldrums now that she faced the reality of it all.

What was he to do? Was it his fault?

He had hoped for an upbeat Sunday with Maureen. He wanted a day filled with laughter and the jokes and anecdotes he had intended all week to share. He wanted a day spent exploring one of the oldest and greatest American cities.

But Maureen had grown colder, more aloof, more irritable with each visit. Even weeks before the old man had broached the idea of his new job and dwelling, Jim had noted a seismic shift deep within her, and it had worsened.

What had changed in her? What had taken hold in that heart, the very heart that announced its love for him so early on? What had changed within that same woman who divulged over glass after glass of wine every last detail of her past and her longings: of her years growing up and at college, of her plans and her private joys and fears?

What awaited him today?

Jim pulled his Blackberry from his jacket pocket. On the fifth ring, the line opened up. Once again came that voice, burdened not with worry but a tangible moroseness, a voice muffled with exhaustion. "Hey, Jim. I guess you made it to town?"

"With Ol' Betty Sue as we speak, in the parking garage by Rowe's Wharf."

"I'm still in bed. Didn't sleep much last night. Wanna stop by?" She breathed the last three words in one long weary sigh, as if she were both tired, and tired of saying it.

"Of course. I'll find a garage or some spot near you."

"Swing by. I'll give you my MGH card. You can park for free in their lot, then just walk over. Just call when you're two minutes away."

"Roger that. Look for my call. Love ya, Maur."

"Love you, too." She delivered her response in that hushed, hurried tone. The consonants and vowels spilled out in such a manner that they struck Jim as one long word.

He was surprised she let him abbreviate her first name. After all, she had, from the beginning, bristled at any mouthing of the epithets hon or honey, babe, baby, or sweetie, even in the most lighthearted of moments. Perhaps she did not mind because her parents often abbreviated her name.

After paying the attendant on his way out, Jim turned left on Atlantic and headed for Beacon Hill, cruising north around the city's easternmost edge. Atlantic became Commercial Street, which separated the harbor from his old neighborhood, the North End. Commercial then turned almost completely westward and morphed into Causeway Street, which skirted the left of the Fleet Center, where he had seen so many hockey games and concerts. It passed Canal and Friend and Prospect Streets to the left with their vaguely seedy sports pubs. Causeway became Staniford, which coursed up through the West End.

He then turned right onto Cambridge Street and passed Massachusetts General Hospital on the right, its surrounding web of streets teeming with researchers, medical students, and young doctors and nurses walking confidently in either scrubs and sneakers or in jeans with leather dress shoes.

Jim swung left under a bridge and headed up the two-laned, one-way Charles Street, one of his favorites. He loved its many shops and coffeehouses and restaurants and pubs, all quaint yet impressive with their painted wooden signs and Victorian façades upon colonial eighteenth-century edifices.

One wintry night he had nearly walked straight into Senator Kerry as he strolled beside his daughter. He and Bryce were embroiled in a deep political discussion as they headed up Charles Street for beers and darts at the Sevens Ale House. The lanky Senator, dapper in his black cashmere overcoat, grunted gruffly at them and glared sternly at Jim for the near-collision. Jim and Bryce whispered to each other their surprise as they stood watching the Kerrys descend the hill toward Cambridge

Street.

Jim braked at a stoplight and called Maureen. She answered after a few rings. "Be right down," she said.

Jim turned from Charles onto Mount Vernon Street and veered left onto the cobblestones of Louisburg Square. On his right stood the townhouse, two down from Kerry's. Jim was cheered to see the four-storied Henretty townhouse facing the diminutive park, with its massive oaks and its black wrought-iron fence. Maureen's head extended from behind the large black wooden door. Jim stopped the truck, left it running, and jogged up the steps.

For a writer, painter, or psychologist, Maureen's face proved an interesting study. Weariness exuded from the eyes. Her full childlike cheeks were a bit more weighed down than usual, as if by either a force of gravity or exhaustion. The mouth was pouty with its full lips. Despite the gravitas and the overall negativity of the face, an air of humor lingered about the eyes. Perhaps she was glad to see him. Perhaps, at her core, she was amused. Beneath the eyes, the faintest semi-circles of black had formed.

Her shoulder-length hair was still damp from a recent shower. She was clad in her Red Sox bathrobe. He leaned forward to peck her on the lips. At the last second, she swiveled her head and he got her instead on the cheek. The skin was soft but tight. It was better than no kiss at all.

"Ah, you got me," Jim said, slightly disappointed.

"Hi there." She extended a small hand from behind the doorway with a plastic MGH identification card. "See you in a few."

She faintly smiled and he stood there, unsure of what to say next. The door shut hard. The lock turned slowly and quietly.

Jim hopped in the truck and moved slowly down the lane as he circled the square. He turned left on Mount Vernon, yet another one of downtown Boston's confusing but charming one-way, colonial streets. He turned left down Joy and began the slow, perilous descent, his foot on the brake the entire way, down Beacon Hill toward bustling Cambridge Street. Lining each side were red brick apartment house after red brick apartment house, and black-shuttered townhouse connected to black-shuttered townhouse, all dating from the early eighteenth century. This neighborhood originated during the same period as the French Quarter. Yet Beacon Hill displayed a far different style altogether: staid, conservative, English. And like Back Bay, every few feet, behind the row of cars lined bumper-to-bumper against both curbs, stood a tall black iron pole crowned by a black lantern, which encased a small flame.

Jim rolled down this gauntlet, where a car could pull out at any second, and passed a trio of young men. They stared his way with curious expressions. Surely it was the truck again.

As Joy Street ended, Jim turned left on Cambridge, going down a ways before turning right down a side street, then left, then into the parking garage. He stopped and waved the card before the mechanical sensor. The board seemed to fight its way erect.

He drove the truck up three levels and parked. Jim gargled with Listerine, spat it as discreetly as possible out of his open truck door, and caught the elevator to the ground floor. He then walked briskly toward a crosswalk and traversed Cambridge. He turned right and then headed up the steep Grove Street, his black leather shoes going clackety-clack on the sidewalk.

He prepared for his discussion with Maureen. What has

been occurring inside her head? An ominous feeling overtook him.

The street grew steeper and Jim started to perspire. After a couple hundred feet, past Phillips and Revere Streets, he turned right, passed a small dry cleaners, and then proceeded until he hit Cedar Street. He then turned left and walked down past the townhouses until he hit Pinckney Street. Once more he turned left and minutes later he was upon the townhouse. Jim stepped quickly up the steps and rapped firmly, five times.

The door opened. The faintly sullen and ever-so-spoiled visage appeared in the doorway. She ran him up and down with her eyes.

Jim stepped inside onto the old dark wooden floor. He tenderly placed his hands to the sides of her jaw and kissed her once on the mouth. She kissed back with a firm press of the lips, but it was nothing like their kisses weeks ago. Almost as if she was forcing it.

"Good to see you." She pulled back and looked up into his face. "How was the trip?"

Maureen wore a nice pink shirt, jeans and heels, and a minimal amount of makeup, less than was her habit. He caught a trace of that perfume that he loved. "You look mmm-mm good!" he said. "Magnificent, I should say."

"There's some green tea on the stove. Want some?" she said, nearly expressionless.

He followed her down the dimly lit foyer, past the small oil paintings and framed family photos, and hooked left into the kitchen. Maureen removed two mugs from a cupboard. At the ceramic-tiled island, which stood under the large copper hood that jutted down from the ceiling, she poured out two cups.

Then she plopped in the teabags, dropped a teaspoon of cane sugar in each one, and stirred.

She handed Jim a mug. "Let's relax on the roof deck."

They returned to the foyer and trudged up the four flights of stairs. Maureen unbolted the door. They stepped into the sunlight and he shut the door behind them. Jim had been there only a handful of times, but each time he could not help but be impressed.

But now was not the time for enjoying the view. Jim opened up the metal chest and removed two of the canvas camping chairs. He and Maureen took their seats, perpendicular to each other.

After four or five seconds of silence, she turned her glum gaze his way. "I'm so sorry to weigh you down with all this drama. I've been crabby lately. I'm actually somewhat surly to begin with. And I can tell it's been getting to you."

Jim sipped his tea, his mind racing. Was she preparing to break up with him?

"It's been just so many things with me lately. No, I wasn't prepared for what I was getting myself into when you moved away. Yes, I helped orchestrate it and... it isn't quite what I thought. At first I was strong, I could take it..."

"Yes," he said softly, signifying to her that he was patiently following. Jim pulled himself farther upright in his seat. He was resigned to whatever awaited. He could almost feel the ax coming down onto his neck.

She looked up from her gesticulating hands, looked down toward her pedicured toes. "Anyway, it's *so* much harder than I thought it would be. I miss all your attention: you stopping by so much, all your little gifts and surprises. I used to hate you springing all your surprise plans on me, but I grew to miss it. I thought we could just meet on weekends but it's now so tough."

Her eyes welled slightly with tears. Then she laughed. "And lately Yoshi at the lab has been such a cretin to me. He singles me out and makes me work on the most grueling of all the experiments and projects, cuts me no slack at all. I don't have to mention he rarely bathes. I swear he does that just to get under the skin of the poor girls like me who have to work with him! I'm sick of inhaling something that reeks of spoiled milk and bad onions."

Jim sniffled but was able to prevent himself from chuckling. Where was she going with this? Was she really about to push him away?

"I'm not calling it quits or giving up on us by any means," Maureen extended her hand toward him as if she was trying to tell him to stop, as if she could really tap into his thoughts. "I would never do that without speaking with you first, or giving you another chance."

"Give me another chance?" Jim said. "I thought I was doing something you were completely behind. Otherwise I would've stayed here."

"I want you to come up each weekend. You didn't *last* weekend."

"I had to help the guys in the shop. Now we're almost finished with the schooner."

"I know, but from now on at least *once* a weekend. And once during the week."

He paused. "Deal." The mug shook as he lifted it to his lips. Then an idea came to him. It wasn't the first time he had conceived it. But he had never voiced it.

"Maureen," he said, "do you ever think that maybe *you* should come down and visit me on the Cape sometimes? Instead of *me* always coming up to *you*? And before I moved to Osterville, you always wanted me to visit you *every day*. Never vice versa."

She folded her arms. "It's hell finding parking in the North End."

"You can take the T, the taxi, or just take a little walk, like I do."

"Well, it was a dumpy place. And you should have dusted more."

Jim was incredulous. He slapped his hands down hard onto his knees. "Maur, I tell you. You are something else. You really are."

"How so?" she almost shouted. "What do you mean?"

"With me, you play the independent, strong-willed New England girl when it benefits you. When it doesn't, you resort to the demure, wilting Southern belle drill you think I'm used to. When it comes to us making decisions, you want it your way almost *always*. Or you will make it known you are just *not* having a good time. But when the workday ends, you always expect me to stop by *your* place, never the other way around."

He paused for a moment. She squinted hard into his eyes, sighing through her nostrils.

"Up here, see, the man and the woman change off: sometimes the man visits the woman, sometimes vice versa. It's an egalitarian culture. But you always want me to pick up the tab and do the driving to visit *you*. Well then, I hope to decide where to eat sometimes and where to go at least. I am a man, you know."

Maureen grew silent. He knew she would never apologize, give ground, or admit any fault. "Anyway, how long are you in town today?"

He was unable to stifle a laugh. "Oh, Maureen. Gotta love her," he said, his smiling eyes on her as he shook his head. "I take it you heard what I said."

"I did. Are you hungry?" She sighed as she posed the question.

He laughed again and she cast him an icy stare. That old line again. She sounded like a hungry child bugging her father for food.

"I'll let *you* pick this time, Mr. Scoresby."

"Seriously? You're pullin' my leg!"

"Go ahead and choose." She smiled despite her irritated tone. "Just us alone, though. None of your buddies need tag along. Not this weekend."

"Okay then. I'll tell you what I'm tastin'..."

"Enlighten me."

"We should get our seafood fix again."

She rolled her eyes. "Ah, Jim, you're so predictable."

"But first we go for a walk. I want to take us someplace first."

"I can only imagine. It involves art, religion, history, or alcohol. I'll place my bet right now."

"Quite possibly. Who knows what the future holds?"

Jim stood and stretched his arms, arching slightly backwards as he released a profound yawn. He walked to the wooden rail of the roof patio. "Just look at that view, Maureen. One of the nation's most beautiful neighborhoods. It's as if you've stepped back into the time of Adams and Hancock."

From his vantage point on the roof deck, Jim saw scores of slate-roofed colonial townhouses, with some later renovations and additions such as granite stairways under the doors. All around were red brick walls and painted black shutters, copper weathervanes and flower beds under windows. He could swear he was in the London of a long-gone era.

Maureen joined him at the rails and rubbed her shoulder affectionately into his. He gave a slight start in shock, his head and torso quivering for a second. Her act ushered in a rush of memories, moments he dearly missed.

"Dad did pay a pretty penny for it. I would get my own place but—the view! It was just too hard to resist."

"Are you good to go out on the town?"

"Are we walking far?" she sighed.

"Just don't wear heels for once. It'll be a whole lot better."

She hesitated, further perturbed. Her predictability never hid for long. "No. They will go with what I put on."

"Ah, Maureen Henretty," Jim shook his head. She had not acquiesced or disagreed. She merely dropped the subject and dodged his request, perhaps out of hunger or obstinacy.

He blinked slowly as he yanked his phone from his pocket. He scrolled down his speed dial and once again phoned Commonwealth Cab.

Chapter Twenty-Five

The taxi sped up Charles Street, passing the boutiques and cafés that were Maureen's playgrounds. It ground to a rude halt at a red light on Beacon Street. To the right were the Public Gardens. A bit to the left, just past the black wrought-iron fence, the famed Boston Common stretched out before them.

"Imagine all the Puritans and Indian braves buried underneath that rolling lawn," Jim said. "Executed colonists, too. And I'll bet there are a few Yankees fans under there."

Maureen turned slowly toward him with narrowed eyes. The light turned green and the cab jerked leftward and sped down Beacon. At the St. Gauden's Shaw Memorial, it hooked right and swooped down Park Street. Jim felt nearly as on edge as he had recently felt on any boat.

"You know," Jim leaned toward Maureen and mumbled, "I've wondered how often Boston taxicabs hit pedestrians or just plain crash. What's intriguing is I've never seen or heard of such a case. And arguably, Boston is the most treacherous American city for any driver."

The cab passed King's Chapel, crossed Tremont, swung left down Province Street, and then stopped. Maureen exited the cab but Jim remained seated, plunging his hand into his jeans for his wallet. He handed the cash to the driver.

"Thanks." Jim shut the door. "Keep the change."

The driver lurched down the street, nearly rolling over Jim's toes. The door had barely closed.

"I suppose that's a 'you're welcome'?" Jim opened his hands, palms-up, in disbelief.

Maureen stood in front of the bar, her arms folded across her chest, a pinched look on her face. She studied the black sign at the top of the façade and the number above the door: forty-seven. Both of these were nearly level with her face. A large wooden flower manger crowned the entire façade, perhaps twelve feet in width. The wood framing of the windows below was painted red. The entire place was literally built into the ground. It seemed the smallest façade of any bar, restaurant, or shop Jim had ever seen. In fact, it brought to mind some curiosity out of Renaissance England.

"The Littlest Bar," she read the words with hesitation and a touch of skepticism. "I heard of this place. It was right under my nose for months."

"That's how it is for most Bostonians. Also, it's actually short for 'The Littlest Bar In The World'." Jim clapped his hands once in excitement. "Place is hell for claustrophobics. But it's worth the discomfort!"

Jim grabbed the door and swung it open. Inside the cramped cellar played a raucous, fast-paced tune, something punk. Ah, he knew the group—the Dropkick Murphys—and he loved them. Five people appeared below, including the bartender, a white-bearded, nearly bald old man in a green sweater.

Filling the air were Irish accents and a Bostonian accent, which, though muffled, was quite thick. There was one accent Jim couldn't quite place. Perhaps it was French or Belgian. Then he thought he had it: was it a Cuban accent?

Two men sat at the bar. A couple sat a few feet away at a tiny round table.

The entire place—not including what was behind the bar—probably measured no more than one hundred and eighty square feet, with the bar about twelve feet in length.

"Mornin', Jimmy. And hello to you, my dear," said the bartender in his thick Irish brogue. "What will you two be having?"

"Hey there, Mr. Finnerty," Jim said. "Maureen?"

"A glass of Chardonnay."

"Very well. You, lad?"

"A pint of Guinness. What else?" Jim said. "By the way, Mr. Finnerty, this is Maureen."

"Nice to make your acquaintance," Finnerty said, nodding. He turned to fetch the wine, and poured out a glass for her. He then filled a pint of Guinness, working the glass in a circular motion in one hand as he pulled down on the draught with the other.

Jim knew full well what the old man was doing and smiled at his skill. He set the glass down in front of Jim, who held it before Maureen's bored eyes. In the cream-colored foamy head rested the raised outline of a shamrock. Jim had only seen this feat performed before in the Littlest Bar and in a few pubs around town.

Maureen sat half-turned around on her barstool. She surveyed the vintage Guinness and Jameson signs and framed black-and-white prints of Irish city and countryside scenes. Three of the five lanterns hanging from the ceiling were lit. One of the walls featured an old rotary telephone, perhaps once part of a phone booth.

"Haven't seen you in here before, young lady," the bartender said, his arms spread out on the bartop as he leaned comfortably toward them. "Now you, *New Orleans*, I've poured you a few in my time."

"But I never get ill, you must give me that much," Jim pointed an index finger in the air.

"That would be true," the old Irishman said. "And you never brawl. Leave that to them punks in the Southie bars."

"I agree," Maureen said. "And you won't find me in those establishments."

Maybe she is finally starting to unwind. Maureen was chatting with a bartender, after all.

"Maybe we could've if you were nineteen and home on college break!" Jim said.

Maureen shot him a mock-cold stare.

"Jimmy, my boy!" Finnerty tapped the counter twice with the palm of his hand. "There's a gentleman here I'd like you to meet."

Jim glanced behind him. Against the wall sat one couple, a tweed-jacketed man with the look of a professor and his much younger girlfriend, embroiled in debate, both full of wild hand gesticulations.

To his right, two men sat looking over at him. The man closer to him was conservatively dressed in oatmeal corduroy pants, a blue button-down oxford shirt, and a hunter green English-style barn jacket with a dark brown corduroy collar. He had gray eyes, graying chestnut hair, and a slightly pinkish complexion. He exuded the impression of a fifty-something English earl fresh from a pheasant hunt.

Beside this man was a more intriguing figure, a tall man,

of an athletic build, and perhaps in his early forties. He sat on his barstool, cradling a glass of amber liquid. He was dressed in a pair of blue jeans, frayed near the bottom, with chocolate-colored alligator boots and a small round belt buckle showing the profile of an Indian brave. His shirt was of faintly wrinkled white linen, its long sleeves rolled up to the elbows. The top button was undone, revealing the man's tanned skin. A brown cord encircled his neck, attached to a small wooden cross and some other symbol Jim could not identify for all the dim light.

When the man turned for a moment, Jim spotted his dark brown hair gathered into a ponytail between his shoulder blades. Gray was barely visible in the beard and the long hair. Something shone in his left earlobe, a golden earring. The slightly arched brows, the high cheekbones, the narrow but nearly aquiline nose, the light brown irises and the brown hair, the look of the face overall was something incredibly familiar to him, a face vaguely French or Italian. The left cheekbone revealed a scar: thin and perhaps an inch long. The eyes were shifty, distrustful, evincing intelligence and humor, and perhaps a hint of violence.

The man spun completely around on his barstool. He looked dead at Jim with half amusement, half expectation.

It was as if the pirate Jean Lafitte was alive and well, fresh from warring with the British, and now sat imbibing in some French Quarter saloon.

"My boy, you're gonna fancy this!" The old Irishman walked over to the men. Finnerty raised a remote control and clicked a few buttons. The wild, thunderous Dropkick Murphys song evaporated. A new tune emerged in the air all about them. Jim knew not the artist nor the song, but the festive accordions and fiddles were completely familiar.

"Jim, come meet these gentlemen," Finnerty said.

Jim descended his barstool and stepped over to the men.

"Jim, this is Bobby Dunleavy in the green jacket. He lives in Newton. He thinks he's some hotshot environmental attorney up here. And last but *not least*—no offense, Bobby—"

Both Finnerty and the attorney laughed. Jim shook Bobby's hand.

"Last but not least, Jean Decareaux, Bobby's good friend. If you've never heard this very talented man's music, you've been deprived, cheated! I'm playing one of his creations right this minute."

"My suspicions were correct," Jim said. "*Laissez les bon temps rouler...en La Luzianne.*"

The man stood, all six-foot-two or so of him, and stretched out his hand. Jim shook it.

Decareaux said in a Cajun-accented English, "The boys of the *Fleur-de-Lis* sniff each other out pretty fast!"

"I know it," Jim said. "That's my girlfriend over there, Maureen."

She stood just behind him. A woman of breeding, she never failed to summon her manners in public when she needed them. Maureen offered her hand. Decareaux bowed slightly and shook it.

"Pleased to meetchawll," Decareaux said. "I had a feelin' you were a Luzianna man."

"How's that?" Maureen said.

"Well," Decareaux parted his hands and looked around in an "I can't believe you don't know" pose. "How that boy went after that cold beer!"

"You couldn't be more correct, my friend," Jim said.

"You're kinda soundin' Nawlins, kinda not. You from the Northshore?" Decareaux said, squinting slyly at him.

"You guessed it. Folsom, just maybe forty-five, fifty miles north of Nawlins."

"Know that place," Decareaux said.

"And you're from... let's see... Lafayette area?" Jim said.

"Yeah, boy, close 'nough." The man gritted his teeth through his smile and, leaning forward, clapped Jim on the shoulder. "Li'l town called Erath."

"One of my best friends, his mama's family's from there," Jim said. "Her grandfather was Senator Dudley LeBlanc."

"Coozan Dudley!" Decareaux cried. "Ol' Mistah Hadacol! He was larger than life, boy! I'll be! Well, what brings you up here?"

"I came up... you know... after *the* hurricane."

"The hurricane?" Decareaux said. "Katrina or Rita? I guess with you it was Katrina!"

Jim nodded, biting his lip.

"Well, strange as it seems, I had a house out in the country, southwest a ways from Lafayette. Rita came just two months after your storm, just flooded the hell outta my ol' house. I sold that place for what I could get. My band and I been tourin' ever since."

"We're both hurricane exiles," Jim said. "I met another in Boston, four weeks after the storm. This one playing right now is yours, isn't it?"

"Sure! It's called 'Mamou', 'bout that town's famous Mardi Gras."

"Always wanted to go. Only went to Mardi Gras down in

New Orleans and on the Northshore. And in Baton Rouge."

"You're missin' out," Decareaux said. "Whoo-hoo, are you missin' out, baby."

"Yep," Jim looked at his feet, his hands in his pockets.

"So Bobby Dunleavy here's a good buddy o' mine. He's one of the main lawyers in a charity in Luzianna I been involved with, called Save The Wetlands."

Dunleavy stood, his hands on his hips. "Yesterday Jean did a show here in Cambridge. I'm showing him around the town today. When he comes to New England, we hit certain old haunts of ours, and one is The Littlest Bar In The World. There's no place like it anywhere."

"I'm with you there," Jim said.

"Yeah, Neil Finnerty's a buddy o' mine and a big fan of my stuff," Decareaux said. "Hey, why don'tchall pull ya stools up to ours. Hang out a little."

Jim and Maureen fetched their stools and returned to the two men, who repositioned their own stools so everyone sat in a circle.

"Ever think of makin' it back down to La Luzianne, Jimbo?" Decareaux said.

"I visit on holidays. I was just there for Christmas."

"No, man, I mean *for good*."

"I've thought of it. Maybe one day, who knows?" For a few seconds, Jim stared past them at the wall. He sensed something unsettling. Some force goaded him into turning toward Maureen. Her eyes were fixed onto him with a piercingly frigid stare.

He started a bit, his head bobbing. "But then," Jim looked back toward his two new acquaintances, "Maureen and I both like it here in many ways. And I landed a new job helping run her father's boat brokerage out on the Cape." Both statements were the truth, after all.

"Wait," Dunleavy said. "You have been here for seven months and you're dating a beautiful young woman *and* you're helping run the family biz for her dad? On the Cape? A boat brokerage... yachts? You might not be leaving, my friend."

Jim studied the floor between them. He could sense a strange feeling build within him.

Decareaux rubbed his hands together, nodding his head in assent. "You seem the type to like this area 'nough to stay. Great part of the country. It's got history like N'awlins. It's even older. You got the whole thing up here with the love of the sea. And people here, man, they appreciate the environment. That's why we got Bobby here bringin' up the cavalry down there in the bayou!" Decareaux punched Dunleavy on the shoulder.

"I know what you're saying, completely," Jim said.

"But you prob'ly gotcha family all down there. An' all the amazin' food and outdoors and jus' the sheer love o' livin'. That slow pace o' life. Workin' to live and play, not livin' to work. And hopefully we got some good music down there."

"We do have that," Jim said. "You'd know a lot about that, I'd say."

"Hear this song here? I wrote this one when I was a student years ago at ULL. That's University of Luzianna at Lafayette, for you N'awlins folks. About a fine Cajun girl I wanted to date, named Maybelle."

"I like the belt buckle," Maureen said. "The Native American there."

Though she seemed intrigued by the buckle, Jim figured

she would murder him if he were to appear on a Boston street wearing one.

"Yeah," Jim said, "that's the one the writer James Lee Burke wears. He's not far from you down there, in New Iberia."

"He gave me this one. Good man, ol' buddy o' mine," Decareaux said.

"I enjoy his novels. That famous detective of his… Dave Robicheaux?" Jim said.

"Burke *is* a fine storyteller," Dunleavy said. "I read him from time to time, when I'm not working twelve hour days."

"You do it for a good cause," Decareaux said. He looked at Jim. "Bobby cares more for the vanishin' Luzianna wetlands than most of us natives do!"

"Good for you," Jim said. "We need more people like you in our ranks."

The attorney, blushing in both cheeks, smiled down at his brown leather dress shoes. Jim downed the dregs of his beer and held the empty glass in his hand, pausing as he felt the warm glow suffuse his forehead and cheeks. Maureen cradled her empty wine glass in her hands. For an instant, she bugged her eyes at him. He rose to his feet as if trying to unhook his body from the stool.

"Hate to say it, gents, but we were on our way to lunch," Jim winced.

"Where are you guys going?" Dunleavy said. The man looked half curious, half skeptical.

"We're headed over to Stephanie's."

"Order the grilled lobster," Dunleavy closed his eyes for emphasis. "Grilled and butterflied right there on the platter. Nice comfort food, too, and right on Newbury. You can sit outside, people-watch."

Decareaux rose to his feet, and his friend followed suit.

"That's just what we planned. I wish we could stay longer," Jim said. Maureen was now at his side. Jim looked at Decareaux. "Reminisce, too."

"One thing, brother." The Cajun pulled out his wallet. He removed a card and handed it to his new friend.

Jim held it close to his face. Dog-eared and lightly soiled, it read:

Jean-Luc Decareaux
Musician and Activist
(337) 555-6731
Acadia63@gmail.com

"I'll keep in touch." Jim handed each man his Henretty & Henretty business card. "Job's changed, but the number's still working. Sign me up for the wetland group."

Dunleavy pocketed the card. "We will."

"Right on, brother," Decareaux shook Jim's hand. "And nice to meetcha, darlin'." He bowed slightly while he maintained eye contact.

"Nice to meet you, too," Maureen said.

"Take care," Dunleavy said. "Look for our group's emails!"

"I will," Jim said. "Good luck on your tour, Jean."

The Cajun smiled affectionately, with a hint of sadness about the eyes. Jim walked back toward the bar to pay his tab. He reached for his wallet.

"Oh, no you don't!" Finnerty said. "Your fellow bayou-dweller already signaled to me. He's got this one."

Jim began: “No, I can’t—”

“I insist,” Decareaux said. “Buy me an Abita down the line.”

Jim laughed gently. “Thanks, Jean. Thanks.”

He waved at Finnerty, Dunleavy, and Decareaux and trudged reluctantly up the short stairwell, with Maureen following. Halfway up, he heard Jean speak.

“Always watch the drink, man. And *never* stop prayin’.”

Jim opened the door. Once again, they stood on the curb. On Maureen’s face was a complex amalgam of curiosity and slight indignation.

What was the reason for such an expression? He did not know. He could barely think now, for all the homesickness that burned like embers through him.

Chapter Twenty-Six

They had been seated at the table for perhaps ten minutes, sampling the crackers and wine and looking out at the theatergoers walking down Charles Street South. Then she brought up their new Cajun acquaintance.

In the growing darkness of his flat, Jim stopped typing on his laptop. He propped his feet up on the arm of his couch. To his left stretched the Nantucket Sound, its advancing waves barely discernible in the scant moonlight. He was still shaken by Maureen's strange reaction over lunch.

After leaving The Littlest Bar, they had walked west back up to Park Street and flagged down a cab. They started out toward Stephanie's, but then opted for Pigalle. The maître d' seated them near the window like old times. Maureen kept silent for over a minute.

"Interesting man, wasn't he? The Louisiana guy?" she said.

"He was that," he said. "That attorney was friendly, too, a bit shy, and not as interesting. Maybe that's just 'cause we didn't give him much of a chance to speak. But the musician... now he's intriguing, no doubt."

"Something you said has been on my mind."

He looked back at her with dread.

Jim swung around on the sofa, set the laptop down on the coffee table, and walked over to the sliding glass door. He put his eyes within an inch of the glass. Out on the bay, gray water stretched for miles, with no hint of a vessel.

"So you might move home," Maureen had told him at dinner. "I mean, you said it right there. It kind of slipped out of you. You may one day move away. But I realize now I could never move away from my parents. Or my mom's parents. You aren't completely anchored to, or *committed* to, this area. *And me.*"

Twenty minutes afterwards, he finally regained his composure. She had done it. She had instigated a quarrel.

When he first met Maureen, on that first date in early January, she had shared far different plans: she hoped to stay on in New Orleans after her graduation seven months before, but she simply assumed she could not land a job there in her field. She admitted she moved back to Massachusetts as a sort of afterthought or default, simply to recoup and rest and maybe circulate her résumé. But now it was clear she would never settle anywhere but New England.

He had indeed enjoyed his time in the Northeast. In a way he could see himself committing to New England. Even so, his heart told him this land was not for him. He felt a pull to a different land, the land of his birth and bloodline. Yet with Maureen's latest declaration, she vied to change the rules and the stakes of everything.

Jim returned to the sofa and sank into the cushion. He took up the rock glass of bourbon and allowed the smoky burn to course down his throat into his belly. As Jim smacked his lips, he realized the Woodford Reserve bottle in his kitchenette was empty. He walked over to the refrigerator, pulled out a bottle of Sam Adams, and opened it. He ambled back toward the sofa and lay down, his back upright against one of the arms, his legs and feet resting comfortably on the cushions.

Stupid microfiber sofa. I wanted brown leather. But Maureen had squashed the idea. After all, as she said on that day months ago, we may very well both be using this furniture soon.

Jim brought the longneck to his lips, raised the bottom high, and guzzled nearly half its contents. The fog within his head grew denser by the minute. How strange to cross paths with the likes of Jean-Luc Decareaux in a tiny Boston watering hole, seemingly light-years from his home. Was it fate? Perhaps he was meant to learn something from the man that day.

Always watch the drink, the man had said, *and never stop prayin'*. Also exiled by a hurricane, Decareaux knew all the many pitfalls that could hound such a person. This line seemed uncanny. The Cajun saw into him better than he expected.

Jim set his Blackberry alarm for seven forty-five. This week or next, he and the men would complete the overhaul of the schooner. Soon the *John Paul Jones* would not only need to be seaworthy, but also in tip-top shape for the voyage up the coast—with children on board.

Random thoughts of Freddy, Decareaux, Maureen and her parents, his own parents and brother, Liam and his Boston friends, and his new sailing team flashed faster and faster through the cinema of his mind. Perhaps it only furthered his exhaustion. In minutes, Jim was lost in sleep.

When he woke, the room was full of shadows, only illumined by a nearby lamp. Jim rose slowly from the couch and slinked toward the bay window. All this turmoil was ruining his sleep, his peace. What had jolted him awake?

He blinked his eyes rapidly, still lingering in the realm of dreams. That last part of his nightmare remained, there several feet from him: the coffin propped upright in the corner, Freddy emerging decomposed in the burial suit Jim had bought him, stepping forth with hesitation. Jim could not see his eyes. He glanced hard, but they were shut, sunken. Then the wraith vanished. Ah, it was the end he could expect, that all should expect. But Freddy had met it too early, too harshly, without comfort...

Outside on the Sound he could see nothing, merely darkness. Again, he imagined his father at that very hour. It was two hours past midnight. George Scoresby had retired to bed, and when the clock struck five, Jim's mother Rachel would rise for the rosary and Mass, and his father would be off to his office to pore over his maps and logs.

Was his father right? If Jim didn't move home soon, would he be increasingly swallowed up in a new life, and in a flash his father and mother and much of his family would be gone and he himself would be an old man, his life almost done?

Nonsense. His father was just pulling out all the stops. Ol' George missed him just that much.

Regardless, he must press on with his life in New England. It would be reckless to give it all up now and crawl back home. And Maureen...

He had commenced the mission. He must, for once, complete the task.

Chapter Twenty-Seven

At twenty past eight, the door of the Melville Boat Brokerage office opened. In walked Jim, his hair still damp from his morning shower.

"Well, look who it is!" Bill laughed like a fiend. "You look a little hung-ovah! Rise and shine, ya highness!"

Jim stopped in the middle of the room, gripping his thermos. "Sleep problems."

"How was the trip, man? Commodore run ya aground?"

"Perfect weather. Kids did very well."

"Those Harbor Islands are pretty nice. Interesting little formations, them drumlins. Formed by glaciers, ya know? Anyway, I guess we're set for the last big push."

"We're on track to finish this week," Jim half stated, half asked.

Bill clapped his hands once with excitement, as if on the verge of declaring some important news. "As long as Donovan don't sleep too late, little Joey DaSilva don't slip out early to meet some hot young broad, and Chief don't sneak some sauce on his lunch break, I'd say, we're lookin' good for finishin' Friday, man."

"Excellent," Jim said. "I'm psyched."

"You should be, Jimmy. We started crankin' on the deck this morning. I s'pose we coulda started with the hull."

"Meh, the order is irrelevant. Long as we work hard and

steady, we'll arrive at the end."

"That's it. We'll get there, man. Let's go check her out, shall we?"

Walking down the stairs, they found DaSilva and Chief on the deck. Chief was hammering a board in place. Their stereo played James Taylor. The earnest, crystal-clear vocals and the minimalistic yet beautiful acoustic guitar chord was unmistakable.

"I, too, have seen fire and rain," Jim shouted to the crew.

"Great folk singer, isn't he?" Bill nodded. "He's a local boy. I've seen him many times, both when he's played out here and in western Mass."

Chief appeared at the rail, joined by DaSilva. They both stood, smiling down at them, Chief's hands at his hips and Joey slouching with his arms at his sides, the faintest timid smile accenting his face.

"There he is!" Chief said. "Commodore Henretty didn't drown ya this time?"

Laughter erupted from various areas of the shop.

Jim attempted to keep his lips fast together but he was unable to prevent them from yielding into a smile. He glanced down at the cement floor and shook his head. "Fortunately, this time I watched for the swingin' boom."

Donovan, in all his ruddy-cheeked, grease-stained glory, appeared at his side.

"Sure ya didn't fall into the deep?" Chief jeered. "At least once? Twice?"

"My eyes were wide open this time, believe me," Jim said. "So y'all already working on the deck?"

"Of course." Donovan raised his brows. "Much progress.

There ain't much left to go."

"I'm comin' on up." Jim walked around the boat.

Donovan and Bill followed, ascending the rolling metal stairwell. Chief stood next to DaSilva, who pointed at the gaping hole in the deck, perhaps ten feet by fifteen feet.

"That's all we got left," the boy said. "Don't fall in."

Jim nodded his head with pride. The men had made much headway. A quarter of the deckboards were brand new, nailed into place, and only needed buffing and staining.

"You men are doing great," Jim said. "All I missed was part of Friday and all of Saturday, but what's our status on the hull?"

"We got a good, I'd say, three, maybe four days left," Bill said. "This deck's maybe two days, with the buffing and the staining included."

"Well..." Jim muttered, narrowing his eyes and holding a fist to his mouth in thought. "Change of plans! Chief and DaSilva, y'all stick to the deck. The next couple days, it'll be Bill, Donovan, and I on the hull. If y'all need another hand on this, gimme a holler. I can help stain or buff. We may finish around the same time."

"We're gonna need some more stain," DaSilva said.

"Six more buckets," Bill said. "We gotta stain the whole deck. And we need a few more buckets of paint for the hull. After the woodwork's done down there."

"Write me up a list," Jim said. "Add what they need, brand, color or whatever included. I'll drive into town at lunch, stop at the hardware store again."

"You may be from Louisiana, but you're still a good guy," Bill said.

Jim shot him a wry grin. "All right, let's attack it!" Jim led

Bill and Donovan down the rolling stairwell.

For the next few hours, Jim helped Donovan and Bill nail the hull boards in place, while Chief and DaSilva worked on the deck. The men passed the list among them. Soon there were eight line items.

At eleven-thirty, the outside door keycode beeped. The door swung ajar. Walter strode inside wearing his khaki shorts and white canvas boat shoes as he fixed his Ray-Ban sunglasses in the neck of his white polo shirt.

"Lookin' very Cape Cod-ish, Commodore Walt," Jim said.

"Gotta look the part, my boy," Walter said. "The clothes make the man, as Shakespeare had it. Well, greetings, gentlemen! How goes it with the old leaky dame, ya damned salty dogs?"

"Actually, we're on target to finish Friday, as you predicted," Jim said.

"I tell ya, men, this fine beaut looks just marvelous," the Commodore said. "It should, after all I spent on her! When my wife caught wind of this purchase, she nearly filleted me alive!"

"So..." Bill emerged from behind the boat. He stood with his hands on his hips, smiling with his trademark mischief. "Seriously, Cap'n. How did ya get back in her good graces this time, if you may divulge?"

"Really wanna know? I made another large donation to the Church. And I booked her and her friends another two-week stay in Tuscany."

A few laughed, but Jim kept mum. Walter's words made him queasy.

"But there's a little method to my madness, gents." Walter clapped once, loudly, his eyes flashing. "I'm giving Kathleen her wish, sendin' her across the pond those same weeks we sail this beauty down to New York Harbor."

A fierce cheer tore loose from Jim and all of his men. The cry of jubilation shot up into the steel rafters as they waved their hands in the air. The Commodore had taken many of the Melville men on two-day, three-day jaunts, but never on a trip of such duration. And never to such an exciting destination as New York City.

"Great idea, sir!" Donovan clapped his hands with gusto.

"This is great, Mr. Henretty!" Bill shouted. "You know who ya real friends are!"

"Nice!" Jim said. "This sounds like an excellent trip. Everybody'll be happy: you, Kathleen, us!"

"Two weeks on board this baby, all the way to the Big Apple! Stopping in ports all along the way. Grilling and drinking on deck *every night*. Everyone can bring a guest! What could *possibly* be left out, my boy? Now, lemme see this old lass!"

"Here, Cap'n," Bill said. "I'll give you the tour."

The men showed him the slowly shrinking cavities in the hull and deck.

Afterwards, at the foot of the ladder, Walter Henretty nodded, his arms joined behind his back. "I cannot deny it. You men are doing just fine. Now don't let me keep ya."

"Actually we were just breaking for lunch," Jim said. "But we'll resume in about an hour."

Walter marched toward the door. He motioned for Jim to follow. "Why don'tcha accompany me to town, sonny boy? We'll grab a quick bite. I'm goin' on a little errand."

"Good idea," Jim said. "I need to grab some things for the men at the hardware store. We should take my truck."

Jim walked faster and pulled alongside the old man. They

headed down the path and up the driveway to the truck. Jim turned the ignition and revved the motor three times.

The old man raised a fist and cheered with glee. "Yes! Let's hear her rooaar!"

"Hahaha! Come on, ol' Betty Sue!" Jim shouted. "Come on, baby!" He worked the shift and eased on the accelerator. The old Chevy rolled forward from where it was backed up against one of the closed garage doors. Jim rolled down his window with one arm. With the other, he steered the truck out onto the driveway, between the oaks, maples, and birches, toward the road.

The old man also rolled down his window. He pulled his pipe from his shorts, along with a matchbox and small tin of tobacco. Walter quickly packed and lit the bowl. Jim looked over at Walter, who sat silently puffing away with the slightest of grins. The old man maintained his silence the entire way to Osterville's Main Street.

After several minutes, Jim said, "So where should we stop first?"

"Let's head to your hardware store. Then to lunch."

"But Walter, will the boxes be safe in the truck bed? And what about your errand?"

The old man puffed away, his eyes shrewd and narrowed with thought as they pierced the windshield. "You don't have to worry much about theft around here. And my errand will just take a second. I'll getcha back to the men in no time."

"I trust you implicitly, Commodore."

"Well, ya should. I've been around a long time."

Jim pulled onto Main Street, a road laid out much like other main arteries in coastal New England towns. Without fail, there was the white clapboard Congregationalist church with its charming steeple. Boxy, brick mid-nineteenth century commercial buildings housed sandwich shops, bookstores, and boutiques. Eighteenth century clapboard houses abounded, as did parallel-parked Subarus, Saabs, Volvos, and BMWs.

Jim parked in the small lot beside Carrington's Hardware Shoppe. They walked across the paved lot and around the brick building. Jim held the door ajar for the old man to enter.

A forty-something man stood behind the counter. Jim had come to the man several times in the last few weeks to buy supplies. Each time, Jim had been struck by his rudeness.

"Hello," Jim said.

Carrington looked back at Jim with large light blue eyes, nearly devoid of any expression save the slightest trace of haughtiness and impatience. The man was very tall, with a thick brown mustache. He was dressed in a white apron over a starched and pressed light blue office shirt. The entire crown of his hairless head was like a gigantic pearl, shiny and spotless and bright. "What'll it be?" the man sighed.

"*Still* not happy to see me? Still so rude after *all* the business I've given you?" Jim said, looking sadly at the man, shaking his head.

"Whaddaya want, kid?" the man said.

Walter appeared at Jim's side, and then took a step forward, his hands resting at his sides, his back ramrod straight. On his face was a look of stalwart pride mixed with fierce animosity.

"Oh, Mister Henretty!" the man held up a hand, palm outward. "How are you, sir?"

"Not so good, Carrington. You addressed my top manager like he's one of your teenage stockboys who didn't show for work."

"Oh... I..." Carrington said. His eyes, all white and light blue nearly to the point of transparence, widened.

"Everyone knows you're naturally a real horse's ass," the old man barked. "But try to keep it in check. Especially for a young man who I *know* always treated you with courtesy. And you knew he was one of my guys. He's been putting supplies on my account here for weeks."

Carrington tried to mouth some awkward apology, but there was no sound.

Jim turned with a faint smile and walked down the aisle. He selected a plastic basket, pulled his list from his jeans' back pocket, laughed quietly to himself, and walked around the store, plopping supplies into the basket.

Walter joined him. Soon they returned to the counter. Carrington shuffled uneasily from one foot to another. Beads of sweat had broken through on the bare egg-like oval of his head.

Jim placed his items on the counter. Carrington feverishly scanned and bagged them and banged the register keys in a kind of nervous fit. He turned to Walter, then to Jim, forcing a smile. "I scanned them so the alarm won't go off. Take these... they... they're all on the house today."

"This man here is Jim Scoresby," Walter said. "He has bought, and will be buying, many of my boat shop's supplies from your enterprise here. As I have long done."

Jim offered his hand. Carrington shook it spastically, and then shook hands with Walter.

"Good gesture, Carrington," Walter said. "Give my regards to Jeannie."

He led Jim back down the aisle and out of the store. As soon as he started the engine, Jim said, "So… interesting scene back there."

"Stodgy, crusty old grinch. You shoulda told me he was being obnoxious."

"Frankly, sir, I've grown quite used to it. I love New England for its culture. Not for its manners, *generally* speaking. Not everyone's a Walter Henretty, a Kathleen Henretty."

"Ya don't need to flatter me, guy. I know we aren't the *friendliest*. Like I told you, our virtues usually lie in other realms."

"I would say inventiveness, resourcefulness, respect for culture and learning, a natural, idealistic bent for social activism." Jim rolled up to Main Street, stopping just before the road. "So where to?"

"Well put! Turn left. I know a good place to grab a snack."

Jim waited for a break in the light downtown traffic. Then he wheeled the truck left.

"Go forward a few minutes, son. I'll tell ya when to park."

"Carrington," Jim said with a strain of humor in his voice. "Crotchety guy did some about-face when he saw the likes of the Commodore. Nearly swallowed his tongue."

The old man stared out of his passenger's seat window, his smile reflected in the window. "I suppose we can attribute his transformation, or near pants-wetting, to the decades of business I've given to his store. Any generic item I can get there for the brokerage, I will. I like supporting small businesses."

"Your fame and stature in the community don't hurt, either."

"Maybe the fact that his brother served under my command

didn't hurt either. Ronald Carrington. Manned an anti-aircraft gun in my flotilla during the Vietnam War. Now, turn into this lot here." Walter pointed a slightly gnarled index finger at a parking lot bordering a white clapboard eighteenth century building. The house sported a unique slate roof, done in a fish scale design. Crowning the roof's center was a small steeple with a burnished gold-colored weathervane in the shape of a sperm whale.

"Very New England," Jim pulled into the lot. "I like the place already."

"I've been coming here my whole life, my boy."

They walked around to the front of the house. A wooden sign attached to the clapboard façade read:

The Bartley Inn
Est. by Josiah Bartley, Whaler
1796

Painted near the bottom of the sign were the outlines of what looked like a cod and whale.

Jim plodded up the three brick steps and grasped the brass door handle, opening the door wide. Walter nodded and thanked Jim as he stepped into the restaurant.

All within swirled the aromas of melted butter, baked bread, and fresh fish. A couple waited in the wooden-floored foyer while a matronly hostess waddled in to escort them into the main dining room just beyond.

She spotted Jim, and then Walter, and her face illuminated instantly with exuberant surprise. "Hello there, Captain Walt!"

"Well, hello to you, Mrs. Gowan," the old man waved.

As if reading his young friend's mind, Walter spoke. "Don't even fret, Jimmy. I called ahead for a reservation. This is like one of my clubs. I eat here at least once a week."

While the couple proceeded behind the hostess into the crowded dining room, its aroma ushered into Jim's mind those first days he had walked through the streets of Boston, three weeks after Katrina had struck. All in the downtown streets near the harbor, around Quincy Market and Faneuil Hall particularly, Jim's nose caught that certain aroma.

He never confirmed what it was exactly. He suspected it was fish some way or the other, whether fish and chips in the pubs, or haddock or halibut prepared the same way. A smell he loved and associated with the city of Boston, much like New Orleans had its own scent: some unforgettable amalgam of coffee roasting in the bean and chicory plants, melting into the smell of Cajun foods like jambalaya, gumbo, and boiled crawfish and crabs, all mixed with the heavenly aroma of the sauce-heavy Creole dishes like Shrimp Creole and Crawfish Étoufée, and the Sicilian scents of stuffed artichokes and massive olive-salad-filled muffuletta sandwiches.

Jim took heart that he no longer smelled those New Orleans scents. They would only bring him sadness.

The return of the high-spirited hostess wrested Jim from his culinary reverie. "All right, gentlemen," she said. "This way."

As they weaved their way through the tables, several diners turned to smile and wave at Walter and to observe his young companion. The hostess motioned to a small table against the room's rear window. She had no need to pull out a chair. The nimble old man had already seated himself.

"Our menus," Mrs. Gowan said. "I don't even need to hand

it to this one! This captain's eaten here more times than there are hairs on your young head." Mrs. Gowan pointed down at Jim's brow, turned, and walked back into the foyer.

Soon a slender young woman appeared at their table. She wore her auburn hair in a ponytail. A natural rosiness in the cheeks accented her cream-colored skin, smooth and shining with youth. The shape of her full, perky breasts revealed itself beneath her white button-down shirt.

She lifted her small memo-pad and greeted them. "Now, how are you guys doin' taday?" she said in a thick Massachusetts accent.

"Just fine, Kelly. I brought a young comrade of mine. He runs my boat brokerage. And dates Maureen, I might add."

"Oh yeah?" the waitress said, glancing at Jim.

"Boy's got his hands full," the old man cackled.

"I wasn't gonna say anything, but..." the waitress raised her eyebrows and looked down at her notepad. "You'll be all right. What'll you gentlemen be havin' ta drink?"

Jim motioned to Walter, but the old man deferred to him.

"I'll take a Dr. Pepper," Jim said.

"We don't carry that," the waitress shot back. "Wanna Pepsi instead?"

"Sure, that's fine."

The waitress scribbled in her notepad and then glanced at Walter.

"A glass of ice water with lemon," the old man said.

The waitress studied him with curiosity and a sort of expectation. "Now I know Captain Henretty don't just want an ice water."

Walter laughed. "I'll take my Fog Cutter along with that."

"That's the spirit." She scribbled further. "Be right back, gentlemen."

Jim vowed to look at her without an ounce of attraction. On the back of her thin neck crawled a tattoo of a small dragon. Jim looked down at the table and took up the menu.

"So, Jimmy," Walter leaned back in his seat, pursing his lips as he studied him. "All seems to be going well with the boat. You're doing an effective job at leading and you're pitching in, to boot. And you're not afraid to learn. The men like you."

Jim was poised to respond but the waitress reappeared. She placed their drinks in front of them. "Okay, you guys know whatcha want?" she droned in her nasal voice.

"All right," Jim said. "I'll take the Portuguese seafood stew."

"It comes with a salad," the waitress said. "Dressing? "

"Italian, please."

"You talk funny," the waitress said. "Where ya from?"

"South Jersey."

The old man snorted. "As for me, I'll think I'll take a break from my lobster thermidor. I'll opt for the seared scallop salad."

"I'll put the order in, gentlemen." The waitress left.

"Oh, you're gonna fancy that Portuguese seafood stew, my boy!" Walter said. "*Caldeirada da Marisco*. It's one of their very best items, chock full of potatoes, shallots, sherry. I mean, you've got shrimp, mussels, scallops, monkfish, wolffish, cod, mackerel, squid, all that good stuff. You'll be full all day."

"Sounds pretty hearty. I only had it once, in the Big Apple. When I took Maureen there."

"But it's more authentic here in southern New England. See, this is where most American Portuguese live. They've been here since the seventeenth century. Like DaSilva, a lot of those guys are descended from people who fished these waters long before Washington was born."

"Donovan was telling me that."

"So, Jim..." Walter leaned forward, resting his elbows on the table, and cleared his throat. "How are things going with Maureen?" He raised his chin ever so slightly. The old man's eyes never left him.

"Not so great. She somewhat regrets letting me move away. It's still taking a toll on her. She's having a hard time at work especially. I was there for her more when I lived in Boston. When I met up with her yesterday, she was actually kind of despondent."

"How'd she leave it with ya, son?" The eyes of the old man brimmed with an unmistakable benevolence.

Jim relaxed. "She needs me to see her more during the week. Or I don't think she can take it much longer."

"What about her visiting you?"

"That's the thing, Walter," Jim said as he winced. "She hardly ever wants to make the drive, or to meet me halfway. Even in Boston, she hardly ever came to see me. She wanted me to come to her, and to stop by her place or to pick her up somewhere."

Walter looked down. "The branch doesn't fall too far from the tree. And *I'm* not the parent that's the tree, if ya follow."

Jim snickered.

Walter winked and sipped from his Fog Cutter. "Whaddaya say," the old man paused, "I give you the opportunity to reclaim your old job? That I give you the *option*. To sweeten the pot, I can plop cash down on a nice apartment in Boston. And I'll move your stuff back for free. If you *choose* to go back to your old job."

"With all due respect, Walter," Jim weighed his words, "what if I don't? What if I want to stay with the Melville Brokerage and commute to see Maureen?"

"Then my full support is behind you," Walter said. "But... what do we do if we try that and she still can't take it?"

"Yes, I see," Jim said, fiddling with his spoon. "What if I stay on with Melville? And leave maybe early more weekdays to drive to see Maureen? And spend most weekends with her up there?"

"As long as you sleep on her couch, my boy," Walter pointed at Jim, looked him straight in the eyes, then burst into laughter.

Jim laughed haltingly, imagining all his intimate nights with the old man's daughter. "Yessir, of course."

Walter slapped his hands lightly on the table. "Now we have a working plan. After all, I moved your butt down here for a reason. I need a *good* man over that shop. I know you love the job. And my little princess can't have her way *all* the time."

"I agree wholeheartedly, sir."

"One must set some precedence, my boy. As Truman once said, 'The buck stops here.'" He jabbed an index finger into the tablecloth.

A woman of perhaps eighty appeared at the table, squinting, her hands clasped before her in expectation. "Is that Walter Henretty?"

She wore a velvet dress, plum-colored and ankle-length. A string of pearls encircled her neck. Her two earrings seemed like Victorian mini-portraits done in some kind of ivory-like material. Jim had seen those before, in antique shops. Her hair was gathered up on her head in a stately, but not excessive, manner and was secured with tortoise-shell clasps. The lady wore scant makeup, in true New England fashion. Her eyes were of a rare greenish hue and emitted a gentle warmth. Surely she had once been a great beauty.

"Is that Ms. Gwendolyn Shippey?" Walter said as he began to stand.

Jim followed suit, but the old woman motioned for them to sit back down. The men sank into their seats.

"And what if it is? How are you today, Walt? Corrupting this young man?" Her voice rose in mock frustration. "Teaching him how to be up to no good?"

"Me?" Walter touched his own chest in disbelief. "But of course, Gwen!"

"Hmmph. Who is this young man?" She stepped closer to the table.

Walter made introductions. Then he continued, "Jim was a star at my securities firm. Now he runs my boat business here in town. He also dates Maureen."

Ms. Shippey said, "They make a cute couple. She moved back home?"

Jim said, "She's still up in Boston."

"Egads! That is a distance, all right. You from down south?"

"You guessed right, ma'am," Jim said.

"A wild rebel in our midst," she said, glaring at Jim with feigned ire.

"Ms. Shippey grew up with me in Osterville," Walter said. "Or at least when I lived in Osterville during the summer months. Hey, by the way, where's Tom?"

"He's around. I'll tell him to stop by," Ms. Shippey said. "He doesn't know you're here." She turned and glided out of the main dining room into the kitchen.

Within moments a man of perhaps sixty appeared in the threshold. He surveyed the room, spotted Walter, and walked into the dining room. The man stopped two feet before them. "Is that Admiral Halsey reincarnate?"

Walter clapped his hands, rose, and then squeezed the man in a bear hug. "Tommy! How are ya, my boy?"

"Tired, but I can't complain," the man sighed. "We just hosted a writer from *Yankee Magazine* for two nights and we had to be in tip-top shape."

Jim studied the man's slightly wavy, silver hair, the piercing blue eyes, the square forehead, and the strong jaw. The man stood several inches taller than Walter, but was somewhat portly. He was clad in pressed light cream khakis and a blue button-down oxford shirt with rolled-up sleeves. All about the man swirled an interesting mixture of unmistakable authority and youthful levity that seemed familiar.

"Jim, meet Tom Shippey," Walter said. "You just met his mother. Tom owns the Bartley Inn."

Jim stood and shook Tom's hand. "I like this place," Jim said. "And I hear y'all do a great Portuguese fisherman's stew."

"Y'all?" Tom laughed. "Where do ya hail from, kid?"

"Louisiana," Jim said. He wondered if he had cringed when he answered the man. Was one of those edgy comments to follow?

"You should taste our bouillabaisse. It's just spicy enough. Probably nowhere near what you're used to, but you might like it."

Jim and Walter seated themselves.

"By the way, Tom," Walter said. "I brought you something."

He handed Tom a small book he had pulled from some pocket.

Tom took it, glanced at the cover momentarily, and then held it close against his hip.

"A little collection by Cheever," Walter said in a hushed tone. "I figured you'd like it."

"I appreciate it, I really do," Tom said. "I better get back in the kitchen, ensure my guys are keeping up with all these lunch orders. We just hired a new sous-chef. See you in a bit."

Soon the waitress unloaded their food.

Jim sampled the stew. As expected, it was superb. When Jim looked up, the old man had stealthily dumped a sautéed scallop, still steaming, onto Jim's empty butter plate. Jim cut a piece from the scallop and tasted it. "Wow. Garlic, butter, a trace of green onion."

"That one's for your good work, son," Walter said. "Now get dirty up to your elbows when you get back. Bust your behind tomorrow on that boat. Then knock off work early and drive up to see my little girl!"

"I couldn't object to that. What of that sounds like work?"

After their meal, when they passed through the dining room toward the foyer, all eyes rested on Walter, a man the onlookers venerated, loved, and to a degree, envied.

"Where to now, Commodore? You had an errand to run," Jim said as they crossed the parking lot toward the truck.

"That was it, my boy!" Walter said with gusto, raising his fist.

"Eating at the *Bartley*?"

"That, and giving the book to Tom Shippey."

Jim sensed an oddness in his friend's response, a certain evasiveness, which flattened into dead silence for half a minute.

"And floating the offer of you moving back closer to Maureen."

Jim felt anxious, even bewildered. He had just grown accustomed to his new role, and a happier role at that.

Walter puffed away at his pipe and stared out the window as the great maples and the white-barked birches and the cranberry bogs shot by in a blur.

Chapter Twenty-Eight

Jim clutched the first of the cardboard boxes of supplies as the keypad beeped. He turned the knob and entered the warehouse. Inside, the men had settled back into their work. A Bob Seger song blared on the stereo. Inside, only Bill and Donovan remained.

"Hi-yah, Jimmy," Bill called.

"We're good now," Jim said. "There's more provisions in the truckbed." After setting the box at Bill's feet, he studied the leathery, ruddy face set in relief against the light blond-and-gray ponytail. "So where are our friends, Chief and Romeo DaSilva?"

"Oh, they'll probably be by any second," Bill said. "How was lunch?"

"Excellent," Jim said. "But first I had to see that old curmudgeon Carrington at the hardware store."

"He's an interesting one, a real doozy. Guy owns a store that caters to tradesmen, but he's got an obvious scorn for men who work with their hands. So was he a pissant to you, too?"

Jim said, "Until he saw I was with the Commodore himself."

"Oh, I bet he changed his act then! Did ya get to see him sweat?"

"Like a turkey on Christmas Eve."

"Your Commodore's given him a small fortune over the decades, that's why. So, where did you guys eat?"

"The Bartley Inn on Main Street. I had—"

"He took ya to the old Bartley?" Bill dropped his jaw and stared at Jim, egg-eyed with surprise. "See that old widow with the earrings like outta some ol' Civil War daguerrotype? Shippey is the name. And her son, Tom? Kinda heavy-set?"

"They seem to like the Commodore a good bit."

"I bet so," Bill said. "Another two souls the old man often helps out."

"So what's their story? You don't like the Shippeys?"

"Nah. Good people. It ain't that," Bill said. He looked in the bags, then snatched them up. "Thanks for getting these."

"This load was on Carrington, by the way," Jim snickered, and went to find Donovan. Jim spotted him by the boat.

The keypad beeped. In walked Chief, with his perennial sidekick DaSilva in tow.

"Greetings, Your Highnesses!" Donovan yelled. "Glad ya could join us!"

Chief sauntered toward them, rubbing his belly with contentment, an expression of regal nonchalance playing upon his face. "Lunch was gooood!"

He stopped just short of the supplies Donovan and Bill had arranged on the cement floor. He stood looking down at the paint cans, sandpaper pads, tape, and other items with curiosity.

"Where did y'all go?" Jim said, expecting a good story.

"Young Joey here has *another* admirer," Chief said.

"She is an older woman to him, twenty-four. She and her roommate, they did some pot roast. It was so good. That new one ya like, Joey, ya oughtta marry. A sweet, hot girl, and she cooks like that? Not many kids today your age wanna cook."

Joey blushed. "Ah, we'll see."

"So you get these ladies to share their food with you, too, huh, Joey?" Jim shook his head.

The boy pulled his hands from his pockets and made a what-me-worry gesture, palms upward. "Well, I can't stand ta cook."

"So, you end up at their places and just outright mention you're ravenously hungry, maybe make a few puppy dog faces?" Jim said. This deceptively shy heartthrob of Cape Cod always amused him.

"Or I mention how great they cook or how I wanna taste their cooking."

"Ah, Joey, you're a man of many appetites," Jim chuckled.

The men all laughed.

"And not all of them exactly wholesome. Now, how are those supplies I got?"

"Good job," Donovan said. "Let's you and me fetch the rest outta the truck. Hey, Jimmy, you up for fishin' after work? Bill and me are goin' out a ways into the Sound again."

"Count me in, podnuh."

"Podnuh? You *are* from south Louisiana. Heard you guys saying that when I was down there in the Navy."

"Joey and Chief aren't coming?" Jim said.

"Chief has ta take his ol' lady to her night job," Bill said. "And, of course, Joey is chasin' his new dame."

"Well, Don Juan," Jim said to DaSilva. "At least you'll get a French kiss and a hot rump roast for your efforts."

"Jim, you're supposed to be a good Catholic boy!" Donovan said.

"All right, all right," Jim said. "Now, before Walter fires

us all, let's jump back to work. After we bring in the boxes, Donovan, I'll help you and Bill on the hull. Chief and Joey Casanova, y'all stick with the deck."

"Aye aye, Cap," Chief said.

Two hours later, Jim plodded up the rolling stairwell and stepped on deck. Chief and DaSilva were working away. For the next few hours, Jim helped them lay, level, and nail the replacement boards. Throughout the shop, the raspy, bluesy voice of Bob Seger resounded from the portable stereo. After Jim returned to the deck with another armful of boards, the radio died out below.

"What happened?" Chief yelled. "We neglectin' you guys down there?"

DaSilva shouted, "You know we can't work without good music!"

Bill's mischievous voice sounded below. "Hey, Swamp Thang up thar! Hey, the hard-livin' and hard-prayin' Jimmy boy!"

"You called?" Jim stood at the rail.

Donovan stared up at him, his hands on his hips. "Bill's got somethin' for ya!"

"Let's hear it!" Jim said.

The stereo kicked on. A very familiar song welled up all around him.

"Now, hah ya like that, Mistah Scoresby?" Bill called.

He looked like an old Key West beach bum with his long hair, Hawaiian shirt, and his leathery skin, red and tanned to oblivion. His blue eyes flashed like the devil's.

"Tune reminds ya of the old homeland, eh?" Donovan said.

Jim laughed just as the first verse began. He clapped his

hands a few times and smiled down at the men.

"'Born On The Bayou'... well done, guys."

Jim returned to Chief and DaSilva. "Well chosen. I love Creedence and John Fogerty. He really had the best attempt at a backwoods version of a generic south Louisiana accent."

"A'ight, professor," Chief laughed.

Jim grabbed a board from the small pile on the deck and slid it into place next to the last one they had nailed. The chorus began. Chief and DaSilva sang along. The boy, with all of his trust in the big man, held the nail in place. Chief drove it home with a few hammer swings. Jim walked over to get the next board. The guitar solo Jim loved had ceased, and his favorite verse commenced, the one about taking the fast train with his Cajun Queen to New Orleans.

For the hundredth time the verse shot a chill down Jim's spine. He held the board in place. DaSilva steadied the nails, and Chief worked the hammer. Then came the final verse. It seemed like Fogerty's appeal to a native son cast by an act of God, man's error, and his own desperation thousands of miles from his home.

Fogerty sang, "Do it... oh, get back, boy."

Jim rose to his feet. He turned, stretched, and walked across the deck for a fresh board from the pile. His eyes welled up, but for a moment.

CHAPTER TWENTY-NINE

That night, Jim returned from two hours of fishing with Bill and Donovan. Sunburned and stinking of brine, fish oil, and fish blood, Jim stumbled into his apartment and called Maureen.

"Yes, Jim, what is it?"

She was not crying. He could not think of a time when she had wept. Her voice merely held that same dull monotone, bereft of any womanly feeling or tenderness. It was as if another spirit, another soul far different from the one he had come to love their first month together, had inhabited her. He could not bear much more. He had reached near the end of his tether, yet it sounded like she might be even further along.

The next afternoon, before work ended, Jim merged from Route 3 onto Interstate 93. The wind whipped inside the truck's cab, tousling his hair. Jim stared ahead, dazed.

Even if the old man hadn't asked him to visit his daughter that Tuesday afternoon, Jim would have done so. He did miss her. But that was not it entirely. Jim knew their relationship was threatened. Maureen had regained her short fuse, that dreaded irritability. When that darker side had first cropped up, their relationship had never quite been the same. Their bond slightly weakened, Jim knew, since those first ecstatic four to six weeks of their courtship.

Yet there had been ephemeral peaks all along, as was that

extended weekend when they rode the Amtrak Acela down to New York City. This irritability, Jim guessed, revealed her unhappiness with their union, and this filled him with worry and frustration.

Jim glanced at his rear view mirror. A green Subaru tailed him in eastern Massachusetts' fashion, perhaps eight feet from his rear bumper. He accelerated by instinct, if only for a second. He realized there was a car in the leftmost lane, just in front of him, perhaps fifteen feet from his bumper. He could move over to the next lane, but then some other car would, in a matter of seconds, accelerate to ride his rear bumper.

It wasn't officially even Boston traffic yet, and it was a no-win situation. Jim cursed once, twice, then three times. He felt a touch of guilt and humor, as he glanced at the rear view mirror. The cross dangled three inches below it, a gift from his brother, fashioned by two nails fused together.

His Blackberry rang in his truck console. Jim activated the speakerphone. Maureen's angry voice shouted that she could barely hear him.

"Wait, Maureen," Jim placed the phone in his lap. He gripped the wheel with his right as he rolled up the driver's window with his left, blocking the sound of the whipping wind.

"Guess you're on your way," she said.

"You got it, *sweet thang*," Jim said. "On my way to you now."

"Sweet thang? I don't know if I've ever been called that before."

"You don't like it?" He feigned offense.

"Anyway, Jim," she sighed, "can you stop and grab me some hot cocoa on the way up?"

"Sure thing, baby," Jim said. "But you gotta—"

"*Baby*?"

"I mean, my dear."

"Okay, so I'll see you up here then? At my place?"

"If these crass, miserable drivers don't kill me first."

"Well, gotta run."

Jim replaced the Blackberry in the console and rolled down the window.

As the truck sped northward, Jim pondered what lay ahead of him that evening. Maureen's state of mind really had deteriorated in the past few weeks. Good thing he was on his way.

Yet Jim intuited that if he wanted to keep her, he would have to make that bold and unexpected move back to the city. Even if he did, he wondered, would it prove too late to salvage the relationship? He could feel her waning passion for him. And he could feel his passion for her begin to ebb, ever so slightly. In a way, he felt at times foolish when he was with her. Perhaps they really were mismatched.

Jim felt cut adrift, without sail or rudder. Looking back at his life after the onslaught of that great storm, it was more that he had awoken to discover he was piloting a ship with no means of navigation: no satellite map, no marine logs, no sextant, no constellation. All he possessed was his own wanderlust—which had brought him to his current point—and his desire to begin anew and to rebuild his life, far away from the life and the city he had lost.

His mind leaped from Maureen to her parents to his friends in Boston and Louisiana, from the job he had left in Boston to the job he might have to leave on the Cape. Yet another car tailing him at a menacing distance jerked Jim into reality. It was an apparently brand-new five series BMW. Its front bumper seemed even closer to him than the Subaru had been minutes before.

Jim felt his breath quicken. If he accelerated, he would be within ten feet of the Saab in front of him. Jim thought to switch into the middle lane, but after turning and looking over his right shoulder, this option was impossible. Next to him was a white commercial van tailgated by an Audi, tailgated in turn by a black Mercedes Benz diesel sedan damaged from a frontal fender bender.

Sweat beads emerged on his brow, chest, and on the nape of his neck. A thought gnawed at him. What would be worse, to die there on that highway due to the callous recklessness of others, or to live and see his grandfather's revamped truck totaled before his very eyes? Jim kept the same distance behind the Saab.

In the rear view mirror, he spied the driver of the BMW, a redhead with a keen squint and a striking beaklike nose. She was dressed in a dark square-shouldered blazer. She flashed her brights once, then twice.

A wave of anger surged within him. He pumped the brake twice and let the truck coast for a few seconds. The woman laid on her horn and made foul facial and hand gestures.

Amused at first, Jim began to grow angry again, with more ferocity than before. This motorist, like so many others on this road, seemed to have little regard for his life or property. Most cared only for getting to their destinations on time, or as it appeared, ahead of time.

On the verge of returning the harshest of the woman's hand

gestures, he let a dark thought enter his mind. A wreck could take out that cold witch, or at least her beautiful sedan. Then he noticed his brother's gift dangling from his rear view mirror, and he relented, smiling. Jim flipped on his right turning blinker. Seconds later, the woman behind him slowed. The lioness would at least allow him to move from her path.

Jim shot a series of feverish glances to his right. The white van slowed. The driver, a corpulent man in a v-neck t-shirt, waved impatiently for Jim to move in front of him. Jim eased his truck gradually into the middle lane. He waved to the man, who nodded ever so slightly.

Another minute passed. Jim again signaled and eventually turned his truck into an open space. He snickered. It was the rightmost lane in the highway, but he still was not free to drive at the speed limit.

His thoughts drifted from the tense drama of metro Boston's rush hour toward less stressful matters. Perhaps the old man was right. He did need to retrace his steps, to retreat to Boston, rejoin his old friends, his former life, and his enviable position at Henretty & Henretty. He would be with Maureen. He could then save the relationship.

The question presented itself: *should* he?

It seemed as though he was losing her, yet it was due to something *beyond* his control. As trite as it sounded, she had almost morphed into a completely different person. Did she still love him? She, the very one who first declared her love for him, perhaps weeks before he would have admitted those same feelings for her? What had happened?

As the road curved leftward, Jim spotted an old rusty Ford LTD stalled on the median. The rear right tire was flat. An elderly black woman stood shaking her head at it, hands on her hips.

Jim put on his right blinker and turned back to the navy blue Beetle behind him. He made a hand signal that he was moving into the median, but the man did not readily slow. Jim gestured wildly with his right arm, pointing to the median, the right blinker still clicking away.

The man slowed ever so slightly. Jim impatiently tore out of the lane onto the median and made a gradual brake. He shoved his cell phone into his pocket, grabbed his lugwrench and jack, and sprang from the truck. He jogged the few hundred feet toward the woman.

She yelled at the tire, which looked like it had been seconds away from disintegrating completely. Her eyes had misted over. She was half dejected, half irate.

"Ma'am, I've got a lugwrench and a jack here. Any spare in there?"

Her face brightened. She spoke slowly, but with a building inflection that revealed a glimmer of hope. "I *do*, sir, as a matter of fact. God bless you! I'd be so grateful if you could help me out here. Just been years since I did this. My back would give out!"

"It ain't no thing, ma'am," Jim said, smiling. "It'll just take a few minutes."

"I got the spare in my trunk, here." She turned toward the driver's door.

"Ma'am, it's best to stand away from the car. My cousin was hit after he'd pulled over. Almost killed him."

"You from Mis'sippi, Luzianna, chile?" She stepped away from the road onto the grass.

"Right on the mark, ma'am! Louisiana," Jim said. "But my cousin I mentioned, he's from Mis'sippi. How'd you know?"

"I'm from 'Bama originally—Opelika—but I know all them accents," she said with a grin. "I live up in Savin Hill now wit' mah li'l girl."

"I've gotta get that trunk there open. Can I pop it from inside?"

"It don't work, chile. You gotta use that key. It's in the ignition there." She pointed a gnarled finger at the car.

Jim opened the passenger's door and slid into the car. His nose caught a faint scent of mildew. Wedged into the odometer was a prayer card that showed a bearded black Christ, smiling pleasantly in his white robes. Jim thought of Mount Zion and smiled. He pulled the keys from the ignition and leapt from the car. After shutting the passenger's door, he jogged over to the trunk. Inside were several old TV Guide magazines, various tools, and that mildew smell.

"You got a leak in here, ma'am," Jim said.

He found the tire jack and the lug wrench and placed them a few feet behind the car. He pulled the spare tire from the trunk bed and placed it on the ground. The trunk shut with a soft click. After he placed the jack under the right frame rail of the car, just in front of the rear right wheel, he loosened the lug nuts. Jim worked the lever until the tire was well off the pavement.

Extracting the tire was no chore. The hubcap was long gone, the rim beneath rusted. After a scant few minutes Jim had taken the tire clean off. He worked the spare into place and tightened the lugnuts with the wrench.

"I tell ya, been a long time since ah seen one o' them trucks, chile!" the old lady said.

"I restored it. It was my Granddaddy's." Jim said. "I can't believe I didn't introduce myself. Jim Scoresby."

"I'm Ms. Mae Pratt." She gave a brief wave as he worked the wrench. "You're quite a nice young man, gonna make some woman a fine husband. You have a real good mutha, ah can tell, an' she raised you right."

"That makes me feel very good. You've got a cell phone, ma'am? You might call your friends and family and tell 'em you got slowed down a bit 'cause of that tire."

"No, suh, it's fine. You helped me so fast, I'll be on the road in no time."

"A thought just occurred to me," Jim said as he lowered the tire completely back onto the pavement by working the jack. He tugged twice, hard, on the newly installed tire.

The old lady's face betrayed a slight unease.

He stood and opened the trunk again and placed the mutilated flat inside and gently shut the door. "Easy part's gettin' that tire off and on."

"Ahh. I getcho drift." She nodded. "Hard part's gettin' back on that road."

"Exactly! Those scoundrels'll run someone over just as soon as slow down for 'em!"

"Oh, this ol' Granny knows how ta hit that gas, you bess believe!" Ms. Pratt said.

Jim stamped his foot once in delight and laughed. "Just what I wanted to hear, ma'am! It's the only way. I mean, just look."

Jim gestured with an open hand, palm up, toward the slowest lane of traffic. Cars zoomed by in a whirlwind, just a mere fifteen feet from them.

"It's almost like," he yelled over the whirr and zoom of the traffic, "even that slow lane's trying to qualify for the Daytona 500!"

She reached out her hand. He shook it, and she held it for a few seconds. "Thanks again, Jim, for all ya hep," she said. "God bless ya, Jim. Have a blessed day."

He handed her the keys and smiled. "You, too, Ms. Pratt," Jim said. "Just please give me your word you're gonna hit that gas and join that 'slower' lane there, when you can get in! I'll gesture for the oncoming cars to slow once you swerve in."

"Oh, you'll see." She wagged a finger at him, eyeing him knowingly, then stepped quickly around the car, and entered the driver's side.

Jim followed and shut the door for her.

She rolled the window down manually. "You may wanna go step in nat grass yonduh, clean o' dis vehicle," she laughed.

"Watch them in your mirror. Don't trust 'em to slow much!" He jogged off behind the car and then hooked left into the grass.

Ms. Pratt started the ignition. She let the car idle there, her left blinker on. Jim looked back at her as the unending column of cars passed by.

During a strange, momentary reprieve in the traffic in the rightmost lane, Jim motioned to the old woman. The Ford LTD had already lurched forward, its tires churning, leaving a thick dark strip on the median and more than a few flying pebbles. The car tore diagonally onto the interstate, its old Detroit motor roaring. The LTD finally straightened, holding its course in the rightmost lane, as it accelerated down the interstate.

A red Geo Metro appeared around the bend, coming at a steady pace, perhaps seventy miles per hour, but there was no threat. Just as Ms. Pratt disappeared around the granite outcrop at the bend, she waved. It was for him.

Jim picked up the jack and lugwrench and strolled toward his truck. He shook his head, smiling. The moment had lifted him and hearkened back to his father's father and a land far away. His Granddaddy Scoresby had attended Auburn University, Class of 1927. It was called Alabama Polytechnic Institute at the time. The town of Auburn bordered Opelika, Ms. Pratt's hometown. Small world, indeed.

Jim laughed as he brought out his key and turned it in the ignition of his Granddaddy's engineer's truck. He laughed so hard that tears welled at the corners of his eyes.

The scene he had just witnessed ranked among the funniest occurrences of his life. Ms. Pratt must have been in her late seventies to early eighties. He loved the look in her eye when she assured him "this granny knows how ta hit tha gas" and then minutes later had torn onto the interstate like a stock car driver shooting from a pit stop onto the track. He could never forget the rusty LTD as it lurched diagonally onto the interstate and then corrected itself, wobbling as the engine roared louder and the tires shed smoke and black trails. Yes, even Maureen would smile and maybe even laugh at his new tale.

He stared back over his left shoulder at the oncoming cars. Minutes later, he swerved into the rightmost lane, accelerating. At sixty-five miles per hour, he held the gas steady. Soon the skyline of Boston rose in his sights. He only had to grab Maureen's Mass General parking card and leave the truck in the hospital parking garage on Cambridge Street. One stop for cocoa in the package store on the walk up to Louisburg Square, and he would be with her again.

Did she feel the same excitement and anticipation? Or did she feel any dread? Jim sighed, as he recognized the same conflicted jumble in his own heart.

Chapter Thirty

Jim plodded up Charles Street, advancing his feet over and over in a kind of cruel staccato. To passersby, he probably looked like he was some fascist soldier goose-stepping his way up Beacon Hill, but it did not matter. She had done it again. As he threaded his way through the stream of pedestrians, clutching the small box of overpriced Swiss Miss hot chocolate, he turned her words over and over in his mind.

When she had opened the townhouse door fifteen minutes before, as the truck idled behind him, she looked him fully in the face as he stood there, one step below her.

"That took a while" was all she had said, driving in the knife to its very hilt.

Jim had opened his mouth to speak, but he had found that he could not. She had passed him the parking garage ID card, with no expression marking her face. He sensed the very faintest glimmer of a smile there, but he could not be sure.

Nor did it matter. She had done it again. She could not help betraying her true nature. Maureen was incorrigible, truly spoiled to the core. What man could change her?

He had left work early, sped the entire way, and stopped for the hot cocoa she requested. That last task cost him perhaps five, six minutes at the package store. What about the detour to help an elderly lady in her time of need? No more than ten minutes.

What would give? Even if he mentioned the old lady, and Maureen was amused, would she apologize for her remark? If he and Maureen were barreling along together in his truck and he stopped for Ms. Pratt, would not have Maureen still complained?

He feared he would make a massive mistake in resuming work at the stock brokerage. All the peace and joy he had found on the Cape and in that shop... was it no career improvement but simply a vacation drawing to a close? A profound sadness built within him.

Yet, moments later, Jim began to breathe easier. On his left, he passed one of his old favorites, the Sevens Pub.

He must move back to Boston. It was too early to break it off with Maureen. He had to move back to give her one final chance. The distance had become unbearable to her. To stay on the Cape, he would lose his girlfriend, and then he would be left employed by her father. How awkward.

He vowed he would keep pushing through. Perhaps she would love him more after he made the move back. He could just ignore her comments and her recent lack of affection. Following the move, he could judge her in a new light.

At least he could be with his Boston friends. That much was sure.

Resuming life in Boston, he would still see the Commodore and Kathleen. He would sail quite often. He just needed to unwind, to enjoy this evening and night in the city.

As he lumbered up the townhouse steps, Jim swore to abstain from argument or decisions. He took a deep breath and rang the bell. After ten seconds, steps approached on the foyer's creaky hardwood boards. The locks were unbolted. The door jerked open.

Maureen let it swing wide as she stepped back and caught the door in her hand. "There you are."

At least she smiled.

"Don't just stand out there looking at me. Let's make some of that cocoa."

Jim stepped into the cool dimness of the foyer. Maureen grabbed the box from his hand. He shut the door behind them and followed her through the hallway. There was no kiss or hug. He still felt unsettled from her remarks thirty minutes before about his tardiness, and his frustration in turn had irritated her. She started down the hall and he followed her. Ah, he thought, she simply had to be unjustly irritated at his justified irritation...

"So, how are you feeling?" Jim grabbed her left elbow and spun her like a top into his arms. Her eyes widened in surprise as he jerked her toward him with one hand on her elbow and the other pressing the flat of her upper back. Jim kissed her flush on the lips, tasting their strawberry balm.

Maureen shook her head and sighed, but her eyebrows rose as if she were impressed over his acrobatic display of passion. "Guess I forgot to kiss, huh?" she said as he looked down at her.

"You did! What did *I* do wrong?"

Smiling, she turned and broke from him, storming down the hallway toward the kitchen. "I'm absolutely craving some cocoa."

"All right then," he plodded behind her with a tired gait. "I could use a cup, no lie."

He collapsed in one of the kitchen's high-backed wooden chairs. Jim stretched out his legs and groaned. It wasn't exactly a recliner.

"What was that for?" Maureen poured water into each mug and placed them in the microwave. She set the time and then turned toward Jim.

"Just needin' ta stretch out those legs!"

"Miss me?" she came around behind his chair and put her hands on his shoulders. "Jim?"

"What do you think, sweetness?"

"Just checking, sailor." She laid her cheek against his as she hugged him.

"I've been doin' some hard thinking. I've gotta move back up to the city."

A moment of odd silence rose and filled every square inch of the kitchen.

"Are you serious?" She swung around in front of him. She looked down at him, her lips parted. Her eyes and white smile widened by the second.

"You are moving back?" she whispered. "When?" Maureen seemed partially elated, her mouth opening into a smile, and peculiarly, somewhat flustered, her nostrils flaring and her brow furrowing. She pulled out a chair from the table, dragged it within feet of his to face him, and sank into it. "What prompted this decision?"

Jim allowed his gaze to drift along the crown molding. "What really precipitated this was... over lunch yesterday, your father flat-out permitted me to cut out of work early and come see you."

"I love him," she said. "Oh, Daddy."

"He's open to me moving back to the city. He said he'd foot the bill, the moving costs, all that. He's sincerely worried about you."

Her eyebrows lifted with excitement. "So... what did you say?"

"I told him I'd consider it. Actually, I was in shock. I also felt awkward, because I was turning beet-ass red in that colonial inn and he just caught me off—"

"Colonial inn? In Osterville, downtown on Main?" Her excitement faded as her face turned downcast with a cloud of worry, almost horror. "The *Bartley Inn*?"

"That a bad thing?"

"Did you meet an ancient woman there? And her son, who runs the place?"

"Indeed I did."

"*Shippey*," she mumbled, her eyes staring past him into the wall.

Jim studied her. She held her chin in one hand, pondering with deep solemnity. Her eyes carried a look of surprise, fused with a sort of discontent.

"What is it? Can I help?" he said.

"Behold one of our family secrets."

He paused.

Maureen jerked up from her chair and walked around the kitchen island. She carried the mugs from the microwave over to the table. After she set one on the placemat beside Jim, Maureen sat again in the chair feet across from him, cradled her mug in her hands, gazing down at her feet.

"Tom Shippey. My half-brother. When Daddy was still in the Naval Academy... he... he slept with this Osterville firecracker by the name of Gwen Shippey. She was quite a looker back in the day. Anyway, I think she set Daddy up. He could've ignored her. But he sent them money every month, from his navy pay—even from his own father."

"Does the whole town of Osterville know? And the guys in the shop?"

Maureen placed her cocoa on the table and placed her reddening face in her hands. "Most of them do know, yes. Daddy used to see Ms. Shippey, or Gwen, as he calls her, during the summers and on holidays home from Annapolis. One night, after a dance on the Cape, she just flat out seduced him. Daddy always assumed Tom was his kid, even though I guess technically back then one couldn't know for sure."

"Oh," Jim said.

Maureen was still sunk into the same stance at the table, her elbows on her kneecaps, her chair turned to face him. Her eyelids grew heavy, came down. She looked as if the subject at hand had already exhausted her.

"Tom Shippey really is his son. You can even see the resemblance. After Daddy retired from the Navy, he settled here in the East. He took over his father's trading firm, spent quality time with Tom, and met and married my mother. He also loans books to Tom. They go sailing and grab lunch."

"Walter gave that book to Tom at the inn, after lunch," Jim said.

"They have a kind of book club. They'll recommend books to each other, see a movie together at the cinema, stuff like that. Daddy feels guilty for not being there much when Tom was young, and later when he was at BC. He wants to make up for lost time."

"That's why the Commodore has that Boston College pennant in his garage?"

"Many of Dad's siblings and cousins were Eagles."

"So how do you feel about their friendship?" Jim leaned forward in his chair, sipping the hot chocolate.

"I should mention how much you really sound like a shrink, Jim." Maureen looked up from her kneecaps into his eyes. Then she reached over and seized her mug of hot cocoa, causing it to slosh a bit over the rim.

"Sorry, Maur," Jim mumbled.

"Actually, it's kind of complicated. I feel above all very happy he didn't just *desert* the boy, he supported him all along. So many men these days would do far less. But I don't think I can ever completely *like* Gwen Shippey. She was just a young hussy then, but still. And at the same time, it is quite strange, the whole thing. I mean, that's my *father*. I always used to feel uneasy, even angry. Like first Gwen tricked him. And that her son had a kind of emotional access to Daddy that... well, it just feels kind of *awkward* that my dad has an 'other family life.' As if having a very old father wasn't really *different* already."

"I understand completely." Jim leaned forward out of his seat and draped his arms around her.

"You *can't* understand."

Jim leaned back. He threaded the fingers of his hands together, prayer-like, and looked at his feet. "So, Maureen, why didn't you tell me all this earlier?"

"It's not easy to disclose. And I never dated a guy long enough to tell him. Anyway, Daddy really nurtures Tom's intellectual life. He visits Tom's kids from time to time as well. I think Mom always trusted that Daddy wouldn't mess around since Ms. Shippey was married for much of her life—and so old—and Mom was so young and beautiful and Daddy just doesn't do infidelity."

"Crazy story. But glad you told me," Jim said. He leaned forward and took her in his arms. He tried to kiss her mouth but she turned her head at the last second.

"What is it?" he laughed.

"Lemme go!" she shot back.

"Why've you been doing that lately, Maur? Just lost that lovin' feelin'?" He stood, shook his head, and walked over to the kitchen's bay window which overlooked the small yet elegant courtyard with its ivy-covered walls and its statue of a cherub bearing a platter.

"I wish I knew *what* was wrong with me," she said.

He walked back around the table toward her. Maureen paused for a second, rose to her feet and stepped boldly toward him.

Jim let himself sink into the cool cerulean blue irises of her eyes. Deep inside was something he had not seen before, neither love nor lust. But he was in no mood for conjecture or speculation. When she leaned forward and put her hands on his shoulder blades, and pulled him toward her, and when she thrust her hot mouth onto his, there was suddenly something more interesting. There was an odd shyness, a timid apprehension, as if she had never kissed him before. But it was almost as if there was an anger there.

They began to kiss passionately. In seconds they had torn their clothes off and collapsed together in a panting, writhing mass onto the kitchen floor. Minutes later they lay together on the cold marble tiles, sweating and in the nude, their breath gradually slowing.

Maureen raised her chin from his chest, and her eyes met

his. Once again that peculiar expression filled her gaze. Inside, there was something… dead. "Tonight I think I want to sleep alone."

Chapter Thirty-One

Wednesday morning arrived with a fierce rainstorm out of the east. Jim sat in his office, perusing the file on the *John Paul Jones*. He did not sip, but instead quaffed his morning coffee, as he struggled to pull himself fully from slumber.

Raindrops pelted the metal roof of the warehouse. Despite the closed door, hammering and men's voices down by the schooner reached his ears. He raised the mug once more to his lips. Three knocks rapped at the door. Jim nearly spilled his coffee. He wiped his lips with the back of his hand and set the mug down on the roll top desk.

"Come in," Jim said.

"Open sesame," said a familiar voice. In stepped Walter, his face and shirt damp from the rain. He carried an umbrella and a raincoat.

"Hey, Commodore!"

"Lemme hang these babies up." The old man walked toward the clothing rack on the opposite wall.

He draped them over the hooks and turned toward Jim with an energetic grin. "How's my man doing this morning?" Walter eased into the chair a few feet from him. "Long drive last night, eh? You look a bit haggard, son."

Jim leaned back in his chair, his limbs feeling heavier than normal.

"The drive wasn't for the faint of heart. But it was worth it, seeing Maureen."

"Let me guess. She wanted you all to take the taxi around?"

"Not quite," Jim mumbled, shaking his head, chuckling, while giving one slow blink.

"Anyway, I wanted to pop in, chat a minute."

The old man stared hard at the ceiling. "Have you given any thought to whether you'll stay on here at Melville or head back to my Boston brokerage? We haven't yet hired your replacement. So I thought I'd check on you. If you haven't decided, I understand."

"I've arrived at a decision."

"Oh, yes?" Walter raised an eyebrow.

"I... I've gotta move back, sir," Jim shook his head, placing his hands, prayer-like, over his lips. He stared at the gray carpet beneath Walter's boat shoes. "I just *have* to. To keep Maureen, I've got to make the move. Another instance where I didn't finish what I started. But at least I will finish the schooner and get her in the water before I move."

Could I have finished the task under the supervising eye of my own father? Jim thought. Perhaps not. The irony of it! Perhaps blood was not always thicker than water. If only his father were more like Walter: encouraging, flexible, understanding.

"You're doing what you have to do, Jimmy. I'd do the same thing. But that doesn't mean this old captain won't miss his best lieutenant." Walter gave a wink and a quick nod.

Jim caught the sadness in the old man's eyes.

"Ya know, Jimmy, I woulda liked to have taught you more about the sea, about boats. We were just getting started."

"I loved it. It doesn't have to be the end."

"I hope ya make it down here some weekends to brave the waters again."

"Of course, I will," Jim said as he felt the pang in his gut. Would his phobia always be with him?

"We can sail out to the Vineyard. And Nantucket. Anyway, lest I forget, when this boat's done, we're gonna flood the drydock, ensure she's seaworthy, get her inspected by the Coast Guard, dock her in Hyannis. Best dock for this old dame is really over there. While I'm doing all this, look into an apartment in the city. I promised you I'd pay the deposit and first month's rent."

"Why, Walter, thanks again, you—"

"I conceived the idea to bring you down here into all this. Maureen was a big part of it, too. We gotta do what's right for her, and for you guys as a couple."

"Walter... I really, really appreciate that."

"And I want you to know, Jim." The old man's face elongated with growing solemnity. "You've really been struggling. You *are* far away from your family. You've had to uproot yourself, make new friends, a new career. You've had a trying time with Maureen. She's put herself through a rough time with the distance and all. And son, you and I... we both bear the scars of battle. Me from Korea and 'Nam. You from that freakish hurricane. I can see it in ya. Among other things, the thousand yard stare. I know that look. I can only imagine how what you lived through down there shook you up. With the old musician, your friend, on your roof. Just know the Henrettys are your family. You're like a son to me."

The old man's sincerity had reached the very depths of Jim's heart. In a way it was embarrassing: it was so sincere and rare and heartfelt, so much and so quickly.

Jim cleared his throat. "Thanks for all this, Walter." He stood, but Walter was already standing, grinning proudly, his hand outstretched. Jim gave it a firm shake, and then pulled closer to the old man, giving him a warm embrace.

"Don't mention it, son." The old man clapped a hand on his shoulder, then turned and walked toward the wall. He collected his umbrella and raincoat and then stopped at the door and turned. "Jack Spaulding's throwing one of his famous cocktail parties tonight. I'm heading there myself with Kathleen. His place at 7:30 in Chatham. Jack specifically mentioned that I invite you. I can give you the directions, or you could ride with us."

"If I have to work late, I'll take my truck. I'll keep you posted."

"Good luck today. And we'll talk soon to solidify moving plans." The old man clicked his tongue once in his teeth, opened the office door, and closed it behind him. For most of the last few minutes, Jim hoped the old man would cease his sentimental talk, yet now that he had departed, Jim felt guilt, as he had neglected to fully disclose his appreciation for all Walter had done. Jim had lacked the immediacy and perhaps the bravery of living in the moment, to thoroughly thank the man who had laid bare his fatherly concern and love.

It was not the first time he had failed to live fully in the present and to give proper thanks. His own father, as intense as he could be, and Freddy—they were now out of his reach—and Jim had never truly shown them the right gratitude, had never truly lived as fully as he could have when he was in their presence...

Jim swiveled in his chair until he regained his previous position at the roll top desk. He looked down at the open file, lost in thought. Spaulding's party would undoubtedly be a good time. The lavish parties at the young man's seaside Chatham mansion had been the talk of the Cape for years, according to Kathleen and Walter. Maureen would probably regret foregoing this one. Jim hoped Natasha wouldn't bait him again.

Jim stood, stretched his limbs, and ambled down the stairwell into the shop. This time, the men were playing the Allman Brothers. "Gents, I thought you'd have on some more local music, maybe Aerosmith."

Bill squinted at him. "I guess I started ta wax sentimental you weren't here."

"Sure," Jim said. "Ohh sweet Mel-liss-saa!"

"I saw these guys perform in Cambridge when I was a young squirt." Bill tossed his long, straight blond hair across his forehead. "Never will forget that night. Skydog Duane was with 'em, ya know."

"That's when they were at their peak," Jim said. "Bill, I'm movin' back to Beantown."

"Ya just started here! You were learnin' so much about all of this! You were havin' a great time, right?"

"Ol' Commodore said the very same thing up there in the office a few minutes ago."

"So you dropped the bomb on him just now, eh?" A concerned, almost flustered look had spread across Bill's face.

"Walter offered me my old gig at the securities brokerage. Maureen's been taking all this distance pretty hard. It was a bold move, coming down here, but she found it was too much. If I want to keep her... well, I have to move back. Luckily, I get my old job back."

Bill peered sharply at him, skepticism emitting from the beady, sun-closed, light blue eyes. "But are ya sure you're ready to get back into that line of work, Jimmy? Wasn't that exactly what you were tryin' to get *away* from? And the city life and the whole Boston 'harshness' thing, as you call it?"

With that statement, Jim's breath quickened as he shuffled from foot to foot. "I moved here because she helped me land this position, but now I've got to sacrifice. Maureen thought she'd be able to endure the distance."

Bill nodded, but seemed crestfallen. "Ah, Jimmy... between you and me and the man in the moon, as you and I've grown to be pals... it's gonna be *no* easy task pleasin' that girl. I been working here many years. I seen her since she was a little girl. But what I'm sayin' is you're just makin' a short-term decision. How is Maureen Henretty..."

Bill dropped his voice to a whisper and glanced about, as if poised to release a long-guarded secret. "How is this girl ever gonna be satisfied with *anything*? She's spoiled rotten to the *core*. Ruined. Over the years she hasn't gotten any better. You really haven't wrapped ya head around who she truly is. When you first fall in love with someone, you see only what that person wants you to see. Mixed with what *you* want to see. As the days go by, the mist lifts and you start to see the real person. She *is* a looker, but she's gonna put you through hell. As if you ain't been through enough o' that with that damn storm."

"I see what you're saying, Bill," Jim paused, hands in his pockets, his eyes boring a hole into the roof. "And I can tell you care. You're a true friend."

"I did bust ya chops a lot. Some of us do that 'cause we're high and mighty smart asses. But others do it 'cause they like ya."

"I have to move back to the city. Eventually, though, I'll need to keep my eyes peeled for an opening out of the phone-brokering thing. It ain't for me. I know it in my heart, despite my skill at it."

"And if you can't put that princess in her place, you gotta get out. She'll run you ragged."

Jim couldn't help but give a shaky hum at his friend's last line. "I hear you." He put a hand on Bill's shoulder. "Some of my buddies back in Boston tell me the same."

"You should tell the men here about your move now. But they're gonna be blindsided."

Jim turned and walked toward the boat. The hole in the hull was mere hours from being completely closed. Then the priming and painting would commence.

As he stepped toward the boat, he spotted Chief and DaSilva working on the deck. Jim hoped apprehension and embarrassment didn't appear on his face. He came upon the stereo on the table and switched it off.

Jim stopped perhaps fifteen feet from the hull. Bill stood just behind. Donovan stood at a worktable nearby, measuring a board he was about to feed into the table saw.

"Gents, your attention please!" Jim called. "Guys, I've got some news. Y'all will take it as good or bad."

"Lemme guess," Donovan shouted. "Mohegan Sun and every casino in Connecticut has barred Chief for life. And DaSilva has five different women calling the shop, waiting outside ta kill him!"

"That all may be true," Jim said, unable to stifle a smile. "But I've got something that's actually *unexpected*."

"Then shoot, Jim," Chief said.

Jim glanced back at Bill. The old hippie stood with his forearms crossed across his chest, their scars of skin cancer surgery clearly visible. Bill's sweaty hair was swept back from his forehead. On his sunburned face was a look of hurt, mixed with a trace of pity.

"I have to give up my position here at Melville to move back to Boston. I'm getting my old job back. Not because I want to leave. Frankly, I like where I am just fine. But if I don't move closer to Maureen, and spend a lot more time with her, we're finished."

"Wait! What?" Chief said, placing his palms against the sides of his head. "Oh, brother."

"You *just* got here, Jim. You're finishing your *first* project!" DaSilva threw his hands apart above his head in a wild gesture.

"Ah, Princess Maureen. That explains it." Donovan said. "Been puttin' the heat on ya ta move back, huh?"

"I've... I've got to," Jim said.

"Ahhhhhhhh jeesh!" Donovan buried his face in his hands. "That girl."

Jim sucked in his lower lip and looked away.

"You'll have completed one great project," Bill pointed up at the schooner. "You should be proud. The *John Paul Jones*. We're almost there, man. Maybe one day more and we can get her in the water where she belongs."

"If you decide to come back," Chief said, his words dribbling out, "Walter probably will give you back your position."

"Yeah, Jimmy," Bill said. "Even if you and Maureen ever went kaput, I wager the old man would let you work here again. He loves you."

"You just moved here, though," DaSilva said. "You're gonna haul your stuff all the way back to Boston?"

"I'm really gonna miss all y'all. Maybe my best time in New England yet. Anyway, I won't serve as any more of a distraction. I'm going back up to the office. Then I'll help with the deck."

"Looks like we finish later today, early tomorrow," Chief said.

"Two days early. Sweet," Jim said. He traversed the shop and ascended the stairwell, feeling cut to his very marrow. As he opened the door, he looked back. The men had not moved from where they had stood. They stared back at him in silence, each with a serious mien befitting a funeral, the eyes of Bill and Donovan drooping with gloom.

"We're gonna miss ya, ya swamp-dwellin' Rebel bastahd!" Bill shouted, then cackled.

As the office door swung closed, Jim laughed so hard he could feel his face crimsoning over. Then tears blurred his vision.

He punched in the code and entered his apartment, then shut the door behind him. In the bathroom, astride each side of the faucet, stood empty longnecks, pointing upward like rifle barrels. He turned on the cold water. Cupping his hands as he leaned over, he scooped water onto his face, as if he struggled to further awaken into a life increasingly, after that morning last August, as strange and unpredictable and illusory as a dream.

Could he be the very person who survived days on a roof of a flooded house? Who nearly expired from exhaustion while swimming for insulin and water for his dying friend?

He was living and flourishing in many ways based on abundant, newfound luck. He had chanced to meet Walter, and thus Maureen, and both brokerages. His life had shot off on a completely new trajectory since that late August day. It was surely no nightmare, just almost... not real... and apparently something over which he had little control. As if he were on a well-provisioned pleasure yacht, yet without any navigation tools. He was cruising along, though by his own use of dead reckoning...

Chapter Thirty-Two

Jim slowed Betty Sue to a roll as he squinted through the dying light at Farragut Drive's mansions, fences, and gates. "Twenty-four...twenty-four...twenty-four Farrugut Drive." He spotted a massive black wrought-iron gate between two large brick pillars. One displayed a faded bronze plaque bearing the number "24."

Jim turned onto the black cobblestone drive and stopped beside the metal box. He punched in the key code. "Ten twenty seven zero four." The wrought-iron fence slid open. He eased onto the accelerator. "Ten twenty-seven zero four," he repeated.

Then he had it. October twenty seventh, two thousand and four, the day the Boston Red Sox clinched the World Series after an almost nine-decade drought. He knew Jack Spaulding to be a die-hard fan.

He caught his first glimpse of the house. Jack Spaulding's estate was truly an impressive monument to the magnitude of his forebears' fortune and culture. Its majestic gray Corinthian columns, stucco facade, three stories, and granite rocks sprawled across a well-groomed lawn resembled some Gothic Revival cliffside mansion on Newport's Bellevue Avenue. Several of the Spauldings lived together in this palace. By the sheer size of it, he now understood why.

A young valet approached him with a smile. "Hey, sir, nice ride!"

"Thanks, my man. My grandpa's ol' wheels. I guess you'd take it from here?"

"Yes, sir. Or you can park it yourself."

"No offense, but I'll take you up on the self-park thing. I prize this ol' girl more than all my possessions. If I let you have her, I won't be able to relax inside."

"Okay sir, if you could park behind that gray Porsche..."

Jim eased the truck farther up the drive. Several guests had spilled out onto the front lawn. They sipped drinks, smoked, chatted, and laughed away. One of them, a leggy young brunette with a jaw-length bob and a black cocktail dress, studied him as she sipped her martini.

Jim veered halfway off the drive onto the grass, stopping a few feet behind the Porsche. He rolled up his driver's window and alighted from the truck, pulling his freshly laundered seersucker blazer with him. Jim donned the sportcoat, shut and locked the door, then walked toward the main house.

The woman in black appeared with six other guests, all elegantly dressed. Two looked to be in their twenties or thirties, four of them middle-aged or older. They chatted and gestured his way, a few drinking and puffing their cigarettes.

Jim caught one of his favorite scents: burning charcoal. Then there arose a certain melody—a clarinet, a trumpet. Jazz. Just a few feet before the front porch, the seven guests moved their stare from him to his truck far behind him.

"Now that truck brings me back in time, young man!" said a tall, white-haired man of perhaps sixty. Dressed in a pressed yellow dress shirt and white slacks, he held a cigarette in debonair fashion a few inches before his face. He pulled his eyebrows upwards in an exaggerated gesture. "Those are hard to come by these days!"

"That thing was pulled right from the set of *American Graffiti*," said a twenty-something man next to the older man. "Better yet, maybe *Sounder* or *Forrest Gump*."

The young man, holding his cigarette down by his hip, flicked the ash onto the grass. His wavy brown bangs hung into his eyes. The face seemed pinched into a sort of sardonic, tart expression, the mouth turned slightly downward in a grimace, the nostrils stretching with contempt, the narrowed eyes hinting at the ivory-white and hazel within. "And the suit's from *Gump*, too!"

"Hey, nice threads, Rhett Butler," said the young woman in black. The woman ran him up and down with a leering smile, her face slightly tilted. Her sly, lynx-like quality increased and her green eyes sparkled as she said, "We know who you are, Jim Scoresby. We've heard about you."

"Good things? Bad things?" Jim held his hands out at his sides, palms up, in expectation, as he climbed the steps to the porch.

"Only good things. So far," the older man chuckled.

A fifty-something redhead, clad in a knee-length green dress, flanked him. Next to her stood two men, their necks and faces and shins deeply tanned, their hair half-bleached golden by the sun. A slightly ruffled, windswept look characterized them, these men with dress shorts and slightly wrinkled, untucked polo shirts, their Oakley sunglasses bound around their necks with elastic cords.

"You dashing young man, come and let us meet you." The dapper white-haired gentleman brought his arm around the shoulder of the red-haired woman. With his other arm, he motioned with his cigarette for Jim to approach. "Don't worry," the man added, "we won't beat you up too badly."

Jim flashed a smile, cast a quick glance at the young woman, and finished with a nod to the old man. "How are y'all today?" he said. "I'm Jim Scoresby. I work for Walter Henretty."

"You work for Maureen Henretty, too, if you date her," the girl deadpanned, a faint tinge of disgust evident in her face.

The older gentleman put out his hand. "Ryland Spaulding. Nice to meet you. My son and Walter both sing your praises. Now welcome to my abode. This is my wife, Susan."

Jim nodded and shook their hands. "Senator. Mrs. Spaulding."

Susan Spaulding gave a faint smile and watched her guest with her large brown eyes.

"You know, I was really just in the state legislature. So, Jim," Senator Spaulding said, "on the other side of me here is Brianna Bradford."

"Great-great great-great great-great great-great great-great great-great great-granddaughter of Governor Bradford," Susan Spaulding added with a slight edge.

"Governor Bradford of the Massachusetts Bay Colony," Jim said. "That's quite a lineage."

"Something like that," Brianna smiled slyly, almost deviously, emitting a purely feline aura. Holding a lit cigar, she extended her free hand, slender and smallish. "If you ask me, Rhett, he was just another chauvinistic, homophobic Christian Crusader."

Jim laughed.

"So you're up here from New Orleans?" Brianna said.

"Yes, indeed," Jim said, a bit vacantly. His eyes drifted down to her dress, slit up the side. "I relocated to New England last September fifteenth."

"Wow. You got washed out?"

"Somethin' like that." Jim snapped his fingers and pointed down at her hand. "How's the cigar?"

"And Jim," Senator Spaulding said, "these two rogues next to me: this is Bob Kimball and Rich Boylan, friends of mine. We do a lot of sailing, fishing. A little golfing, too. We're out there so often, these guys could impersonate steamed lobsters for Halloween."

"Well, they wear their sunburns proudly," Jim shook their hands. "They earned 'em."

"Would you like a drink or something to munch on?" Susan Spaulding said. "There is a load of food out behind the house. Jack and Natasha are inside watching the Sox game. Or you can hang out with us here."

"I'll start by saying hello to Jack and Natasha, maybe grab me a drink," Jim said. He nodded and waved at the group as he walked toward the French doors. Partygoers stood just inside the windows, chatting and cradling their drinks.

"I hope you've caught that Red Sox fever," Bob Kimball said. "If you haven't, you should watch an inning or two in there."

"I haven't got the fever yet, but I'm getting into all the old traditions," Jim said. "And I love Fenway Park. A storied, fascinating ol' place."

"Good to hear!" said Rich Boylan, the other horribly sunburned, disheveled sailor standing next to Senator Spaulding. "Just whatever you do, don't become a Yankees fan!"

"Yes, twenty-first century Rhett Butler," Brianna said.

"Would you really want to become a *Yankee*?"

Jim threw his head back and laughed. He took the remaining few steps and opened the French door.

The rather spacious sitting room contained a group of adults of all ages. Several turned to watch him. Some sat, some stood, some spoke with half-inebriated voices but all conversed, holding their beers, martinis, glasses of wine, and mixed drinks. In the center of the room was a rectangular cloth-covered table, heavily laden with cheese, dips, baskets of chips, and other appetizers.

Jim threaded his way between the sitting and standing guests. He caught a few expected words, "seersucker," "Louisiana," "Katrina," "Maureen" and "Walter." The next room turned out to be a considerably larger living room of high ceilings, dark wooden walls of bookshelves, and a deep brown oak floor. A vast crowd stood in this room, filling it with their din.

Even louder sounds emanated from the titanic flat-screen television. The Red Sox were embroiled in a fifth inning skirmish with the Tampa Bay Devil Rays in Fenway Park. As the Red Sox pitcher neared the mound, the few guests on the Victorian couches, and the crowd assembled in a semicircle around them, erupted into a burst of whistles, cheers, clapping, and shouts, a fierce audio volley of passion and pride. In Louisiana, Jim had only seen such a display at LSU football games.

A group had amassed against the rear of the couches. As this group whistled and shouted, its crescendo built ahead of Beckett's pitch. Jim snickered upon spotting Natasha in the crowd. Jack's typically composed face contorted with passion as he screamed at the television.

At the opposite side of the room, a cluster of guests had

congregated around a long, rectangular table. When Jim reached this group, he recognized no one. Where were Walter and Kathleen? Walter had phoned hours ago to say they were about to depart, and Jim told him he was still waylaid at work.

Jim veered around a young couple and stepped up to the table, laden with caviar-smothered crostini, jumbo shrimp, remoulade sauce, crabcakes, escargot, chips and various dips, olives, and other hors d'oeuvres. Standing behind the table was a man with thinning white hair combed back on his head and attired in a white button down shirt, black bow tie and black trousers. His eyes were large and solemn. A tiny American flag pin hung on his shirt's right chest pocket, and the left chest pocket held a small nameplate that read "Joseph." He opened an Amstel Light longneck for a young blond-haired man and attempted to uncork a bottle of white wine.

"Yeees, gooood. Almooost there. I know it's really hard for you but it's not that hard, know what I mean?" said the young man, still clad in his corporate pinstripes.

The old man's cheeks flushed a mottled, unhealthy red. His gaze fell tableward and he scrambled to pierce the cork and push down the arms of the corkscrew. The harder he tried, the more apparent his anxiety. The wet, chilled bottle slipped in his half-gnarled hands.

"Damn, man. Wow. Here, let... let me do it," the young man motioned with his fingers to hand over the bottle.

Jim's eyes bulged and his heart surged as the bartender surrendered the bottle and corkscrew to the young man. Just for a moment, the man's bloodshot, slightly watering eyes rolled to meet Jim's fierce stare. Then the wounded eyes, with the wounded spirit behind them, fixed back onto the table.

His hand started to shake, and he tried to hide it by folding his black hand-cloth.

The young man's face evinced physical exertion and disgust as he finally worked the cork from the bottle. He sighed as he poured the wine into a glass. "See... not too hard... in actuality." His tone turned nasty as he poured the wine to within three inches of the rim of the tall clear glass.

"You forgot somethin', bud," Jim said in a soft voice. He seized the wineglass from the table, and without spilling it, brought it close to his chest. Jim forced his face into a tender expression as he politely nodded his head.

"See... you corked it," Jim looked at the glass for a second. "And you left a piece floatin' in there."

"Here, give us that glass, son," the old bartender's cheeks flushed. "I got a clean spoon heeyah."

The young man's eyes widened, his skin turned ghost-white as if drained of all blood. He seemed like a half-felled tree, wavering before a pausing lumberjack.

"Allow me." Jim took the spoon from the bartender, his eyes fixed on the perpetrator. Jim brought the spoon nearer to the top of the glass. At the last second, Jim laughed as he transferred the spoon to his other hand and instead stuck an index finger two inches into the wine. He pulled his finger from the glass and brought it dripping into his mouth.

"Corked, but sooo *good*!" Jim gritted his teeth and flashed his eyes. "*That's* how we do it in the bayou. Now, get goin'!"

The young man took a step back, blinking rapidly. He looked as if he wanted to shrink within his pinstripe suit and hide.

"You're a real ass, seersucker boy!" the young man said as he moved away from the table. "Who in the hell *are* you?"

"You get goin' before I crack you hard in front of all these folks." Jim wagged an index finger in his face. "Want a new dental plan?"

The young man turned, his opened Amstel Light still on the table, and marched off across the room, past the crowd shouting and gesticulating at the widescreen. He glared at the onlookers before he opened the French doors and stepped outside onto the front porch, closing them after him.

Sensing himself beam with deep pride, Jim turned to the bartender, whose eyes wrinkled in a grateful and amused smile at his new friend. Jim raised the wineglass. "To the victor... go the spoils." He took a sip. "Kids don't respect their elders much these days."

"Some do, like yaself. Really, ya don't have to finish that wine, son."

"I'll finish it, sure. And I can polish off that Amstel in a bit."

"No ya don't, friend. Gimme that!" he held out his hand. "Whaddaya really want? Come ahhn!"

"You got any Woodford Reserve back there, sir?" Jim handed back the wine, his eyebrows rising. "I'll take it neat."

"Now we're talkin'." The bartender fetched the whiskey. "I'm gettin' slower in my old age. But still Senator Spaulding employs me. And I ain't really *that* slow. That kid was a real brat, I tell ya, spoiled as hell. Don't know what he got. He's one of Jack's star sales guys. Jerk's name is Ford Brinkley. He's from an old family here on the Cape and he thinks he's royalty."

"But he sure got his little comeuppance today," Jim said. "Boy was a real horse's ass."

The bartender placed a rock glass on the tablecloth and poured out the bourbon. "I'm Joseph Riordan. Friends call me Joe." He stretched out a hand.

Jim again noted its crooked, weathered fingers, and shook it. "Jim Scoresby. I work for Walter Henretty. And I'm lucky enough to date his beautiful daughter, Maureen."

"Henretty? Old Captain Henretty, good man. See him here all the time. People just love Walter. And he's got a smart, pretty wife and kids. So where you livin', the Cape? Boston?"

"I was in New Hampshire, then Boston, now Osterville. But I'm returning to Boston. Long story, I must say." Jim sipped the bourbon.

"Where ya hail from, my man?"

"Louisiana."

"I can see it in the suit. And the accent. And the choice of spirits. Ya from New Orleans?"

"There and a town about forty miles north of it," Jim said. "But if I was a true New Orleanian, I would have requested a Sazerac or a Hurricane."

"I prefer the Sazerac," Joe said. "Katrina sent ya up this way, I guess?"

"She did indeed," Jim said. His eyes drifted from Joe's dour face to the window beyond. "There's Walter now. I was wondering where he'd gone."

"He and Mrs. Henretty are just out that door."

"I'm gonna stop and see 'em," Jim said. "Great to meet you, Joe. Put a li'l liquid soap in that Amstel in case our boy comes back for it."

The slate patio jutted out perhaps fifty feet and ran the entire length of the mansion. The three steps bordering it led down to a great green on which children played. On one side of this lawn, a game of croquet was underway. On the other side of the green, children in a spacewalk jumped and howled and laughed.

Just before Jim, a large crowd chatted on the patio in the ebbing twilight as jazz resounded from loudspeakers. Flames flickered in the gas lampposts ringing the patio. Two waiters weaved through the group, distributing hors d'oeuvres. Walter held court among a cluster of couples, relating a tale from his years on the open sea. Neither Walter nor Kathleen had spotted Jim.

A familiar face appeared in the audience. Reverend Cordell Ward listened, his scholarly eyes focused somewhere downward.

Glass of bourbon in hand, Jim launched forward and meandered around several guests, finally appearing before his Dorchester friend.

"Jim, how are you?" Reverend Ward whispered as Walter continued his tale, still oblivious to Jim's arrival.

The pastor's eyes exuded a quiet peace.

"Not so gloomy, Reverend. Enjoying a little libation. And today's completion of our work on the *John Paul Jones*. Can you believe it?"

"I can't wait. We'll have a great time. The boys are gonna love it."

Surely the tale met its end, for the crowd erupted in a swell of laughter, applause, and a few sighs of relief.

"Jim! There you are, my boy! Glad you could make it," Walter shouted, clapping his hands once in excitement and stomping a foot.

"Yes, great that you came, Jim!" Kathleen said.

"I wouldn't miss a Spaulding party," Jim said. "I've heard these events are among the best on the Cape."

"I would have to agree," an old man nodded.

"Except for mine over in Hyannis." A woman laughed, fidgeting with her pearl necklace. Jim could detect a face-lift in her past.

"But you can't compare the two!" Kathleen said. "You throw the majority of your parties on your yacht."

"With that *excellent* sound system, I might add," said another guest, a sixty-something man in wire-rim spectacles. He wore a starched, striped, blue-and-white button-down oxford with walnut khakis and sockless penny loafers. His hands hid in his pockets, his chin pointed slightly upward, his eyes half-closed.

"Well, Jimmy boy!" Walter said. "Ya see we got the Reverend over here, eh?"

"The one and only," Jim said. "I'm glad to see him. Long drive, huh?"

"It was worth it," Reverend Ward said.

"You tell Reverend the good news about the boat, Jim?" Walter puffed out his chest.

"Just did!" Jim said in an upbeat tone.

"I couldn't be more proud," Walter said. Then he turned to address the small crowd. "Ladies and gentlemen, meet Jim Scoresby. I've told some of you of Jim, my star broker in Boston. He dates my daughter Maureen. So you can imagine the trust I have in him. And the amount of surveillance I had on the poor boy!"

Everyone laughed, including Jim and Walter.

"You know, I had to can the guy who used to run my boat

business. Soon I fixed my eye on Jim for the position. Maureen lobbied for Jim to relocate to the Cape to run it. So his first project—and it was a biggie—he and the boys just finished today."

"Walt, is it true," said a short man with a reddish comb-over and huge brown eyes, "you recently purchased a tri-masted Herreshoff schooner?" He cradled his martini as he spoke.

"Dr. Wentworth, I did indeed, and braved Kathleen's wrath," Walter looked at his shoes, shaking his head, laughing gently. "Ah, I tried to keep it a secret. But word does travel, does it not?"

"I am curious to see this vessel in action," said Dr. Wentworth. "Will you race it in the Figawi?"

"Ah, yes, the Figawi," Walter nodded. "Well, that's this Saturday. Haven't decided if we're gonna pull the trigger on that one."

"But you've raced every year for the longest time, Walt," Kathleen said, peering up into his face. "Why not this year?" She looked out at her captive audience. "I've been telling him this all afternoon. Evidently to no avail."

"But Walter," Jim said, "I thought you were definitely participating this year. What happened? You've won so many of 'em, besides."

"Things have changed, Jimmy. I'm getting old, breaking down. And there's that stress that comes with skippering in a race. And the joints just don't always hold up to the wake anymore. I'm not what I was." His face assumed a wistful expression.

"Commodore Henretty, I do understand," Reverend Ward said.

"Please call me Walter."

"Okay, Walter, I don't want you to strain to take all my kids on that trip coming up. Now I feel guilty."

"That's different. I really wouldn't have it any other way."

"We'll make it worth your while then," Jim said. Some faces appeared curious, even puzzled.

"Oh, I'm sorry, y'all. Commodore's takin' me and Reverend and Jack and Natasha sailing from Chatham to Boston soon. We're bringing children from a Baptist church in Dorchester and from a youth group in Southie."

A few replies of approval shot up from the crowd. Dr. Wentworth raised his martini in a toast. "I heard about this. May there be no infighting, then. You mustn't have a Belfast situation there. Or even more so, a South African one."

Some nervous chuckling arose in the crowd.

"We'll be just fine," Reverend Ward said. "The boys had a tiff about to pop open during our last trip. But Walter, Jim, and I stepped in and squashed it."

"Gotta instill order. And a little fear," Walter said. "After all, I can't motivate our boys with two daily cups of navy grog. Now, Jimbo there, my Luzianna boy, I can with *him*."

Another wave of laughter rippled through Walter's semicircle of hangers-on. Someone asked Walter about his children. Jim seized the opportunity and excused himself, ducking out of the crowd and walking, empty glass in hand, toward the door.

Jim spied a trio of two men and a woman, all three black, standing toward the opposite end of the patio. The woman wore a white chef's hat. They stood behind a table, grilling shrimp and lobsters on a black cast iron wood smoker: a fifty-gallon oil drum connected to a much smaller drum, and to a cone-topped black iron smokestack.

Jim strolled toward the table and smiled when the woman, slightly graying and with a matronly figure, looked his way.

"Hey there," Jim said. "How y'all doin'?"

Neither of the men turned as they pulled the shrimp and lobster off the grill and onto two large platters with their tongs. "Not bad, sir," she said. "Care for some lobster or shrimp?"

"Just a little bit of both, if I could. But please don't call me sir!"

"Sho' thing, hon," she said. "We'll hook ya up. An' ah'll take that glass."

She took his empty glass and placed it on a tray behind the table. She grabbed a plate while one of the men placed a platter of steaming shrimp on the table. The woman tonged five onto the plate. She placed two tiny metal cups of butter and sauce beside them.

"You gotta taste you some o' that lobstah!" She turned to her other side. One of her helpers had removed much of the meat from a butterflied lobster and forked it onto the platter. She transferred two large dollops of lobster meat onto the plate.

"Ah can tell you hungrier then you lettin' on, shug," she said, chuckling.

Jim hesitated. His father's favorite word. Shug. "How could you tell?"

"The eyes. You looked like you were gonna snatch one o' them lobstahs off that grill there."

Jim took the plate with a chuckle. He grabbed a fork from the table, speared a piece of the steaming white meat, and dipped it in one of the cups of sauce. Jim chewed, savoring it before swallowing. "*That* is delectable. Y'all chose charcoal, not propane."

"You got it," one of the men said. "No propane with our stuff, no way."

"Haven't seen one of those Oklahoma Joes in a while," Jim pointed to the grill, remembering a similar model he once bought for his grandfather's backyard before Katrina. "Last time was back in Louisiana."

"*That's* where you from," the woman said. "I was wonderin'. Yeah, Bobby here, his granddaddy from Shreveport taught him how to use this grill."

"They like those grills a lot down there," Bobby said.

"They sure do," Jim said. "Even more so in Texas. But as many in South Louisiana say, Shreveport's part of Texas anyway."

"Ah gotta agree with ya there," Bobby laughed. "Or part of Arkansas."

"Well, I might be comin' back for seconds," Jim said. "Or thirds."

"I don't blame you!" Bobby said. "I'd do the same. Come on back."

Jim waved, turned, and proceeded down the patio. The Commodore still held the crowd spellbound. Nobody noticed Jim as he walked by and opened one of the back doors.

Inside, the Red Sox-crazed guests remained amassed, layer upon layer, around the Victorian couches and the flat screen. Their attention held fast to Josh Beckett, atop the pitcher's mound. He struck out another Tampa batter. The partygoers burst into a wild blaze of cheers, whistles, and shouts.

Jim found a spot near the crowd's outermost ring. He attacked the shrimp and lobster, dipping them with his fork into the two sauces.

"Let's go, Beckett!" someone yelled from deep within the crowd.

"Come on, Tampa!" someone else screamed mockingly. "You guys don't even know how to pronounce 'baseball' down there!"

Jim cringed as he forked a chunk of lobster tail into his mouth. He made sure to savor what he recognized was the taste of the oak charcoal, hickory chips, butter, and Old Bay spice.

A Devil Ray batter cracked a ball high over Beckett's head. The room unleashed a barrage of "get it!" and "catch it!" and "come on!" and even an "is that all you got?!" As the ball arced toward the fence, the Red Sox shortstop sprinted, catching it just in time as he dived. The living room exploded like an artillery shell, a hundred words like red-hot shrapnel hurling outward from the clapping and leaping throng.

Jim's gaze seized upon a movement in the center of the crowd. A handful of guests parted. Out jogged Jack Spaulding, dressed in a hound's tooth blazer, burgundy button-down dress shirt, and blue jeans. A green Red Sox cap crowned his head, his trademark blonde curls spilling out of its sides and back.

"Luzianna Jim," Jack half-shouted. "How goes it, man?"

Jim shook his hand. "I've heard about these Spaulding bashes the whole time I've been out here on the Cape."

"This is just a last minute, weekday one. Come to a weekend party here." Jack pointed at Jim's plate. "You got some of that good stuff, eh? Those guys cater a lot of our parties. We pay 'em extra to come all the way from Canton."

"That's a li'l hike, all right," Jim said. "Hey, so I met the senator! I like him."

"Yes, *The Senator*, as he's been dubbed. Dad is a cool cat in many ways, young at heart. Want a drink?" Jack walked toward the table where Joe stood.

Jim joined him. "I don't believe I've ever refused."

"Joseph!" Jack said. "Have any left for us, my man?"

"Better hurry," the bartender proclaimed across the living room as they approached.

"So whaddaya say?" Joe slapped his hands on the bartop.

"Jim, what's your pleasure, buddy?" Jack thundered, alcohol in his voice. "Joe, my good Celtic chieftain, our Hibernian hero. Let's give the lad a beverage."

"I better downshift," Jim said. "I'll take a Shipyard. In the bottle's just fine."

"And I'll take a Harpoon IPA, good sir," Jack said. "That's the spirit, Jim. So have you gotten into the Sox yet? You've been in New England now for almost... nine months, right? Haven't caught the fever yet?"

"Gettin' there," Jim said. "But I suspect most here were raised with it."

"You psyched about the trip? Sailing on that old wooden schooner—is that gonna be nice or what? Always wanted to sail a Herreshoff."

"It'll be great, Jack. We just finished on her today. Now we've gotta test if she's seaworthy."

The men both turned and picked up their longnecks, and then thanked Joe.

"I'm sure she's fine," Jack said. "Nice threads, by the way. Well, I gotta catch the rest of the game. You should, as well!"

Jack winked hard at Jim with the whole left side of his face and made some kind of slick clicking sound. He marched back to the cheering crowd, whistling as hard as he could.

"Come on, Sox!!" Jack boomed, a clenched fist and an index finger raised toward the ceiling's wooden beams.

"He's right, son," Joe said. "If ya ain't got that feevah yet, work on gettin' it!"

"Maybe I'll contract it with time," Jim said. "It was quite a story when they won the World Series a couple years ago."

"Glad I lived to see it," Joe said.

"Catch you in a bit, Joe," Jim said and walked toward the television. The seventh inning commenced, with the Sox leading with a few runs ahead of the Devil Rays. Jim watched for a minute, but succumbed to his restlessness and headed for the front patio door.

The original crowd of guests smoking and gabbing and drinking on the front patio had grown. Perhaps thirty people stood in the nearly extinguished twilight both under the columns and just beyond them on the green. Patio lights overhead illuminated the mass of partygoers in all their sartorial finery: strings of pearl, Italian leather shoes, designer suits and sportcoats, an occasional tweed blazer, silk dresses. His sweeping gaze came to rest on a familiar face. Jim walked toward the older man just beyond the columns.

"Mr. Scoresby, there you are," the senator nodded once. "Enjoying the party?"

"It's a grand time. Grilled shrimp and lobster, all the libations a young man could desire, a good baseball showdown, and a nineteenth century 'summer cottage' reminiscent of Newport."

"Glad you like it, son. You see Jack in there? And Walter?"

"I did. They're both in good spirits. Especially Jack, as the

Sox are pulling this one out, apparently." Jim felt a tickle on the nape of his neck and whirled around.

Brianna smirked. "Hi there, Jim Scoresby. I mean... Rhett."

"Well, hey, Brianna. What's new?"

"I'll tell you what's new, Rhett. You spooked my date, Ford Brinkley, that's what's new. He said he had to run back to his place to let the electrician in, but I know better. After he drove off, some guy told me what you did inside."

"I caught your beloved tongue-lashing the bartender in there. Really degrading him."

"I heard you put a finger in my wine."

"My apologies. I'll get you another."

"Someone else already did." She raised her glass of Chardonnay. "Ford can be a real ass. I've been dating him about a month, but now I'm getting what he's all about."

"Let me hazard a li'l guess. Money, status, power. Maybe a little lust thrown in there somewhere. Often accompanies power."

Brianna fought it, but her lips gradually formed into a smile. "Okay, Cajun boy, enough of the wisecracks and all the pleasantries. Is it true you're dating Maureen Henretty?" Brianna held her glass to her chest and placed the other hand on her hip.

"I take it you know her?"

"We attended Phillips Andover together. You have your work cut out for you."

Jim blushed. He wondered if the many people who said that ever detected any confirmation in his face.

"She's great," Jim said. "She just comes off the wrong way to some people."

"I don't believe you, Rhett. I think you're taking it day by day."

"Not at all. I'm even moving back to Boston in a few days to be closer."

"That's unfortunate. But at least you'll be near more of the action. Boston's a fun town."

Jim hummed in assent. His hand trembled as he held his beer.

"I was getting my MFA in painting from Amherst but the college pace became a bit too much. I took a year hiatus to clear my head. I'm staying in my parents' property on the Cape, in their mother-in-law cottage. Not in their house, or we'd just fight endlessly."

"I was a broker at Walter Henretty's securities firm in Back Bay. Now I'm in Osterville running his boat business."

"I also heard you're a writer. Fiction?"

"Primarily."

"Interesting." Her sly, leopard-like quality increased as she batted the long lashes of her green eyes.

"Hey, where's the restroom? All this bourbon and beer is gettin' to me."

"Bourbon and beer," Brianna said in her best Southern accent. "Go through that door there. Take a right, then a left. Then you'll see a stairwell. Go up the stairs and the bathroom's right there."

"Be right back."

The crowd still mobbed the television, immersed in a fit of shouting and clapping. Jim followed his recommended route through the downstairs and up the stairwell. After he flushed the toilet and washed out his mouth with a handful of tap water, he realized the bathroom was not meant for guests. A towel lay on the tile floor and a toothbrush rested on the countertop.

He shook his head, chuckled, and opened the door. Jim knocked into something. He took a step back, blinking rapidly.

Brianna placed a finger on his lips. Her mischievous eyes narrowed, her lips parted. She pushed him with both hands into the bathroom and shut the door.

"Brianna, come on now—"

She thrust her face forward, her lips onto his. Grabbing the nape of his neck, she pulled him even closer. Jim yanked his head backward. In his mouth swirled the taste of cherry lipgloss, wine, and a trace of cigar.

"Brianna, back off!" Jim whispered as loudly as he could. "I can't."

"Sure you can," she shot back, half in anger, half in amusement. "She doesn't deserve you and you know it."

Jim untwined her arms and started for the door.

She grabbed his open hand and planted it on her breasts. "You're just letting life pass you by, Jim!" she hissed as he pulled his hand away. "You need to get rid of that bitch Maureen Henretty!"

He jerked her aside, lurched for the knob, and yanked the door open. He stepped sideways through the door, and then turned back. Panting, Brianna's eyes flashed with outrage, as she leaned against the wall in a half crouch.

Jim walked down the stairwell, through the downstairs and out onto the front patio. He waited for an awkward moment at the crowd's edge. The senator stood in the midst of the crowd, which chattered and laughed away under the porch lights.

Jim approached him, said that he was feeling ill, and excused himself from the party.

Chapter Thirty-Three

Jim kicked off the covers. The nightmare's remnants lingered for a few seconds. He turned over on the bed, his eyes wide open.

In his dream, Jim attended a party one spring afternoon in the well-landscaped backyard of a great Uptown New Orleans home. Freddy played trumpet, before a jazz quartet. In the yard, all of Jim's closest friends assembled, from down south and from New England, and a few from his Sewanee days, including Damon. A great table on the lawn featured catered étouffée and jambalaya and a well-stocked, fully-manned outside bar. In an instant, the yard started to flood. Moments later, they all fought to reach the surface. Jim did, but Freddy and many of his friends did not...

It is Friday, he thought. We finished the boat with time to spare. The old man will want it tested in the water fairly soon. At least Walter didn't enroll in this year's Figawi. That ought to free him up a bit.

Jim rolled over once more. He recalled phoning Maureen as he drove from Jack's party toward Osterville. To Jim's surprise, she did not turn out too grumpy or snappy. Perhaps she was happy over his upcoming move.

The wine he consumed at his apartment before bed left him with a decent hangover, thankfully not one of the caliber following a long, wild night of partying in Boston. It bore no similarity to those following his old weekend benders, the kind he began to indulge in after his evacuation last September to New Hampshire. And it was not one of the vicious hangovers after his move to the North End last November. Those wild times all ceased when he met Maureen.

His Blackberry rang. Such a harsh sound for so early in the morning. Surely it was Maureen. Jim groaned and snatched the device near his head.

"It's MEEEeee," his mother's voice sang. "How are you, sweetie?"

"Not bad, Mom... morning," Jim said. "'Bout to start work at the shop."

"Oh, I'm so glad you love that new job of yours," she gushed. "I think you will for some time to come. More than the one you had with investments."

Her voice was musical, and too upbeat for his throbbing cranium and his grogginess. "I just got back from Mass. Who do I see out here on the patio but someone you know well. I'm handing off the phone. Love you, Jim."

Before Jim could reply he heard a quite different voice on the line.

"Rise and shine, *shuuuger*," it sang. "*Now you know ah miss mah sonny boy.*" Jim knew the voice well, its musical inflection, its soft baritone accented by its first two decades in Georgia, South Carolina, and Mississippi.

"Morning, Dad," Jim said. "How's it goin'?"

"James Ewell Scoresby. Well, I'm sittin' out here enjoying my Fresh Market coffee and it's still nice and cool out and I'm lookin' up through all these magnolias and big oaks out here and I've got my trusted li'l buddy Pooh on the table here beside me. He's guardin' me," referring to his loving companion, his adopted tabby cat.

"Been thinkin' here, dreamboatin' a bit before I set in on my logs. I love that old sea captain Walter, I love that you're seein' more of the world but I wantcha to come home. Be with me and take another stab at Paw Paw's house. It's gutted but nothin' more's been done. And grab beer and oysters and crawfish at Morton's with me, and we'll catch all the festivals around."

"Haha, Dad," Jim said. "I love you, too."

"Ah miss ya, boy. Time's runnin' out. Ah, and it's so precious, more than you know. Well, I'll have a few cold ones and some raw ones in your honor in a few hours."

Jim could hear the protests of his mother and his father's infectious laugh. She was perpetually opposed to their affection for raw Gulf bivalves.

"Now someone wants to talk to you, shug. Love you."

"Jimmy, how's it crackin', man?" said his brother's voice, already well caffeinated. As many noted, it sounded eerily like his own. "I'm having Dad's roof replaced by my guys this week. Hey, you're missin' out on lots of good work, not here on the Northshore but over in the city, Uptown. Some good profit. Anyway, when are you coming to visit?"

"I just started that new gig here but I want you to come up soon, now that it's warmer. I've got to run to work now but let's talk tonight, make a plan."

Paul agreed and they said their goodbyes. Jim lay there for a few seconds longer, staring at the ceiling, his spirit aching, remembering his mother and his brother but even more so, his father's voice and words. What was it? What troubled him about them? Regardless, the man could be overbearing to those he loved but he sure was a charmer. And that life-loving, dynamic spirit—it reminded him of another charismatic man he had seen much, as of late...

A cold shower and two large cups of coffee later, Jim descended the stairwell into the shop.

"Don't look so groggy, ya Highness," Bill glanced up and smiled. "The journey's over. The ship's finally come home. Or rather, it's about to set sail. We did it, pal."

"We did indeed," Jim murmured, keeping his eyes half-closed to further illustrate his fatigue. The two men reached out and half slapped, half shook hands.

"Too much enjoyment, my friend?" Bill said.

"Well, *how* does one put it?" Jim rubbed his eyes. "I *have* had more."

"I bet you have!" Bill gave a belly laugh.

The outside door alarm beeped. In stepped Walter, thermos in hand, and clad in his shorts, green polo shirt, and brown boat shoes. "How are ya, men? Tired? Happy? You guys should be proud!"

"Morning, Commodore!" Jim said. "I'm very proud. Of the men."

"I am, too, Jimmy. Look at this beaut! Man alive!" Walter raised a fist aloft as his eyes greedily scoured the boat. "Look at the new paint on that hull! Now only one task remains."

"We gotta see if she floats," Donovan said, striding up to Walter.

"Yes. I must confirm she's seaworthy. That's precisely one reason I stopped by. I wanna flood the graving dock here, put her out in the Sound. Today."

"We could do that," Jim said in a shaky voice. What if the boat took on water in the dock? And if not, he would have to be ready to be out on the water immediately.

"I caused a stir yesterday at Spaulding's when I disclosed that I wasn't racing this year in the Figawi. Very early this morning, I reconsidered. I have one race in these old bones yet!"

Jim hesitated. "My, that's great, Walter." He wondered if the weather conditions would be sound, and if Walter would run into any danger.

"Spaulding is absolutely elated. Last night he gave me the offer. If I race, I can skipper his boat, use his crew. It's a marvelous racing yacht, a fifty-six foot Pearson. He's raced her a few times, just never won. Racing's not his bag. But his crew's pretty practiced, pretty strong."

"Now I can see," Bill said, "why you wanna close the book today on the schooner."

"So let's flood this drydock and lift her off those blocks," the old man said. "We'll see her leak in the dry dock here if she's not ready. Assuming all is well, we get her in the water."

"She ain't gonna leak, no way," Chief said. He and his ever-present sidekick, DaSilva, watched them from the ship's rail above.

"My team has done quite well." The Commodore slapped Bill's shoulder. "More work, and at a faster pace, than I could've asked for."

"On behalf of the men, we thank you," Jim said, his heart warmed yet again by the old warrior. "But the work I did was nothing compared to what you guys did here."

"You can say that again," Donovan cracked. He peered at

Jim with mock hostility. "Just joshin' ya, guy!"

"Hey! I just heard Jim say 'you guys'!" DaSilva exclaimed from the rail above. "He's on his way."

"Kid's got a point," the Commodore said. "Jim will be one of us soon enough. Now let's get cranking, lads! Billy, you flood the dock when I give the word. Jim and I will join the others up there in the boat and keep an eye open for leaks. We'll get this baby in the water, assuming we don't meet any surprises."

Walter climbed the stairwell and swung deftly over the rail. Jim followed suit.

"That looked easy, son," Walter whispered, "but it felt worse than you might suspect! Those old captains of yesteryear were just gritty. Or that's why they drank their grog!" Louder, he said, "Now, flood it, Billy!"

A siren rang out. The dry dock, like a square concrete valley, slowly filled with water. Jim's heart thudded faster in his chest as the water reached the blocks and began to rise around them. The old man stood at the rail, his arms proudly on his hips, looking straight down off the boat, as if he aimed to see the keel.

"Be watchful for any leaks, men," Walter shouted.

He ordered Donovan and DaSilva to station themselves below deck at opposite ends of the vessel. "Now Jim," Walter said. "Let's conduct a run-through of the ship. The engine room, the galley, all the cabins, everything."

As Jim turned from the rail to follow the old man toward the hatch, he glimpsed Bill watching him from across the dock. He stood, one hand holding a cigarette to his lips. Bill blew out the smoke, smiling.

Chapter Thirty-Four

"So you guys made it to Hyannisport." Bryce turned toward him, away from the window. They just finished dining at one of the most coveted tables at Sonsie on Newbury Street, while watching the passersby outside the huge patio door, which management had slid open.

"She was more than seaworthy," Jim said. "And she made great time. And passed Coast Guard inspection."

"Obviously," Maureen said. "Or you wouldn't have come to Boston to enjoy your Friday night. And to spend the weekend with me."

Jim put an arm around her shoulder.

"Yeah," Patrick said, "now you can hobnob with all of us city folk. In the hottest lounge in Back Bay. You never know: Tom Brady and Bridget Moynahan might enter at any second."

"I'd rather see Teddy Kennedy or Whitey Bulger," Case added. "But if it was Senator Teddy, man, I don't know if we could drag him from the bah."

Patrick blinked slowly and shook his head from side to side.

"Bryce," Jim said, "you once told me Brady lives a block away and used to pop in here all the time. But I think he moved to New York, to be with his girl."

"His stay here was kinda short-lived," Bryce said. "He and a lot of the other Pats, and a lot of the Sox, they love 'Daisy Buchanan's' pub down this street. I've seen them there."

"I like that place," Jim said. "You and I've gone there, remember? "

"So, Jim," said Bryce's girlfriend Cara, "will you miss the Cape? And your boat job?"

"Always. I had a great time down there. Made some lifelong friends, those guys in the shop. And I got to better know a friend I already had. He's truly a fascinating, amazing man: Maureen's father, Walter. Or the Commodore, as I call him. I'm not ashamed to say I'm a little crestfallen to leave him. He's like my father away from home."

A memory appeared in Jim's mind: his father taking him to eat his first raw oysters, then to hear Mark Knopfler perform at the Saenger Theater one May night five years back. Afterwards, his father took him to the Roosevelt Hotel's Sazerac Bar, once the favorite haunt of the legendary Governor Huey "Kingfish" Long. There they talked and joked and Jim enjoyed his first Sazerac. If only Jim could forge a great friendship with him as he had with Walter...

"Walter sounds great," Cara said.

"You'll see him again, Jim," Maureen said with a dismissive wave of her hand.

Jim pushed his pint of beer a few inches forward. "It's just... well, the Commodore, in other news, had decided to sit out the Figawi race this year."

"The sailboat race from Hyannis to Nantucket?" Bryce said. "Every Memorial Day weekend?"

"Maureen's dad has won that race several times, and he's been saying he wouldn't be competing this year. Last night, a crowd at a party in Chatham couldn't believe the news. Just this morning, Walter tells me Senator Ryland Spaulding's offer proved too tempting. Walter can use the Senator's boat and well-trained crew. Spaulding didn't feel much like racing anyway."

"Maybe Daddy had all this orchestrated as a publicity stunt," Maureen said, raising an eyebrow. "Just joking. He has been feeling his age lately."

"Walter claims this is his last competitive race," Jim said. "So I feel bad he's taking us afterwards on that trip up the coast from the Cape to Boston."

"That's the one you guys are taking with all the at-risk kids, right?" Bryce said.

"Yep. But that trip won't be as hard on his joints. We won't be racing, just cruising. We'll have a few days to get from Hyannis to Boston Harbor. Then all the men from Melville and I will help him sail the boat back down to the Cape. It's a tri-masted vessel, over one hundred feet long, after all."

"Whose idea was it to do this trip with the kids?" Patrick said.

"My father's," Maureen said. "He's involved in all sorts of charities. He knew those two churches, a Catholic one in Southie, and a Baptist one in Dorchester. Their youth leaders were into sailing. Their kids still needed help and a new direction. Dad sensed Jim was the man for the job, the one who could help him lead the kids' sailing lessons and the last trip."

"And then he asked you for your opinion." Jim placed his arm again on Maureen's shoulder. "And you lobbied for me."

Maureen shrugged, uncomfortable with his hand on her in such a public place. He let his hand fall to his side. Jim sighed and excused himself from the table and headed for the bathroom. A woman walking past him into the dining room bumped shoulders with him, though Jim at the last minute veered slightly away from her.

"Oh, I'm sorry," Jim said by instinct and grimaced.

The woman paid no notice, too busy calling someone's name. Jim chuckled and walked into the corridor.

When he returned to the table, Cara said, "You sure weren't down on the Cape very long."

"It just flew by in a flash," Jim said. "Maybe a month and a half."

"So Maureen, your dad paid for the move down there and back?" Bryce said, an impressed look playing in his eyes.

"Moving him down was part of the original terms of Daddy's offer, then he added the move back."

"That *is* pretty impressive," Cara said.

"On my drive up today," Jim said, "I called one of my broker friends. He needs a roommate in the only surviving clapboard carriage house in Back Bay, between Beacon and Storrow Drive. I might take him up on it."

"I know just the place. Light blue clapboards. Sweet spot." Bryce rested his chin on his index finger. "You'll have a great view across the Charles and Harvard Bridge toward Memorial Drive, that domed building at MIT, and Cambridge. I've hit a few wild parties in those carriage houses. Barely escaped alive!"

"Nice," Jim said, half-lost in thought as he sipped his beer.

"And you'll be right around the corner from us," Cara said with a sunny inflection.

"We'll all have to catch up, hit the town like old times," Jim said. "And Bryce, we can go grab lobsters and ten cent wings after work at Whiskey's. And trivia at Crossroads Pub on Beacon."

"Roger that," Bryce said.

"So you guys are off tomorrow morning to Maine?" Patrick said.

"First I have to check out the carriage house. Then we're blasting off up ninety-five toward Portland and Yarmouth. We probably will stop in New Hampshire."

"In Exeter? At Liam's?" Case said.

"He wants to show me his friend's house that he moved into last year," Maureen sneered. "Jim slept in his attic, you know."

"The same attic where Liam found a lithograph of Lincoln in a closet?" Bryce said. "Where the closet door had been nailed shut?"

Jim nodded. "I slept in that attic until autumn turned too cold. Then I stayed in a room in the parish house across town from the rectory and church, where I had gotten a job doing maintenance."

"They tried to make a priest out of you up there, if I remember," Bryce said.

"The priests, staff, and much of the congregation wanted me to enroll at Saint John's Seminary in Brighton," Jim stared down into his beer. "I actually considered it, attended a retreat there. But it's just not for me."

"He found something he fancied a bit more." Maureen smiled and waited for Jim to agree.

Jim studied what was left of his ale.

"So how about we kill our drinks and scoot over to Vox?" Patrick said. "Over on Boylston?"

"Then maybe we can go to Saint and let Cara dance!" Bryce

said.

Jim's eyes rose slowly from his glass. He turned his head and allowed his gaze to sweep the breadth of the restaurant. Spread out before him was a panorama of vanity, ambition, and egotism, of empty chatter and cold glances Jim recognized all too well. How weary he had grown of that emptiness! How very different from the soulfulness and laissez-faire of the New Orleans of his memories.

But still he longed to further explore the variety and excitement of Boston. And as Jim downed the dregs of his beer, he thought how he loved the slower pace of southern Maine, with its seaside lobster pounds, its craggy shores with their dark, frothy waters and mysterious coves, its Portland pubs and chowder houses. He recalled Exeter, New Hampshire, with its plenitude of colonial houses and quiet lanes, and his mood somewhat lifted.

"Sounds excellent, podnuh," Jim said.

"Let's go, sure," Maureen said as Cara cheered. They rose slowly, and navigated through the crowded tables beside the vast open window. A thirty-something man dressed in a suit, walking the opposite way, stepped on Jim's foot.

"Ow!" Jim winced and shot the man a hard, puzzled look. The man made brief eye contact with an odd, faintly hostile look, and stepped quickly away in silence. Jim shook his head and walked on. They passed the doorman and emerged onto Newbury, with its flickering gas lamps and its two streetside rivers of pedestrians.

Jim thought of the man's face, and the disturbing look he had detected in the eyes...

Chapter Thirty-Five

Jim snickered as they drove past the throngs of twenty-somethings and thirty-somethings coursing up and down the sidewalks through the light fog. After an evening rain, the mist now rose from the wet concrete and cobblestones and the fog blew steadily in from the ocean.

"Maureen, almost every time I come up here to Portland, it rains. But I still really love visiting. Interesting architecture, too. All these gray and brown nineteenth century buildings. They're not as old as what's in Beantown, though. Reason being this city burned the first Fourth of July after the Civil War. The fire ignited in one of the boathouses over there. Spread across the city."

Jim stared at the crowds. Their attire was not as conservative and professional as in Boston, but instead generally somewhat relaxed, even at times bohemian and grungy. Their pace seemed slower.

"There's one place I must take you next time, here on Commercial Street. The one and only J's Oyster. The jewel of the Old Port! The oysters are better across the street though. At J's they only serve Chesapeakes. But the atmosphere's what I like most. Laid back, unpretentious. The barmaids have a lot of spunk, too. Pretty entertaining lot, if you ask me."

Maureen remained silent. Why had she fallen into another strange mood? She probably didn't feel like stopping at Liam's house.

"So Maur, I wonder how the old warrior's faring at the race."

"Right now the Figawi's still underway for some, over for others, no doubt. Mom's in Nantucket by now at some fête, awaiting the outcome."

Jim slapped a hand on the dashboard. "I say the old man wins it all."

"You might have spoken too soon. He's older, slower. And it's not his boat. He doesn't know most of the senator's crew."

"Ah, Maur, sweetie," Jim said. "Where's your faith in the Commodore?"

"I'll go with realism."

"So, excited about my new digs? In Back Bay, no less?"

"Your new place could use some work. The carpet needs replacing. The walls need spackling and a few coats of paint. And it's just crazy how those floors aren't level. I guess a ton of settling can happen in an 1880s garage. But your roomie seems just fine. And the view is really something to write home about."

"Location, location, location is the crux of it," Jim said. "I take a few steps out the door and I'm on Newbury or Charles, or on the Common or Public Gardens."

"We'll ask your roommate and the landlady if we can refurbish the walls, at least?" Maureen turned and her gaze seared into his. "Well, it'll be a bit strange now. I'm just so used to you having a place to yourself."

"But Franco's giving me a month-to-month. That deal in downtown Boston's worth more than gold. We've worked together and he knows I'm good for the rent. And besides, we get along."

"You have had some good luck, if you think about it all," Maureen said, her eyebrows raised in emphasis, "from the time that you first landed in New Hampshire last September."

"I have, haven't I?"

In a few moments Maureen was asleep. Jim drove on in silence. Soon he pulled up in front of Liam's house and parallel parked. Maureen awoke with a start. Even at the front door, she still looked half-asleep.

"Greetings," Liam said in a near whisper, opening the front door. "Come on in. Glad you guys could make it. Good to see you, Maureen."

"Nice to see you again, too, Liam."

She and Jim walked through the door. "Exeter really is beautiful. I like the house."

"Why, thanks. It dates from 1844. There are lots of stories about this place. But many Exeter homes are much older."

"Liam! Good to be back on Court Street!" Jim stood just inside the corridor, holding up the six-pack of Geary's Ale. "A little somethin' for the hospitality."

"Thanks," Liam mumbled, taking the beer with an approving nod. "Come on in, take a seat." Liam shut the door and motioned down the foyer toward the parlor on their left.

Jim followed Maureen down the creaky dark boards into the parlor. Maureen chose the refurbished Victorian couch. Jim sat at her side and threw an arm comfortably across the top of the sofa.

Liam walked to the kitchen to store the beer in the fridge, and returned to a wooden rocking chair. "So how was the trip up?"

"You mean the trip *down*," Maureen said. "Not so bad. Except Jim devoured *eight* pieces of fried chicken at that Popeye's just off the interstate in Kennebunk."

Liam's eyes shone with a familiar twinkle. "I've seen him in action many times with that stuff. In college, in Tennessee. Down in New Orleans for Mardi Gras, and in Kennebunk. I've seen this fool eat a whole box, usually after a long night."

"I know the sight." Maureen smiled and shook her head.

"Should we take a little drive to the market, get some lobbies and some treats?" Liam looked from Maureen to Jim.

"Sure," Jim and Maureen said together.

"Then maybe," Jim said, "you can show Maureen here some of your treasures."

They piled into Liam's old Subaru station wagon parked in the driveway. Inside lurked a faint smell of mildew and some other stench, much like spilled milk.

As Liam zoomed down Court Street, Jim came close to exploding in a fit of laughter when he looked into the backseat. Maureen's face contorted, her lips grimly sucked inward. Her eyes squinted as if she had taken a massive bite of a lemon.

"Maureen, roll down that window," Jim said as he manually cranked down his own. "You look like you could use a li'l fresh air, sweetness."

Maureen shot him her death glare. Jim bit his cheek to keep from roaring with delight.

"See this brick hotel on our left, Maureen?" Liam said. "That's Blake's Inn. The Republican Party, very different in those days, was founded there in 1853. It was converted into an apartment building for a time. My dad stayed there when he was a kid, while my grandfather renovated the house you just saw."

Jim, of course, knew the story. Newly home from the war, Liam's grandfather combined his G.I. Bill money with the savings he had accrued years before as a plumber, and he purchased the home. The old man died several years back. Just last spring his widow passed on to join him.

Liam became the caretaker of the old house, something to which he did not entirely object. He fell into a situation where he could restore an old house, while operating his business as an antique and militaria dealer.

The Subaru turned right onto Front Street, continued a few hundred feet down the hill, passed the old white clapboard Congregationalist church and the gazebo on the left, and hooked right onto Water Street.

"This was once the capital of New Hampshire, Maureen," Liam said, "during the Revolution."

"This is one pretty street," Jim said as they passed colonial inns and the nineteenth century brick buildings housing bookshops and delis. They crossed the Swampscott River Bridge and passed a yellow colonial festooned with three Betsy Ross flags. Liam turned left onto Portsmouth Avenue. Soon, Liam stopped in a very familiar parking lot.

"Remember this joint, Jim? On The Vine Marketplace. Maureen, your boyfriend probably spent a few thousand bucks at this place in his first months in Exeter. Oh, they love him in there!"

"Let me guess," Maureen smirked. "Seafood?"

"You've got that right," Liam said.

Inside they navigated through the rows of vegetables toward the rear section, which boasted a great variety of meat and local seafood. Basket in hand, Liam veered away from them into another aisle. Jim toted his handbasket back to the produce section and selected some asparagus, a couple of lemons, and a large bag of salad greens. He led Maureen over to the seafood and meat counter.

Jim approached the curved glass. The large bowl of sea scallops, the tank boasting lobsters even twenty-five pounds in weight, and the section of filet mignon, prime rib, haddock, halibut, bluefish, swordfish, and a wide variety of clams sparked remembrance of many great meals that previous autumn.

"Hey, I remember you," said the young man from behind the counter. He was a Mainer, from the Casco Bay area. He wore a slightly stained apron. His black hair was austerely shorn in a half-inch-long crew cut, topping a pale face that drooped with an unmistakable somberness.

"Tommy, whatcha say, man? I was just thinking how long it's been. You haven't been around the last few times I shopped here."

"I'm usually in Durham, at UNH. Classes taking all my time. Hear you moved down to the big city."

"I did. Tommy, meet my girlfriend Maureen." Jim placed his hand gently on his girlfriend's back. "Maureen, this is Tommy."

Maureen gave him half a nod and even less of a smile.

"I've witnessed quite a few of Jim's record purchases here. I've seen him buy a ten pound lobster, but his friend there never buys more than a pound and a half."

"I ate the ten pounder by myself," Jim laughed. "I got quite sick. After five pounds, you feel queasy."

"Gross," Maureen said. "I've seen the photos. Unforgettable."

"Ha!" Jim said. "And we haven't addressed all the clams I've bought off y'all!"

"Littlenecks, mahoganies, cherrystones, quahogs, steamers, Essex clams," Tommy said. "Jim here was the human vacuum cleaner! Well, what can I get you guys? Five lobsters and thirty pounds of clams?"

"Actually, Tommy, let me consult with my queen here," Jim said, swinging his gaze slowly around to Maureen. "Want a lobster? And some clams? Or would you like some breaded haddock or some swordfish?"

"I'll take a little swordfish and some clams."

"Easy 'nuff," Jim said. "I'll take lobsters: a pound-and-a-half and a four-pounder, then a half-pound of swordfish."

Tommy paused, his eyes twinkling with humor as they fixed expectantly on him. "That all, chief? Just that?"

"And I'll take five pounds of steamers, and two pounds of littlenecks."

Tommy laughed. He grabbed the littlenecks with his gloved hand and began tossing them into a hanging scale.

Liam appeared beside Jim. "Recognize this distinguished gentleman of Exeter? An old friend of yours."

Jim turned and felt his heart leap, and then begin to pound within his chest.

That morning Jim had feared he would run into Father Ben around town. But Exeter wasn't a tiny country hamlet, and Jim gambled he could slip in with Maureen and show her around and not introduce her to his first new friend and employer in New England, a man who had fervently prayed Jim would join the ranks of the priesthood.

"I recognize this guy," Father Ben said. "But does he

recognize me?"

"Of course, Father Ben." Jim gave him a warm hug.

He spotted the disappointment in Father Ben's face. So he was still frustrated with him after all, that Jim vacated the parish house and moved into the oldest neighborhood of the very worldly city of Boston, to end his religious discernment and resume dating.

"Parishioners ask about you all the time. Ken Stockbridge, Elizabeth, Father Francis, and all the others. You should stop by and see us sometime."

"I will, I promise. I'm sorry, Father," Jim mumbled, glancing about. "I've meant to."

"Is this your new lady?" Father Ben smiled warmly at Maureen.

Tommy continued to toss the clams into the scale, casting curious glances at the scene before him.

"Maureen Henretty," Jim said. "I've written you about her. Good things, Maureen, don't worry." Jim winked. "Meet Father Ben Shaughnessy, pastor of St. Stephen's Catholic Church here in Exeter."

"You have a very good man here. He can sleep and eat and drink too much at times, but he's a good soul, no doubt. And Jim, you have a lady of charm and poise. You two feel free to visit us sometime. And you, too, Liam."

"We will, Father," Jim said. "We'll see you soon, definitely."

Father Ben gave Jim a look that mingled skepticism, sadness, and affection. "Now I must return to my shopping. I'm having Dave Emmersley over for dinner. We're still planning the construction of the new church."

"Good luck with the project. And please tell Dave and the

others I said hey."

"I'll do that... *No Blood,*" Father Ben said.

Maureen shot a quizzical glance at Father Ben, then Jim.

Father Ben laughed. "Ask your boyfriend for the source of that old moniker. Nearly the entire town of Exeter called him that. Now take care. God bless." He turned back toward his cart, and wheeled it around a corner toward the bread section.

"*No Blood*, eh?" Maureen looked with amusement at her boyfriend.

"Yep, I remember No Blood," Liam said. "This bayou boy didn't adjust very well to the cold. As they sometimes say here in northern New England, Jim had no blood."

Jim stared in silence at the spot his old friend had left. Had it merely been a refuge, that period of priestly discernment months ago? Or had it been a period of serious introspection? Or had Father Ben pressured him into a discernment program once he learned it was something Jim had lightly considered for years?

Jim knew all three were true, to some extent.

But perhaps he should have told Father Ben his thoughts last year in real time: that he increasingly did not feel the priesthood or even the diaconate was for him. Had he led on Father Ben? He didn't think so.

Had he led on Maureen? His growing sense of their relationship being threatened—was he keeping that from her?

Jim looked over at her. She was staring uncomfortably at the ground.

Chapter Thirty-Six

"So, Liam." Maureen broke her silence, cutting herself a small slice of Cabot Extra Cheddar and placing it on a shredded wheat cracker. "You must give me the tour I've been hearing about from No Blood here. Let's begin with this room." She pointed behind Liam, her glass of Chardonnay in her other hand. "Say, with that print on the wall."

"Oh, that daguerreotype? That's Colonel Elmer Ellsworth," Liam said. "Lincoln's friend. He was the first reported casualty killed in action in the Civil War."

"He's kind of handsome," Maureen said, "in a mid-nineteenth century way."

"The ladies of the North agreed. He was a cross between a heartthrob and a war hero—"

"Nah, Liam!" Jim said, already halfway finished with his first beer. "First you should show her your man room!"

Liam led them through the cellar door and down the stairwell, and flipped the light.

"In-ter-es-ting," Maureen said, drawing out the syllables with sarcasm. She stood with one arm on her waist, the other lifting her glass of Chardonnay like a diva. "Actually, this is neat. In a *guy* sort of way."

The basement spanned the entire outline of the house. Brick pillars punctuated the floor every twenty feet in each direction.

Despite the low ceilings and the concrete floors, Liam had expended much effort in outfitting the room. Against the wall, topping a wide dresser, rested a flat-screen television. Black leather couches formed a square in the basement's center. Inside this formation lay a grizzly bear rug. Liam's late grandfather Norman, an avid hunter, had brought it from Alaska decades before.

Against the other wall stood a dark oak hutch containing a few bottles of high-end bourbon and Scotch. Beside this stood a 1960s-era refrigerator, in remarkably good condition. It contained enough cold beer, Jim and Liam often joked, for a post-game celebration by the entire Boston Red Sox.

Next to it rested a large wine rack holding an eclectic and expensive assortment of wine. Beside the rack stood an antique table topped by a square humidor, with two compartments. Cigars from the Dominican Republic, Brazil, and other countries filled one, and in the neighboring compartment, strictly Cubans. Liam often opened the basement windows and puffed one after he made a big sale, or scored a big purchase, in his antiques and militaria business.

The walls displayed all manner of treasures: old metal signs advertising Smuttynose beer and Remington and Browning firearms, and an old wooden sign advertising "*Bayley's Lake Winnipesaukee Boat Rentals*." A painting of Portsmouth in the eighteenth century hung near the 1865 lithograph of Lincoln that Liam's grandfather had found locked in the attic closet. Taxidermied small game also decorated the walls: beaver, muskrat, fox, and squirrel, hunted or trapped by Liam, his father, and grandfather. Liam once complained to Jim that his collection contained no moose. He also lamented that all of the Eastern Cougars once populating New Hampshire were no more, that one would have been the perfect addition to the man room.

Jim's gaze swept back and forth across the walls, and he reflected that the room seemed like a rustic version of Walter Henretty's garage workshop.

Liam steered them through the room, showing them various curiosities, including a samurai sword Liam's grandfather captured in Okinawa. Propped in the corner was a flintlock musket, perhaps five feet long, from the French and Indian War. Liam showed them a large, rusty bear trap his father once found while hiking in northern Maine. Two snowshoes, once worn by Liam's great-great uncle in the Yukon gold rush, protruded from a basket in another corner. A faded, framed campaign poster bearing a black-and-white photographic image of FDR hung on one of the brick pillars. Underneath the image were the words, "*Carry On With Roosevelt*."

Liam led them upstairs. They passed through the kitchen, into the dining room, and across the creaky but finely finished boards to a closet. Inside hung several American uniforms, mostly from the First and Second World Wars, complete with insignia.

Maureen said nothing. Liam led Jim and her into the sitting room. "We were in this room earlier today, but I want to call attention to one small feature."

Maureen and Jim drew alongside of Liam, who stood right before a window.

"If you look closely at the panes here, and on many of the other windows, you can see etchings of initials, even some names and dates."

"What are they?" Maureen said.

"Those were done by Phillips Exeter students. As early as 1844," Liam said, fascination in his voice. "My grandpa Norman bought this house in 1946, but it had only been a house for twenty-seven years. Before that, it was a dormitory, run by a resident dorm master. Generations of Exeter students scratched their names, initials, nicknames, dates, even tiny cartoons into the glass. See this one here?" Liam pointed at one set of numbers.

"1-21-1905," Maureen said. "January twenty-first, nineteen oh five."

"Rough Ridin' Teddy Roosevelt," Jim said, "had just been inaugurated commander-in-chief for his second term the day before. It was probably the talk of the town when that kid etched that one. He was probably tryin' to pass time in the dead of a New England winter."

"Good job," Liam said. "You're probably right on that one. Now let's make a little detour back into the corridor to see the TV room."

Liam led them into the hall, then hooked right into the neighboring room. "I refurbished those Victorian couches myself. Tried to make 'em look more authentic with that fabric."

"My," Maureen said. "I like that crimson one."

"Thanks. Come and see the foyer you first entered." Liam led them back into the hallway, past the sitting room, and then into the main foyer. "I just put a nineteenth century doorknob on that front door. Got it in Brimfield, Mass. Excellent place to buy antiques and solid military items. The sellers often don't know what they're selling."

Liam then led them up the stairwell. The wooden rail was just above waist level, and had been sanded down.

"Hold tight to it, but don't count on it to support you if you fall," Liam said with a cackle. "Hey, just being honest! You may want to hold on to Jim, too!"

"You've been sanding that rail," Jim said as they ascended to the second floor.

"You're peeling off that old wallpaper?" Maureen said.

Liam paused just above them. "It's a work in progress. I'm trying to turn the dial back well into the nineteenth century on this entire place, peeling off all three layers of wallpaper and applying Victorian-era design." He pointed to the wall. "That red wallpaper's from the late forties. My grandparents put that stuff up. The yellow one's from the 1880s. That blue layer dates from before the Civil War. Probably the original stuff, dating to 1844."

"Didn't the really old wallpaper contain arsenic?" Maureen wrinkled her nose.

"I don't know, Maur." Jim clapped a hand onto her shoulder. "There's only one way to know. Lick!"

Maureen cast Jim a mock-furious glance.

"Hey, you lick it, Jim," Liam said. "It really might give you a good buzz!"

They proceeded to the top of the creaking stairwell and turned left down the dark corridor. To their immediate right was a closed door, which Jim had rarely seen open.

"How's Ms. Gloria these days, Liam?" Jim whispered, pointing to the door.

"Keeping to herself as always. Quiet as a church mouse."

"Oh, Liam! Liam!" Jim whispered in a witchlike voice,

impersonating the eccentric, reclusive old widow. "Maureen, Gloria is Liam's only tenant. And her son crashes here. Often. She relishes any opportunity to torment poor Liam with unsolicited advice."

Liam turned left and followed the rail around toward a door on top of two walking steps. "Here's my room, Maureen." He opened the door at the end of the hallway, revealing the room containing the nineteenth century bed he bought at an antique sale in northern Vermont.

Liam pointed at the fireplace. "I still use it from time to time on winter nights."

"Or when he tries to impress a lady guest!" Jim said.

Maureen sniffled, smirking.

"And that little cubbyhole over there is where I buy and sell all my wares, every day. And many nights." Liam pointed at the desktop computer in the tiny room connected to his bedroom, just to their left. A window beyond the desk overlooked the street. Several of the panes also bore some of the students' etchings.

"And now, last but not least, I'll show you, Maureen, where this swamp creature crashed last fall."

Liam returned to the hall. At the attic door, he unfastened the latch. "This ancient device here's original to the house. You'll never see such a latch manufactured today. My dad's little brother Bruce would undo this every day. His room was up there. Bruce passed away in a car accident at seventeen. I never told Jim that, 'cause I wanted him to actually get sleep up there."

A tremor coursed like an icy trickle down Jim's spine. "My," was all he could muster. What truths proceed from a tongue loosened by the drink.

"Shall we ascend?" Liam said, smiling. He opened the door and continued up the narrow stairwell. Even the steps themselves seemed suitable for children or a diminutive adult. Jim could fit a little over half of his foot on each step, unless he turned that foot sideways. "You may want to lean forward, Maureen, use your hands on the steps," Jim said with a serious tone. "That's how I used to have to do it."

Maureen set down her glass on the small hallway dresser and returned to the open attic doorway.

"This is odd," Maureen muttered as she took Jim's advice, following Liam up the staircase, ahead of Jim. "Blue wallpaper still on the walls."

"No owner ever removed or replaced it," Liam said. "Or even renovated the attic."

Maureen reached the top and stepped onto the floor of the attic hallway. Two seconds later, Jim emerged. Liam stood nearby, waiting. The ebbing twilight filtered through a lone window in the next room, highlighting the silhouette of the great sugar maple outside the front door. Under the window, the mattress lay upon the wooden floor, its sheets pulled back as if someone had just risen.

Liam yanked a cord dangling from the ceiling. A bulb overhead filled the attic with soft light. He pointed to a cubbyhole in the wall, now filled with old books and toys, and spanned by cobwebs.

"That was constructed as a sort of safe by the original builders. Even Grandpa was unaware of its existence. One day he moved a bed frame and gouged the wall, right there. He discovered a hidden closet, filled with some old books from a professor and army lieutenant who once owned this house. His saber and Federal army uniform were there, too. My dad has them all locked up down at his house in Connecticut. But there was one last item in there—"

"What was it?" Maureen said.

"That framed lithograph you guys saw hanging down in the man cave."

Maureen stared into the cluttered cavity, its walls thin slats seemingly composed of balsa wood.

"That lithograph was produced in Washington in the springtime of 1865, just after Abe's assassination. Lincoln lithographs were especially popular in this town. I don't know about Jim's hometown, though."

Liam shot Jim a sly look.

"Lincoln's party was born here, just at the end of this street. His son Robert studied at Phillips Exeter. When Lincoln died, a long spell of mourning hit here. The townspeople always entertained the President and his family on their visits. And I should mention, there's a chance Robert Todd Lincoln roomed in this house."

"My," Jim said. He was impressed every time he heard the story.

"That is something," Maureen said.

"And now, next, but not least," Liam paused to create an air of suspense. "There's the makeshift bedroom over there, where Bruce lived." He led them across the creaking boards into the room. "The first soul to sleep in this attic in forty years was Jim here."

"Did you guys happen to *clean* before he took up residence?" Maureen said.

"I did when he emailed that he'd accepted my invite and was flying up here," Liam said. Jim caught the discomfort in his face.

They three stood in the center of the room. Jim and Liam looked down at the mattress on the floor, with its blanket torn back, like they were looking at a body in a coffin. Liam turned and stepped toward the closet, its door ajar.

"You left one of your shirts in there, I see," Liam said. He took the shirt, still on its hanger, and handed it to Jim. Holding up the shirt, Jim whispered what was printed on its front.

SEWANEE
CLASS OF 1999
ECCE QUAM BONUM!

"Liam, how could we ever forget those times, my friend?"

"That would be impossible. Consider our time-honored motto, after all. *Ecce quam bonum*. 'Behold how good!'"

"Ah, man," Jim said, "so many memories of this room, so many memories." He felt the emotions crash within him like a great wave.

Hands on her hips, Maureen pivoted. Jim followed her gaze, wondering what she was thinking. She glanced at the room's disheveled bed, then its floor of robin's egg blue one-by-twelve boards, its lone third-story window, and its low cracked ceiling, which sloped diagonally downwards as it reached the walls. A serious expression dominated her face, manifesting both reflection and irritation.

"Mmmph," she muttered, barely audibly, as she stepped into the doorway. Then she spoke in a louder voice, in the midst of exhaling. “You guys thinking of getting that seafood ready? My stomach’s just *growling*.”

Liam paused. “You bet.”

She turned and started down the stairs, breaking the proper solemnity and sanctity of the moment. Liam walked reluctantly behind, his arms folded across his chest. Jim’s eyes met his friend’s, as Liam pulled the cord of the overhead bulb.

The tap and thud of shoes on steps drifted through the attic. Jim lingered for a few seconds. He looked down. He could barely make out the mattress with its lone pillow and its ruffled sheets half pulled back. He recalled the roof membrane pulled back off the Superdome, but quickly purged the thought from his mind.

Jim clutched the shirt as he stepped toward the window. The old sugar maple was still rooted in the grassy patch out front, a branch reaching within feet of the window. He couldn’t remember ever seeing the great tree verdant and bursting with leaves.

Beyond the tree, on the other side of Court Street, lay a row of homes dating back to the eighteenth century. In the evening’s fading twilight, Jim stared out at the town that was once like a second home to him, the town that once took him in as one of its own, on that night of the fifteenth of September.

He twitched, then drew in a quick breath. Court Street below filled slowly with dark water. With sirens blaring in the distance, the Orleans Parish school bus plowed down the road, dividing the water. In the windows were women and children, staring with wide eyes and open mouths through the glass.

He turned his back to the window and slowly walked past the mattress toward the stairwell. It was not the first dark vision he suffered in this room. Jim glanced down at the mattress again. He imagined himself thrashing and jolting awake and sweaty between the sheets.

The voices of Maureen and Liam drifted up from the first floor, speculating on his absence.

Chapter Thirty-Seven

That evening Jim and Maureen had driven as far south as Stoneham when Maureen's cell rang. They both had lobbed calls in to Kathleen Henretty all day, to no avail.

When Maureen's phone lit up, an unfamiliar number appeared. "It's a 508," she said.

Could be the Cape, Jim thought, looking over at her from the steering wheel. Or it could be from west of the city: Framingham, Westborough, or thereabouts.

"Hello?" Maureen said into the phone.

There were a few seconds of silence.

"Mom, we've been *trying* to reach you all day long! And some of yesterday! Yes, we're in the truck... yes, he's here with me... okay, one second..."

Maureen whispered. "Mom dropped and broke her phone. She's borrowing somebody's. She wants me to put it on speakerphone." Maureen punched a button and held the phone aloft between them. "Go on."

"Hey there, Kathleen," Jim said. "How're y'all?"

Some commotion arose in the background and then Kathleen's slightly hoarse voice came on the line. "I'm at a party down here on the island, not too far from Smith Point. So guys, would you believe me if I told you Walter won the whole thing? Again? At his age? With a crew and boat he didn't know?"

Jim laughed. "I told you he'd take it, Maureen!"

Maureen shook her head and smiled. "Daddy never ceases to surprise even me."

"So Walter and I have been at been at parties late this afternoon and evening," Kathleen said, "visiting all our old friends on the island. It's great. Walt's so happy. Not even tired! He's off with Spaulding and Jack at the Schwartzmanns'. I brought the car with me onto the ferry, so we'll drive tomorrow to the eastern side of Nantucket."

"When will you be back in Osterville?" Maureen said.

"Monday evening. We'll be here two more days at some parties, and Memorial Day late afternoon we'll ferry it back. Spaulding is yachting back to Chatham tomorrow with his son and the crew."

"It must be a hard life for them. And for you, this weekend," Maureen said.

Jim chuckled.

"You guys have fun today in Portland and Exeter?"

"We shopped in the Old Port. Jim ate his body weight in fried chicken at a Kennebunk Popeye's and seafood everywhere else."

"That was to be expected, dear," Kathleen said.

"His college friend Liam, who visited Jim in Boston, had us over to his house," Maureen said. "Tons of historical treasures inside. I can see how he and Jim became friends. I also saw Jim's first room when he evacuated to New England. Did you know our Jim slept on a mattress in a dusty attic for *five weeks*?"

"Sometimes you do what you must do, Maureen. I got to scoot, so tell me you love me and that you can't wait to see me."

"I love you, and I *can* wait to see you," Maureen said.

"Ha. Love you, too. Take care, Jim," Kathleen said.

"Thanks, Kathleen! I sure will. Give Walter my congrats!"

"Take good care of my little girl, young man." Kathleen hung up.

"I can't believe he won again," Maureen said.

"I just had a feeling the old salt would pull it off in the end," Jim said. "Wonder by how many seconds, or minutes."

"We'll soon learn," she said, looking out of the window.

Jim wondered what she was staring at, it being pitch black outside, save for the silhouette of the tree line. They were just south of Medford on Interstate 93, entering Somerville. In a few minutes they would hit Charlestown, then cross the Charles. They would park on Beacon Hill at the Henretty townhouse.

Other than fatigue from the long day, Jim did not know why he was so eager to reach his destination. Another night with the very person who regularly uttered comments such as the one about the mattress—he felt an ember within his gut. Where had her heart gone? What had happened to the girl he had fallen in love with months ago?

Back in the Louisburg Square brownstone, dangling his legs in the hot bath, Jim felt the need to get moving up out of the water, but where, he knew not. Bryce and Cara were in Connecticut for the weekend. Patrick was probably up to his usual mischief, lurking about town for his next female victim, someone he could use, or someone who could use him. Case probably was unloading luggage at Logan Airport or unwinding at his place in East Boston. Duff might still be in town, just a few streets away, off of Bowdoin.

Maybe he should have taken Maureen farther north along

the Maine coast to Bar Harbor or at least Camden. And what would they do tomorrow? Better yet, what would they do tonight?

And what did he expect to find at Maureen's place? Did he expect to find refuge with her, to relax and receive comfort? Perhaps he was like a dog coming in from a cold wintry night to warm himself against another dog, but instead finding only a hissing viper. Perhaps that metaphor was too extreme. But what pity or heartfelt affection or solace did he expect to get from her?

When he failed to pull her away from her laptop, he grabbed a volume of the old New England Transcendentalists and ran the warm water in the jacuzzi bath. For a few seconds, Jim cradled the book. As a boy, he read those writers with pleasure, but he had neglected them for years.

Jim warmed his legs in the water, striving to forget that the one who so recently wanted him moved back to her side was now ignoring him. He gently turned the pages of the old volume until he found an Emerson quote he loved, "*Give all to love; obey thy heart.*"

Had he not done this with Maureen? Was he now any happier for it? He had followed his heart and it had deceived him as to the worth of its object.

He found two more, Emerson's "*Hitch your wagon to a star*" and Thoreau's famous "*Go confidently in the direction of your dreams. Live the life you have imagined.*"

He had followed the latter in the past year. He had long dreamt of moving to the Northeast, to live there even for a few years. So far D.C. and Maryland were the closest he had come, nearly four years ago. Then business brought him away from the East to the Midwest and California for a few years. He had just moved back to Louisiana, at the dawn of 2005, and had worked eight months writing, renovating the house, and selling insurance when the great storm hit.

In the end, Jim *had* honored Thoreau's exhortation. He moved with confidence in the direction of his dreams—to explore more of the world. Jim attempted to remove himself from the insanity of Katrina's aftermath. Sadly, the insanity followed him. Or to his chagrin, he carried it *within* him. With the new fear.

Jim laid the volume aside and let the warm water run. After removing his clothes, he shut off the faucet, and lowered himself into the water.

The heat welcomed him, coursing along his nerves with a healing effect. But he was not hoping to savor it alone.

"Maureen?" he called with optimism.

"Yes?" she said from her bedroom, beyond the half open bathroom door.

"I ran us a bath. It feels amazing. Why don't you put that thing down and come on in?"

"I've got to return some emails. Just enjoy it. I'll shower later."

Jim let his chin fall to his chest, and wiped some water onto his face. He was disappointed, but not dejected. He expected as much.

On their first few dates, they had remained abstinent. Despite her involvement with the Boston social scene, she forged the impression she was a conservative girl, albeit an independent and modern one. They even attended Mass at St. Cecilia's on their second date. After a month together, they grew very physical after all the wine consumed one dinner at Number 9 Park. And it had just happened.

She was not much of an imbiber, nor did he aim to get her inebriated. But that night, drink nevertheless brought them over the line. They made love frequently for weeks thereafter, and it was quite good, but the run abruptly died off.

She insisted it was her guilt, and he understood, as he interacted so often with her father. Jim felt increasing guilt himself, as the old man continued to do everything in his power to help him. And with the relationship's new physical dimension, Maureen grew testy. Much of what Jim said or did irritated her. Yet once they ceased having sex, her moods did not much improve.

What is more, in the last few weeks her attitude had deteriorated markedly. What was it? Did she not completely trust him? Had she fallen out of love? She sometimes told him she loved him, when a phone conversation was ending, or when he kissed her goodbye. Yet now that he decided to move back to Boston, as she had desired, she seemed to be pulling away from him.

Jim lowered himself into the water, save for his head. He paused, then sank all the way under. He imagined how it must have been for those who drowned in those murky, vile waters nine months before. A fierce chill shot through him, and he surfaced, blowing the water out of his nostrils and wiping his eyes with his hands.

"Having fun in there?" Maureen said. At least her tone now seemed playful.

"What are your thoughts about tomorrow? If we want to end up at the Cape with everyone else in New England, we'll have to leave in the wee hours of the morning, beat the traffic. Or we could stay here in town, find something to do. We could head west to the Berkshires. Arrowhead is open now, Melville's home over in—"

"Actually, Heidi and some others from work are throwing a cookout in Cambridge. I kind of owe it to her to come, as I missed her birthday party last week."

Jim cringed. He had braved insults in New England, but never so many callous remarks by a previously unknown couple hosting him at a party. He barely escaped her boyfriend Chris' presence without committing an act of assault and battery. Surely Maureen *must* know the last place he hoped to go on Memorial Day weekend would be to a Cambridge cookout to be further probed and cross-examined by Maureen's circle of haughty friends.

Jim teetered on the verge of objecting, of calling her out on her lack of consideration and emotional intimacy. But he decided not to protest. What was the use? He would find something else to do.

He inhaled and sank once again beneath the comforting warmth of the water.

Chapter Thirty-Eight

At seven that Wednesday morning, Franco departed for the Henretty & Henretty Brokerage. Jim stood at the large window in his black pinstripe suit, sipping his coffee as he gazed out the back of their carriage house apartment.

Commuters sped down Storrow Drive. Just beyond, a smattering of joggers made their way down the grassy Esplanade, where elderly couples strolled the paved pathways. Daysailers skirted about on the Charles River just beyond, their sails swollen with the morning Atlantic winds. Beyond those jogging down Memorial Drive on the opposite bank were Cambridge and MIT's Great Dome. To his left, the Harvard Bridge, covered with all manner of walkers and joggers, spanned the Charles.

Jim clutched his briefcase and stepped down the narrow, brick-paved alleyway toward the asphalt lane behind the carriage house. After he circled around to Exeter Street, he commenced the few blocks' walk toward the John Hancock Tower on Copley Square.

Jim had never taken this exact route, although he was quite familiar with the neighborhood, one of his favorites in Boston. As he swung left off Exeter, up Beacon and toward Dartmouth, he let his eyes crawl around the copper bay windows, the bright red bricks, and the fish-scale slate roofs of the Victorian-era brownstones. He studied the lampposts and the black wrought-iron fences in front of the buildings. He peered down the cobblestone alleys, each marked with a sign bearing a different number.

And though he loved Back Bay, something gnawed at him.

Relocating to Boston had been a mistake. He felt guilty that he could be so pessimistic regarding the future with Maureen.

Yet in the deepest corner of his soul, he sensed his time in Boston was somehow past. He was destined to move on, but he was running from his destiny. Maybe he belonged back on the Cape with the boats and the sea. Maybe he belonged elsewhere, in a place he had not yet seen. And what if—just what if—Jim found true love in that novel place, a heart that fully returned his love? And what if he found a pursuit that fit him more than sales and seacraft? He could envision happiness and fulfillment in that land, that realm yet unglimpsed.

Jim crossed Commercial Avenue, or "Comm Ave," as the locals called it. People walked their dogs down its wide green median. He crossed Newbury, glancing to the right and left at the stores of designer clothes and sunglasses, the fine restaurants, the chic lounges. He did not miss the hard edge of the city, the impersonality. But he missed city life, its variety and diversions.

Jim continued up Dartmouth. On his left was a twenty-four hour Seven-Eleven, where he and Patrick had often stopped for hot dogs and sandwiches after long nights clubbing. Homeless men loitered outside the door. One man sat on the filthy pavement, his back against the concrete wall.

Just as Jim passed, the man lifted his eyes from the ground. Sorrow and exhaustion lengthened his sooty face, and his watery blue eyes were full of resignation, of surrender.

Jim tightened his grip on his briefcase and walked faster up Dartmouth. The homeless man said nothing as Jim passed him. Moments later, Jim recognized him.

Months ago, in the dead of winter, the man had been sitting at the entrance of a bank. Jim handed him a box of chicken wings. New to Boston, Jim had not yet met Maureen or Walter, Bryce, or Duff. He had just quit his job at the church in New Hampshire.

What had changed within him in Boston? Had he attained a rough edge, an impersonality? He quickened his pace.

Jim reached Boylston. Copley Square stretched before him. On his left rose Trinity Church, the Romanesque treasure of H.H. Richardson. Beyond this loomed the John Hancock Tower. To his right stood the Boston Public Library, the Lenox Hotel, and the many Boylston Street bars and restaurants. Thoughts of the homeless man faded. Memories of long, wild nights rushed in upon him.

The electronic sign signaled to walk. Jim pursued the small group of pedestrians attired in business formal and business casual, surely bound for work. Listening to their iPods or chatting, students heading to Emerson, Suffolk, or Boston University crossed Boylston and diverged right and left, walking half as fast as the suits.

Jim power-walked across Copley Square toward the John Hancock Tower, dispersing a small flock of wandering pigeons. Soon he stared at the elevator door, as he rose toward Henretty & Henretty's offices.

A series of memories flashed, one after the next, on the screen within his imagination. He first met Walter over drinks, blocks away at the bar at Abe and Louie's Steakhouse. His first date with Maureen was at Strega. Weeks later, they made love for the first time at her townhouse.

At Salty's at Faneuil Hall, he had introduced himself to Bryce. He envisioned Father Ben with arms outstretched, praying over him at Mass. He first met Duff at the social hour at St. Cecilia's in Back Bay, and helped his newfound blind friend down the stairwell. On those nights when Maureen stayed behind at her place, he wrote and read as he listened to music on his stereo.

Alone in Liam's attic, on the mattress until autumn turned too cold, he had dreamed of New Orleans every night and what he had left, what he had lost. He imagined Freddy gasping his last on that Mid-City roof, his mouth opened wide like a drowning man's. Then there appeared the panorama of his native city as the National Guard chopper and its cord spirited him through the air and over the flood.

The elevator beeped and the doors parted. A new secretary sat behind the lobby desk. He flashed his badge, and then walked forward and held it to the scanner. The glass door slid open.

"Surprise!" The greeting exploded throughout the room. Everyone stood and clapped.

"Welcome back!" a female voice screamed.

"Hey, Jimmy!" a man shouted.

Many wore party hats, as if for a child's birthday. Jim walked toward them, greeting everyone by name. Each one offered him pats on the back, handshakes, a few hugs, or words of welcome delivered in both sincerity and fakery.

Franco appeared, his hand extended. "Good to have you

back, man. There's cake in the break room."

"Nice surprise, this welcome here. Your idea?"

"Nah," Franco said. "It was his."

Standing in the doorway of the corner office, above the walls of cubicles, Walter Henretty smiled at Jim. Dashing in a navy blue suit and yellow tie, he leaned against the frame of his doorway, gripping his coffee mug with his left hand.

"'Scuse me a sec, bud," Jim told Franco, and walked toward the corner office.

As Jim rounded the large block of cubicles, the old man maintained the same position against the doorframe, smiling away. "Welcome back, Jim."

"Great to be back, Walter. I appreciate the party."

"They missed ya here, son."

"You got my voicemail on your cell, right, congratulating you on your victory? I knew you'd pull it off."

"Thanks. Come on in, take a seat."

Jim sat in one of the two black leather seats facing the desk, which Walter circled and sat behind.

"That really was my last Figawi. Joints are absolutely killing me." The old man winced and massaged his lower back with one hand. "You all settled in at your new place with Franco?"

"I devoted all of yesterday to moving and touching up some things around the apartment."

"Are you happy with it?"

Jim nodded. "I love the view, too. I'm very indebted."

"Well, you deserve it. We won't forget you down in the shop. But sometimes a man's got to hold fast to his duty. And priorities."

"Very true," Jim said.

The old man made a pensive face and leaned slightly forward. "Maureen confided last night she's been a little off the last few days, still in shock you're back. Getting used to her old life all over again. But I think she's getting happier, Jim."

"That's what I wanted."

"Now, I just rallied the troops before the party here. I'll depart momentarily. Anything I can do? Dewey wants to go over some client files with you. Obviously, your colleagues will keep what you gave them, but we have several other leads and a few current client accounts to provide to help you rise back to the top. Just ease into it. Because your first full week is next week."

Jim leaned back in his chair. Could it really be this easy? "Thank you, Walter."

"Don't mention it. I look forward to our boat trip this weekend."

Jim could feel his own eyes enlarge, just for a moment, at the thought of the open water.

"So, Jimmy, I'll call you tomorrow morning. We'll get it all queued up for the kids and the meeting place and the carpooling and everything else. Now if you'll excuse me, I've just got to meet with one more person."

Walter rose. They shook hands firmly, and Jim headed down the hall toward Dewey.

When lunchtime arrived, Jim left the office for the Copley stop, rode the T to the State Street station, and walked up the stairs to the street. He took heart that friends had answered his texts so quickly.

Jim quickened his pace down State Street, hooked left down Congress, turned right on North, then finally took a left on Union. Jim's heart warmed to see the old four-storied landmark, the oldest restaurant in America. Huge glowing red letters spelled out its name on the roof: *UNION OYSTER HOUSE.* He did not know which he loved more, the small semicircular oyster bar once frequented by Daniel Webster himself, or the second floor, where a French royal had dwelled in exile.

Inside, Bryce, Case, and Duff were seated at the oyster bar next to an empty stool. They sipped water and enjoyed bowls of chowder.

"Hey hey hey!" Jim slapped each on the back. "Great to see y'all again."

"Whoo hoo!" Case cheered.

The others greeted Jim as he sat. Bryce smiled expectantly. Behind his dark sunglasses, Duff listened, facing forward, his kneecaps pressed together to secure his walking stick. Case seemed un-Bostonian as always with his long, shaggy hair and ruffled University of New Mexico t-shirt.

"Y'all sure got here fast," Jim said.

"I cabbed it over here from Franklin Street," Duff said. "I wanted to catch you on your first day back."

"I took the T here. Ride was mere minutes," Bryce said. "Gotta love it."

"I'm a free man!" Case shouted. "For a few hours I'm free from seedy-ass Eastie and my soul-numbing job unloading luggage at tha *Low-gen aya-pawt*!"

Jim laughed at his friend's impression of the working-class Boston accent. Practicing it was one of their most cherished pastimes.

Jim had met Case after a job interview months back.

Chatting and drinking Guinness together in the great Irish pub downtown, the Black Rose, or the Roisin Dubh, Case uncannily declared, "You are from southern Louisiana, not too far from the Big Easy."

Case had studied linguistics at the University of New Mexico. He had just returned that week from several months in Slovakia teaching English, and like Jim, was scouring Boston for employment. Jim had revised Case's résumé for a teaching position but Case instead took a job at Logan Airport loading luggage onto planes. Over the winter, Case de-iced the planes' wings. He now lived in a messy East Boston hovel and spent much of his time bemoaning the rudeness of his miserable colleagues. He always related his yearning to climb more of the mountains out west and to find love with one of "the many naturally gorgeous, unpretentious women of Eastern Europe." Patrick constantly ribbed Case that he had never kissed an American woman. Jim couldn't help but snicker at the joke, whenever it was told.

"Look at the bright side, Case," Duff said. "You'll soon be free of that roommate of yours, the obsessive compulsive cab-driver, and—"

"I'll be climbing peaks and skiing the slopes full-time out in the Rockies. And no more crazy roommate, no de-icing planes, no unloading luggage, no soulless coworkers."

"What kind of hassle could anyone encounter in Crested Butte, after all?" Bryce laughed.

"So Jim, I'm glad you texted me about lunch," Case said. "You know, Bryce, Duff, if I got along better with my family, I would've taken the rail up to visit my brother Wade. He and his wife in Newburyport don't really want me around. My mom up in Nashua has her own gig with her new husband. My dad's just too far away, almost in Canada. Hey, speaking of getting along, Jim, things any better with Maureen?"

"She's been showing me almost no affection or interest, especially for the last few days. Even weeks. Maybe she's fallen out of love. Maybe she just wanted to somehow extricate me from her dad's business and property down there, pave the way for an easier break-up."

Bryce shook his head, almost dazed. "That's pretty dark."

"Jim, you gotta be free. Just let her go," Case said. "Move out with me to Colorado. I'll teach you how to ski. We can work at one of the lodges. Meet some of the cool girls moving there from all over the country. No more probing as to whether you graduated Ivy or if you belong to the right country club. You can write and I'll show you some of the reservations, the mountains. We can road trip it to Utah and Arizona and Taos, check out the petroglyphs."

"Maureen's really just going through a phase," Jim said.

"Watch out for making excuses for her," Case said. "No one can fully watch out for you but you."

"Whatever the case, I need to keep working for her father. He's just helped me out so much. And he comped my move back to Boston."

"He's doing it for his daughter, Jim," Duff said. "Hey, I'm sure he's a nice guy—"

"He's most likely looking after his family, his little girl, first and foremost," Case said. "Don't lose sight of that. He wants what's right for Maureen."

"Don't be so cynical. He cares about my welfare, too."

"But you weren't exactly liking that investments job.

Remember all the times you ranted to me about it, and—"

"What else right now will give me the income I need to live in this city?"

"That's one reason you've gotta split. For you especially, Beantown's unlivable. Look, I know you. Haven't you read your Kerouac and your Edward Abbey? You need something different, man."

The bartender approached, pad in hand.

"I'll go for a bowl of lobster bisque," Jim said. "And a half-dozen Pemaquids and a half-dozen Wellfleets."

"There you go!" Duff said.

"Anything to drink?" the bartender said.

"A Sam. Boston Lager, please."

Bryce shook his head, laughing. "Good having you back, James. So how's the first day back at the old job?"

"Oh, not too shabby." Jim sighed, folded his arms, and rested his elbows on the bartop. He blankly stared down at its smooth wood.

"You don't look so well," Bryce said. "Is it just Maureen? The job? You miss the boats?"

"Is it that you miss your family?" Duff said. "Hometown?"

A long moment of silence ensued.

Jim finally turned, and his friends were waiting for his answer. "More and more by the day," Jim said. The spent sound in his own voice surprised him.

In the eyes of his friends he noted a tinge of worry, a certain disappointment. He must show his appreciation.

"But... I am really happy to see you all. And this weekend, I'll be on the open seas."

Jim felt better that the truth was out. The bartender handed him the frosty pint. Jim mumbled a thank you, brought it to his lips, and drank deep.

So he had voiced it. Up until now he had kept it within, submerged. What he could not disclose to them was that fear he felt building in the last few days for the coming expedition. Time and grit and experience had lessened, but not quelled, his anxiety over the water.

But there could be no room for bowing out. The fear ignited and spread within him. Jim paused, and with ferocity, drank another long gulp of the lager.

Chapter Thirty-Nine

At nine on Friday morning the two Club Wagons pulled into the Hyannis harbor parking lot. Tanya Ward drove the van carrying her husband, Jim, and the Mount Zion boys. Sarah Murphy drove the other van, with her husband, Jack Spaulding, and the St. Brendan boys as passengers.

Walter Henretty stood on the dock, beaming a broad, toothy smile. "Mornin' to you guys," he said as the vehicles emptied.

The boys sprinted toward him, some of them gleefully leaping like grasshoppers.

They all looked at the schooner, anchored out in the harbor. All about Jim were sighs and expressions of wonder.

The hum of a boat motor sounded across the water. The dinghy zipped toward them, and a familiar figure manned the motor. His long light blond hair and flinty face brought to mind a Viking set upon a morning raid.

"Ladies and gentlemen, Bill is coming. My best and most experienced worker and sailor from my boat shop, to ensure the trip goes smoothly. And on board is one other worker from my shop, Chief. He volunteered to serve as donkeyman, or the one who mans the engine room and the generators. Chief knows more about boat engines than anyone. So tell me," Walter said, "are you young sailors ready for the ultimate expedition?"

"Yeah! Yeah!" the boys cheered.

"Yes, Commodore Henretty!" Jack Spaulding said with gusto, saluting the old man, who cackled with delight.

"Clown," Walter said with a crooked smile.

"Aye aye, skipper," Jim joined in, walking up to Walter. He felt in better spirits. He loved that Maureen arrived that morning at his apartment on her way to work to see him off. It seemed like a throwback to the Maureen of the first days, scarcely six months ago. Perhaps things would turn around. And it could start with this weekend when he would indulge in his favorite aspect of New England life, the close bond with the sea.

"At the ready, Cap'n!" Tim Murphy shouted, giving a salute. Reverend Ward stood beside Tim, smiling.

"We'll have a blast, gents," Walter said. "I'm grateful for your help, Tanya and Sarah, in dropping everyone off safely and on time. I'll make sure to return 'em to you in the same manner."

The wives thanked him and, having set the boys' gear on the ground nearby, stayed to observe.

"Now Reverend Ward, Jim, Jack, Tim, please see to it that all gear's put into the dinghy bit by bit. Bill and Jim will take trips to the boat and get the gear up on deck. Then Bill will take the crew out there, two at a time."

Jim gazed out at the three proud masts and all one hundred and six feet of her. She was truly a sight to behold. He never felt such a thrill standing before a boat, not an ocean liner or even the U.S.S. Constitution in Charlestown.

A hand slapped his shoulder. Bill laughed as giddily as one of the boys. "Good to see ya again, bud."

"Same here, Bill!" Jim said. "Let's get this boring part over with and set sail."

After thirty minutes, with all duffel bags stowed below deck and crew accounted for, everyone stood on deck wearing a life preserver. Walter made one last run-through, checking all of the equipment and provisions. Several boaters amassed on shore, chatting and observing what some probably recognized was an authentic Herreshoff schooner.

Walter returned to the bow. He ordered Jack and Bill to untie the dinghy, and told Jim and the Reverend to winch it up from the water.

"Lieutenants Scoresby, Murphy, Spaulding!" Walter said some minutes later. "Take these positions. Scoresby to the aft, Murphy to the mizzenmast, Spaulding to the foremast. Lieutenant Ward, stand by on the aft deck with Jim. Bill—I mean Lieutenant McGreevey—will see to it the anchor's aweigh and he'll float around and help where it's needed."

Jim sneaked a look back. Clad in his nautical gear, Walter stood with his hands fixed at his hips. Though his face reddened as he barked out the orders, he mouthed the words through a smiling face. The old man clearly loved it.

"Now, Lieutenant McGreevey, raise anchor!"

The anchor loosened from the harbor floor and rose upwards toward the bow.

"Now men, at my command, unfasten halyard knots! And raise sails and tie down. Now, get ready, set... *go!*"

The men pulled the halyards down with all their might. The sails rose bit by bit to the tops of the masts. In moments, the wind billowed the sails.

Walter stationed himself in the cockpit and turned the

wheel a few degrees. The great ship veered even farther away from the shore. In a few minutes, Walter spun the wheel hard. The ship turned until it moved directly south.

The men and boys glanced shoreward. A great cry of jubilation arose from the onlookers, about twenty of them now. Perhaps they picked up on the semi-military decorum of the ship's departure. Walter had not acted so in all the days of their training. Perhaps the old captain aimed to ham it up for the crowds and, in turn, he wanted the boys to feel like they were part of an authentic, bold expedition.

Soon the harbor and Hyannis itself were barely discernable in the distance. The quasi-military atmosphere vanished. Four of the lieutenants—Bill, Reverend Ward, Jack, and Tim—congregated on the foredeck, along with the boys. Everyone clutched the rails and stared past the bow. The boys pointed at circling gulls and at what looked like a porpoise moving far off in the water.

In the cockpit, Jim grasped the wheel. The old man stood beside him, puffing his pipe contentedly, watching the ship slice windward through the waves. Neither man spoke for several minutes as the ship progressed on its southerly route.

After they ventured farther south, away from the shore toward Nantucket, and away from Uncle Robert's Cove just to their port side, he must turn the wheel until they headed due east. Once they reached a few miles east of Chatham, he would turn the ship directly north, pass the Cape's tip at Provincetown, and then head north-northwest toward Boston. If they did not make good enough time on this route, Walter had decided, they would dock in Plymouth harbor and call Tanya and Sarah to meet them.

"So, I know you puff a cigar every once in a while," Walter said. "But pipes are an enjoyment in themselves. I almost like pipes enough to introduce you to them, but that's a habit ya don't need, son."

"I bought one in a smoke shop in Portsmouth. A cheap Grabow, that's all. I puff it sometimes, but Maureen detests it. Hey, you really do look quite the captain with one. Both Admirals Halsey and Nimitz smoked pipes at sea."

"Correct you are. Ya see this pipe here, son?" He held it up to Jim's face. "A little scuttlebutt for ya. This belonged to my father, a navy captain in his own right. A 1922 Dunhill, bent style, with a rusticated bowl. Dad bought this to celebrate crossing the Panama Canal into the Gulf of Mexico. He was on his way back to Boston. When they docked for the weekend in Mobile, Dad spotted this in a shop. Early Dunhills, made by Alfred Dunhill, they're considered by many to be the very best pipes in the world. After 1915, they started putting this single white dot on the vulcanite stem, see? It's their trademark. This dot's made of ivory but eventually they started using plastic. After 1955, you know, Dunhill bowls weren't made from the same kind of briarroot. Though they still tasted great, they weren't quite the same."

"That's intriguing," Jim said. He stared at the white dot. "I knew vaguely of those pipes. My Granddaddy Scoresby smoked one during his decades with the Tennessee Valley Authority. He built dams and bridges and roads as a civil engineer. All across Tennessee, Georgia, Alabama, South Carolina, Mississippi. I've seen Granddaddy puffing the pipe in pictures, but somehow it was misplaced."

"I have another Dunhill below deck, Jimmy. It's a '51. I

bought it in San Francisco on my way out to Korea. But I want you to have this one. Have a *real* pipe. After I finish this last bowl, of course."

"But what about Davie? I bet he'll want to—"

"He would have none of it. He makes fun of me, says it makes me look more like a geezer. I've got other things to give him anyway. He won't appreciate this like you would."

"Thanks, Walter. I really, really like it."

"That's why it'll be yours. So how ya like steering this baby? I can't offer you the *ship*, ya know."

"I understand that! Well, yes, I really like handling the wheel," Jim said. "Sailing seems to me a lot like golf, or fishing. Or smoking a pipe. It's a meditative thing, for an introspective person. Something not suitable for someone impatient or wound up too tightly."

"That's pretty insightful," Walter said as he nodded. "Hey, handle that wheel for a few. I'll be back shortly. I'm checking on the men up front. It won't be too long 'til we swing this old gal due east."

"Aye aye, Cap."

"That's my boy." Walter slapped him hard on the back, then strutted out of the cockpit, across the deck toward the bow.

"Are we having fun, or what?!" the old man yelled, raising his fists high above his head in jubilation and pumping his arms in excitement. "This beats anything else we could've done, gents! You're all sea-ready New Englanders now, even the crazy Cajun manning the wheel back there. Look at him!" The old man pointed at the cockpit.

The kids cheered and laughed.

"Come join us, Jim!" one of the St. Brendan boys screamed.

"Yeah, just leave that wheel and come and hang out here," one of the Mount Zion boys shouted.

Jim shook his head and motioned "no" with his hand. He smiled, looking out at the waves that no longer seemed to scare him, and recalled Walter's spontaneous gift of the Dunhill.

His thoughts drifted toward the Boston brokerage.

It would be tougher going this time around. He was not built for such work and, if he were honest with himself, he was even starting to dislike it. But he once rose to be the top broker at Henretty & Henretty. He could do it again. It could bring Maureen and him a great living.

But when would he write? Trading drained him of time and energy. And he always remained on standby with his cell phone. A good night's sleep and three meals a day were so rare, they were sacred.

He studied the wheel in his hands, its polished wooden handles pointing outward from the circular center like rays of the sun. What a truly meditative pursuit sailing is, he thought. It lacks the sheer adrenaline surge found in powerboat racing, or even power boating. But sailing suits those of my ilk.

Walter left the group at the bow and walked toward him. He pointed at Jim and winked, then veered across the deck and disappeared down the hatch. He reappeared several minutes later, emerging from the stairwell on Jim's side, with something in his hand.

"Here, Jimmy boy," Walter said, handing him his father's Dunhill. "Told you it was yours. I just cleaned it. Treat it well. Give it to your son one day. I've got mine here, the '51."

"My, thanks again. Now that's a gift." Jim took the pipe and placed in it a side pocket of his cargo shorts and buttoned it in.

Walter held another pipe in his hand. He sat down on one of the benches next to the wheel and withdrew a small plastic bag from his pocket. After pinching some tobacco from the bag, he packed the bowl. He returned the tobacco to his pocket and placed the pipe in his mouth. With one hand he cupped the bowl, with the other, despite the wind, he lit the tobacco.

"That was the hardest thing to learn, would ya believe it?" Walter said, raising his eyebrows. "Lighting one of those babies on deck."

"I can imagine," Jim said.

"I checked on Chief. He's fine-tuning something on the engine. And I visited with the kiddoes. They're just elated. They've never ventured this far out. They've all swam before, but no trips in rivers or lakes or the ocean. They're proud of ya at that wheel. They can't wait for their turns. I might make a Navy man out of one of 'em yet."

"Hey, Walt, think we may still get rain today?"

"I checked the radio again," Walter said. "And I checked the Net right before we left. Possible drizzle, fifty percent chance, for the evening. Not enough to postpone the trip. If the sky leaks a bit, son, it won't last long. We'll just put the kids below deck, have 'em play cards or something while I steer us along."

"Doesn't sound bad."

"We'll never be too far from shore anyway. And ya know, Jim, it rained a little during the Figawi, Sunday and late Saturday. Some boats dropped out."

"Apparently, you didn't," Jim said.

They both looked at each other and grinned.

"Wonder what Maureen's doin' right now," Jim said.

"Hopefully thinking of you."

"She saw me off today," Jim said. "I think she's emerging from her slump."

After a moment of silence, Walter raised a finger. "Let me see that wheel a second. Never mind, you steer it. Pull us east now, fully parallel with the shore, per that GPS. We're far enough out in the sound."

Jim turned the wheel steadily with both hands.

"Ah, good, son. You've come far. My latest pupil! Tell ya what, Jim. You go up to the bow and visit with the guys. Be my eyes on the ground. Do a little reconnaissance for me. Are they getting along up there? None of 'em better misbehave or mouth off to each other like last time."

Jim strode across the deck, past the booms and under the three great masts, which rose like massive pillars above him. "Hey hey hey, gentlemen!" His words carried an upbeat lilt.

"We saw a whale!" Lance cried.

"It was jumpin' over there in the distance!" Dwayne shouted, pointing starboard into the horizon.

"Wow... seriously?" Jim said.

"Yeah," Scott said. "Then it crashed into the water. It musta died of shock when it saw our big ship."

The laughing LaRon clapped Scott affectionately on the back. On their last trip, the two had not been exactly friendly with each other, nearly coming to blows. Now Scott buckled over with laughter.

"What great fun this is!" Reverend Ward said. "Right, Dwayne?"

"Yeah!" The diminutive boy screamed with delight.

Reverend Ward shot Jim an animated look of amusement

and glee.

"This is the life!" Tim Murphy pumped his fists above his head. "And no burning buildings or five-alarm fires out here."

"You're home free from that." Jack looked back at Jim. A hint of weariness lingered about the eyes.

"How're you likin' this, Mr. Spaulding?" Jim said.

"Can't complain, really," Jack said, forcing a smile. "We've got great sunshine, strong winds. We've got the open seas and a legendary vessel."

Jim studied Jack's face. Natasha was at it again. Jack was finding it harder to conceal. At least Maureen wasn't the only one.

He glanced sternward at the lone figure gripping the wheel. If only he could one day achieve what the old man had. A happy, healthy relationship, success in one's career and hobbies, and nearing retirement with wealth. Where could these be won? On his current path?

The old man stared past Jim into the horizon, his expression hardy as a seawall.

Chapter Forty

An hour had passed since they anchored in Chatham harbor. Reverend Ward, Tim, and Jack had taken the boys below deck for dinner when the rain came. Not an intense rain, but instead little more than a drizzle ensued, enough that the men shut all of the portholes anyway. Only Walter, Bill, Chief, and Jim remained above deck, clad in their raingear and seated under the wooden-roofed cockpit.

"We could've pressed on," Bill said. "We still got some good winds. Conceivably, you and I could've taken turns, Jim. One fella sleeping, the other steering. But it really isn't worth the risk. And sailing alone at night? You got some experience, but not *that* much. We were too close to Chatham to keep going. There isn't enough light to maneuver around those damned shoals. They can be treacherous."

"Agreed," Jim said.

"We better grab some chow, son," Walter said. "And catch some z's. All night in!"

Below deck, the boys were tucked into bed in their respective cabins. Walter motioned for Jim, Chief, and Bill to follow. He pointed to the galley, where they removed their raingear and piled it into the sink. Walter opened the pantry drawer and removed some bananas, cans of tuna and ziplocked bags of sandwiches. The four men stood in the galley in silence, wolfing down the food and downing bottled water. Sheets of rain pelting the deck overhead were the only sounds.

The old man pointed at Jim. "Get some good sleep, my boys. Rest your bones well. I'm waking you guys first."

They tiptoed down the hall. Bill and Chief entered their cabin. Near the end of the corridor, Walter pointed at the guest cabin. Jim entered and heard Walter shutting the captain's cabin door. Jim shut his own door, and removed his clothes and shoes. He tore back the blanket and shot under the covers.

Yet sleep did not come for nearly two hours. In the haunted corridors and chambers of his mind lurked the familiar demons and wraiths. A cascade of thoughts crashed against each other—thoughts of Maureen, his friends in Boston, his parents and brother, Liam and Father Ben and the townspeople he remembered in Exeter. Eventually, Jim drifted off to sleep.

Jim found himself lying on the hot roof, eating from a bag of sliced bread. He pulled slice after slice from the bag, feasting away while he watched the clouds above creep by. Jim suddenly realized a flood had risen around the house. Freddy lay feet away near the edge of the roof, pleading for help, but before Jim could reach him, the waters engulfed him.

Somehow Jim stood in St. Louis Cemetery Number One at twilight. He ran through the labyrinthine lanes and alleys, weaving between the temple-like burial crypts, many of them cracked and crumbling, in search of his friend's grave.

A familiar voice arose nearby, old and deep and gravelly. "Lookin' fa me, podnuh?"

His old friend stood about one hundred feet down the lane. With one arm, he held his guitar pointed to the ground, a look of grief on his face.

"Freddy? Freddy!" Jim screamed. "Where did you go?"

"I wanted to live, Jimmy. I didn't want to leave just yet. Almost none of us did. I wanted to live! You know I wanted to live..."

Jim's mouth opened. The tone of Freddy's response was among the saddest he had ever heard.

He sprinted toward the ghost. He was halfway there when it vanished. Jim wept feverishly as he continued toward the end of the lane. The twilight gave way, second by second, to pitch black.

Jim jolted awake. He lay in bed, wet with sweat, despite the cool air of the cabin. He must have been weeping aloud. Jim wiped his eyes and peered at the crack under the cabin door. The corridor light was on, and he recognized the outline of two feet. Seconds later, the feet were gone, the steps fading down the corridor.

Chapter Forty-One

Morning commenced with a rap on the cabin door. Jim rubbed his eyes, slid out of bed, and turned the knob. Walter and Chief looked caffeinated and well rested.

"Rise 'n' shine, Jimmy!" Bill said.

"That's right!" Jim said. "We've gotta be up before the others. I'll meet y'all in the galley in five."

Jim dressed and walked to the galley. Walter was waiting.

"Hey, Jimmy, let's wake everyone. Have them all meet us here in ten minutes. You and I can grab some grub here later. You take cabin rooms one, two, and three. I'll wake up the rest."

Jim rapped on the three doors. Tim opened one. Reverend Ward and Jack opened the others.

"Mornin', gents," Jim said. "Walter and I will have a li'l breakfast prepared in the mess room. Let's all meet up there in ten."

Back in the mess room, Walter, Bill, Chief and Jim pulled out the table, set it, and arranged the chairs. Walter pointed Jim toward the galley counter, where cereal had been poured into bowls. The men grabbed some bananas and ate standing. Walter then greeted the remainder of the crew as they filed in.

"Hey there, sleepyheads! How's everyone feeling?" Walter said. "Take your seats. There's cereal and fruit and drinks for everybody. Dig in. Don't save a spot for us. We've eaten and we're going on deck. But we'll be back shortly."

Everyone complied, chattering and joking. Some boys recounted pranks from the night before. Some teased each other. But when the old man returned, the mess room fell absolutely silent.

"Good to see everyone in such high spirits," Walter said. "Hope you men enjoyed your first night on a ninety-four year old Herreshoff schooner!""

"It was awwwwesommme!" Dwayne said.

The adults chuckled.

"That's good, Dwayne!" Jim said. "Air was a little cooler than in our neck of the woods."

"Oh, yeah," Dwayne said.

"Shameful Seamus wouldn't stop with his singing," Lance said. "I almost wanted to get my eardrums removed."

"Now, lieutenants, please ensure you and the boys grabbed enough grub. Then throw away the plates and bowls and meet Jimmy and me here on the rear deck. We set sail in about thirty, forty-five minutes to points east."

Jim, Chief, and Bill followed the old man out of the room, into the galley, through the corridor, then up the stairwell. Scant rainclouds loomed in the morning sky, and generous sunshine and a strong westerly breeze greeted them.

Jim joined the other three men where they stood just before the bowsprit, and marveled at the scene before him. Chatham Harbor boasted a broad variety of seacraft, from power yachts to sailing yachts, from daysailers to yawls to schooners, from dinghies to ketches to sloops. Hinckley yachts that had probably drained their owners of millions of dollars, in both purchase and upkeep, rested at anchor and at their moorings. There were a few wooden sailing yachts, probably from the early and mid-twentieth century, but none came close to outshining the *John Paul Jones*.

People on the docks, about to board their own vessels, paused at length to gawk at the treasure in their midst, the wooden tern schooner's great beauty and rarity, her three majestic masts, her lengthy bowsprit, her figurehead depicting the great colonial hero, her wood-and-glass boxed cockpit, her vast network of rigging, the white painted hull with her name displayed in gilded gothic characters near the bow. A few of the more knowledgeable onlookers probably guessed the yacht to be a Herreshoff.

"Jim, do me a huge favor," the old man said. "Get Jack and you two go grab me a copy of *The Globe* in that chandler's shop over there. And some half-and-half for the coffee. Kathleen and I forgot to pack it. And a third thing—one bag of ice. Meanwhile, Bill and Chief and I'll get the crew in gear."

Walter pushed a twenty-dollar bill at him, but Jim waved it away. "My treat. Be right back."

He jogged toward the stairwell and shot down the steps. The sleepy-eyed Jack was emerging from the mess room. Back on deck, Jim and Jack lowered the dinghy, small motor included, into the water.

"After you, podnuh," Jim said.

Jack descended the small stern ladder and sat in the dinghy. Jim tossed down the cords to Jack, who held the ladder with one hand as he gathered the four cords into the boat. Down the ladder, Jim stepped into the boat and sat at the stern, one hand gripping the gunwale and the other grabbing the motor's pull cord. He yanked twice and the motor started.

Jack pushed off hard from the ladder and plopped onto the bench near the bow. The dinghy rotated until it faced away from the yacht. Jim turned the handle. The motor geared up, sending them slowly across the harbor toward the docks.

"Over there!" Jack yelled over the whirr of the small Evinrude. He pointed toward the small building with the dark green asphalt roof and sided with wooden shingles. "That's the shop!"

They gained bit by bit, and then slowed. Jim weaved in and out of the anchored boats like a serpent. Soon they reached the docks. A few spectators, among them a couple with their two teenage sons, stood just feet away. Jack knotted the dinghy onto a cleat, stepped onto the dock, and nodded at them.

"That's a real sight out there," the father said. He was a tall, thin man with longish snow-white hair. Like the others, he was dressed in boating gear.

"Thanks," Jack said. "It is something else. My friend's boat."

"Your friend here?" the man said, pointing with interest at Jim.

Jim smiled and shook his head. "The owner's out there."

"That's a Herreshoff, isn't it?" the woman said, a hand held over her eyes to shield her vision from the growing sunlight. She was a petite blonde, somewhat sun-weathered, with an intelligent expression.

"You guessed right," Jim said. "One of the last tern schooners the brothers built. Launched in 1912."

"He get that baby around here?" the man said.

"It was purchased in Casco Bay. We just overhauled her in Osterville. Actually it's a *he*. The *John Paul Jones*!"

"Wow," one of the teens said.

"Y'all take care," Jim said, waving. "Gotta grab us some provisions for the road." He turned to Jack. "Or for the *sea-road*, as the great poet in *Beowulf* calls the ocean."

"Now I seem to recall that term," Jack said. "Mrs. Hartley's English class at Groton."

"Funny how the nautical history aficionados come out of the woodwork when that boat's in the water," Jim said as they walked down the dock.

"I could probably handle *one* more encounter," Jack said. "And no more."

Inside the shop, an old man sat behind the counter on a worn brown leather chair. He had a ruddy face crosshatched with wrinkles and eyes so very squinty Jim could not even discern the color of their corneas. A small pair of spectacles rested at the tip of his red nose. His grey beard hung at least five inches long. A yachting cap crowned his head. Jim guessed it had once been black before sunlight or washing faded it to a dull gray. The old man shot them a flinty glance over his newspaper, but uttered no greeting.

"Mornin', sir," Jim said.

The old man nodded and returned to his paper.

Jim turned right toward the refrigerated goods. On his way back to the counter with a pint of Borden's half-and-half, he grabbed a *Boston Globe.*

Jack stood next to the counter beside the magazine rack. "I thought we were going to have a nice rain-free weekend," Jack said, "but alas, we got rained out a bit here in the harbor last night."

"Ah hah," the old man said. After a brief pause, he put

down his paper and looked hard at Jack. "You men going out on the water this morning?"

"In a few minutes, yes," Jack said.

"It's unseasonably hot and humid out. Weather seems like it's actin' up a bunch. Cool, then warm, then temperate, then hot and rainy for some of the Figawi. Then warm and a bit rainy yesterday and last night. Strange weather, I tell ya."

Jim immediately turned from Jack to the old man. Then he was comforted to catch a glimmer of humor in the old man's eyes.

"I agree," Jack said. He seemed amused the man had opened up. "It is uncommon for this time of year, isn't it?"

"But it should be warm for you today."

Jim placed the newspaper and the cream on the counter. "Any way we can get a large bag of ice, too?"

"Ice box is unlocked just outside the door."

The old man took Jim's cash and banged a few keys on the register. He fished out some change and handed it to Jim. He then bagged the cream and paper and handed it to Jim with the faintest grin.

"You have a good day, sir," Jim said as he and Jack departed.

The door swung shut. Jim handed the paper bag to Jack and then pulled a bag of ice from the box outside. They headed back to the dock.

"NECN's forecast says no chance of rain today or tomorrow, you know," Jim said.

"That crusty old codger just probably wants to put in his two cents," Jack said.

A few people lingered on another wing of the dock, staring at the schooner.

"No rest for the *John Paul Jones*," Jim said. He stepped into the dinghy, sat on the rear bench and gunned up the Evinrude. Jack sat down on the front bench, and unknotted the rope from the cleat. They slowly spun around, and then were off toward the schooner.

For a moment, Jim studied his friend's face, angled sideways at some unknown object. At parties, Jack seemed lighthearted, even carefree. Yet outside of such occasions, he seemed troubled, weighed down by unknown worries and forces. Even now as he sat in the dinghy, Jack seemed incapable of looking at something without soon allowing his gaze to drift pensively, worriedly downward, with knitted brows. Now Jack stared hard at the water flitting past the bow.

Here was a man with all the moxie and endurance required to found and lead a successful software company. But it was indisputable. His relationship with Natasha weakened him.

Jim killed the motor. The dinghy coasted the few yards toward the stern of the schooner. Jack crouched, his arm outstretched, ready to grab the ladder. He deftly scampered up the ladder, even with one of his hands gripping the plastic bag of ice. Jim followed just a moment behind, one hand clutching the cords and paper bag.

After they raised the dinghy, they saw that the boys and lieutenants had assembled on the foredeck, dressed in their life vests. All the boys sat on the deck. Walter stood before them, holding one hand aloft, illustrating a point. Jim and Jack strolled toward them in silence.

"Jim and Jack," Walter said. "Glad to see you. All is well?"

Jim gave two thumbs up.

"You guys join me by the cockpit in a minute. But

first, I need some young backs and strong arms! Lieutenant McGreevey, anchors aweigh!"

This time, Jim could not feel the vessel drift. "No wind?" he called.

"Affirmative," Walter said. "Big Chief is down in the engine room and is gonna gun us outta here. We still will raise sails, however. Bill, go down and tell him."

Bill went for the hatch.

"Now, at my command, if you four could raise the foremast sail. Lieutenants Ward, Murphy! Scoresby and Spaulding! Resume your mast positions. At my command, raise sails... go!"

A flurry of halyard-pulling erupted on deck. Each man and boy pulled hand-over-hand as the sails wound their way up the three towering wooden masts.

"Now, tie down!" Walter bellowed. "Tie down and knot 'em, lieutenants!"

Reverend Ward tied down and knotted the shroud of the mainmast. Tim Murphy did the same on the mizzenmast. Jim and Jack bowlined the shroud onto the foremast's large cleat.

All of the men and boys looked up at the sails. They were in place, just without a trace of wind. How fickle was Mother Nature, Jim thought. And how mysterious and cruel.

He glanced at the Commodore. The old man stared directly at him, his arms at his sides. He smiled a proud, worldly-wise smile, a narrowing and twinkling of eyes and a faint grin without the showing of teeth. He placed the pipe in his mouth. A dark grey plume rose right over his right ear and past the bill of his dark blue baseball cap that read "NAVY."

The twin diesel motors surely were at work. The ship drifted forward, turning and pulling away. A great cheer shot from the nearest dock, where spectators still remained, many of them waving. Minutes later, the *John Paul Jones* encountered decent winds. They snagged the sails which slowly, steadily billowed open and wide. A collective sigh rose from the crew. The *John Paul Jones* was once again making good time.

Minutes later, they moved south at a speed of about fifteen knots. As if bidding their farewell, a flock of seagulls dived, turned, climbed, and circled the schooner as it progressed farther from shore.

Inside the cockpit, the Commodore puffed away at his pipe. Jim stood beside him, steering. Jack rested a few feet away on the teak bench, lost in thought. At least he looked in better spirits.

On the foredeck, the Reverend and Tim and their charge of six boys leaned against the bow's rail, studying the few boats on the horizon. After twenty minutes passed, Walter ordered Jim to turn the wheel, to steer directly eastward, parallel to the dune-and-grass coast of the Cape Cod National Seashore Ponds Preserve.

"This," Walter said, "aims us directly out into the Atlantic."

Jim drew in a deep breath and held it, imagining the schooner capsizing in a great storm, hundreds of miles from land.

Following thirty minutes on this course, the old man gave the order to tack directly northward along the Preserve's coast toward the Cape's tip at Provincetown. The ship listed slightly to port as it righted its course.

A great cheer burst from several of the boys at the bow. Jim heard and felt the mighty push of the wind, which further filled the sails.

Smiling at the vessel's progress, Jim turned to Walter. "I know the plan's to anchor outside Truro, but at this rate, hell, we may even be west of Provincetown by twilight!"

"Ah, you may very well be right, sir," the old man said, his eyes twinkling with delight. "We are making way, for sure." Walter was clearly elated at their good fortune. Their only mishap had been last night's rain.

Jack excused himself, strolled toward the bow, his hands buried in the pockets of his linen pants.

"I wonder," Jim said, "if our friend's feigning a look of happy-go-lucky comfort there."

"We both know what's weighin' down the guy, don't we?" the old man said, and turned a pair of gloomy eyes toward Jim.

"I'd say we do," Jim said. "Maybe this trip will do him some good."

"Spaulding's son has been mopin' around all hangdog like that many a time in the last few months," Walter said, shaking his head and closing his eyes. He made a hissing sound. "The man needs to free himself of that virago."

Jim let slip a laugh, just for a second, and stifled it by contorting his mouth.

"Ah, look at this day, son. Look at this day, will ya?" Walter said, pulling the ziplocked bag of tobacco from his coat pocket.

"It's some beautiful out there. We've been blessed today. Just a few clouds, much sunshine, decent wind."

Walter proceeded to pack the bowl. With one strike of a match, and his other hand shielding the bowl, he lit the pipe. "We have, son. We have," the old man said.

They stared through the square front window of the cockpit. Nearly everything beyond was some marvelous shade of blue, the frolicking waves of dark blue and the sky of royal blue, interrupted only by the scarcest number of grayish-white clouds in the distance.

"We've both been blessed in another way," Walter said, looking over at him. "We're both blessed to be here, to be breathing. I know you were having a nightmare last night in your cabin. I could hear it. And I know why. I lived it, Jimmy, for decades. Still am. We carry guilt—we survived while someone we cared about passed on right in front of us, in a catastrophe. And war is always a catastrophe.

"I know you had Freddy. Many of my men died under my watch. I'll tell you about one. Chester Wilkins, from Gloucester. Twenty years young, and his forebears had been sailors for centuries. He served alongside Carrington's brother as a gunner. Used to have panic attacks sometimes when we were close to enemy boats and sometimes planes.

"One day he came to me and said he'd had enough. It was the last day of his tour. Wanted to go home. I persuaded him to enlist for another tour, as he hadn't conquered his fear. Two days later, our tin can hit a mine my flotilla had missed. He screamed on impact. It was honestly more like a shriek. A squeal. Wilkins lost both of his legs and an eye and it ripped his guts to shreds. Took him two days to pass. But not after I visited him and saw that hazel eye staring at me, expressionless. Son, I have seen that eye stare me down for decades now..."

Jim said nothing, just watched Walter as he focused his gaze out past the bow into the horizon.

Chapter Forty-Two

At quarter past noon the pipe fell from Walter's lips and clattered across the finished floorboards of the cockpit. The old man bared his teeth like an angry wolf and gripped the wheel, as if the ship was about to plummet off the edge of a waterfall.

"*God save us all. Oh, the children*!" Walter blurted in a half-whisper, half-gasp.

"Walter, what is it?" Jim said. He had never seen the old man in such a way. Perhaps, in his old age, he was overreacting.

"*White squall. Look at those scuds.* We may be *done for*," Walter stammered in the same tone. He reached over and yanked the brass shaft from where it was attached to the cockpit wall and banged over and over at the brass bell.

The lieutenants and boys, who had been lunching in the mess room, surfaced on deck. With several frantic waves of his hand, Walter ordered all on deck to hurry to the cockpit. "All hands, get over here! Get in here, all of you! Sit down on the floor by the wheel! Hurry!"

"Shouldn't I batten down the main hatch?" Jim shouted.

"No," Walter thundered. "Stick with me, son, right here."

Jim stood there feeling helpless, his hands at his sides, as he felt the fire grow within his belly. Yet he saw nothing on the horizon, or in the water before them, save a cluster of low-hanging clouds and something he had never seen: a strange, large patch of white-capped waves, of broken water.

Tales of white squalls, accounts of tornado-like storms that struck on lakes and oceans, without warning and often in good weather, filled Jim's mind. He had watched a film on the subject years back.

The old man still bashed the brass bell when the men and boys clustered around them at the cockpit's entrance.

Walter boomed, "Everyone, listen to me! It's an emergency! All lieutenants, secure the lifejackets of the boys in your charge. And then secure your own and get on the floor in this cockpit. We're heading into a squall. We're almost in it!"

A wave of exhortation and cries of desperation moved through the group of boys, who now sat on the deck next to the wheel.

"All vests are secure," Tim Murphy said.

"My guys, too," Reverend Ward said. He enunciated with strength, but his voice still wavered.

Jack Spaulding crouched just beside them. His face displayed an unmistakable expression of terror. Jack knew full well what a white squall was.

"Okay, now listen to me, men!" Walter yelled. "I'm going to radio news of the squall. I need you boys to hug your hands around your knees, like Lance over there. Sit up against each other. Good. Now Tim and Jim and Bill, Reverend and Jack, you interlock hands like this, form a canopy over them. We're gonna hit the squall in a minute. That thing's wide as hell so we can't avoid it."

Walter grabbed the VHF radio and began to bark into it. Jim paid no mind to the words, as he was lost in thought. Surely this couldn't be happening to him again. And now to more friends of his, and now to children!

The lieutenants got into formation and shielded the boys. The Reverend prayed out loud, rushing boldly through his orations but pronouncing them with great clarity.

Jim glanced at his watch. It seemed like an hour had gone by. Yet only two minutes had passed.

The wind gusted. Jim trembled as he looked up. Walter stared down at him, the eyes steeled with a fierce, resolute intensity.

"Should we move below deck?" Tim said.

"You don't wanna be below deck," the old man spoke in staccato. "She may capsize. Many do in squalls. She may even founder."

One of the boys under the pile began to weep.

"It's all right," Jim said, "we're gonna get y'all through this. You'll see."

Walter said, "It may just be a wee one. We've got our life vests on. If we stick together, we'll be okay."

"Wait!" Jim shouted. "Where is Chief?"

"Ah, damn!" Walter said. "He never came up. Good God."

"Chief!" Walter yelled.

The whistling grew louder. All at once a massive wind from the stern jolted them forward, but they did not break out of formation. Two of the masts snapped and slammed across the deck. A cockpit window shattered, raining shards and splinters of glass upon the backs and the arms and shoulders of the adults atop the huddle.

Jim kept his head tucked down between his shoulders, with one arm grabbing Tim's, while his other arm linked through Jack's. The fierce whistling and tearing and whipping of the wind, the clinking sound of the broken glass upon them, and the shouting and cries of some of the boys persisted. Despite the din, the young Reverend's effusive thread of prayers sounded out like the bold, deliberate, forceful call of a foghorn in the night.

"Hold tight, men!" Walter yelled. "It should last only a few minutes. Hold tight! Bear it, men! Bear this, now!"

The Reverend's prayers came faster and faster, resounding like the plodding of a charging stallion. Jim recognized the twenty-third psalm of King David:

He maketh me to lie down in green pastures: he leadeth me beside the still waters. He restoreth my soul: he leadeth me in the paths of righteousness for his name's sake. Yea, though I walk through the valley of the shadow of death, I will fear no evil: for thou art with me; thy rod and thy staff they comfort me. Thou preparest a table before me in the presence of mine enemies: thou anointest my head with oil; my cup runneth over.

Deep inside the huddle a boy, LaRon or Jeffery, echoed the words, praying along with the Reverend. Dwayne wept, now in the midst of his second vicious storm.

A great lashing sound, almost like that of a bullwhip, cut the air, and then a great flapping noise ensued. The lines of the downed masts flailed about in the violent winds, and the sails slapped against the deck. Once more, the great schooner lurched fiercely forward. It began to sway, then list slightly to port.

"Ah no. Ahhh," the old man said, sounding exhausted. "Hold tight, don't you dare let go! I fear she mighta broken open."

"My God," Jack said within the huddle with an air of doom.

"Should one of us get ready to lower the lifeboat? Should we stay in here? I need to find Chief now!" Jack poured out his words in a sort of half shout, half supplication, to the old man.

"Hold tight for a minute longer," Walter bellowed. "Hold tight, I'm ordering you. We leave on my order. We need to stay in here as long as we can. That wind could blow us clean overboard."

"I'm gonna get Chief, damn it!" Jim yelled with anger. He glanced up but Walter was gone.

At that moment the roof of the cockpit ripped open, then wafted away. The walls collapsed, one of them landing on the Reverend's back. A second blast hit them from starboard.

In a heartbeat, their formation disintegrated. They plunged into the dark blue deep, chilly despite the warm June day.

Jim held his breath, and his spine stiffened with an almighty terror, as he felt the cold grip of his old foe. Water had kept him on that New Orleans rooftop the summer before as his friend lay expiring from shock and exhaustion, water had murdered so many innocents in the city that he loved, water plagued him with dread for days and nights since. Once again water was on the verge of robbing him, and those he cared about, of life and peace. His lungs felt like they would burst if he could not curse the water aloud.

Jim kicked to the surface. "Everyone swim away from the ship!" he screamed. "It's heelin' over! It'll go down!" He counted Bill, Tim, and Jack in the water, and spotted Reverend Ward some distance away. Between them, five boyish heads bobbed in the water. The old man was nowhere to be found among the waves and floating debris.

"We need to get Chief and the old man," Bill shouted,

paddling in place and blinking water out of his eyes, looking like an old dog swimming.

"Where's Dwayne?" Jim yelled. "Where is Dwayne?"

"I don't know! I don't know!" Tim Murphy yelled. He, Bill, and Jack had formed a circle in the water with LaRon, Jeffrey, and Scott. Reverend Ward clung to the floating wooden roof of the cockpit, perhaps twenty feet away. He had pulled Lance and Seamus to his side. Their shaking arms held fast to the roof in turn.

The winds had stopped and the squall had broken up. The old man had been right—only minutes in duration.

"Watch the boys here!" Reverend Ward shouted. "I'm gonna swim and find him!"

"I am, too!" Jim yelled. "Tim and Jack, get the boys to hold fast to that. I'm swimming back for Dwayne!"

"Where's the Commodore?" Scott screamed, clinging to the floating roof.

"Yeah, where is he? And where's Dwayne?" LaRon cried as he appeared, swimming freestyle toward the floating roof. Swimming with one arm, Jack towed Jeffrey slowly toward the Reverend.

Jim launched into a fierce freestyle swim toward the listing ship, stopping just short of the hull. He spotted Dwayne. With a splash he went under about fifteen feet before Jim, just against the hull of the ship.

Jim forced himself forward. He could not find the boy in the opaque waters. Jim surfaced. He spotted Dwayne about twenty feet away, alongside the hull, just as the boy again submerged with a strange sound.

Jim swam as fast as he possibly could, and just feet shy

of the mark, unfastened his life vest and dived. He swam diagonally down, kicking his legs backward and forward like a sprinter. With an outstretched arm, he found and clutched the boy's shirt and then his arm. Jim's own heart leapt as he pulled Dwayne close, kicking and exhaling through his mouth.

They shot toward the surface. Jim found the light. The boy gasped, coughing vehemently.

Jim half laughed, half wept. "Ah, Dwayne, we almost lost you, friend."

Dwayne coughed again. Jim held him tight to his chest with one hand and stroked through the water with the other, kicking the whole time. "Soon we'll all be eatin' at Bob's again. Why no life jacket?"

Nearly a minute passed, with nothing but Dwayne violently coughing and spitting up water. "Couldn't... swim...with any with it," Dwayne finally said.

"Dwayne, that was so against the rules, buddy."

The others began to shout for joy. Jack and LaRon clung fast to a large piece of wooden flotsam, just feet away from the cockpit roof. Jim handed Dwayne over to Reverend Ward, who grabbed the boy and held him close.

Jim said, "Little guy lost his vest."

Reverend Ward smiled, clinging to the floating roof with his other arm.

"What about Walter and Chief?" Jim said. "And Walter was wearing his vest. He's got to be out there. He couldn't have gone under."

"Jim, *you* have no life vest, brother," Reverend Ward said.

"Doesn't matter. Lost it so I could actually swim. I'm goin' find the old man."

"I'm comin', too," Bill said.

"Swim with me, damn it," Jim said. "But keep that vest on."

"Hurry," Jack said. "Trust me, the boat's about to go down. It's taking on water as we speak."

Jim and Bill swam toward the ship, still afloat about one hundred feet away. Its three once-proud masts were downed. The ship listed slightly but steadily to port. A single line from one of the sails draped over the port side into the water.

"Why don't ya climb that line, if it holds?" Bill shouted, several feet behind Jim. "I'll swim around the boat. I got the vest. If I don't spot Walter, I'll climb the line."

"All right," Jim said, then pulled himself slowly up the line, hand over hand. He collapsed onto the deck, struggling for a moment to breathe. Below him, he knew, Bill swam the perimeter of the ship.

Jim pulled himself to his feet. He shot across the boards. He saw the spot where the wind had shorn the cockpit clean off the deck. Only a lone collapsed wall and the steering wheel remained. Hadn't Walter been swept into the water with them all? Or had he been snagged on the rail, and again gone below deck to radio?

Jim grew frantic as these thoughts fired within his mind. He ran sternward. Then something caught his eye. Jim halted and slowly turned his head to the left. Under a spar from the collapsed mizzenmast lay a soul-crushing sight. Jim broke out in a sprint for the center of the deck. He stopped just short of the wreckage of Walter Henretty, with the hulking figure of Chief kneeling a foot away.

"Walter," Jim whispered in a hushed tone.

Lying on his back, Walter still breathed. The wooden spar had broken off the mast and pinned his abdomen to the deck. A piece of the mast had crushed his thighs. Walter gurgled blood with each breath, a trickle running down from his mouth. His face was a strange ghost-white. His head rested on the deck, his hands motionless at his sides. The eyes narrowed, glassy with death. Not a shadow of fear or horror showed in them, solely an expression of fatigue and resignation, of final and humbled surrender.

Strangely, Jim also caught a glimmer of humor in the squint of the man's eyes. "W... Walter?" he whispered, barely able to form the words. He leaned over and tried to pull at the spar, to no avail.

"Aye aye, Cap," Walter croaked. "I was caught by the rail... and didn't go overboard... then I crossed the deck. I was going for Chief. Spar came down. Crushed me."

"Oh, Walter..."

"'S'all the crew together?" Walter was barely audible now, and slurring his words. The lids were coming down, growing heavier.

"Every last one of them. I came back for you," Jim said. "Me and McGreevey here did."

A thud sounded on the deck. Bill, dripping wet and out of breath, jogged toward them.

"That's him right now," Jim said.

"Walter," Bill said, drawing up alongside of Jim, his eyes displaying tenderness and deep shock.

"Give my love to my two girls and son. Give my love to... all the others down there... and all my friends..."

"Walt..." Jim whispered. "Walt..."

The lids drooped until they almost closed.

"You find your way now... my son..."

The lids shut completely. A new, thicker stream of blood—nearly black it was so very crimson—welled up and ran from the old man's mouth with his last breath.

Bill squatted and placed an index and middle finger to Walter's throat. He stood, closed his eyes, and let his chin hit his chest. "He's gone."

They were silent for a moment.

"We gotta jump off this death trap before she goes under," Chief said. "The surge slammed me against the work table in the engine room. Messed up my hip, my leg. Otherwise I'd try to get this off him."

"Can you still swim?" Bill said.

"I'm gonna have to," Chief said.

"Damn," Jim said. "I want to get that ax in the hall, chop him loose."

"It's too late, and you know it," Bill said with resolve.

"It'd take probably ten minutes to free him. This thing's goin' to the bottom any second. Come on, Jim."

Bill broke for the side, toward the dangling line. Jim took one last look at his expired friend, the shell of a once strapping man who had traversed the seas for over half a century, now lying blood-soaked, spent, vanquished under a fallen mast.

Bill reached the rail. Jim started to run, then turned and dashed for the stairwell. He grabbed the ax hanging on the wall just inside the entrance.

"Jim!" Bill shouted back as he waited at the rail.

"I'm not leaving anyone behind again!" Jim yelled. He sprinted back toward Walter and brought the ax down upon the spar—just to the side of the body—over ten times until the spar broke in two. Jim grabbed a piece with both hands, crouched, and strained with every measure of his power. He rose, and with him the spar, which he tossed aside.

"No, Walt would want it this way," Bill shouted. "A watery grave with his ship. His last vessel, too, man. Now let's get off this boat!"

Jim tugged with all the strength he could muster, gritting his teeth and growling like a flustered wolf. He rolled the rest of the mast off Walter's lifeless legs to the deck.

"I can't lift him, Jim," Chief said, grimacing and straightening his life vest. "I'm messed up. It's got to be you."

"Then do it, Jim!" Bill screamed. "Hurry, damn it!"

Tears blinding him, Jim knelt and gathered Walter's arms around him and lifted him to where he was nearly upright. He threw the limp body—still clad in a life vest—over his shoulder and stepped shakily toward the rail.

Jim grimaced. He could feel Walter's broken femurs shift.

Bill, followed by Chief feet away and moments later, leapt off the rail into the deep. They hurtled toward the now-calm waves and disappeared, reappeared, and commenced swimming.

Jim stepped cautiously over the rail, which he grasped with one hand and Walter's bloodied legs with the other. A sound, strangely familiar, emerged in the distance. He peered through the midday sunlight into the horizon.

A helicopter approached. And a powerboat—some sort of speedboat—motored his way. The famed Chatham Coast Guard had intercepted the old man's radio call.

Jim grinned, knowing Walter, though deceased, was

coming home with him. He looked down at the dark blue waves, spotted here and there with floating debris, and once again saw that flooded street as he was raised by cord into the helicopter. He gripped his friend tightly with both arms and leapt out as far as he could.

Chapter Forty-Three

A week had passed since the funeral. It seemed like an entire year. Jim had yet to return to Henretty & Henretty. He admitted to Dewey he needed several days off. Dewey understood, Jim surmised, since he wrestled with his own grief. Jim still sometimes fielded calls and received orders from the Back Bay carriage house.

That Friday night, Jim and Maureen sat on the roof deck of her Beacon Hill townhouse, splitting a bottle of Chateau Calon-Segur. They spoke sparingly, mostly listening to the street sounds below. Occasionally, a car passed, or a couple or small group strolled down the sidewalk of the narrow cobblestone streets, leaving or approaching some party or bar or restaurant. From time to time, the wind would blow, tousling their hair, grazing them as they sat beside the parapet wall.

Lounging there languidly, with a chill, Jim remembered the violent, almost supernatural gale that took down the great schooner and the old captain.

Maureen did not react to his shudder. She had been quite distant since the incident, even more than in the weeks preceding Walter's death. She seldom spoke, never smiled, and rarely showed affection. She spent nearly all of her free time visiting with girlfriends, or sleeping alone.

"I just don't understand," Maureen said, her speech slightly slurred as she reclined in her lawn chair, "just *why* Daddy *had* to run for Chief. He had *already* radioed for help. If he wasn't so hardheaded, he'd be alive."

"He was the Commodore," Jim said. "He wanted to save all his crew. And he wanted to get Chief at least near the hatch in case the boat started to break apart."

"And a *white squall*! They happen usually in the Great Lakes and the tropics. I've researched them, Jim, the last few days."

"White squalls do occasionally occur here, but my sentiments exactly. You know that I've turned the same thought over and over in my mind."

Jim recalled the etymology he had uncovered behind the word. Squall. From the Old Norse *skvala* or "squeal."

His stomach grew uneasy as he remembered the whistling shriek, like a banshee's scream, that had cut through the schooner's rigging as they hugged the cockpit deck. That was the very scream that cut the air just as a twenty-foot surge leapt over the starboard side and swept the cockpit, and those inside, into the deep. Then Jim recalled the sailor from Gloucester Walter had commanded, and his scream, his shriek that tore through the Navy destroyer as it contacted the mine. Now he felt queasy.

To Maureen, he did not completely confide what the storm meant for him. It was the second time his life had been upended by the sudden arrival of a cataclysm of nature, a catastrophe of the weather. The first exiled him from his homeland, robbing him of one of his closest friends. The second thieved nearly all that he had found recently found—a chance to help wayward youth, renewed confidence on the open water, the vessel he had painstakingly repaired and remodeled. But the greatest and most painful loss was his irreplaceable friend, Walter Henretty.

A man who called Jim his son, even in his last minute of life.

Not a night passed that a nightmare did not plague Jim. Freddy used to haunt his dreams. Walter had joined him.

What he still had, Jim ruminated as he sipped the wine, was Maureen. He harbored a small ember of love for her, despite that he felt she tried her damnedest to smother it. Jim hoped and prayed that ember would grow again into a roaring fire within him once again. Maureen did have many faults, but he couldn't give up on her just yet.

She lifted the bottle from the small glass table between them and poured herself another glass. She reclined in her chair, watching the illuminated windows of the surrounding brownstones.

"I've often thought it was his time. I hate to say it, but he would have loved that he went out in that way. He would've preferred to be left out there in that wreck, on the sea floor. But it's a good thing you recovered him. For us. And I know I'm boring, Jim," she said with exhaustion, as she struggled to her feet. "But I've got to return some emails."

"Love you, Miss Henretty," Jim said as he grabbed her hand, brought it to his lips.

Through the dark, Maureen smiled weakly at Jim before she opened the stairwell door. He found himself alone again to reflect, and to stew in his thoughts.

How he had loved the old captain. To be sure, their friendship proved one of the few things that made Jim's recent life tolerable. Despite the other friendships he forged, Jim tasted harshness, mockery, callousness from many.

And now the old man was gone. In the midst of his last voyage, Walter gifted his young protégé with his own father's

Dunhill pipe—almost as if the old man knew his time had arrived.

Jim tilted the glass upward, draining his wine. He emptied the bottle into his glass, and set glass and bottle both on the small table. He reached deep into his left pants pocket. He produced the coveted object and held it before his eyes. Its silhouette revealed itself against the light of a brownstone's third story window.

The 1922 Dunhill had remained in Jim's buttoned shorts pocket from the moment the old man presented it until Jim stood wet and shivering in the Coast Guard station with the crew. While changing into fresh clothes, Jim discovered the pipe, and he wept silently there in the bathroom stall. He would never again see Walter. Or Freddy.

Jim drew the small bag of dark English tobacco from his right pants pocket. He packed the dark rusticated bowl of briarroot. With his left hand he shielded the bowl and held the matchbox. With his right, he struck the matches, first one, then two, then three. Jim puffed until thick plumes snaked from the bowl.

At least the old man saved his crew through enforcing the life vest rule. And Walter did radio for help. All the children and lieutenants survived.

Jim met them at the funeral in Holy Cross Cathedral in the South End. Cardinal O'Malley and Walter's parish priest concelebrated the Mass, a memorial complete with Navy honor guard and a beautiful yet gut-wrenching bagpipe procession.

How strange it was that the crew stood there and probably thought the same thing. That each of them escaped while the old man met the full force, the full fury, of the storm—a tempest sent from above to that time and that place specifically for *him*, and for them.

It was whispered among the survivors and the funeral service's congregation: it was a great deed and feat that Jim had salvaged Walter Henretty's body from the sinking wreck. Kathleen and Maureen had ensured it was cremated and committed to the sea, just off Nantucket.

Maureen later admitted she couldn't bear to imagine her loving father as food for sea creatures. And neither could her boyfriend. It was one of the main reasons, Jim told her, he had refused to leave without his friend.

But just why had the ship sunk? Had that massive surge against starboard cracked or compromised the hull? Was there a defect in the new hull planks and fasteners? The boat had passed inspection, and then days ago, the formal investigation had exonerated Walter and the Melville team, both in the final voyage and in the overhaul of the vessel.

Just what did God want from Jim? What had God wanted from Walter, to send that squall, to let that spar crush his chest and his life? Would Jim ever know?

Jim remembered his father's old line: "Life is but a mystery, filled with mysteries. And in the end these mysteries are probably all connected... in some honeycomb pattern."

How had he come to realize, in the last year, the wisdom in the words of the old engineer and geologist.

His father returned to the silver screen within his mind. He saw his father standing on the back porch in the dusk, as he liked to do, looking out across the grassy yard and up through the vast branches of the great loblolly pines, magnolias, sweet gums, and white and black oaks. The man who had created him and forged him into all he had become—had Jim rejected him? Perhaps he had become a heretic. He had rejected and—unwittingly—even twisted the image and likeness of his creator.

Jim had ceased praying after Walter's death. Or rather, he had refused to pray. What if there were no God? What if there were a Creator, but no afterlife?

The thought was brutal: what if all that awaited Freddy and Walter on the other side were oblivion and the total annihilation and disintegration of consciousness? He wished he could have some sort of sign.

In the end, Jim still had youth and health. He had this life, and while he still drew breath, why not spend every moment enjoying those things nearest and dearest to his heart? In this he could take comfort. In this there was some victory.

Jim cradled his pipe in his palm and brought it to his lap. I need to visit more with my friends, he thought—Liam, Case, Duff, and the others. Do more than speak with Reverend and Jack and Tim on the phone. Check on the boys. Take another drive with Maureen down to Osterville to check on Kathleen, the kids, and to visit my friends in the shop. Get *outside* of myself. And I should see my family and friends down south—I drift further from them, day by day, and the vibrant, rich life that was mine in New Orleans...

After Jim finished the bowl, he spilled the charred tobacco into the ashtray. He returned the pipe to his left pocket, stood, and downed the last of the wine. He placed the glass on the table, told himself he would clean the mess in the morning, and disappeared down the stairwell. Hours later he woke on the living room couch.

Upstairs, he found Maureen asleep on her bed. Her empty

wineglass sat on her dresser. Next to her lay her laptop, in hibernation mode.

With his own laptop in for repairs, Jim took up her computer and tiptoed out of the room and down the stairs.

He placed the laptop on the kitchen counter, pushed the power button, and prepared to search for a news site.

Maureen had been reading an email from a John Day. Jim did not recognize the name. By instinct, Jim went to exit out of her email account, but something made him linger. He glanced at the end of the email.

Maureen, all I can tell you is that you need to cut it off completely (and soon!) with Cajun Man. I know this is the hardest, darkest time for you with your father's passing. I would have loved to have met your dad, too, Maureen. I know he meant a lot to you. That's understood. I am sure you've been a great daughter. Good thing you never told him about me. He would have no doubt leaked it instantly to his Cajun sidekick.

I digress... love, you know you cannot keep both me and your old flame. I'd been hanging on for weeks even before the accident with your dad, waiting for you to end it with Jim like you vowed you would. Even though you're the prize you are, I can't hold on forever. Anyway, cheer up. Call me tomorrow. I know you can't talk tonight. I haven't seen you in days and I can't wait until I have your sweet self and your sweet body all to myself again! Maybe we can take another day trip back to Newport. Anyway call me tomorrow! Love you.

P.S. I've said my piece with all this. Now on a funny note: I am attaching a pic Frank took of me on those slopes in Killington late last winter. Back long before I met you...

Jim scrolled down, his eyes watery and wide with horror.

The last time Jim felt this pain was the moment he spotted the pale head resting on the deck of the doomed schooner.

He held his breath, shut his eyes, and exhaled hard. He recognized the young skier in the photo. It was the well-dressed man that had run into him, literally, weeks ago at Sonsie. John Day must have been spying on his "prize" and spying on him, to boot.

Jim's gut turned, but he decided to grieve no longer. He had done enough of that already. One must save sorrow and tears for those souls that merit them. He had loved the old man and always would, and owed it to Walter to be gentle with his eldest child. He must not retaliate. But he could not act oblivious. She had been found out.

Jim unplugged the laptop and trudged with it up the stairs. He shouted her name angrily as he entered the room. Maureen was immediately awake, though noticeably quite tipsy.

After a few seconds she processed that he stood before her, glaring down menacingly at her. But when she saw the open laptop, turned in his hands toward her so that she could see the illuminated screen, she bolted upright in bed.

"The writing of John Day makes for edifying reading, I must say," Jim said, and tossed the laptop onto the bed beside her. "You won't read my writing, but you'll remember this. Enjoy your daytrip to 'the island' with Johnny. And enjoy your life from here on out. You're on your own. I wanted to be a part of it. Too bad I ignored the fact that you left mine—and you deserted me—some time ago."

Maureen opened her mouth but uttered nothing. She even seemed to be choking.

He took one last look at the face—that strange mixture

of child and fox—and stormed from the room, down the stairwell, and out into the street.

Chapter Forty-Four

That Monday morning Jim laid yet another burden on Dewey. He would move on from employment at Henretty & Henretty. Dewey impressed him with the undeniable grace and humanity of his reply. "You don't have to say a word, Jimmy. I know your heart, son. And it is good. My brother would want what's best for you. And you know I do, too. May the wind be at your back, son."

Jim thanked him.

"But I'll hold something against you if you don't visit. Don'tcha know, I'm ya old Irish uncle, Jimmy boy."

Dewey stood and extended a hand. What a man old Dewey had been. And his manager had made it a point not to mention Maureen. No doubt he knew nothing of his niece's infidelity. Maureen could never admit a fault, much less a cardinal betrayal.

And it was a good thing Jim heard no word from her.

He had spent that weekend visiting with friends: Liam, Case, Duff, Tim, Jack, Father Ben, Patrick, the men in the shop. Bryce did not answer his phone.

Luckily he could depend on Reverend Ward. The preacher, though young, was wise enough to sense the hurt in his friend's voice.

"Jim, I've been meaning to catch up. Look, what are your lunch plans today? Tanya and I are takin' you out to an old familiar place I think you'll like."

By noon, Jim found himself doing the last thing one would expect to be doing on a Monday in the heart of Boston, Massachusetts—savoring collards, fried okra, candied yams, and black eyed peas with diced smoked ham, while listening to Fats Domino.

"Sure you thought this through? Now, Jim?" Reverend Ward said, his face solemn as he leaned slightly forward over his plate toward Jim.

"I have," Jim said softly.

Jim explained how he had phoned the movers days ago, mere hours after he left Maureen. He resigned at the brokerage that morning, and the movers arrived at nine o'clock. In a hushed, humiliated, but faintly relieved tone, Jim told the Reverend and Tanya of the shocking email.

The conversation soon turned to brighter, more important things.

"Jim, the charity work you've offered is a great thing, a good thing, with the folks down at Bethesda Baptist, even though we could use you up here with us. Those guys down there—I know 'em. They're hurtin'. They could use an ol' Luzianna boy lendin' em a hand!"

"Really, Jim," Tanya said, her eyes the picture of pathos.

"And I'll admit, Jim, I didn't think you'd take so easy to life up here. You're a Luzianna man, and you missed it too much to stay away. I have a feeling your destiny lies down there. Go finish that first novel."

"I suspect you're right, Reverend."

"Call me Cordell, Jim. And I think mine does lie up here in Boston. And a little bit in 'Nawlins, too. Tanya and I both."

The grinning pastor put his arm around his wife. "We'll catch you down there from time to time, doing mission work. But years from now, you'll increasingly appreciate how special a place Boston is. And one of the greatest things about this nation... is this region."

"I actually agree with that," Jim said.

"Now, you did often take things too seriously here," Cordell said. "But I knew all along you'd be happier closer to your roots. You're not meant to be a denizen of the big city."

The waiter arrived with the bill. Jim tried to snatch it. Cordell and Tanya argued with him back and forth over it, but Cordell insisted.

"You win, you win," Jim said. "My treat, next time I'm up here. Or when y'all are down in the Crescent City, Reverend."

Cordell laid cash on the table and they walked out the door. "Remember, not Reverend," he told Jim. "Cordell, my friend. Cordell!"

He stretched out a hand to him. Jim shook it firmly, then hugged Cordell and Tanya goodbye. Minutes later, Jim rolled west in his old Chevy truck along Interstate 90—the Massachusetts Turnpike—on what he knew would be a very long but exciting road home.

It would be a quiet journey, too. Two days later, just at the point of crossing south over the Georgia line on Interstate 24, Jim received a text from Maureen. No apologies, only a demand that he meet her at Sonsie that night at eight.

Jim hurled the phone, along with an unopened bottle of bourbon, through the passenger's open window into the Tennessee River.

At twilight the next day, he pulled onto the long oyster shell drive, through the dense tract of magnolias, sweetgum, thick longleaf pines, white oaks, live oaks, and cypress, the latter two dripping with Spanish moss. The words of his preacher friend echoed in his ears:

"You're a Luzianna man. And you missed it too much to stay away. I have a feeling your destiny lies down there."

Jim parked his truck alongside the tin-roofed Acadian cottage, his passenger door facing its front door. The weeping yet smiling gray-haired man and the pale, black-haired woman who once gave him life burst onto the porch. They stood, embracing each other, waiting for him to emerge from the truck. Smiling at him with narrowed eyes, just next to them, stood his brother Paul. Suddenly Jim froze, his gaze directed through his windshield for nearly half a minute. Far down the long horseshoe drive, side by side, stood two unmistakable figures. They stared back at him, grinning slightly, their chins raised. Freddy "Foghorn" Beasley and Commodore Walter Henretty waved once and nodded. Walter in his formal Navy Captain's uniform. Freddy in his guayabera, linen pants, guaraches, and porkpie hat.

Jim gave a start and wiped his eyes.

Then they turned—and with Walter draping a relaxed arm on Freddy's shoulder—walked and vanished around the bend into eternity.

About the Author

Born and raised in New Orleans and its suburbs—and working and residing there during Katrina—Chad has written for the *New Orleans Times-Picayune, The Sewanee Purple, The Riverside Reader, The Baton Rouge Advocate,* and most recently, *Austin.com.* After living in many cities and regions, he counts himself lucky enough to reside in the laid-back yet vibrant, friendly and creative city of Austin. There he spends many of his days and nights either holed up like a hermit, reading or writing away, or prowling around, investigating all of the live music, delicious cuisine, and cultural hotspots he can find.

www.ingramcontent.com/pod-product-compliance
Lightning Source LLC
Chambersburg PA
CBHW070358260626
47161CB00001B/184

* 9 7 8 1 9 3 8 7 4 9 2 0 9 *